A Violent Act

A Violent Act

ALISON JOSEPH

First published in Great Britain in 2008 by
Allison & Busby Limited
13 Charlotte Mews
London W1T 4EJ
www.allisonandbusby.com

A CIP catalogue record for this book is available from
the British Library.

10 9 8 7 6 5 4 3 2 1

13-ISBN 978-0-7490-8063-1

Typeset in 11/16 pt Sabon by
Terry Shannon

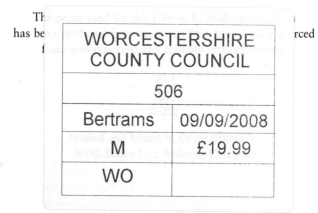

ALISON JOSEPH was born in North London and educated at Leeds University. After graduating she worked as a presenter on a local radio station then, moving back to London, for Channel 4. She later became a partner in an independent production company and one of its commissions was a series presented by Helen Mirren about women and religion. Alison also writes original radio drama, including 'Sister Agnes Investigates', and has adapted novels for BBC Radio 4, including the award-winning production of *Captain Corelli's Mandolin*. She has also published various short stories. Alison lives in London with her husband and three children.

'*Permit me, therefore, to repeat, as having been proved,*
these two propositions:
All organic nature moves in a circle.
Creation is a violent irruption into the circle of nature.'

From *Omphalos* by Philip H Gosse, 1857

Acknowledgements

The ideas expressed in Agnes's father's (fictional) book, quoted in Chapter 12, refer to *The Sacred Theory of the Earth* by Thomas Burnet, 1681.

Thanks are due to Dr Jonathan Barber of the University of Leeds, Dr Amyas Bray, and Detective Sergeant David Brown of Holborn Police Station.

I would also like to thank the staff of the British Library.

Lastly, I wish to thank Timothy Boon.

CHAPTER ONE

Upstairs a door crashed open. There was a burst of music, loud and fast, then the door slammed shut again.

'You were saying, Doctor—' She leant back against the sofa in the sudden quiet.

He stared ahead of him. 'I just worry that she won't survive.'

Footsteps passed in the street. The morning was grey and damp with mist.

'It's up to us to make sure she does,' she said.

His gaze met hers, his pale eyes fringed with blond lashes behind his wire-rimmed glasses. 'She's so vulnerable, Sister. If there was a cliff and a sign marked danger, you'd find her there, walking towards it.' He shivered at the thought, or perhaps because the central heating of the hostel lounge was defeated by the autumn chill.

'But you reckon she's been clean for at least a month.'

He nodded. 'She's done very well. Very well.'

'So, we can think about the next stage.'

Again, the direct stare. 'It's not just up to her. She's at the mercy of that young man. The thing is, Agnes, I've been working with addicts for years. You know where my practice is, down the road in Bermondsey – of all the young people I see down there, drug abuse is at the heart of nearly all of their problems.' He smoothed his fingers through his cropped hair. 'I'm very fond of Abbie. And to me, yes, she seems to have turned a corner. She seems honest about having kicked the stuff, and she's trying not to see that ghastly dealer of hers any more, although God knows he's terrifying enough...' He flicked a brief smile at Agnes. 'But I've trusted people before when they've sworn blind they were free of it, only to write the death certificate six months later.' He rested his hands on his knees.

'She's talking of leaving the hostel,' Agnes said.

He raised his eyes to her. 'Leaving?'

'We've been discussing finding her a flat of some kind, to get her out of the area, away from Murchie.'

'But if she leaves...' he frowned, rubbing at the side of his head, '...who'll keep an eye on her?'

She nodded. 'That's the problem, of course. But then, so is Murchie.'

He curled forwards in his armchair, all elbows and knees. 'Murchie,' he said. 'Why they can't just lock him up now – he's got form for dealing as long as your arm.'

'Yes. And he's got all those kids working for him. Most of his customers never see him. The only person who could really give evidence against him is Abbie herself.'

'And she's terrified.' He uncurled himself. 'Poor girl.' He leant back in his chair. 'Do you know she got an A in her Art GCSE? She told me herself. It's the only exam she ever passed. She had a really nice teacher. She let her call her Fiona instead of Miss.'

There was a knock at the door, and a face appeared. 'Dr Kitson...' A young man shuffled into the room, his trainers trampling baggy trousers. 'There's a phone call in the office. Marianne, from your practice. Sorry to interrupt, Sister.'

'That's OK, Gilroy,' she said.

'I was going anyway.' The doctor stood up, tall as a pillar, shrinking the room around him. 'Well, Agnes.' He picked up his case and went to the door. 'It's a busy morning at the clinic. I'm surprised Marianne's left me in peace all this time.'

'Thanks for coming,' Agnes said.

'Even though I was no use.'

'That's not true.' She got up and followed him into the hall. 'Everyone here is worried about Abbie.'

'She's a nice kid.' Agnes saw the flicker of concern cross his face.

'Keep in touch,' he said. 'Try and get her to eat, at least.' He opened the front door, braced himself against a gust of wind, then descended the steps to the street.

She shut the front door.

'Anyone out there?' Gilroy was leaning against the wall, his heels kicking the skirting board.

'All quiet,' she said. She glanced at him. 'Are you sure it was him – last night?'

He nodded. 'Couldn't mistake him. Bastard.'

'You look exhausted,' she said. She followed him back into the lounge, where he flopped into an armchair.

'How's anyone going to sleep when there's fuckin' stones being thrown at the windows? S'all right for me, I was on the night shift, I can go home – but our residents, they ain't got no place else to go.'

'Why didn't you call the police?'

He whistled air through his teeth in answer. 'Man, you just don't get it, do you?' He rubbed the top of his head, his fingers following the lines in his shaved black curls. 'It weren't just Murchie out there on his own. Him and all his boys, it was. Feds is just going to make it a whole lot worse.'

She sat down opposite him. 'You tell me, then – what shall we do? That's the third night running we've been under attack.'

He shrugged. 'It's Abbie that's the trouble. Murchie thinks she belongs to him. And all that was cool till Mots came to live here.'

'Dermot?'

He nodded. 'Murchie thinks Mots is moving in on Abbie, right? And he ain't happy, innit?'

Above them, the loud music started up again. Gilroy yawned. 'And if it ain't them rude boys keeping me awake, it's Eddie with his 50 Cent. Non-stop, man, he's got it on repeat.'

She rested her arm on the sofa cushions. 'You should get some sleep, Gil. Aysha can cover your shift.'

He stood up. 'Sleep, yeah. That's where I'm going.'

'And I might just put in a call to our local police station.'

'You think feds is going to make a difference?'

'Yes. I do.'

He smiled down at her. 'Man, your faith, Sister.'

She smiled back. 'It's my job.'

'Maybe.' He went to the door. 'The God thing – the God thing I can do. The feds...' He shook his head, sighing. The door closed softly behind him.

She sat, alone, in the hostel lounge. Sunlight filtered briefly through the curtains, then faded again. There was a smell of bacon frying.

She recalled what Sister Michaela had said after Mass at the convent house last night. 'Back at the hostel, eh, Sister? No wonder you're looking so well.'

It had sounded like a reproach.

Agnes looked at the soft green carpet, the pale cream walls, the simple, wooden crucifix hanging in one corner, the only sign of the Order's influence.

She thought about Abbie, and Dermot, and Eddie upstairs, and the other residents, Paz, Sari and Lizzie; and Gilroy. Gil, who'd once been a client and now was a co-worker; who at an early age had tumbled out of school and subsequently drifted into drug abuse, criminality and eventually, homelessness. One midnight he'd appeared on the hostel doorstep, drunk and bleeding; now, two years later, here he was, a trusted member of the hostel team. For a while he would tell anyone who'd listen that without the Lord Jesus he'd still be on the streets. The story varied; sometimes it was a pastor at his mother's church who'd saved him; sometimes a vision of Our Lord himself, one wintry night by Blackfriars Bridge when he was considering throwing himself into the river.

Agnes had noticed that Jesus had faded from his more recent accounts of his salvation. She settled further back on the sofa. It wasn't something she'd ever experienced, a vision of Our Lord, despite being a nun, and a nun who'd taken her final vows at that. No longer a novice; no longer poised in a state of uncertainty between the world and the Order. Her friend Father Julius had remarked recently how well it suited her, being 'fully paid-up' as he put it. She'd asked him what on earth he meant, and he'd frowned at her over the top of his gold-rimmed glasses and said, after a while, 'You seem more yourself, I suppose. Yes, I think that's what it is.'

More myself. She blinked up at the window, which suddenly flooded with pale sunlight.

It was Julius too who'd said, 'The great thing about having made your final vows is that at last there's nowhere left to run.'

As if it was that easy, to call a halt. To draw a line.

Outside she could hear a distant peal of bells, the City churches across the river chiming noon. She checked her watch, wondering whether to join Aysha in the kitchen, making lunch.

The door squeaked open. A young woman stood hunched in the doorway, her hands wrapped around each other. 'Sister – they said you were in here.'

Agnes looked up. 'Abbie – come in. How are you?'

The girl took tentative steps to a chair and sat down, perched at the edge of the cushion. Her mousy hair fell in wisps around her thin face. Her legs looked brittle in their skinny jeans.

'I've been thinking about what to do, and I've decided the best thing is if I leave. Like, soon.' Her voice was reedy and uncertain.

'Abbie, we've talked about this. You know what I think.'

'I'm only causing trouble here.'

Agnes shook her head. 'If various men around you choose to behave badly, that doesn't mean it's your fault.'

Abbie gazed at her with wide blue eyes. 'If I went away, then they'd go away too.'

'And how would that solve any of your problems?'

She pulled at a thread on the knee of her jeans. 'Dunno,' she said at last.

'We're trying to find you a flat. Surely you should wait till then.'

'That'll take ages.'

'It's not as if you've got anywhere to go in the meantime.'

'My dad lives over in Brixton.'

'Your dad? You've never mentioned him before.' Agnes searched her memory, trying to recall the file. Mother dead, father absent, ex-army, known to have a criminal record for assault.

'Never had much to do with him, that's why.'

'Do you want to have anything to do with him?' In her mind Agnes ran through the options; to send a vulnerable teenager back to a violent ex-soldier—

Abbie interrupted her thoughts. 'No,' she said. 'I don't.'

'Well, then you should stay here for a bit longer. Dr Kitson says you're making good progress.'

Abbie's crooked posture softened slightly. She nodded. 'He's been good to me,' she said.

'He says you've done really well on his withdrawal programme.'

'He's been very nice to me.'

'So, if you don't need the drugs any more, you can kick Murchie out of your life too.'

She stared at the floor, her hands knotted together in her lap.

'I take it he doesn't want to go.'

Abbie shook her head.

'And is that why he's causing all this trouble?'

'Yes.' The voice was barely audible.

'I suggested to Gil that we call the police—'

Her head flicked upwards. 'Don't do that.'

'That's what Gil said.'

'He'll only take it out on me.'

'Abbie—' Agnes leant forward, resting her elbow on the arm of the chair. 'You don't need Murchie. He knows that. That's why he's playing up. He can't bear to feel that he's losing control of you.'

She shook her head. 'You don't know nothing about it. I mean, I'm not being funny or anything, but it's all right for you to say, isn't it, when you're one of them nuns—'

'My husband was just like Murchie,' Agnes interrupted. 'The more he sensed he was losing control, the more violent he became.'

The blue gaze settled on her.

'I would have died if I'd stayed with him,' Agnes said.

'When…?'

'A long time ago. In France. I was very young.'

Abbie leant back on the sofa. She crossed her arms. Outside there was a screech of brakes, the hoot of a car, an engine revving, fading into the distance.

'I thought you couldn't be just a nun,' Abbie said at last. 'When they said you were a nun, I thought well, why doesn't she wear one of them things, you know? And you've got that nice hair, kind of short and dark like that. And your jeans are really well cut, and I like them ankle boots, are they new? My friend Lindy, she's one of the girls, she was asking me which one you were, and I said, she's the nun, right, only I said, she'd be quite pretty if she weren't a nun. I said you looked like that woman off the telly, that one about people's houses and doing them up, you know, those ones with the swimming pools and stuff in the south of France only then they find the neighbours have killed their puppy. But she's younger than you, and anyway, you're not allowed on the telly are you, it's against your religion.' She stopped, breathless, as if she'd run out of words.

'I suppose so.' Agnes wanted to ask what it was about being a nun that forbade being pretty too, but Abbie turned to her.

'Your husband, then—'

'Yes?' Agnes waited.

'How did you get him out of your life?'

'I was rescued.'

'Who rescued you?'

Agnes met her eyes. 'Father Julius.'

'What, him, that nice priest what comes here sometimes?'

'Yes. I met Julius, back then, in France. He'd come over from Ireland to be a curate in the village there. We became friends. I turned up on his doorstep one night…he hid me from Hugo, got me on to a boat to England.'

'Is that why you became a nun, then? To hide?'

The sunlight faded, and the room became dull again.

'I hope not,' Agnes said at last.

Abbie stretched her fingers in her lap. 'I don't want to hide neither.'

'Well, you don't have to. You should stay here until we can find you somewhere appropriate to move on to.'

'Dr Kitson said he'd be sad to see me go.'

Agnes leant towards her. 'You don't have to go.'

Abbie picked at a fingernail.

'You're not responsible for Murchie,' Agnes said.

Abbie pulled her phone out of her pocket and glanced at it. 'I told him I'd see him later.'

'You don't have to have anything more to do with him.'

Abbie looked at her. 'It's all right for you. You got away.'

She looked at her phone again, then went to the door. 'I'd better go. I'll see you later.'

In the doorway, Agnes squeezed her arm. 'It'll be OK, Abbie. We'll look after you.'

Abbie gave her a thin smile. She seemed about to speak, then turned away. Agnes heard the front door close behind her.

In the kitchen, a young woman was stirring a huge saucepan. She was dressed in black from head to toe, apart from an apron which the hostel had acquired and which for some reason showed all the best-known sights of Paris in red, white and blue. She looked up at Agnes and smiled. 'Soup again,' she said.

'We need to do a midnight supermarket run.' Agnes looked at the wide pine table in the hostel kitchen, set for six, a bread roll in each place.

'Eddie can do it. He likes it when they give us all the free stuff.'

'Reminds him of his shoplifting days.' Agnes sat down at the table.

Aysha looked at her, her brown eyes dark with concern. 'You all right?'

Agnes picked up a roll. 'I was thinking about running away.'

'Don't do that.'

Agnes glanced at her, then laughed. 'I mean, I was wondering whether becoming a nun is just a way of hiding from the world.'

'You aren't hiding, though, are you?'

'No, but—'

'You don't even dress like a nun,' Aysha said. 'When I told

my nan about you, she said, how does anyone know she's a religious woman, then?'

'Your nan?'

'My mum's mum. She lives with us. Twenty years now, she came over when I was born, and she still reckons she's homesick for the village. She said to me, Aysha, there you are wearing hijab and everyone knows you're a believing woman, and there's this nun, a woman who's given up her life to God and no one knows.'

'So, she thinks I'm hiding too?'

Aysha smiled. 'But then, it makes no sense, because if I'm wearing the headscarf I'm hiding more than you are.'

Agnes shook her head. 'No, because whenever you walk out into the street, everyone knows you're a Muslim. Whereas, no one knows anything about me. I'm just a woman with short, dark hair and jeans. So I'm the one who's hiding.'

Aysha smoothed the Eiffel Tower over her long black skirt. 'I don't know,' she said. 'People just have to do what feels right, don't they – oops, the soup.' She turned back to the cooker and stirred furiously. 'It always burns on the bottom of this pan, and they all complain. And that Abbie eats next to nothing as it is.'

'She went out,' Agnes said. She got up from the table. 'It would be nice if she came back for lunch.'

Aysha sighed. 'Poor girl. There's a letter for you,' she added, as Agnes went to the door. 'Parcel thing. In the office. One of your Sisters dropped it off for you.'

The sky had clouded over, and leaves danced circles in the gutters. Agnes pulled her scarf tighter around her neck. Her bag was slung over her shoulder, weighed down with a large brown paper envelope, which was covered with a chaotic array of American stamps, and bore a postmark from West Virginia.

She reached the main road and waited for the lights to change. She could see the spire of St Simeon's, Julius's church, a needle of Victorian gothic against the post-war grey of Southwark Bridge Road.

I don't know anyone in America, she thought.

I don't know anyone in West Virginia.

Except for my father. And he's been dead for years.

I'll open it after Mass, she thought.

Father Julius stood before the altar. The folds of his purple robe echoed the curls of blue and red stained glass on the window behind him. The chalice sparkled with candlelight as he held it up.

Around her, Agnes heard the murmured responses of the sparse congregation, their words floating upwards with the incense smoke. She glanced down at the envelope which peeped from her bag. She was aware of a sudden scent of tobacco; a flash of memory, of her father, in his London flat, long after he had left the family home in France, leaning back in his antique rocking chair, framed by the marble mantelpiece, lighting his pipe.

Agnes breathed in the smell of smoke, and her throat tightened, as if the past itself was seeping out from the envelope beside her.

'Aren't you going to open it?' Julius poured boiling water into a large teapot. They were sitting in his office, a tiny room at the side of the church, down a curved staircase. Agnes sat beside his desk, which was deep red mahogany. It was tidy; a blotter, an ink pen in a tray, a solid black old-fashioned telephone. Above it, set into the Victorian brickwork, was a leaded window, through which she could see the almost bare trees outside waving their chilled fingers.

Julius came over to the desk and handed her a small porcelain cup patterned with blue. He set one down for himself. She heard the sharp out-breath as he lowered himself into his chair.

He glanced at her, and his blue eyes smiled. 'What?'

'I was just thinking, we must be much older than we were.'

He peered at her over the top of his glasses. 'Well, Agnes, I think that's indisputable.'

'But I thought you were old when we met,' she said.

'That's because you were young,' he said.

'You had white hair even then.'

He touched the top of his head. 'Did I?'

She smiled at him. 'And now it's sticking up.' She looked into her cup. 'What's this, then?'

'Green tea. I hope I've made it right. One of my parishioners insists on it – Mrs O'Leary. She says it'll save my life, after my "health scare", as she puts it. She's given me packets of the stuff, and I'm still not sure I like it.'

Agnes sipped it. 'Well, it tastes as if it's doing good, I suppose.'

Julius watched her. 'So,' he said. 'This envelope.'

'Oh. That.'

He reached across to her bag, pulled the letter out and passed it to her. 'Go on, then. And there's no point looking at me like a sulky child. So, as you told me before Mass, it's been sent to your convent house, and it's come from the States, where your father spent his last years. So now you think it's something from your family's past that's going to trip you up again, just when you'd found an equilibrium. I know what you're thinking. You're worried that some kind of vortex to do with your parents and their difficulties is going to open up and drag you down into its core.'

Agnes took another sip of tea.

'You don't have to be frightened of them any more,' Julius said.

She looked up at him.

'Go on,' he said. He held out the envelope again. She took it and tore the end open, and pulled out the contents. It contained a series of yellowing printed pamphlets, which she placed on the desk. There was also a letter. The letterhead said 'Reisberg Institute, Department of Geology'. It was signed Dr Bretton Laing.

'Geology?' Agnes said.

Julius's phone rang, a solid black, old-fashioned ring. 'Father Julius?' he said. 'Ah, yes...'

Agnes read the letter, which addressed her as Sister Agnes, apologised for intruding on her life (she could hear the polite American tones), and explained that he was taking the liberty of returning some of her father's property to her, as the library which housed it in America was closing down, and he really didn't know who else should have it. Dr Laing also explained he would be coming to London in the near future and would be very happy to discuss the enclosed with her, if she felt this would be at all helpful. However, he respected her calling in life, and if she felt such contact would be inappropriate, she must rest assured he would understand perfectly...

'...Yes, of course,' Julius was saying. He glanced at his watch. 'I can pass by later on today if you like. Three o'clock?

See you then.' He hung up. He looked at her. 'Still here, then? No vortex?'

Agnes was leafing through the pamphlets. 'These were my father's. In fact,' she looked at the name printed on one of the covers, 'they're written by my father. Some of them. "Male and Female Created He Them – an argument in support of the Adamic Language." They're religious tracts. How very odd.' She threw a glance at Julius. 'Who was that?'

'Oh...' He frowned, rubbing his eyebrow. 'A parishioner. Jeremy Stipes. His wife had cancer a while ago, they found out last week that it might have recurred. She's only in her fifties. He's a cradle catholic, but the idea that his wife might die seems to be testing his faith rather severely. His main response at the moment is rage, which, although understandable, is rather unhelpful to everyone else.' He reached for his cup and took a mouthful of tea. 'It wasn't a happy marriage at the best of times. I said I'd pop round, they've had some more test results.' He pointed at the pamphlets. 'So he was religious, your father?'

'He always had an eccentric belief system. But this—' She picked up another pamphlet. '"And the Evening and the Morning Were the Third Day – How the Lord placed the Fossils in the Crust of the Earth".'

'Goodness.' Julius reached across and picked up the booklet. 'He was a creationist?'

'It seems so. But why would this geologist end up with all this? My father died ten – no, eleven – years ago.'

'Funny place, America,' Julius said. 'They do things differently there.' He got up and brought the teapot over, and refilled both their cups. 'Do you think you'll see him?'

Agnes picked up Dr Laing's letter. She put it down again.

'You don't have to,' Julius said. 'I can write to him and explain that you're in an enclosed order and only have permission to speak once a year, and then only from behind a grille...'

Agnes laughed. 'Oh, Julius,' she said. 'I was thinking on the way here about the choice we've made—'

'Worrying about it, no doubt—'

'I was thinking,' she said, 'that monastic life is just as much a running away as a running towards. It's a turning away from life, instead of a celebration of it.'

Julius leant back in his chair; he touched his fingertips together. 'I know what you mean,' he said, after a while. 'Because our faith is about the life after this one; because we believe in the part of us that survives death – it's easy to accuse us of death-worship. We try to live this life in an awareness of the next one, but it can look like a deliberate decision not to engage with life at all.'

She began to gather the pamphlets into a neat pile.

'You're not...' Julius reached out a hand towards her. 'You're not regretting your decision to take final vows?'

She raised her eyes to his. 'No,' she said.

'No one can accuse you of choosing death over life,' he said. 'All you have to do is go shopping with your friend Athena, and you come back a new person.'

'Am I so shallow?'

He smiled at her. 'Even a nun needs a new pair of ankle boots from time to time.'

'You don't miss a thing, you terrible man.' She tilted her foot towards her. The boots were in soft black leather with a low heel. 'Athena knew they'd suit me. And they were in the sale anyway.'

He watched her, his head on one side.

'Just because you're so spiritually advanced, you can see this life as an illusion—' she began.

His hand went up to stop her. 'No,' he said. 'Not an illusion.' His tone was harsh. 'When I nearly died, the year before last...' his voice faltered, then he continued, '...everything changed.' He picked up his empty cup, and traced circles around the rim. 'And even though all my tests are coming back clear, and even though my doctor says I can start going every six months for check-ups rather than every three...' He put his cup down. 'I caught a glimpse of death, in those weeks. And now I know, more clearly than I've ever known, what it is to cling to life.'

His eyes seemed distant; his face had become grey.

Agnes swallowed. 'Oh Julius,' she tried to say, but her voice was thick. She reached out her hand to his, and his fingers locked with hers.

They were sitting like that, both gazing ahead, unseeing, when a sudden tinkling ring broke the silence. Agnes jumped, blinked. 'My mobile,' she said, rummaging in her bag, pulling it out.

'Hello? – Oh, Gilroy – I thought you were at home – what?'

Julius watched as she slumped over the desk, leaning on one hand, the other holding her phone tight against her ear. 'She can't be,' Agnes was saying. 'How can she be?' She listened, for a minute, maybe two, shaking her head. Then she said, 'I'm on my way.'

She clicked her phone off, stared at it in her hand as if surprised to see it there. 'It's Abbie.' She looked at Julius.

'She's dead.'

CHAPTER TWO

A fog had descended with the evening. The streets were dark and slowed, the air difficult to breathe. Agnes ran, dodging the rush hour crowds at the bus stops, darting across traffic lights, pounding the narrow road that led to the hostel.

There was noise, shouting, harsh blue lights, sirens.

And then there was the calm of the hostel as night fell. People were talking, repeating the story, how it was Eddie who found her, how he got no answer from her room, everyone saying 'but she came back', Paz swearing he heard her come in. And Eddie, knocking and knocking until, forcing the door, he saw her there, blue and cold and eyes staring.

At the centre of the talking, there were the police, a young man with short, mousy hair, who wore his non-uniform with a nervous, upright correctness. He made notes, listened, occasionally turned to the WPC at his side, whose easy manner and Afro curls gave the impression that she, too, was in civvies and not in uniform at all.

'Detective Sergeant Rob Coombes.' He held out his hand as Aysha came into the kitchen and sat down. 'This is WPC Martha Rice.'

Agnes handed Aysha a mug of sweetened tea.

'We heard her come home, soon after you left,' Aysha glanced up at Agnes, then went on. 'She went straight to her room, and then we called her for lunch and she didn't come, and after a while Eddie said she must eat so he went up there, and...and...' Aysha burst into tears. She buried her head in her arms. The police waited, solemn and patient.

Agnes left the kitchen.

The hallway was dark. From the lounge came hushed conversation, the scent of cigarette smoke even though it was banned.

Agnes went into the office. She switched on the anglepoise lamp. As she turned, a young man was standing in the doorway. His pale face was tense, his blue eyes looked haunted.

'Dermot—' she said.

He stumbled to a chair and threw himself into it.

'You've heard,' she said.

He was immobile, his hands clasped between his knees, his gaze fixed on them.

'The police are here,' she said.

Still he was silent. Outside sirens blared, then faded. He raised his head. 'She were dead scared,' he said.

'Of whom? Of what?'

He met her gaze, shook his head, stared at his hands in his lap once more.

'Murchie,' Agnes said.

'We were out on the street, out there...' he jerked his head towards the window. 'She wanted to leave him. He got angry. When that guy's angry...' He glanced up at Agnes.

'When was this?'

'Earlier today.'

'It still doesn't explain—'

He interrupted. 'The guys are saying she OD'd.'

'That's what it looks like, yes. There was a syringe there, Eddie said.'

'Why would she shoot up now, though? She gave that up a long time ago. Why go back to injecting? Even if she was going to relapse, she wouldn't do it that way.'

'Unless...'

He looked up at her. 'Unless she wanted to die?'

Agnes was silent. From the lounge came a sudden blast of music which faded just as suddenly.

'So,' Agnes said, 'you were there, with this scene in the street, then?'

He nodded, hunched in his chair.

'What happened afterwards?'

He shifted his weight. 'I had to go. I walked her back here, said goodbye...' He looked across at Agnes. 'Said goodbye,' he repeated. 'I never knew it really was goodbye.' His voice faltered, and his eyes reflected the low lamplight.

'You really cared about her?'

He nodded.

'You'll need to tell the police all this.'

'Feds?' His expression hardened. 'What can they do?'

'It's an unexplained death...'

He met her eyes. 'If only it were.'

'You mean—'

'That girl had every reason to do what she did.' His face softened once more. 'If only I could have stopped her.' He stood up, glanced down at her, hesitated, then left the room.

It was late when she left the hostel. She walked through the rain-soaked streets, through the traffic noise. Even her block of flats seemed unwelcoming, its inter-war low-rise lines uneven and drab.

Her flat was cold and dark. She walked around, putting on heating, lighting, feeling it come to life again, feeling the polished floorboards warm under her bare feet, the soft wool of the rugs she'd brought over from the Provence house all those years ago when she'd first taken up residence here.

She sat at the desk, glanced up at the white walls, the icon of St Francis.

It was good to be home. All last year she'd lived in community at the convent's main house. She'd craved solitude, but tried to tell herself that it was part of her spiritual training to eat the Order's cheap cornflakes for breakfast instead of the croissants and French apricot jam that she would normally choose. She had tried to be reasonable when Sister Christiane had explained that a visiting abbot needed to live in her flat; and when, at last, at the end of his stay, it was suggested that because Agnes was once again needed to work in the Order's hostel, it would be convenient if she took up the flat again, she had simply bowed her head in acceptance, and waited until she was sharing a celebratory glass with Athena to admit that, yes, she was very happy.

Athena had worried that the visiting abbot would have made off with her antique silver teaspoons or the French-linen tablecloths, but as far as Agnes was aware, everything was just as she'd left it.

It was good to be home.

She lit a candle. The traffic rumble seemed to fade into the distance, as she took out her prayer book. She closed her eyes with the familiar words.

'Yea, though I walk through the valley of the shadow of death...'

Her eyes flashed open. She saw Abbie's face, blue and motionless, her empty eyes staring.

'...I will fear no evil. Thy rod and staff will comfort me.'

To cling to life. That's what Julius had said. That now he knew clearly what it is to cling to life.

Abbie had relinquished her life, whether in error or by choice.

She finished her prayers, got ready for bed, lay down. But all she could see was Abbie's face; and when the dawn broke over the tower blocks beyond her window, she had the feeling that the image had been with her all night.

The morning was sharp and cold. Agnes wrapped her coat more tightly around her as she headed for the hostel. She found herself wondering where Abbie was now, wondering how long the police would need to keep her, wondering whether Julius would do the funeral, as Abbie had claimed to be Catholic by birth. She wondered about next-of-kin – would she have to contact her father? Would he care?

The police tape was still strung across the street outside the hostel. At the top of the steps lay a tangle of roses. They were pink and bedraggled and they'd been stuffed into an empty vodka bottle. Agnes saw a tattered card, which she picked up. Scrawled on it in pencil, it said, 'To our Abs. There are promises that no one can break.'

Gilroy stared at the roses in their makeshift vase as they sat on the desk in the office. 'We should tell the feds,' he said. He reached a finger towards the card, then withdrew it.

'Who might have left it?'

Gilroy shrugged.

'One of the girls? Someone who cared? Murchie?'

Gilroy sucked in his teeth. 'Not that bastard. He don't care about no one. Except his dog.'

Agnes leant back in her chair. 'What made Abbie do it?'

He shrugged. 'Something changed. She went out to see Murchie, she seemed OK. When she got back she did what she did. It makes no sense, man.' He gazed at the roses. 'I think Dermot knows more than he's saying. He's already gone out, it's early, man, too early for him. And he needs his sleep, we're on the soup run tonight.'

'He must be upset.'

Gilroy nodded. 'They were good for each other. All that dealing and business he was doing before he came here, he's really worked hard to get out of it. He was looking after himself. And Nige, the old Mots wouldn't have been able to look after Nige the way he does.'

'Nige?' The name was familiar.

'You know Nige, man. The rat.'

'Oh. The rat.' Of course. Sweet, albino, a liking for baked beans...

'And her,' Gilroy was saying, 'Abbie would have

straightened herself out too if she hadn't…if this hadn't…' He swallowed. He stared at his feet, then back to Agnes. 'I said I'd get breakfast. Not that anyone wants to eat.' He stood up and went to the door.

Agnes breathed out. 'I spoke to her yesterday. I encouraged her to tell Murchie…' She stopped, then went on, 'I told her to be brave. And look what happened.'

'I said the same. And she said to me, Murchie would rather kill her than set her free.' He hesitated by the door, then left the room.

A brief burst of sunlight filled the hallway, glinting against the glass in the office door. She could see a shape silhouetted in the glass, and it took her a moment to realise that it was Dr Kitson. He pushed the door open and headed for the other desk, and she realised he hadn't seen her.

'Dr Kitson.'

He jolted, turned towards her. 'Agnes,' he said. 'I didn't notice you there.' He smiled, came towards her, took hold of her hand.

'I'm so glad to see you,' he said.

He relinquished his hold, and in silence they settled into the shabby office armchairs. They sat for a while, Agnes staring at the floor, Dr Kitson leaning on one arm. At last he raised his head.

'There will always be the thought,' he said, 'that we could have prevented it.' He gave a heavy out-breath. 'Always.'

Agnes leant back in her chair. 'I told her to challenge him,' she said. 'Murchie. I told her about my life, as an example, about leaving a violent man, and then…' Her words drifted into silence. In her mind she rehearsed the story, how Abbie had set out that day to meet Murchie, how she'd stood up to him, and then: a heated exchange, the threat of violence, perhaps the reality of violence too, enough to drain her of all courage, rob her of all hope. Enough to—

Dr Kitson interrupted her thoughts. 'I mean,' he was saying, 'could that little tyke make her feel so hopeless that she just gave up? It seems so unlikely. She was making such progress.'

'She seems to have OD'd.'

He nodded. 'Heroin. That's what the police told me. Though it wasn't the stuff she'd been using before, I've asked them to investigate where she got it from.'

'Do you think they should be writing it off as an overdose?'

He gazed ahead of him. 'What else can they do?'

'I've been wondering whether anyone wanted her out of the way.'

He flashed her a glance, then shook his head. 'Why would they? And anyway, there's no evidence that anyone else could have got in,' he said. 'Although, if you're asking me whether Murchie is in some way implicated, then I'd say, yes. Every time that poor girl made any progress, that nasty boy managed to undo it.' He shook his head.

There was a quiet ticking in the pipes as the central heating cooled. Upstairs a door slammed; someone thumped down the stairs to the kitchen; there was subdued laughter.

'It must be hard for you, all this,' Dr Kitson said.

She glanced at him.

'I mean, the reason you went into this work, I imagine, was to make people's lives better, not to oversee a world of criminality and death.'

'It must be the same for you,' she said. 'You want to make things better too.'

'I have no illusions, though.'

'And I do?'

He met her eyes. 'I just meant, with faith, you know...the belief in a benign God...' He looked at his watch. 'Oh, dear, I'm expected at surgery in ten minutes.' He stood up. 'Well, look...' He waved an arm towards her in a vague farewell. 'I'll be back. If people need to talk, you know...residents. I can be here if you need me...' He went to the door, his hand on the door handle. 'Although I imagine you people here can organise that.'

Agnes stood up too. 'Thanks for your help,' she said.

'Let me know if there's news from the police, won't you?' He stood in the doorway.

'In the end,' Agnes said, 'we have to know we did what we could.'

He bit his lip, frowning. 'But there's always the thought we could have done more. Isn't there?'

Agnes met his eyes. 'It's a hard one to get away from,' she said.

He took a few steps into the hall, then turned back.

'The problem with Abbie was that it was between me and Murchie. And in the end, Murchie won.' He went to the door, and opened it. 'Take care,' he said. 'I'll ring you.' He trod down the stone steps, and then was gone.

She shut the door behind him. She went back to the office and slumped back into an armchair. The sun had gone in, and the room was grey. A ringing noise cut through the silence, and she took her phone out of her bag.

'Hello? Oh, Athena.'

'Heavens, kitten, you sound terrible.'

'One of our residents—' Agnes began.

'I know, I know. I just bumped into Julius, bless him, and he said some poor girl had died. Poor you. Poor everyone.'

'Yes,' Agnes said. 'Poor everyone.'

'Well, poppet, there's only one thing for it. Cake.'

'Cake?'

'I've found this fab place, not far from you, just near Borough Market – it's all pink, and it does fairy cakes on those tiered things, and proper cups and tea-strainers and everything. What do you think? Three-ish?'

Agnes looked at her watch. 'You know, that would be wonderful.' She wrote down the address as Athena dictated it.

'It'll be such fun. We can pretend we live in a time when everything was elegant. I might even wear a tea gown. If I possessed such a thing.'

Agnes put her phone away in her bag. There was a knock at the door and Gilroy put his head round the door.

'There's someone asking for you. He says he's Abbie's dad.'

'Oh. Goodness. Well, he'd better come in.'

A moment later a figure appeared in the room. He was broad-shouldered, with a lined, weathered face. His head was silvery with closely shaved, grey hair. His eyes were blue; the same blue as Abbie's.

Agnes stood up and held out her hand. He grasped it firmly. 'Paul Moffat,' he said. 'I'm pleased to meet you.'

She gestured to a chair. 'I'm Sister Agnes,' she said.

'I know.' He sat heavily into the chair.

'You know?' Agnes sat down opposite him.

'She told me all about you. You made quite an impression.' He smiled, but it seemed to take some effort.

'I didn't know you were in touch.'

He passed his hand across his forehead. Agnes noticed the tattoos across his knuckles.

'We weren't. Not really. I saw her about a month ago. We talked, she told me about living here, about what you were all like. You were her favourite.'

'She didn't say she'd seen you.'

He shook his head. 'She wouldn't have.' His voice faltered; he leant on his other hand, which was untattooed.

'What happened?'

He was silent for a while, then he looked up at Agnes. 'I was her dad. I was all she had. I let her down.' His voice choked, and again he fell silent.

Agnes waited. After a while he said, 'This won't make much sense to you. You being a nun and that. But I've worked it out, now, you see. When Abbie was born, I were made up, I were. The happiest man alive, me. She was the cutest little baby you ever did see. They handed her to me, the midwife did, and I held her in my arms and I thought, nothing can touch me now. It was like I was invincible.' His face was illumined with the memory, a brief lighting up which faded almost at once. 'But it didn't turn out that way. Because, for it to turn out that way, I'd have had to change. And I didn't change. All the things that made me what I was, they were all still there. So I carried on being a villain, being angry with the world. I carried on taking my anger out on the people around me. I were still drinking then, and when I drank, for a while it were better and then it were much much worse...' He stopped, breathing heavily.

'She said you were a soldier.' Agnes tried to make out the lettering on his knuckles, but it was blurred into his wrinkled skin.

He met her eyes. 'Yeah. Yeah, I was a soldier. It seems like a long time ago now. Another lifetime.' He clenched his fist and the lettering almost came into focus, then relaxed again. 'Thing is, Sister. I can blame all that. I've had counselling, here and there, when anyone was patient enough to put up with me. I can say, yeah, it's post-trauma. The things I've seen, the things I've done; sure, I've seen my best mate's arm blown off and him dying there in the street, calling for help, bleeding to death in front of me... And worse. These two women I saw once, in the marketplace, in Bosnia—' His words cut out. He shuddered, his eyes distant. Then he looked back at her. 'The point I'm making, Sister, is that I can blame all that if I want to. But it just avoids things, don't it? All them years ago, I held that baby in my arms and I promised her the earth. And in the end, it was a promise that I broke. Like all the other fucking promises I've ever made.' His voice cracked, and he covered his eyes with his hand. 'That's what she said to me. Abbie. Last time we met. She said, she's had enough of waiting for me, only for me to let her down again. She said she was tired of it, and she wasn't going to put herself through that again. And then she got up and walked out. And that was the last I ever saw of her. Her walking through the doors of that café on the High Street there. I can't walk past it now without crying.' He struggled to contain the tears which welled in his eyes, then turned back to Agnes. 'And what I wanted to say to her – what I should have said to her – what I say to her now, all the time, in my head – is that I feel the same way now as when I held her in my arms all those years ago. Nothing ever changed. I carried on caring about her, and I carried on making the same old mistakes. And you know, what I think now, and you might understand this, being someone who's run away from it all too – what I think is that it was all too much. When I held that baby, when I felt that feeling – it was too big. Bigger than I could handle. What I saw, when I looked into her baby-blue eyes, was that she was asking something of me. 'Cos that's what it is, isn't it? The minute you're a parent, you realise there's someone out there who you care about more than anything else in the whole world. And in the end, I couldn't hack it. And I ran away.' He breathed out, then looked up at her. 'I think maybe that's why she liked you. Because you'd evened it all out. You've given it all up, you don't have the highs and you don't have the lows.' He glanced at her. 'I hope I ain't speaking out of turn...'

'No, not at all.'

He fell silent.

'What about her mother?' Agnes said, after a while.

He sighed. 'She should never have been a mother. She couldn't look after herself, let alone anyone else. They took Abbie into care when she was four. I pleaded, I begged, I argued...but they weren't going to listen to me, an ex-soldier with a criminal record who was off his face half the time. And then her mother died, as you know. And I tried to stay in touch, but it weren't easy. They made me so fucking angry, those social workers...' He shrugged. 'Anger, see? My constant companion.' He smiled, briefly. 'I've taken up enough of your time. All I really wanted to say, was, here I am. I'm her dad. And she was my baby.' His voice cracked. He clenched his fists together in his lap. The four letters came into focus. L-O-V-E.

In the silence, Agnes heard herself say, 'You only had one hand done.'

He blinked at her. Then he looked at the backs of his hands.

'I went to have both done. Love on one hand, Hate on the other. Me and a mate, years ago, for a laugh. I got as far as Love, and then I stopped.' He smiled.

Agnes followed him out to the hall. 'Why did you stop?'

'I don't know. Maybe because it hurt too much. Always was a coward.' He offered her his hand. 'She was right about you, Abbie was.'

Agnes shook his hand. 'We still let her down.'

He looked down at her, and tears sparkled in his eyes. 'I've made a promise to myself. If I ever get another chance, if I ever find myself in a place where someone needs me – I'll allow myself to feel it. All the highs and lows, whatever life throws at me. I won't fight it any more. It's the only thing I can do for her...' He swallowed back his grief and stumbled out of the door. She watched him go down the steps and out into the street, his head bowed, not looking back.

She went back into the office and sat at her desk. She leant her head on her hands and closed her eyes. In her mind she saw the curls of pipe smoke, the grey whorls of marble, she heard her father's tight English vowels. She wondered whether he'd ever held her as a baby and promised her the earth.

Her mobile phone cut through her thoughts.

'Hi, am I speaking with Sister Agnes?'

She heard the cultured, American voice.

'Yes,' she said.

'This is Bretton Laing.' There was a silence, then he went on, 'I wrote to you.'

'Yes. Of course.'

'I'm sorry,' he said. 'They gave me your mobile number, I have no idea if this is appropriate. As I said in my letter...'

Agnes had a vision of herself, veiled in black, sitting behind a grille. 'It's fine,' she said. 'Really. I'm glad you've rung.'

'Oh.' She heard the relief in his breathing-out. 'Great. That's great. I'm in London, my schedule changed. I was hoping – I thought maybe we might meet.'

'That would be lovely.' Agnes tried to warm up her voice, banish the fatigue. 'I was very glad you sent me those documents, I was going to call you, only we've been rather...'

'How would this evening be?'

Agnes thought about her flat. She remembered the dull sleeplessness of last night, alone and dwelling on Abbie's swollen staring face.

'This evening would be fine.'

'I could buy you dinner. If you people are allowed... I wasn't sure whether...'

Agnes thought about dinner, and food, and pink cakes. 'Maybe we could meet for a drink. My life's rather complicated at the moment, and I'm a bit tired...'

'Sure, yes. Of course. My hotel has a very good cocktail bar, if you don't mind meeting me here. It's just near Tower Bridge. A fine view of a true English landmark – cliché, I know. How would six-thirty be?'

'That would be fine.'

'I mean, when I say cocktails, obviously, they do soft drinks too...'

'Oh. Good. Right.'

She heard him breathing. Then he said, 'It's really very good of you to meet me. Your father was—' He seemed to check himself, then he went on, 'I don't know much about the way of life you've chosen, but please rest assured I have no intention of disturbing your peace.'

'Thank you,' Agnes said.

'See you at six-thirty.' His phone clicked off.

Again, the picture of Abbie's tortured form. An hour or so with an educated American in a hotel bar, far from disturbing her peace, would probably go some way to restoring it, she thought. She found herself wondering what it was about her father that he'd stopped himself from saying, and why a few funny old pamphlets written by an English eccentric should prompt such an urgent need to see her.

She thought about the 'very good cocktail bar' in Bretton Laing's hotel. She hoped that a bar catering to American tourists would know how to keep a decent single malt.

CHAPTER THREE

'I mean, honestly, what does one wear to meet an American –
what did you say he was?'

'Geologist, I think. That's what his letter said. Although
what he thinks he's doing dabbling in creationism I don't
understand. I would have thought the two things clash.'

'Creationism,' Athena repeated. 'And cocktails. One really
ought to be quite smart. Sharp suit, perhaps? Or maybe more
feminine.'

Agnes looked at her friend. 'I hadn't thought.'

'I mean, really, you can't wear those old things. What if he
turns out to be absolutely gorgeous?'

Agnes surveyed the table in front of them. A tiered pink
stand was laden with little cakes. She turned it towards her
and considered whether to take another. 'I was thinking of
wearing a veil, actually. Just so everyone knows I'm a nun.'

Athena looked at her. 'I hope that's a joke, kitten.'

Agnes reached for a cake. 'You know me.'

'Oh. Phew, what a relief. I'm never quite sure. Since you
took those final vows, you've been saying very odd things.

Most disconcerting.' She licked pink icing from a fingertip. 'So, what exactly is a creationist?'

'Well, these papers of my father's make out that he was putting forward the view that the Bible is literally true and God made the world in six days, about six thousand years ago.'

'Oh.' Athena paused, mid-lick. 'And this American believes that too?'

'I can't think he does. He's a scientist of some kind. I imagine he's just researching it.'

'Hmm. In that case...' She frowned. 'Maybe black, then, and obviously not low-necked, but feminine, you know, you've got a good figure, even in that scruffy jumper. And a bit of lipstick.'

'I don't own lipstick, Athena.'

'I do think it's important to make the right impression. I've planned a whole outfit for Nic's return. It's so exciting.

'I bought this tweed skirt the other day, I wouldn't normally think of it, except that it's extremely well cut, I just think he'll like it, it's a lovely mix of dark grey and green and I've got a fab black top which will be just the thing with it...but who knows, sometimes it seems as if I can throw on any old things, a pair of jeans and an old shirt and he's just as happy.'

'When's he back, then?'

'Tomorrow evening. It's so exciting. I'm going to pick him up at the station in my new Audi. Such a treat to drive, I don't know why I didn't upgrade years ago.'

'And Nic's back for good?'

Athena nodded. 'It was awfully nice of you to give up your old house in Provence for his therapy centre, but he and I have finally worked out that it's just no good for us living that far apart. So now that sculptor, Jake, you remember, he's taking over the lease. And I know you're not allowed to own anything, poppet, but the minute you want to leave the convent and have a place of your own, I shall relinquish any claim to your family home, you know that, don't you sweetie?'

Agnes smiled at her.

'Anyway,' Athena was saying, 'it suits Jake and his brother Justin very well. Jake asked whether we'd mind if they built a new foundry for the bronze casting in that funny old brick building, grain store, whatever it was.'

'Grain store...' Agnes found herself repeating the phrase. An image flashed into her mind, the low outbuilding with its terracotta-tiled roof, from which you could reach the first few branches of the umbrella pine. A sudden memory, of losing her grip on a branch, swinging briefly, before getting a toehold and clambering back down to the roof, shaking, pulling at the torn edge of her skirt, cold with fear, wondering what her mother would say...

'Are you all right?' Athena was looking at her over the rim of her cup.

Agnes picked up the teapot. 'That house,' she said at last. 'Such memories.'

'You'd better be wary of this lovely American, then,' Athena said. 'You don't want to be tripped up any more.'

The teapot was white in colour with tiny pink roses. Agnes refilled both their cups.

'At least Nic's got work here,' Athena said. 'I was worried about him giving up the therapy centre and being bored, but it's OK because he's going to work with Janis in Primrose Hill, doing regression work like before.'

Agnes glanced at her. 'Janis?' she said.

'No, really, it's absolutely fine,' Athena said. 'Janis is about sixty and has grey hair in a bun, and she wears these floaty clothes and she's a Virgo or something, and Nic says she has the gift of making her clients feel safe, and when you meet her you can absolutely see why.'

'Ah.' Agnes reached for a white-iced cake with little yellow daisies on it. 'And will he live with you?'

Athena put down her cup. With a fingertip, she gathered up some cake crumbs that had landed on the linen tablecloth. 'The thing is…' she looked up at Agnes. 'He's very keen to live with me. And—'

'And you're not sure?'

Athena sighed. 'As ever. One of these days I'll just have to decide that he and I are a couple, and jolly well put up with it. I mean, I absolutely adore him, poor man, and it's not as if I want to spend my life with anyone else. It's just…' Her words tailed into silence.

'I know,' Agnes said. 'You and me both.'

'But at least he'll be in London, and I'm very busy at the gallery at the moment, we've got a new exhibition coming up, Simon really needs me to put in the hours, it'll be nice to have Nic there to come home to, and anyway, his mum's not well, down in Devon, and it'll be jolly for him to see her too, and there's his son Ben too, did I tell you, he's living in London with his wife and they've got a new baby, their first, a little girl, and Nic's hardly seen her what with being in France, so really it's absolutely the right time for him to be here.' She paused for breath.

'Even if he does have to live with you?'

'We'll manage.' Athena's voice seemed rather thin. 'I'm sure he's right, we've lived apart for far too long, and really, he absolutely doesn't think it's wise to leave me lying around any more, as he put it.'

Agnes laughed.

'Well, he's right, isn't he? All that silliness last year with Jake, awfully sweet, but really it's just as well I can stash him in the south of France. The truth is, I do need Nic to keep an eye on me.' She dabbed the sides of her mouth with a linen napkin, then surveyed Agnes. 'Do you still have that grey pencil skirt? Maybe, with that nice black cashmere sweater. I could lend you some shoes, even.'

Agnes sighed. 'Really, Athena…'

'It'll be nice. Get you out and about a bit, take your mind off all these awful goings-on at your hostel.

'I suppose that's rather what I thought.'

Athena checked her watch. 'Do you know, if I had time I'd drag you off to that lovely new store by London Bridge and find you a lipstick. Something to make a statement. Scarlet. Crimson. Make sure this gorgeous American creationist geologist knows he's met his match.'

Agnes raised her hand. 'Athena – he's giving me back some papers of my father's. There's nothing to say he's gorgeous. And even if he were…'

Athena watched her. 'Yes?'

'I'm a nun.'

'Yeah, yeah—' Athena began, but Agnes interrupted.

'It's different this time. Even Julius has noticed. I feel I've at last begun to let go of something. I think, even being in religious orders, I've spent the last few years clinging to a false self, a self that was nourished by the world, in some way. Julius and I were talking about this earlier – how monastic life can be all about running away from life, which isn't the idea at all – and I feel that maybe I've just begun to glimpse how it might be, for me, as a nun, to feel that I'm really embracing monastic life instead of just hiding in it.'

'Ooh dear. Darling, that's terrible. Who am I going to discuss my new shoes with now?'

'What are they like?'

'Well, the thing is, I went to this warehouse sale, I thought I'd get some sensible black boots for the winter, anyway, of course, they didn't have any in my size, but what they did have were these jewelled red-suede peep-toe wedges, such a stroke of luck it was.'

'Mmm. That is luck.'

'And you see, it was meant to be, because they cost exactly the amount I had left over after I upgraded to the A3. I'd wear them to the exhibition opening, except I can only stand up in them for about forty seconds...' She leant back in her chair. 'See? I knew you'd be interested. All this pretending it's going to be sackcloth and ashes from now on, please don't give me a fright like that again.'

They parted on the corner of Borough High Street and Newcomen Street. Athena kissed her on both cheeks. 'Have a lovely evening. Don't do anything I wouldn't do.'

Agnes brushed raindrops from her hair. 'I've never worked out what that means.'

Athena patted her arm. 'I think it means nothing at all. At least, when I say it.' She turned towards the rush hour crowds. 'I hope I can find a taxi amongst all that lot. I need a cardboard sign saying Fulham, that usually works.' She set off through the mass of people, turned briefly and waved. Agnes saw a cab draw up almost immediately.

* * *

Her flat was warm and light. Agnes poured herself a glass of mineral water, and wandered into the tiny bedroom. She opened her wardrobe.

Cashmere sweater, she thought, taking it off the shelf. Athena's right. It suits me.

It's only a black jumper, she thought. It doesn't matter what I wear, she thought, as her eye fell on the grey pencil skirt hanging on its hanger. She remembered when she'd bought it, nearly ten years ago, before...

Before I decided that none of this mattered.

I'll comb my hair, splash my face with water...

She took the skirt from the wardrobe and held it up against her.

She had a sudden jolting memory. A full-length, ornate mirror in the house in the Loire valley, where she'd lived with Hugo. Behind her, the heavy walnut wardrobe; holding up outfits against herself, getting ready to go out for dinner, the butterfly nervousness as she anticipated his response – 'I can't believe you thought you'd dress like that'; 'People will think I can't afford for you to dress properly'; 'You look like a whore...'

She'd make a decision, a demure, well-cut dress, a pair of elegant heels, knowing, always, that it would be the wrong decision because Hugo would choose to make it so; descending the wide staircase with a tightening in her stomach, a rising terror, knowing what he'd say, what he'd do.

And yet, the violence, when it came, always brought a sense of relief, the knowledge that it was over.

Until the next time.

She wondered what it would be like to get dressed knowing that you'd be admired; that rather than fear, one would feel only delight. Like Athena, she thought. She tried to imagine what it would be like to throw on a pair of jeans and an old shirt and know that even then your partner would think you were lovely, even if you didn't wear the new tweed skirt you'd planned to wear.

She looked at her watch. She pulled off her jeans, pulled on the pencil skirt and the cashmere jumper, found a pair of black tights, decided to wear her new ankle boots.

She was glad she didn't own any lipstick.

The hotel foyer was a muted space of subtle sofas in beige and cream; there was a background sophisticated murmur of conversation. A massive arrangement of white lilies seemed to reach up to the glass-atriumed ceiling.

She hesitated by the sweeping curve of the reception desk.

A man was sitting on one of the sofas, his legs angular in sharply tailored trousers. He rose from the sofa and approached her, his head on one side, a questioning smile. 'Sister Agnes?'

She nodded, returned his smile.

He offered her his hand. 'Bretton. Most people call me Brett. I'm so glad you could see me.' They shook hands. Behind him she could see the hotel bar, all dark wood and low candlelight.

He waved her towards it. 'Of course, they do loads of non-alcoholic things...pomegranate juice stuff they have, it's really healthy too—' He was flustered, now, pink-cheeked, under his pale, floppy hair.

She smiled. 'Actually, I've had a really hard day, and what I'd most like is a decent single-malt whisky. With ice.'

He studied her, standing there in the wide, bright space. She noticed how his eyes were light green, almost golden. Then with a touch of his hand he ushered her towards the bar.

She sat at a low table, and he brought a whisky and a glass of white wine to the table. 'It's an Islay,' he said. 'I hope you like it.'

'I do.'

'Your father liked it too.'

She looked up at him. 'Did he?'

'I thought you'd have known...' He began to fuss at the handkerchief in his breast pocket.

'In that case it's probably the only thing we had in common, him and me.'

He sat down, smoothing his trousers, then looked across at her.

'You're not how I imagined you,' he said.

'Oh,' she said. 'And how did you imagine me?'

'More like a nun, I suppose.'

'Ah. Yes. People do.'

'All that...' He waved his hand towards her clothes. She thought perhaps that he was blushing but the light was dim.

'And you look more French than I imagined too,' he was saying.

'I am half French,' she said.

'I forget. Your pa was so English.' He took a large gulp of wine and Agnes wondered again why he was so nervous. 'I hope...' he began. 'I hope it wasn't a shock, my letter. I got the feeling that perhaps your relationship with your father wasn't quite...'

'We weren't close. He didn't leave for good until I was in my teens and living here at boarding school, but he'd been so distant up till then...' She swirled the ice around in her glass. In her mind she saw the long corridor of the house in Provence. Sunlight through open windows, soft white curtains twitched by the warm breeze, her father in the distance, nodding to her vaguely before disappearing into the shadows of his study.

'His study,' she said. 'He had this armchair, one of those heavy leather ones, it swivelled when you pushed it round with your feet...' She remembered creeping alone into the room, she could feel her bare toes on her father's oak desk, laughing as she went round and round; and then there he was, standing in the doorway. It was the end of the game, but she couldn't recall rage or disapproval, just running out barefoot into the sunlit landing.

'I must have been about nine,' she said. 'I remember laughing, running away down the corridor. But I might be wrong. It might be a dream, not a memory at all. It's the problem with being an only child,' she added. 'No one to back you up. No one to put you right...' She found she was gazing directly at Bretton, and looked away.

'Yes,' he said. 'I'm an only child too. Another of those?'

'I haven't finished this one—' she began, but she noticed his glass was empty. 'Yes, thank you,' she said.

She watched him cross the bronzed polished floor, watched his rangy American charm as he chatted with the barman.

A conversation washed towards her from the next table: '...and then Mother was shouting at the television, but it's only because she hates time-lapse. Clouds and things. Flowers opening. And then my father left the room, so you can imagine...'

He came and sat back down, sliding her whisky across the table to her. He took a sip of wine.

'What did you want to tell me?' she said. She hadn't meant to say it out loud, she realised.

'I'm sorry?' His eyes met hers.

'I just thought—' She stopped, searching for words.

He stared at the table. He pushed the silver tray of nuts and olives towards her. 'Maybe we could get some more of those,' he said. He glanced back towards the bar, as if planning an escape.

'Just tell me,' she said.

'OK.' He leant towards her. 'I knew your father quite well. In his last year or so, when he was...when he was dying.'

Agnes stared at him. 'He – my father – knew he was dying?'

Bretton closed his eyes, opened them again. He nodded. 'He had cancer. He was in denial until the last few weeks, but then...'

'He didn't contact me.'

'No.'

'No one told me. Until afterwards.'

'I know.' He reached across the table, as if to take her hand, but stopped short, his long fingers resting on the shiny wood. 'What you must know is that it wasn't his wish. In the last few days he was trying to trace you, he was asking anyone he could think of —'

'My mother was still in the house in France.'

'Yes.'

'She knew where I was.'

'Yes.' He frowned at his hand on the table.

'You mean…' Agnes stared at the glass in front of her and said, 'My mother was the only person he didn't ask.'

'He felt he couldn't.'

Agnes picked up her whisky and chinked the cubes of ice together.

'I'm sorry,' he said.

She met his eyes. What else, she wanted to say. What other secrets will there be, if I begin to ask? Here you are, sitting there, having known my father in his last few months when he, too late, chose honesty. What do you know?

'Oh, well,' she said. 'It's so long ago, isn't it? It must be…ten years now…?' She smiled at him across the flickering candlelight. 'So, how did you come to meet my father?'

He leant back with an out-breath of relief. 'Your father was involved with a society that promoted creationism. He'd got all these nineteenth-century pamphlets, rare ones. Not to mention the ones he wrote himself. When I was doing my research, someone put me in touch with him. Then, when he was…dying…he said I could have them. So, I was rather burdened with finding a home for them all. And of course, by then, he'd told me all about you. Anyway, I found a place for them temporarily, but I'd always meant to contact you at some point, in case you might have a view about what to do with them, particularly with such a definite religious viewpoint…'

'It's very thoughtful of you,' she said.

'And now the library that was storing them wants to dispose of them, and they've come to me, and I thought you'd better have first refusal seeing as you're his daughter.'

He picked up a cocktail stick and speared an olive.

'I wasn't sure what you'd think of it. I mean, with you being a believer.'

'I'm not someone who takes the biblical account at face value.'

'Ah.' He nodded at her. 'I wasn't sure.'

'I don't see a conflict between Darwin's views and my faith.'

'Neither did most Christians at that time,' he said.

'It's not a subject I know much about.'

Bretton toyed with a second olive. 'Your father...' he said.

'What?'

'Apart from the books, he had a collection of very rare objects. Shells from various important geological strata. A chunk of the original Noah's Ark. Fossils which he claimed were created within the six days.'

Agnes stared. 'How can that be?'

'I've got them. They're a box of stones, ammonites, that kind of thing. He was adamant that they were created by God at the same time that he created the crust of the earth. He said he could prove it. That's how I got involved, with my background in carbon dating. The piece of the Ark would be quite easy to date, I thought.'

Another flash of memory; yellowed pages within a leather binding, her father reading to her, her toes, barefoot against the warm wood of his desk. 'Genesis. He used to read it to me. The King James version. It was something we shared, the language of it, that old English...'

'The irony is,' he said, 'that your father's view is gaining ground. What would once have appeared to be an eccentric belief held by a tiny minority, has turned into this argument we keep hearing about "intelligent design"...Where I come from, the evolutionists are on the back foot.' He glanced up at her. 'Perhaps you're pleased at that?'

'Oh, no.' She shook her head. 'I don't like to see religious beliefs gaining political power.'

'No,' he said. 'Neither do I. Unless it's on the side of the underdog.'

She smiled at him. 'Liberation theology. We can agree on that.' She finished her first whisky and started on the next. 'So, how come it was you who ended up with all this stuff?'

'I don't know. I suppose he trusted me.'

'Didn't he have family – friends – anyone?'

He put down his glass. 'You know what he was like.'

'Do I?' She met his gaze.

'Distant. Shy. A bit forbidding, although I don't think he realised it.'

'Yes.' Forbidding. Distant.

'You know his writings on Gosse, I suppose?'

'Gosse?' She blinked at him.

'Philip Henry Gosse.'

'I'm sorry, I've never heard of him.'

'Important nineteenth-century writer, took on the whole Darwinian thesis, insisted that the world was created in six days. I'd have thought they'd let you read that in the nunnery.'

'Our "nunnery" library isn't as extensive as it should be.'

'He wrote a book called "Omphalos". It's all about the fact that Adam the first man was created with a navel, ie with all the signs of having had a history, a past within the life cycle of men. It's a stunning argument, actually. Gosse's view is that when you ask the question "Where does the story start?" you're asking the wrong question, ie your starting point is wrong. He argued that God's narrative isn't based in human time. God can start the story wherever he wants. So, the way he saw it, creation is what he calls a "violent interruption" to a cycle that is continuous – hence the first man was created with a navel. And trees were created with all their rings.'

'Oh.'

'Your father searched for fossils that would prove the Gosse thesis.'

'And he reckoned he'd found some?'

Brett nodded. 'Guess so. It's all about time, you see.' He brushed back his floppy hair. 'Even if there is a moment of time in which creation took place, it can't exist without another moment before it and another after it and so on to infinity. And I guess your Pa's view was that that's really no problem, if you're God.'

'No. I can see that.' She noticed him glance at his wrist, checking the watch that peeped out from the expensive shirt cuff. 'You have to go, don't you?' she said.

He looked up at her and smiled. 'And so do you, I expect,' he said. 'I can't imagine they allow you out late.'

'You'd be surprised,' she said.

He placed two notes on the waiter's tray. He held up his hand. 'It's on me,' he said. 'I insist.' He glanced across at her. 'Or does your Order give you an expense account? Would I be surprised by that too?'

She laughed. 'I'm afraid not.'

'Relying on the kindness of strangers,' he said. 'I guess it's not a bad way to live.'

She watched him collect the change, watched him leave a generous tip. As they stood up, he reached for her coat, held it for her to put on.

She slipped her arms into the sleeves, then turned to face him. 'It's quite clear to me that you knew my father better than I ever did.'

He stood, tall against the low light. He looked at the floor, looked back to her. 'Perhaps,' he said. 'But then again – perhaps we all know our parents better than we realise.'

'Even one as distant as he was?'

He offered her his arm. She linked her arm through his as they walked slowly through the darkness of the bar to the lights beyond. 'There's always an imprint,' he said. 'Genetic, you might say.'

'Unless you're a creationist,' she said.

The foyer was busy with dark-suited men. He glanced down at her. 'Even then,' he said. 'Even creationists like the idea of inheritance. The first Adam and the last,' he added, as they approached the wide revolving door. He stood back to let her go through first.

The outside air was cold. A mist hung over the Thames, pin-pricked with light from the buildings beyond.

'What do you mean?' she said, as he joined her outside.

'The idea put about by all this nineteenth-century lot was that Adam was thirty-three when he was created. And Jesus was thirty-three when he died. The circle of redemption was complete. And the Wood of the Cross came from the original Tree, the Tree of Knowledge. It's all symmetrical, you see.'

'You'd make a good monk,' she said, as they began to walk along the quay.

He smiled down at her. 'Oh, no. Not me. You forget, for all that I've brushed up against your father's world, I'm a scientist. If I wanted to study the wood of the cross, I'd carbon date it first.'

She laughed. 'Symmetry,' she said. 'I can see how that would appeal to my father. He liked order.'

'At the expense of feeling, maybe?'

'Yes.' She glanced up at him. 'Perhaps that's how it was.' They came to a halt at the end of the road. 'I can get the bus from here,' she said.

'Is that monastic life? A glass or two of decent whisky, and then you catch the bus?'

'That's on a good day,' she said.

He shook his head. 'It's not for me.' He scanned the street for a taxi, raised his arm as one approached. He opened the door for her. 'But—' she began.

He leant into the driver's side, exchanged a few words, passed some money across to him.

'There you are,' he said to her. 'Safely home.'

'The kindness of strangers,' she said, getting into the taxi.

'It's always worked for me,' he said. He shut the door, leant into the open window. 'I'll call you. There's loads more of your father's papers, if you want them. Thank you for a lovely evening.'

The cab pulled away. Agnes watched the passing yellow haloes of street light in the mist. She could feel the warmth of his arm against hers. She heard the low foghorn of a boat on the Thames.

CHAPTER FOUR

'...You established the moon and the sun; you fixed all the boundaries of the earth...you made both summer and winter...'

In the convent house, the Sisters' singing floated upwards towards the chapel roof. As Agnes joined in the psalm, she caught a cadence of her father's voice, seemed to hear him reciting the same verses, loud in the belief that he was uttering a literal truth.

The chapel windows were muted with a chill dawn. She felt a sudden wave of loss, for what exactly, she couldn't say. She was fifteen again, standing in the chapel in her English boarding school, trying in her homesickness to imagine the warmth and light of Provence, knowing that in her absence her parents' marriage was unravelling.

It was fear; an old fear that nothing stood between herself and chaos. She found she was standing with her fists clenched, her eyes tight shut, the way she did as a child, believing that she could hold it all together just by thinking about it, knowing that if she ceased to concentrate then it would all erupt into disorder once more...

She opened her eyes, breathed again.

'...The Lord was so merciful that He forgave them their sins; for He remembered that they were but flesh, a breath that goes forth and does not return...'

She joined in the amens, grateful to her community for giving her a place to be where the chaos would be kept at bay whether she was concentrating or not.

The convent kitchen was busy with Sunday morning. Sister Mary wanted to ask her about a new setting for the 'Ave Maria', it would involve some harmony singing, and I know it's a bit of a challenge now that Sister Thomasina has gone to the house in Germany, but I do think we're capable of a simple G minor triad, don't you, Agnes? Sister Helen wanted to know if she'd seen Jonah the kitten, he's always running off, serves us right for naming him after a prophet, although I don't suppose there are many whales roaming around Hackney, he's more at risk from cars these days, oh and by the way, Agnes, have you met Sister Louisa, she's joined us from our sister-Order in Yorkshire, American but been here for years, she was here a minute ago, ah, yes, look, there she is, come and say hello...

Sister Louisa had a kind, lined face, and thick grey hair, tied loosely back. She was sitting in a corner, her mug of tea held neatly in both hands, her white collar giving her a starched, upright look.

She smiled up at Agnes. 'I've heard a lot about you.' Her voice was quiet, with a soft American accent.

'People usually have,' Agnes said.

Louisa looked at her as she sat down next to her. 'And is that a good thing?'

'For a nun, probably not.'

Sister Helen had drifted away; Agnes could hear her in the hall, tracing Jonah's last sightings, I definitely saw him yesterday morning, and some of his food's gone, but that might be one of the others stealing from him, naughty things...

Louisa was speaking to her. 'You think we all crave anonymity?'

Agnes looked into her clear grey eyes and suddenly wanted to tell her everything, about her father, her memories in chapel, her insight that convent life had let her off the hook.

'Do you?' Agnes said. 'I mean, do you crave anonymity?'

Louisa stared at the mug that she still held in her lap. 'Yes,' she said. 'Most certainly I do.'

'For any reason? Or just generally?'

Louisa continued to stare ahead of her. Her face seemed heavy, as if weighed down with sadness.

'Let's just say, that where convent life is concerned, I have resolved to tuck myself away. I am attempting to find a modicum of peace.'

'I live alone.' Agnes heard her words blurt themselves out.

'They told me.' Louisa was looking at her now. 'I thought, lucky you. And how determined you must have been to get your own place. And now I've met you...' Her voice tailed off.

'So,' Agnes said. 'How long have you been in England?'

She smiled. 'Oh, some years. Mostly in Yorkshire. I've been based in Bradford, working on a health project for street women. I'm starting a similar thing here. The Sisters tell me I should ask you about the hostel.'

'Anything you like.'

'How do you get round the laws about the age of your clients? In Bradford we were seeing girls of thirteen, fourteen, it was very difficult not to be forced into returning them to the very families they'd fled.'

'It's an endless debate. The police know us. They're usually very helpful. But we've been concentrating on the over-sixteens for a while, it's more straightforward legally.'

Louisa nodded and sipped her tea.

One of our residents died. The words formed in her mind, unspoken. Abbie, she was called. Agnes almost said the name, out loud, as if somehow that would bring her back, back into this world. She felt her throat tighten with tears, turned back to Louisa. 'And America?' she said.

Louisa put her mug down on the window sill. Then she turned back to Agnes. 'I ran away. Everything since can be traced back to that.'

Agnes met her open gaze. I was just the same, she wanted to say. I ran from my husband into an enclosed Order, I ran away from that into this one. She wanted to tell her everything; about her father, and how he, too, ran away, from England to France, from France to America; and now, she wanted to say, I've met someone who knew him in his last few years, who can tell me how he was, how he lived, how he died…

Louisa spoke first. 'They said you'd want to know everything about me,' she said.

'They did?' Agnes was jolted back to the present moment. 'They were right. Where do we start?'

Louisa smiled, but then Sister Helen was there again, approaching Agnes, breathless. 'Agnes – the hostel's phoned. Can you go there at once?'

Agnes was on her feet. 'What's happened?'

'It was that nice Gilroy. He said there'd been another incident. A threat of some kind. The police have been called.'

'I'll be right there.' She picked up her bag and turned to Louisa. 'We'll catch up later,' she said.

'I very much hope so,' Louisa said.

'His rat? Dermot's rat?' Agnes stood in the hostel kitchen, her voice loud.

'Poisoned. Dead.' Gilroy was leaning against the kitchen table, the palms of his hands flat against the pine surface. Three of the hostel residents, two girls and a boy, were sitting on a bench, silent, watching.

'How—?'

'He was injected, we think. Mots was keeping him outside 'cos he'd got allergies from being in his room. He found him this morning when he got back from the soup run.'

'Where is he now?'

Gil flicked a glance at the young people sitting on the bench.

'He's in his room, innit Sari?' the boy said to one of the girls. He had soft, brown eyes which peeked out from under a woolly hat pulled down almost to his nose.

'Nah, Paz, he ain't.' The young woman had a sheet of jet black hair that swung at her cheeks as she spoke. Strings of beads hung from her neck, and she fiddled with them, turquoise, pink, amber. 'He went out. Lizzie heard the door go, didn't you Liz?'

Lizzie nodded. She was silent, porcelain-skinned under red curls.

Gil turned to Agnes. 'Sergeant Coombes is in the office, if you want to talk to him.'

The office was unlit. Agnes bent to switch on the heating. 'Aren't you cold?'

Rob shrugged. 'Not so's I'd notice.'

'I bet uniform would be warmer than what you're wearing.'

'I've been out of uniform eighteen months now.' He spoke with pride.

Agnes came to sit down opposite him. 'It's nice of you to give up your Sunday over a mere rat.'

He appeared to blush. 'It's not so much that it's an animal, you understand. It's the connection with what happened before. There seems to be a pattern of bullying going on round here.'

'Yes,' Agnes agreed. 'There has been.'

'I take it that the boy Murchison is involved?'

Agnes nodded.

'And we know he was involved with Miss Moffat too.'

'Yes.'

'If you don't mind me asking, what was the nature of their relationship?'

Agnes met his eyes. 'What do you think?'

'You mean, like most of the girls who hang around with Murchison?'

Agnes nodded.

'He's scum.' Again, the colour rose to Rob Coombes's face. 'I may be speaking out of turn, but people like that kid see everyone as money. They see all relationships in terms of what they can get out of them. With the other lads it's getting them to work for you, getting your cut. With the girls…' He shook his head.

'Perhaps if you spend your young life being treated as a commodity, you end up treating other people the same.'

He flashed her a look. 'Is that what you think? That it's always caused by hardship?'

'Well, I—' Agnes stopped, taken aback at the strength of his response.

'I used to think like you. Where I'm from, east side of Leeds, you'd see deprivation just bringing about more deprivation. But then, one day I met Syrus. White lad, he were, tall, jet black hair. He came from one of the richest families in Leeds, his granddad was in textiles, his dad was in property. Lovely home, lovely mum, lovely brother and sisters. All great kids, all went to college. Except Syrus. He was running one of the most successful drugs rackets in Chapeltown. Not that he lived there, of course. And no one in Chapeltown ever saw him there.' He leant down and rubbed his ankle in its ribbed grey sock. 'There weren't now't wrong wi' that lad's life. He were loved, he were cherished. I were a volunteer in them days, special constable. When he first got brought in, his parents were there at his side. Weeping, they were. Asking, what have we done? What did we do wrong? And I heard my boss say to them, old Flaherty, he said, sometimes people just choose to be bad.' He leant back and looked at her. 'Soon after that I came down south, joined the Met. And the more I do this job, the more I think Inspector Flaherty was right. Not all the time, mind, a lot of them are poor saps all right. But with this Murchison character – I'd save my sympathy for someone who deserves it.'

The heater was roaring away at full blast. Agnes bent to switch it off. In the sudden hush she said, 'So this rat business?'

'From what those kids in your kitchen said, Murchie's been plaguing young Mr O'Hagan for some time.'

'Dermot? Yes, he has.'

'And that young woman was involved too?'

'She came to live with us as part of a move to get her off the streets. And she met Dermot here, who's also a resident. And they became a couple, and Murchie didn't like it.'

'He knew Mr O'Hagan before?'

'Yes. I'm not sure of the background, but Dermot declared himself homeless and came to live here some weeks ago, as a way of escaping from Murchie.'

'It's obviously quite difficult to get away from this Murchie.'

Agnes looked at him. 'Yes.'

He stood up. 'Well, we'll keep in touch.'

'You could...' She hesitated, then went on, 'Couldn't you take the rat away for forensic tests?'

He looked down at her. 'Culpable homicide doesn't extend to rats, I'm afraid.'

'No, what I thought was, if you can trace the poison, you could make a connection with whatever Abbie OD'd on.'

'And what would that tell us? Just that there's been some purer-than-usual stuff around recently? So, what's new?'

'But if Murchie drove Abbie to suicide, surely he could be charged. And then the rat...'

Rob stepped towards the door. 'He's a nasty piece of work, our Murchie. Sounds like he'd be pleased to have Abbie out of the way, and it's just like him to make more of it. But that doesn't mean we can charge him with anything.'

'And the roses?'

Rob glanced back at her. 'The roses?'

'That note that was left?'

'Oh, that.' He looked at his feet. 'In my experience, trouble attracts trouble.'

'You mean, the Abbies of this world don't merit a police investigation.'

'A junkie who's found OD'd after a row?' He looked at her. 'From what we know so far, that stuff she injected was purer than what she was used to. Even if she didn't mean to kill herself, she still got a lethal dose. What can we do?'

Agnes followed him out to the front door. 'What if Murchie wanted her dead?'

'From what I know of Murchison, if he wants someone dead he arranges it. Usually with a Mach 10 and a round of ammunition. Subtlety is not his strong point. Even with rats.' He opened the front door and glanced out into the street. A sharp wind kicked at the fallen leaves. 'It's time for me to go back to my Sunday morning, I think. Which in my case means back to the office. Keep in touch, eh?'

The hostel kitchen was subdued. Lizzie was slumped at the kitchen table, flicking through an old magazine. A mug of tea was growing cold at her elbow. Paz was making toast, helped by Sari.

'You should have brown bread, not white,' Sari was saying. 'It gives you cancer, white bread, they put stuff in the flour, I saw it on telly.'

Lizzie looked up from her magazine. 'I just keep thinking about him. Poor little thing.' She crossed and uncrossed her legs in their skinny black leggings and clumpy trainers.

Sari turned to her. 'Who?'

'Nige.'

'Oh. The rat. Yeah. I saw Mots earlier, he were that upset he were – oi, Paz, it'll burn on that number, turn it down.'

Lizzie went back to her magazine. Sari was talking to Paz. 'I want Marmite on mine, and don't tell me it's disgusting 'cos I know what I like, right? Oi, Agnes, do we have any Marmite?'

Agnes greeted them all from the kitchen doorway, then went to a cupboard and took out a dark glass jar. 'I think it's a bit old. We should put it on the shopping list.'

Sari took it from her. 'Ta. Here, Paz, put this on mine. Lizzie, do you want some toast, girl?'

Lizzie shook her head. 'Too upset.'

Sari looked at her. 'God, I wish I cared that much about animals. I'd lose loads of weight, I would.' She turned to Agnes. 'Do you want some toast?'

Agnes shook her head. 'I'm not staying, I'm meeting Father Julius for lunch.'

'Lunch?' Sari stared at her. 'But it's Sunday.'

Agnes smiled at her. 'And?'

Sari shrugged. 'Dunno. Just thought he'd be doing more holy things than eating, that's all.' She picked up the slice of toast and Marmite that Paz handed her and took a large bite.

'Sari at the hostel thought you shouldn't have lunch.' Agnes turned to Julius as they stood at the bar of The George. 'So Heaven knows what she'll think of you having a pint of Guinness too.'

He smiled at her. 'Better not tell her,' he said. 'When she asks, say we had dry bread and water.'

'So I won't say I had fish pie and you had roast beef, then?'

'I think if you do that we'll lose any authority we might once have had. Shall we find a seat?'

They settled into a warm corner by a misted-up window.

'So,' he said, and waited.

'What?' She glanced at him.

'Well?'

She sighed. 'The American? Or the hostel?'

'Both, please.'

She picked up her glass of white wine and sipped it. 'The hostel is a bit grim because Abbie's dead and because Dermot is upset and now someone's gone and murdered his pet rat by injecting it with something, which has made everyone feel very jumpy.'

'They broke in?'

'It was outside, in a cage. They got over the fence. He'd been living in Dermot's room, Nige had, but they decided he needed the air, didn't like cigarette smoke, or something.'

'Oh dear.' Julius picked up his glass and took a large mouthful. 'And the American?'

In her mind Agnes saw the sparkling sweep of the hotel bar.

'Was he nice?' Julius said.

'Yes,' she began. 'Yes, he was nice.'

'Will you see him again?'

Agnes looked at Julius. 'You've got a Guinness moustache,' she said. She watched as he took out a large cotton handkerchief and dabbed at his upper lip.

'What did he have to say about your father, then?'

'They were friends. Towards the end of my father's life. He said my father was difficult.'

'Oh.' Julius nodded. 'Good.'

'Why good?'

Julius leant back in his chair. 'It would be awful if everyone but you thought he was a lovely old man – ah, here comes lunch.'

Dishes were put before them; forks were prodded into roast potatoes.

'So,' Julius resumed. 'How well did he know your father?'

'From what I can gather, he oversaw his last few years. He seems to have been trusted by my father with all those pamphlet things. He tried to trace me when my father knew he was dying...' She put down her fork, blinking at her plate in front of her.

Julius looked at her. 'So, he knew him very well, then?'

She nodded.

'I remember when he died, and you tried to get permission to go to his funeral.'

Agnes looked up. 'You were in the middle of arranging for me to leave my enclosed Order at the time, do you remember? And they said I couldn't go. We agreed it was revenge, you and I.'

'I didn't get the impression you minded very much.'

She shook her head. 'I didn't mind. I was relieved. It was all too much.'

'And your mother did go. Surprisingly.'

'Yes. She stood at the back for the whole of the service, and left immediately afterwards. Didn't speak to a soul, even though there was an old family friend there who she knew quite well. He was sort of my godfather. He told me later in a letter. She ignored them all and then got the first flight back to Nice.'

'I'd say, typical, but one shouldn't speak ill of the dead.' He turned to her again. 'So, is this man a creationist too?'

'Brett? No. He's a geologist.'

'Ah. Good.' Julius speared a cauliflower floret with his fork.

'Good? Again?' Agnes glanced across at him.

'I prefer evolution. As a model of God's intervention, I mean. Adam having to name the animals, for example. It puts us in a very odd relationship with God. I'd rather God did it. I don't see what's so funny,' he added, as Agnes began to laugh.

'I'm not sure that's the true Darwinian view of evolution,' she said. 'God naming the animals rather than Adam.'

'Oh,' he said. 'Darwin. Yes. Well…' He picked up his glass and took a sip. 'It's all stories, isn't it? I mean, there are different ways to tell a story, aren't there?'

She carved a neat square of pastry from the top of her pie. 'Go on.'

'Well, no one these days is going to start looking for geological evidence for the Garden of Eden, are they? On the other hand, as an account of our relationship with God, one might say there's a great deal of truth about the story of Adam and Eve. That it is human nature itself that has exiled us from Paradise. Had we chosen to behave simply on the level of the animals, without fully exploring our human capacity for knowledge, we would still be there, but we wouldn't be fully ourselves. The Fall was inevitable, arising from our very humanness…' He stopped and took another mouthful of beer. 'But it's not true in terms of evidence – you couldn't say that it happened in any kind of provable way. All I mean is, there are different ways in which a story can be said to be true.' He looked up at her. 'Will you see this man again?'

She smiled at him. 'I should introduce you to him. You'd get on.'

'Oh,' Julius checked his watch. 'I forgot to say. Jeremy Stipes. Promised to meet him here around now.'

'Your unhappy parishioner?'

He nodded. 'But it's OK. We can tell Sari in the hostel that in his misery he had two main courses and we only ate crisps.'

'I think even crisps might be a bit much.'

'What is she, a Calvinist? Do we have to prove we're saved by showing it in our impeccable behaviour? Ah…' He glanced towards the door. 'Here he is.' He stood up as an ambling figure approached, his raincoat unevenly buttoned, his hand outstretched. Julius took the hand that was proffered, gestured across the table. 'This is Sister Agnes. Sister Agnes, Jeremy Stipes. Have a seat, can I get you a drink?'

Despite protests, Julius had gone. They watched him as he took his place in the queue at the bar.

Jeremy Stipes turned to her. 'You wouldn't believe he'd been so ill, would you?'

Agnes looked at him. He seemed shabby, although it was difficult to say exactly why; something about the stoop in his shoulders, his lank, greying hair. His face was plump and moist-looking. 'Gives us all hope, I suppose,' he said. 'Julius's recovery.'

'Mmm,' she agreed.

He studied her with eyes that were small and narrow set. 'I expect people say that God was on his side.'

Agnes had a flash of memory, of the room in Intensive Care; bright lights and beeping, and at the centre of a web of wiring, Julius himself, blue-lipped, immobile, shrouded in bed sheets…

For a moment all she could feel was the terror that he might die. Jeremy seemed to be waiting for her reply. 'If only one could be so sure,' she managed to say.

'Julius says he's praying for my wife,' Jeremy said. 'He says he's praying for me too, although last time I told him not to bother—' He was cut short by Julius's return.

'Pint of guest ale, as you requested. Another glass of white wine...' He put the glasses down on the table, went to retrieve his half of Guinness.

'Not to bother?' Agnes turned to Jeremy who was already starting on his beer.

Jeremy shrugged. 'I'd rather put my faith in doctors these days.'

Julius reappeared and settled back on his seat, puffing slightly with the effort. 'Doctors, did you say? They saved my life, there's no doubt about it.'

'And they'll do the same for Pauline.' Jeremy's voice was quiet against the background noise.

Julius sipped his Guinness. 'Yes, of course.' His eyes were on Jeremy. 'How is she, your wife?'

His face seemed to tighten. 'She'll get better,' he said, after a moment.

'Is she in pain, still?'

Jeremy's hands went to the side of his head. 'It's terrible to see. They've got to do something. Dr Kitson's been wonderful, he says he won't give up, there's a new prescription he's going to try, but now it's in her bones...' He straightened up, picked up his glass again.

'And...' Julius seemed oddly determined to pursue the conversation. 'What does Pauline think?'

Jeremy was staring into his glass. 'She... I keep telling her not to give up. I can't bear to see her like this. And then she gets angry.'

'Angry?' Again, Agnes wondered at Julius's cross-examination.

'Yesterday she was shouting at me. She said it's not about me, it's about her, but as I said to her, I'm the one trying to do the caring. When she's crying out in pain sometimes, it's awful to see. I told Dr Kitson and he said he was going to find something more powerful to help her.' He seemed to droop, deflated by the effort of speech.

'Perhaps she needs to talk to someone,' Julius said.

So that's what all this is about, Agnes thought. He could have asked me first.

'There are various people who come to the house.' Jeremy's voice was wan. 'She's tired of it all. Nurses, counsellors...'

'An outsider might be helpful. Agnes, here, for example,' Julius said. 'Someone just to listen.'

Jeremy flicked a glance at Agnes. 'I don't know about that,' he said. 'You know my views.' He turned towards Julius. 'You know the difficulties I've been having with the Church in all this.'

'But Pauline...' Julius prompted.

He picked up his glass and drained it. Then he faced them both. 'I can't see what a nun can do to make things better when all the doctors in the world can't cure it.'

'And is that Pauline's view?'

Jeremy's shoulders slumped. After a moment, he shook his head. 'I suppose it can't do any harm,' he murmured.

'Tomorrow?' Julius said.

'Tomorrow?' he echoed. He shrugged. 'I suppose so.' He glanced across at Agnes. 'When would suit you? Not that she goes anywhere these days... Julius says you work in a hostel.'

'I'm free in the morning,' Agnes said.

He nodded. 'First thing, then. She doesn't get up very early. Ten-ish do you?'

'That's fine,' Agnes said.

He finished his beer, then stood up, his arms awkward at his sides. He thrust out a hand towards Julius. 'Bye then.'

Julius shook his hand.

'I suppose I should thank you,' Jeremy said. 'Although I can't see what good any of this will do.'

'You don't need to thank me—' Julius began.

'No,' he agreed. He straightened up, his hands in his pockets. 'Well,' he said. 'Tomorrow, then.' He nodded briefly at Agnes, then turned to go. They watched him cross the pub, his worn heels dragging on the polished wood. The mirrored door flashed his reflection as he left.

Agnes took a large mouthful of wine. 'Thanks,' she said to Julius.

'I knew you wouldn't mind,' he said.

'That's all right then.'

He gave her a searching glance. 'You don't mind, do you?'

'No, but—'

'Oh. Good. I wouldn't like to think I've embroiled you in something distasteful.'

She threw him a look. 'He's rather...'

Julius met her gaze. 'I know. But his wife is an interesting woman. She was a teacher. Before she got ill. You'll get on with her.' He shook back his sleeve and looked at his watch again. 'I ought to be getting back to church,' he said. 'How are you spending the afternoon?'

Agnes drained her glass. 'At home,' she said. 'Relishing my hard-won solitude.'

'Ah.' Julius smiled.

They stood up to go. In the street, Julius took her arm. 'I suppose in any other person it would seem presumptuous, my insistence on including you in my attempt to help a parishioner.'

'Whereas,' Agnes said, as the pedestrian traffic lights beeped, 'it's not presumptuous at all when it's you.'

'It's very kind of you to say so.' He looked down at her and smiled.

'For someone who practises humility, your arrogance can be quite breathtaking at times,' she said. 'I'll get the bus from here.'

They paused at the bus stop. Julius let go of her arm. 'Agnes—'

'What?'

'It's not arrogance,' he said.

She smiled. 'I didn't mean it—' she began.

'No,' he interrupted. 'What I mean is – I'm very worried about Pauline Stipes. I've been racking my brains to find a way to help her, and in the end I realised you were the answer. I'm sorry if it seemed like arrogance.'

She looked at him as he stood there. Behind him the traffic sped by in a swish of wet tyres. She breathed in, as if to speak, breathed out again.

Her bus appeared at the corner of the street. She smiled up at him. 'Silly old Julius,' she said.

CHAPTER FIVE

The candle guttered in a slight draft, throwing shadows on to the white-painted walls.

Agnes sat in the silence of her flat and opened her prayer book.

'The fool has said in his heart, there is no God. The Lord looks down from Heaven upon us all, to see if there is any who is wise, if there is one who seeks after God. Everyone has proved faithless; all alike have turned bad...'

She thought about Jeremy Stipes, resisting prayer. She felt a tightening in her chest at the thought of having to encounter him again the next day.

She thought about her father, for whom it all became so clear, so easy; so straightforward that he was able to believe in the story of Genesis, not as a parable, as Julius had asserted, but as a historical, factual truth. She turned to the Old Testament reading.

'...So God created man in His own image; in the image of God created He him; male and female created He them. And the evening and the morning were the sixth day...'

She recalled the English Bible that always lay on the desk in her father's study. Did he take these words literally even then, when they still shared the same house? She had no memory of him saying so; he was more likely to pour scorn on the Catholic teachings that her mother attempted to pass on to her. She remembered a row between them after the local priest had been persuaded to come to the house and give Agnes some kind of religious education. She remembered raised voices, accusations of brainwashing, indoctrination, her mother fighting back with blame, predicting a terrible future for their daughter, condemned to Purgatory for living a life outside our Mother Church...

'Your Mother Church!' her father had yelled. 'Not mine!'

Agnes had watched their faces creased and red with rage, and after a while had wandered out to find her pony in the field instead.

And yet, she remembered now, at some point he had come to be religious. She recalled a visit to him in London, in that in-between time when he kept a flat in Pimlico, 'for business', sustaining the fiction that he hadn't left the marriage, all the while allowing her mother to retreat into solitary eccentricity mixed with bitterness. She must have been sixteen, perhaps, visiting London in a school vacation.

'South Carolina,' he'd said, pointing at a map of the United States. 'That's where I'm going. Just for a bit. Research, you know. For my book.'

His book. She wished she'd asked him more, now.

Again, that distant memory of pipe smoke, and now she could see in her mind his room in Provence, the heavy desk, the fossils arranged neatly in a line. She remembered picking them up, the disappointment that they felt like stones and not like bones or shells or the things they resembled.

Fossils, even then. And even then, there was a book. 'I suppose you're telling the poor child all about that book of yours,' her mother used to say. And the young Agnes, faced with the implied obligation to take sides, backed away, until after a while it was easier never to ask any questions of him at all.

She returned to her prayers. '...Have they no knowledge, all these evildoers? See how they tremble with fear, because God is in the company of the righteous...' She wondered if her father had gone to his death in the firm belief that he had joined the company of the righteous. It would be something to ask Brett next time. She wondered if Brett would call her, or whether she should call him. She thought she might ask Athena, and then smiled, because she knew what Athena's advice would be: when it comes to men, don't call, ever – wait until they phone you, even if you have to wait days, weeks, months even, sweetie – it's always worked for me...

She turned the page of her prayer book, determined to concentrate.

'Lamb of God, you take away the sins of the world, Grant us Peace.'

Peace.

She thought about Sister Louisa, tucking herself away and aspiring to peace. She hoped she'd see her again soon.

On Monday morning it was still raining. Agnes got off the bus at the end of Atherton Road and began to walk up it, checking the house numbers, pulling her scarf tighter around her neck. She knew it was a compliment from Julius, that this visit was something she might do, but the thought of encountering

Jeremy Stipes again made her feel tense. And Dr Kitson too, she thought. Would it be a breach of confidentiality to admit to him that she was now involved with one of his patients? Should she have told Jeremy that she was acquainted with his doctor? It's hardly surprising, she supposed, as his practice was nearby.

Number 134 had a neat front lawn, and a perky-looking hydrangea, in spite of the persistent drizzle and the chill in the air. The porch was painted white, with a green front door. Agnes rang the bell and waited.

The door was opened by a pale woman with untidy, dark hair and a tight, anxious face. 'Ah,' she said. 'It's you.'

'Sister Agnes,' Agnes said, although it seemed unnecessary.

'Yes, yes. I'm Pauline.' Her hand went to the door latch to close it behind them; the loose sleeve of pink candlewick dressing gown fell away to reveal a skeletal wrist. 'Come with me.' She led the way into the living room, tugging her sleeves back over her fingers, the long gown sweeping the parquet floor.

'I wouldn't have agreed if it wasn't for it being Father Julius's idea. That's what my husband said, anyway, and I didn't think he was lying this time, as it's not the sort of thing he'd have come up with at all, a nun coming to visit me. And he's gone out now, anyway.' The living room had sliding French windows, which gave on to a patio. The rain-soaked garden extended towards a distant row of trees. She stood in the middle of the room. The carpet was chocolate brown with a swirly design; the walls were cream in colour, and oddly bare. 'He did say not to expect the full works.' Her eyes scanned Agnes's jeans, her old grey sweater, her ankle boots. 'I said I don't care what she wears.' Her voice was strained, her face unsmiling.

There was a silence. Even the birdsong from the garden sounded waterlogged and desultory.

'I don't have to stay,' Agnes said.

Pauline shrugged. 'You can do what you like. There's tea and coffee in the kitchen, you can help yourself, I don't know how fresh the milk is.' She flung herself into one of the armchairs, which was broad and covered with green velveteen.

'Can I make you anything?'

'Me? Oh, no.' She patted her thin stomach. 'Peppermint tea is the most I'm allowed these days.'

Agnes sat down on the other armchair. 'Then I won't bother either.'

Pauline surveyed her through eyes that were dark brown and piercing. 'He gave nothing away about you,' she said at last.

'I hardly saw him, only for a few minutes, with Julius yesterday.'

'He usually has a view. Even after a few minutes.' She leant to one side, resting her elbow on the arm of the chair. 'It's doctor this, and doctor that, and some are OK in his view, sound, he calls them, and some he takes against and then I'm not allowed to see them any more...' She took a deep, weary breath. 'Doctor Kitson he swears by, can't quite see why. But you –' Again, the sharp look. 'He said nothing at all.'

Agnes settled herself in her chair. 'So,' she said. 'You go to Julius's church.'

There was a brief softening of her face. She nodded.

'I gather...' Agnes searched for the right words. 'I gather your husband's faith is being tested by your illness.'

Pauline leant her head against the back of the chair. Her

voice, when she spoke, was quiet. 'If you want to know my view—' she began. 'What I mean is – it's not faith, is it? The Lord giveth and the Lord taketh away. There are no conditions. What I mean to say is...' her fists clenched together in her lap, '...I don't think my husband has ever really believed. Only when it suited him – to be someone in the church, to read the lesson, to shake hands with visiting bishops. And now the Lord has dealt him this blow, and he's going around stamping his feet and having a tantrum.' Two spots of pink appeared on her cheeks.

Agnes studied her for a moment. Then she said, 'And you?'

'Me?' The question seemed to surprise her.

'Well, I can't begin to know what it's like being you, but aren't you cross with God too?'

Pauline blinked at her. 'Oh,' she said. She frowned at her fingers in her lap. Then she said, 'Perhaps. Perhaps I was once. Yes,' she said, nodding as if recalling a distant memory. 'When it was all new. When I thought life was about being well and not ill. When it didn't hurt so much...' Her voice shook slightly.

'And now?' Agnes prompted.

She turned and looked out of the window. The rain had eased, and the tops of the trees swayed in the breeze. A branch of overgrown rose bush tapped at the edge of the window. She turned back to Agnes. 'I've just refused another bout of chemo,' she said. 'And they're all very cross with me. Jeremy accused me of wanting to die. And I don't, that's what they don't understand, I don't want to die at all. It's just I never want to feel that ill again, the way I felt with the last chemo, and they can only say it'll give me a few months, maybe, maybe not...' Her fingers curled around each other in her lap. 'Jeremy keeps accusing me of giving up. Yesterday I got very cross with him, very angry, I said some cruel things, and afterwards I thought I shouldn't have said them.'

'What things?'

She met Agnes's gaze. 'I said the only reason he wanted me to survive was so that he didn't think he'd failed. He wanted this marriage, this house, everything just so, no children… He had a plan, and now my illness has wrecked his plan and he will be widowed and that wasn't part of the plan.'

She looked so thin, so cold. Agnes wanted to wrap her in soft blankets and keep her warm. 'And – you regretted saying all this?' she asked her.

'At first, yes. But not after a while. Not when I thought about it. Because it's all true.' She raised her eyes to Agnes. 'Mostly, I'm in pain. Sometimes it's worse than others. Sometimes it's bearable. But the thing I can't bear…the thing that weighs me down every minute of the day, that makes me feel that I can hardly carry on, is the knowledge that I should have left my husband years ago. I waited and waited, I thought there was a future, I thought the right time would appear, I thought the decision would make itself. And now it's too late. I am destined to die as his wife. And that's what hurts. It hurts me to the very heart of me. Sometimes I feel I can hardly breathe.' She leant back in her chair and closed her eyes.

Agnes waited. Then she said, 'What are you going to do?'

Her eyes opened again. 'What can I do? I think about leaving, but whenever I imagine it, I'm in an ambulance. Or sometimes, a coffin.' She seemed to be about to speak, but then there was the sound of the key in the door.

Pauline looked at her watch. 'On the dot,' she said. 'You'd better go.'

They heard Jeremy in the hall, hanging up his coat.

Agnes crossed the room and grasped Pauline's hand. 'I shall think about what to do,' she said, in a low voice.

'Hello?' Jeremy called.

'We're in the lounge,' Pauline replied. Agnes let go of her hand.

He appeared in the doorway, damp and puffing slightly. 'Ah – still here?'

'She's just leaving,' Pauline said.

'Good. Right. Well...lunch?' He looked at his wife, as if expecting her to get up.

'I'm not hungry,' she said.

'Got to eat, though, haven't we?'

'I'd love a cup of coffee,' she said.

He looked at her, surprised. 'Coffee? You know we don't allow you coffee any more. I'll make you a nice sandwich.'

He gave Agnes a thin smile and went out to the kitchen.

Agnes touched Pauline's arm. 'I'll come and see you soon,' she said.

'Thank you,' Pauline said. 'I'd like that.'

The clouds were lifting as she walked back to the bus stop. She had managed a polite goodbye to Jeremy, who was making sandwiches in the kitchen, and then had let herself out. She stood at the bus stop, watching the sky lighten above the rooftops, taking deep breaths of urban air.

Sometimes I can hardly breathe, Pauline had said.

Agnes thought of her sitting in her chair, her husband in the kitchen, unravelling wafer-thin ham, cutting slices of bread; the rose bush tapping at the window.

* * *

The hostel was bright and loud and full of people. Aysha was standing at the stove, stirring a large saucepan. This time the apron was striped, in shades of blue.

'Isn't it someone else's turn?' Agnes put her bag down on the table, unfurled her scarf from her neck.

Aysha smiled. 'I don't mind. If it's not soup, then it's heaps of paperwork in the office. I'd rather be here. Anyway, everyone's so sad about Abbie. And now Dermot's in the office and there's high-level discussions going on.'

'Dermot?'

She nodded. 'Gilroy and him, they went to see the police earlier.'

'That's not like Dermot.'

'No,' Aysha agreed. 'But he's that upset about the rat. Gil said it's what Nige would have wanted.'

'He's got a point. I suppose.'

'They went to see that young copper that was here before.'

'Did they get anywhere?' Agnes switched on the electric kettle.

'All I know was that Dermot was saying that at least now those gangsters will know he means business.'

'I'm not sure that's so good for Dermot, is it?'

Aysha shrugged, stirred the soup.

Agnes carried her mug of tea out to the office. '...that bastard Murchie thinks he can get away with anything...' Agnes heard as she approached the door. 'But as far as I'm concerned, he's reached the fuckin' limit now...'

Dermot looked up as Agnes came into the room. 'Sorry, Sister,' he muttered.

'Don't mind me.' Agnes drew up a chair. 'You were saying...?'

Dermot shook his head. 'Poor Nige.' He frowned, staring at his hands in his lap.

Gilroy stood up. 'You heard we went to the police?' He went over to the door. 'About time we pointed a finger at Murchie. Shame it was just over a rat – a very important rat,' he added. He glanced at Dermot, then left the room.

Agnes sipped her tea. 'You and Murchie,' she said. 'You were friends once?'

He nodded.

'What changed?'

He shrugged.

'Abbie,' Agnes said.

He looked at her. He nodded again.

'Murchie likes things to go his own way,' Agnes said.

'He thinks he owns the bleedin' street. Not just the street, the whole of the 'hood. Not just the 'hood, the whole fuckin' city...'

'And you'd had enough.'

'It was Abbie. Me and her wanted to make a go of it. We'd have had a life together, we'd have got away from all this...if she hadn't...' He screwed up his eyes. 'And now Nige.'

Outside a fire engine screamed past.

Dermot leant forward, his fists gripped together. 'The only time I have anything, and it gets taken away. All my life, I've had to fight. And I still lose.'

Agnes tried to remember what she'd read in his file. 'Liverpool, wasn't it?' she said.

'Yeah.'

'You're Irish?'

'I was born here. My dad met my mum here.'

'Exile,' Agnes said. 'It can be hard.'

'You're telling me. My dad used to say, remember, boy, you're fighting for Ireland. At school, you know, when the other boys beat me.'

'Didn't he try to stop them fighting you?'

Dermot threw her a harsh smile. 'Him? Nah.' He laughed. 'My dad, protecting me?... Nah.' He picked up a biro from the desk.

'What about your mum?'

'Didn't have no mum. She died when I was little.'

'In Liverpool?'

He nodded. 'I don't remember her much.'

'Why did your dad leave Ireland?'

Dermot began to unscrew the biro. 'He fell out with his dad. We was in fairgrounds, his dad had had the business for years, his dad before him. And my dad got chucked out, and his little brother took over. It weren't right, everyone said so. No one knew what his dad had got against him. So he came here and made a fresh start.'

'Was there just you and your dad, then?'

He nodded.

'And it didn't work out?'

His fingers worked on the pen in his hands. 'Nah.' He looked up at her. 'People said he were doing his best, but if that was his best I'd like to see what his fuckin' worst was. He was an angry man, see. After what happened in Mayo...it's like he never stopped being angry. He was angry with his dad, and then he was angry with my mum for dying, and I reckon he was angry with her before that too... And he was angry with the construction blokes who gave him work, so they stopped giving him work, and then he was angry with the security companies, so they wouldn't give him work neither.

And then he was angry with me...' The spring from the biro
flew across the room. He stared at the bits of plastic in his
hands.

'So you left?'

'I ran away to London.'

'And is he still in Liverpool?'

'Nah. He's dead now. Lung cancer, they said.'

'Do you miss him?'

'Do you miss yours?'

Agnes blinked at him.

'I shouldn't have asked that. Only I thought you being quite
old, your dad must be dead –'

'Yes,' she said. 'He died some years ago.'

He crossed the room and retrieved the spring from under a
chair. He went back to his seat and began to reassemble the
biro.

'I don't suppose...' she began. 'What I mean is, you get used
to not having a dad. So, no, I don't miss him. And anyway, he
wasn't around that much when he was alive. I was already
used to not having a dad.'

'You were lucky.' He forced the spring back into the barrel
of the pen. 'Having no dad must be better than having one
that belts you.' He screwed the pen back together, and smiled
at her. 'There you are. Good as new.' He stood up and
sauntered to the door. 'The only good thing about my dad is
that he taught me not to let people push me around. And
that's what Murchie is about to find out.'

The office was suddenly quiet. Even the smell of soup wafting
from the kitchen failed to lift the chill in the room. The ringing
of Agnes's phone cut through the air.

'Darling, it's me. I'm running an errand for Simon in Borough High Street, there's a lighting designer he wants us to try, and I thought as I was so close maybe we could meet for a coffee or something afterwards? Not that I want to drag you away or anything…'

'Athena, right at this moment I can think of nothing better than being dragged away.'

'How about the market itself? That sandwich place down the end?'

'Fine.'

'Make it about twenty minutes. I can't imagine a lighting designer can detain me for any longer than that.'

Rain dripped from the awnings, from the passing umbrellas. Agnes wrapped her hands around her paper cup.

'I mean, poppet, it's all very well Simon saying he was at college with this boy, but that doesn't mean he's not going to rip us off, does it? The prices he was quoting just weren't competitive, and I told him so.'

'And what did he say?'

'He said if I could get better quality elsewhere then I was welcome to it. And his clothes were more barrow boy than Balenciaga too. So off I went. I hope I haven't ruined a wonderful old friendship, although knowing Simon, he'll soon find another one. Anyway, how are you? You look tired, you know? I do think those tiresome nuns ought to give you a holiday.'

'I'm fine, really. How's Nic, did he get back OK?'

'Yes. Last night.'

'And was it lovely to see him?'

'Fine. Yes. Lovely.'

Agnes glanced at her, but before she could ask any more, Athena said, 'So, this creationist?'

'Geologist,' Agnes corrected.

'How was he?'

'Nice. Really nice. Interesting.'

'Rich?'

Agnes frowned. 'I've no idea.'

'He must be pretty OK to stay at that hotel. Nice clothes?'

'Yes,' Agnes conceded. 'Nice clothes.'

'So, what happened?'

'Well, we had a drink at his hotel.'

'Surely, more than one?'

'Yes. More than one.' Agnes laughed. 'And he talked about my father, and his last years, and...' She hesitated. 'It was difficult for him. It turns out my father was trying to get in touch with me, towards the end, but not trying very hard...'

Athena pursed her lips. 'I know that one. My family in Greece – they were always hopeless at letting me know anything important. So – what did you talk about, you and this—?'

'Bretton, he's called. Brett for short.'

'Brett. Mmmm.' Athena smiled. 'Very...what's the word? It's all a bit Scarlett O'Hara. How old?'

Agnes sighed. 'Forties. Maybe. Early forties, I'd say.'

'Mmmm.'

'Listen.' Agnes put down her paper cup. 'If you think he's so gorgeous, you can flirt with him.'

Athena looked at her. 'Oh, no. No I can't. None of that now. Nic's back and it's serious.'

'What do you mean, serious?'

A shadow passed across Athena's face. 'He's talking about

getting married. I know,' she said. 'My face looked just like yours does now when he said it. Him and me. We've never even lived together properly. And now this.'

'Marriage?' Agnes stared at her friend.

'I know what's brought it on – his son, you know, lovely Ben, and Julia, and their new baby, well, now they're back from Melbourne, planning to buy a place in London... And I think—' she paused. 'I think he likes the idea of him and me being proper grandparents. I mean, obviously, his ex-wife is around, but she's got her own life and it's all very amicable... I just think he likes the idea of it all being orderly and regular.'

'Grandparents? You?'

Athena managed a smile. 'I know. Ridiculous, isn't it? At my young age. I mean, it's true, the idea of a wedding is rather appealing. A castle in Scotland, I thought. All very romantic. Bagpipes. Tartan... But that's just a wedding, not a whole bloody marriage – oh, kitten, don't laugh...'

'What are you going to tell him?'

'Well, luckily I don't have to say anything for a while as he's off to visit his mum, and we had a lovely romantic evening last night, and it's absolutely fab he's back in London instead of living in France, and he's very excited about his new practice, and also it turns out his mum is really getting very frail, his sister's been doing all the caring, and he feels it's his turn to do his bit now... So,' she finished, 'I think there's enough to keep him busy without having to decide about getting married just yet.'

They sipped at their paper cups in silence.

'Perhaps it's like taking final vows,' Agnes said after a while. 'Getting married.'

'Perhaps. With a few significant differences,' Athena said.

'Well, yes. But that sense of closing off options that you never wanted anyway...'

Athena looked up at her. 'Yes,' she said. 'You're right. I only want him. I know that now. Do you know, I even lent him my car?'

'What, the Audi?'

'My pride and joy.'

'It must be love,' Agnes said.

'Yes. It's just all the other stuff that goes with it, the domestic stuff, the everyday life of it all... I'm not sure I'd be very good at it.'

Agnes considered this for a while.

'So, this creationist—'

'Geologist,' Agnes said.

'Are you seeing him again?'

'Well, I'd like to. I think there's lots of stuff he could tell me about my father, for a start. But he hasn't phoned, you see, and I was thinking of calling him, but—'

'Oh, no, sweetie,' Athena interrupted. 'Don't call him. The thing with men is, you *must* wait until they phone you, even if you have to wait weeks, months even – it's always worked for me. In fact, look how well it's worked – Nic wants to marry me. I ought to write one of those best-sellers for women who are desperate to find a husband—'

Agnes's phone trilled in her bag, and she pulled it out. 'Hello – Oh, Brett, hello – yes, that would be lovely.' She heard him suggest that they meet later, agreed to a time, tried not to laugh as Athena made exaggerated thumbs-up gestures across the table. 'That'll be fine. See you later. Bye.' She clicked her phone off and looked at Athena. 'You'd better write that best-seller,' she said.

Athena fished in her bag. 'I meant to give you this,' she said. She produced a small box made of gold cardboard. 'Lipstick,' she said. 'Yves St Laurent. It's very neutral, just a nice shine, nothing that your Mother Superior could possibly object to.'

Agnes took it, opened the packaging, admired the glossy tube.

'Even if we're both going to be people who've taken final vows,' Athena went on, 'we might as well look our best.'

CHAPTER SIX

Agnes stood in front of her mirror, holding her new lipstick. She twisted it up and looked at the shiny colour. She tried to remember the last time she'd owned lipstick, wondered when she'd thrown the last one out. She couldn't remember a rite of passage, a discarding of her worldly self. It was more a drift into finding that she didn't really think about it any more.

She imagined herself walking into the bar to meet Brett. It's hardly a big deal, she thought; it's only like my having expensive face cream. I could either wear it, or not. It makes no difference, really.

She leant towards the mirror, lipstick in hand, about to apply it.

A sudden flash of memory; of herself in identical pose; of Hugo's hand crashing towards the mirror, dashing the lipstick from her hand, a torrent of abuse. *Painted trollop, going out whoring, are we? No wife of mine is going to appear in public dressed like a tart...*

Agnes looked at the lipstick in her hands, put it into its box and tucked it away into her handbag.

* * *

The hotel's revolving door swished with light. Brett was in the foyer; he rose to greet her, smiling at her as he took her hand briefly, then led the way to the bar. 'I'm glad you could make it,' he said. 'Single malt?'

'Yes please,' Agnes said. 'The Islay was very nice.'

'We need a big table,' he said, and she noticed the large parcel under his arm.

He carried their drinks to a wide corner table. 'I thought you'd better have a look at all of it, or as much as I could bring over from the States. There's loads of his papers...' He placed the parcel on the table. 'There's extracts from the book he was writing, although I don't think he'd ever have finished it.'

'I was going to ask you about that,' Agnes said. 'I remembered, after our last meeting, my father used to talk about his book. I could never quite pin down what it was about, it seemed to keep changing.'

He smiled. 'I think it always did. There are various bits of chapters here, but the subject matter is quite wide-ranging. There's lots of mathematical formulae which seem to be biblical in some way, going through the genealogy of all the people mentioned, how long they lived, who begat whom...adding up the years to prove that we're in the year six thousand and something, although that keeps changing too. There's stuff from Judaism too, Kabbalistic stuff, all numerological formulae and things. And then there's this—' He bent to his briefcase and pulled out a small, clear plastic box. It seemed to be full of stones. 'The fossils,' he said, sliding back the lid. 'The ones that he reckoned are only six thousand years old.'

Agnes peered into the box. She reached towards one, looked up at Brett. 'May I?'

He nodded, and she chose one. It was small and round, a curled shell-shape, stony grey, with a pinkish, marbly sheen. She studied it in her hand. 'It doesn't seem that different from any other fossil,' she said. 'But I don't know much about it.'

He took it from her. 'No, you're right. Just a fossil, I'd say. A common or garden ammonite, one of his Dorset ones. Although there is something odd about the colour of the stone, that hint of violet in there.' He put the fossil back with the others and slid the lid shut. 'Your father was so vehement in his belief, however, that I'm going to do what I can to prove the age of this stuff.'

'How?'

'The institute where I'm based has access to a carbon-dating lab. I'm going to start with the piece of Noah's Ark and give it a go. And then I'll see what we can do with this stuff.' He tilted his head towards the box where it lay on the table.

She picked up her glass and took a sip. 'If you don't mind me asking—' She looked across at him, then continued, 'Why are you going to so much trouble?'

He stared at the table in front of him, then he looked up at her. 'I don't quite know. Deathbed promise, I suppose. In a way. He kind of relied on me, at the end, to carry the flame—'

'Even though he knew you were a scientist?'

His eyes met hers. 'There were very few people in his life – at the end.'

'You mean, he'd managed to alienate everyone but you?'

He smiled, briefly. 'You could put it that way.'

'And—' she hesitated, then went on, 'why did you wait so long after his death?'

'Oh, that's simple. Money. I had no way of getting over here, no funding. I was just a graduate researcher in the States,

I knew if I came over here I'd have to do it properly, stay a while...it was only with this grant from the Chambers Vestiges people that it became possible.'

'And who are they?'

'It's a funny old English academic institute, set up after the publication of Robert Chambers' seminal work in the 1840s. It funds research about the age of the universe. My work is geological but I made my funding application fit their criteria.' His eyes were alight with amusement.

'Did they mind?'

He frowned at her. 'Mind what?'

'That you're just a geologist really?'

He laughed. 'They're desperate to fund people. These days there aren't that many people willing to take on research that "supports the Church in welcoming new theories of God's creation". And anyway, I have great respect for those guys in the nineteenth century. Amateur scientists, some of them clergymen, finding themselves at the frontiers of knowledge about this huge, huge subject, and having the courage to investigate it and the imagination to think of a way of telling the story that had never been told before.' He picked up his glass of white wine and drank from it.

Agnes watched him. He looked young, excitable and honest. 'Stories,' she said.

'What?'

'A friend of mine was talking about how different stories can carry different truths. Like Adam and Eve – his example – a myth which carries meaning for us even though as a story there is no evidence that it ever happened.'

He studied her. 'Who is this friend?'

'A priest I know. You'd like him, actually.'

'The thing is...' He leant back in his chair, '...your father never used words like myth. Or metaphor. It was all true. It all *had* to be true. He thought he was a scientist. That's what he used to say. "Bretton, you and I are both men of science. We understand each other." There were no shades of grey with your father.'

Yes, Agnes thought. No shades of grey.

'Another drink?' He stood up.

Agnes watched him at the bar. It was like being with two people – one, the bright-eyed scientist, open and honest and keen; the other, a hidden, shadowed person, skirting around a version of events he was reluctant to reveal, shutting down whenever she asked a question concerning her father.

He reappeared, settling down again at the table, passing her another whisky. 'Would they mind, your fellow Sisters, if they knew?' He smiled at her.

'The whisky? It breaks a few rules, I suppose. Next time I'll try the pomegranate juice.'

He laughed. 'I will if you will.'

She looked at him. 'So, to continue your story: you got the money from this institute, then you came over and took advantage of being here to contact me and honour my father's memory in some way?'

The mask came down, the laughter stopped, cut short. He nodded. 'That's about it.' He indicated with his head the papers. 'You can take away with you any of that you want.'

She eyed the parcel on the table. 'If I thought I might come to know more about my father—' she began.

'Oh, but you will. At least, intellectually.'

'But not about his life. How he lived. Who he loved...'

Brett's hand went to his glass. He circled it on the table, round and round.

'You must know all that, though,' she pursued.

The glass continued to circle.

What are you keeping from me? she was about to say, but was interrupted by the ringtone of her phone.

'Hello? Oh – Aysha—'

She listened to the distress in Aysha's voice; she was phoning from the hostel, Dermot had been attacked, he was in the office on their first-aid stretcher but he needs to go to hospital, he's bleeding, he's refusing to go, we don't know what to do—'

Agnes was on her feet. 'Give me ten minutes – five, maybe,' she said.

Bretton was looking up at her.

She put her phone back in her bag. 'It's the hostel where I work. It's for homeless people, particularly the young – there are times when it gets dangerous, and this evening is one of those times.'

He stood up, reached for her coat, helped her on with it. 'You are a most surprising person,' he said. He picked up the parcel and the box of fossils, and then was hurrying next to her, out of the bar, out into the street, and she was aware as she hailed a cab that he was behind her, opening the taxi door, getting in after her, sitting next to her as the cab swerved through the narrow lane and out into the main road.

She looked at him, his profile lit up by the soft yellow rhythm of passing street lights.

'I know you didn't invite me,' he said. 'But I thought if it was dangerous, you might need a hand.'

'That's very kind of you,' she said. 'The worry is, that you might just make it worse.'

'Well, if that's the case, I'll just pay off the taxi and disappear into the night.'

She smiled. The luminous splendour of Tower Bridge receded behind them; the darkness thickened around them as they headed for the hostel.

There were lights on in every window. As she opened the front door, Sari and Paz appeared, their expressions pinched with anxiety, then curiosity, as Brett loped into the hall behind her, his long pale green raincoat flapping. They stared at him, then Sari took her arm and led her into the office.

Dermot was lying on the stretcher on his side, facing away from the doorway. Sari stretched up to whisper to Agnes, 'There's loads of blood, it's horrible...'

Aysha was kneeling next to him, a bowl of hot water at her side, towels on the other. She looked up as Agnes came into the room.

'He's got to go to hospital. He's barely conscious.' Her voice was low.

'I'll call an ambulance—' Agnes began, but was interrupted by a moan from the stretcher.

'No,' Dermot murmured.

Agnes strode over to the stretcher. Dermot's face seemed to have changed shape, and the skin across his jaw was blackened and torn. She glanced up to see Brett slip out of the room.

So much for being good in a crisis, she thought.

She knelt down and took hold of Dermot's hand. 'Why won't you go to hospital?' she said.

'Tired of being brave,' he mumbled. 'Told me not to.'

'Who told you not to?'

'Murchie. Not to breathe a word. No feds.'

One eye was completely closed under the swelling, and the other seemed to be staring blankly ahead.

'Can you see anything?' Agnes tried.

There was a silence, a rasping breath. 'No feds,' he said, after a moment.

'We must call an ambulance.' Agnes got to her feet as the door opened and a man in uniform appeared, followed by a woman, also uniformed. There was the crackle of a radio operator; from the window, the blue shadows of a flashing light.

They knelt next to Dermot, looked at each other, lifted the stretcher, then turned to the room. 'Who can tell us what happened? Who did he talk to first?'

Paz cleared his throat. 'He came in about half an hour ago, he was staggering, going on about Murchie and his bredren—'

'Can you come with us? The duty doctor will need someone to fill in the detail.'

'He's a resident,' Aysha said. 'He can't be responsible—'

'Then you come too, lady.'

They filed out, a solemn column, Paz following the stretcher, Aysha last, down the steps, into the back of the waiting ambulance. The doors slammed shut, the ambulance sped away into the darkness.

Brett was standing by the hostel steps. Agnes went and stood next to him. They watched the last flash of blue light as the ambulance turned on to the main road.

'Do you hail ambulances the way you find taxis?' Agnes's eyes were still fixed on the distant street.

'I got on my phone. I knew it was 999 over here. I watch a lot of your television.'

She looked up at him. 'Thank you.'

'And at least you Brits don't have to pay.'

'Would that have stopped you?'

He was silent.

'Thought not,' she said.

They sat in the warmth of the hostel kitchen, grouped around the table; Sari and Lizzie, Agnes and Brett, Gilroy hovering by the kettle, endlessly refilling the teapot.

'Are you from New York?' Lizzie was leaning on her elbows, gazing across at Brett.

'It's like Spiderman, isn't it?' Sari was surveying him from under her black fringe.

'Spiderman?' Lizzie giggled at Sari.

'Yeah. He just flew in in his cape, with a whole ambulance crew, just when we needed one.'

'Batman more like.' Lizzie stirred two large spoonfuls of sugar into her mug of tea. 'He's the one with the cape.'

Agnes turned to Brett. 'You don't have to put up with this, you know.'

He smiled at the young women. 'On the contrary, I'm greatly flattered.'

'Yeah, well,' Sari reached across and took the sugar from Lizzie, 'it's not often you get compared to a superhero, I bet. Not at your age.'

'And don't think I'm ungrateful.'

Agnes went over to Gilroy. 'You must know it's not your fault.' She spoke softly. 'Get some rest.'

He turned to her. 'I encouraged him. I made him feel OK

about standing up to them. I was wrong.' He shook his head. 'I've just put him in danger, that's all I've achieved.'

'We'll have to get the police involved—'

He interrupted her. 'No. You heard him.'

'I'm not having those thugs rule this area.'

'It won't make anything better for Mots.' Gilroy sank into a chair. His skin looked grey and papery.

'Maybe not in the short term. But we can't go on like this.'

Brett stood up. 'I should leave you in peace.' He gathered up his briefcase and raincoat.

Agnes glanced at Gilroy, then followed Brett out into the hall. He paused by the front door, looked down at her, rubbed his forehead. 'Well, I guess I didn't think it was going to be like this.'

'Like what?'

'I suppose I really thought that London would be all quaint Victorian streets and smiling cops in those funny hats, and the Queen coming out to wave from her balcony.' He managed a thin smile. 'That guy on the stretcher was in a bad way.'

Agnes nodded.

'When I heard that Ralph's daughter was a nun...back then, before I ever thought I'd meet you...' He stopped. He looked down at her, then went on, 'I always thought monastic life was about avoiding trouble. I had no idea that being a nun meant deliberately walking right into it.' He touched her elbow, then opened the door and gazed out into the night. The sky had cleared to frosty starlight. 'Well—'

'Will you be all right?' she heard herself say.

He turned back to her and smiled. 'Do your London cabs dare to come this way?'

'Failing that, I've heard it's pretty easy to hail an ambulance round here.'

He laughed. 'See you around,' he said. 'At least, if my superhero duties permit.'

Agnes shook her head. 'I wouldn't let those two go to your head. Their admiration is usually fleeting.'

'Story of my life.' His attention was caught by the trundle of a diesel engine, a streak of yellow light. He dashed down the steps, raised his arm, spoke to the taxi driver, turned back and waved to her. 'Well, what do you know?' he called. 'There's always a batmobile just when you want one.' He got into the cab, slammed the door shut. The taxi made a sharp turn and accelerated back towards the embankment.

She switched off the light in the hall, shooed Lizzie and Sari up to their rooms, went into the office and dialled Aysha's mobile.

'How is he?'

Aysha sounded exhausted. 'He's asleep now. They're keeping him overnight. They say there's no huge damage, but he's got some degree of concussion. Paz told them what he could. They asked about police statements, but I told them it was part of an ongoing situation at the hostel and we'd talk to our community officer here. I didn't want to upset Dermot any more. Paz is still here, we'll both come back soon, I reckon. What about there?'

'Gilroy's gone to bed. I'll sleep here too, I think.'

'See you in the morning.' Aysha hesitated. 'Thanks for being there.'

'It's just being a nun,' Agnes said. 'Deliberately walking into trouble.'

'It must seem like it at times. Night, then.'

'Night.' Agnes replaced the receiver. She went into the kitchen. Brett's parcel was still on the table. She gathered it up, switched off all the rest of the lights, went up to the spare staff bedroom.

She sat on the newly made-up bed. She held the parcel on her knees, then opened one end of it and drew out a sheaf of papers.

She picked out a small, bound bundle. It had a cardboard cover, on which someone had painted a border of insects in watercolour, now rather faded. There was a bee, an ant, a daddy-long-legs. A butterfly perched in the top left-hand corner; a snail, complete with silvery trail, seemed to be trying to make its way up the right-hand side. In the middle, her father's name, Ralph Gardner, painted in the same delicate colours. Above that was the title:

'For it is Written in the Book of Names'.

Agnes opened the cover. The pages were closely typed on thin paper. She flicked through the pages.

'And I will fight for my beliefs in front of God and in front of mankind, so that the truth be known. The lava flows around a mountain are like the rings of a tree, a measure of time itself, a message from our Creator written at the time of creation and available for us to know if only we use our eyes and our knowledge that we are His children.' There followed a series of mathematical calculations: 'Circumference 75 miles = 75 flows of lava, each a mile wide...'

She turned the page. 'It is a gift from God, that he has allowed us to live within the cradle of his creation; and that, in spite of our exile from Eden, we are still living out our days within the creation of our Father.' Beneath this was a small stone, taped to the page with yellowing sticky tape. As she touched it the tape came away and she was left holding the stone, the size of a pebble, in her fingers. It too had a fossil imprint, like the ones from the box that Brett had kept. Under the mark where the sticky tape had been, there were more equations. Then, at the foot of the page, she read, 'It is a gift from the Lord, and I have come to see it as true, and I will make known this truth, for I shall be grateful to the Lord till the end of my days.'

She closed the book and put it back into its envelope. She placed the fossil on top. She lay down on the bed, her head resting on her arms. She wondered what had happened; how had her father changed from the dry, laconic Englishman, detached and quizzical, to this impassioned writer of quasi-Victorian natural philosophy?

She yawned. The change that had been wrought in her father seemed greater than any volcanic eruption, even if the fossils did prove that the universe was several million years younger than anyone had imagined. There would be more questions for Brett, she thought, more pressing than the age of the stones.

As she closed her eyes she saw Dermot's swollen face, Aysha's terror, the blood-soaked towels. She rolled on to her side and pulled the covers tightly around her.

CHAPTER SEVEN

'As soon as your lad's back, let us know.' Rob Coombes's voice sounded rough on the phone. 'And if he doesn't come back this morning, we'll go and talk to him at the hospital.'

'He's very reluctant,' Agnes said. 'He said he didn't want to talk to any of you.' The big chair creaked as she rocked it to and fro. She stretched her feet out under the office desk and yawned.

'Late night, was it?'

'I don't think I slept much,' she said.

'No, well, I'm not surprised. I've asked for a meeting with my officers here. It's time we called a halt to the kind of behaviour you've been witness to.'

'Well, that would be nice,' Agnes agreed.

'There's no doubt that if your lad hadn't come to talk to us, he wouldn't have been attacked.'

'I think that's what he feels.'

'Leave it with me. And call me when he's back with you.'

Agnes replaced the phone receiver. She leant back in the chair and closed her eyes. She wondered whether to try out the hostel's brand new shower room that they'd somehow found the money for, although Sari had been complaining that there was nowhere to put your shower gel and the water wasn't very hot.

She heard a faint cough. She swivelled the chair round.

'I'm sorry—' Dr Kitson was standing in the doorway. 'I thought you might be asleep.'

'I feel like it.' She smiled at him as he sat down in the other desk chair.

'I heard about poor Dermot,' he said.

'They reckon they're discharging him today, though he was in a very bad way,' Agnes said.

'Probably just bruising. I'd like to see the X-rays if I get a chance.'

'The police are promising some kind of extra help to get rid of all this trouble.'

He pushed his glasses up his nose, his finger resting on the bridge. 'It's very simple, it seems to me. Murchison's view is that if he can't have Abbie, then no one will.'

'But Abbie's dead.'

'And he wants revenge.'

'Why should he blame Dermot?'

Dr Kitson's hands rested together in his lap. 'I don't know.' He looked at her. 'This poisoning of the rat – do we know what was used? What kind of needle, if any? Or might it have been in the poor thing's food?'

'I don't know how much forensic work they've done.'

He drew out a handkerchief, patted at his forehead with it. 'It seems to me that it's a major clue. These low lifes out in the street would have access to all sorts of substances that would kill a rat. I'm surprised the police haven't been more thorough about it.'

'You could ask Sergeant Coombes later on, when Dermot's back.'

'There are many unanswered questions.' He folded the handkerchief into a tiny square and replaced it in his pocket. 'I keep asking myself about poor Abbie. I keep thinking about her.'

Agnes nodded. 'They seem happy to treat it as an overdose,' she said.

'I've no doubt it was an overdose. But that's not the point.' He jabbed with one finger on the arm of the chair. 'I keep wondering what happened in between my talking to her, and her coming back to the hostel. She seemed so much better. What can have happened in those few hours to make her go out, score some heroin and then be so careless with it as to kill herself? She hadn't touched the stuff for weeks...' He shook his head.

There was a silence. Then he said, 'Worse than that. I've been wondering if she meant to do it. If something so terrible happened that morning that she lost any will to carry on. And she was doing so well, too...' He raised his eyes to Agnes's, his expression troubled.

'We know how she was that day. She was wanting to leave. Frightened of Murchie. And I encouraged her to stand up to him...'

He nodded. 'I know, I know. She was talking that way to me. Something happened to make her feel either suicidal, or at least sufficiently hopeless to decide to drug herself again.'

'Well...' Agnes stifled another yawn. 'Perhaps if the police manage to pin down Murchie, we might get some answers.' She stood up. 'Coffee, I think. It's the only answer.' In the doorway, she turned to him. 'I met one of your patients. Pauline Stipes.'

'Oh. Mrs Stipes.'

'I felt I should let you know, because Julius has put me forward as a kind of counsellor to her…'

His face seemed to relax slightly. 'Ah.' He nodded. 'How did you find her?'

Agnes hesitated, standing in the doorway. Behind her she could hear the sounds of the hostel awakening, radios blaring, water running in the hot pipes.

'She's a brave woman,' Dr Kitson said. 'But then, she needs to be. And at least she has her husband to support her.'

Agnes glanced at him. She wondered whether to share with him her impression of Jeremy, but he seemed to think the conversation was over, as he swivelled to and fro in the chair.

'Well,' she said, after a moment. 'Coffee, I think.'

Two mugs of coffee later, there was still no word of Dermot, and Aysha's phone was switched off. Agnes made Gilroy promise to call her the minute there was any news, and headed out into the street, hoping to find a bus to take her to the community house.

A boy was cycling towards her on a bicycle that seemed much too small for him. A dog galloped along behind, tied to the bike with his lead. The boy stopped at the hostel, leant his bike against the wall. He stood in the street, scanning the windows.

Agnes took a step towards him, and the dog began to bark. A bull terrier cross, she thought, squat, dark brown and unfriendly.

'Can I help you?' she asked the boy.

He stared up at her, under a fringe of black hair. 'Who are you?' His voice was surprisingly deep for someone so small.

'I work here.' She gestured with her head to the hostel. 'Who are you?'

'No one,' he said. He reached for his bike. To her surprise, she grabbed his arm.

'Why are you outside our hostel, then?'

The black eyes narrowed as he looked at her. 'I wouldn't do that if I were you.' He wrenched his arm away and got hold of his bike handlebars.

'The police are watching out for you lot,' she said.

He sneered, a flash of white teeth. 'Oh yeah. And what are they going to do, then—?' He stopped as a voice shouted from the end of the street.

'Oi – Kav – what you doin', blad? I said over by the shops—'

The smile left the boy's face. He turned round. The dog barked and jumped up and down, still attached to the bicycle, as a young man approached. He was wearing a short silvery jacket, low-slung black trousers, large trainers.

'She grabbed me, Murch,' the boy said. His voice was child-like now, plaintive.

The young man faced him. He had shorn black hair, striped with bleached-blond streaks, and blue eyes which startled against his brown skin. He strolled closer, a smile playing on his lips, several heavy chains of jewellery jangling at his neck and wrists.

'She grabbed you, did she? Poor little you.' The dog barked some more, and the young man bent down to it and untied its lead. It jumped up at him, and he petted it and rubbed its sides. 'Hello, Baby,' he said. 'How's my Baby?' The dog growled and squealed and jumped some more. He straightened up, holding the lead. 'Kav, man, you get your ass over to Joel's like I said, right, blad?'

The boy nodded, flung himself on to the bike and cycled off. The young man looked at Agnes.

'Murchie?' Agnes looked back at him.

He rolled his shoulders, fixing her with a stare. 'Who's asking?'

'You knew Abbie,' she said. 'Abbie who died.'

The gaze didn't falter. 'Yeah. Abbie who died. Stupid whore.'

'You were one of the last people to see her alive.'

He gave a tight smile. 'Lucky me, eh?'

'She was frightened of you.'

He scuffed the pavement in front of him, then looked back at her. 'Yeah, well. People are, aren't they?'

'You've been throwing things at our hostel. You've been harassing Dermot, just because Abbie was growing fond of him.'

He nodded, still smiling. 'Guess I have.'

'Why did Abbie mean so much to you?'

His expression was taut as he met her eyes.

'She seemed frightened that you wouldn't let her go,' Agnes continued.

A shrug. He adjusted his jacket at his waist, as if trying to get the look just right.

'And you know Dermot too,' she pursued.

His eyes narrowed. 'He's a tosser.'

'That doesn't give you an excuse to harass him.'

'Harass? Me? Do you know what that boy's like?'

'I know he's trying to clean up his life.'

'Yeah, well, he better try doing better than mouthing off, picking fights with my bredren. Him no angel, that boy, you hear me?'

'He still doesn't deserve—'

'I mean it, lady.' His eyes were wide, almost tearful. 'Him going around playing the innocent, all this time now, him trying to dump me and Connor in it, and Connor his cousin an' all, innit? What they say about blood being thicker, not in his case, man, no way.' He shook his head.

'You still have no right to do what you did. And there's all this trouble you've been causing around our hostel.'

He studied her, his head on one side. 'Listen, lady. When this trouble start? You tell me, eh?'

Agnes faced him. 'I imagine,' she said, 'when Abbie started trying to escape from you.'

He took a short step towards her. The dog moved towards her too, looking up at his master as if awaiting instructions.

'It weren't like that. You want to hear the truth, I'll tell you, man. Abbie was happy with me. It was only when your lot started giving her other ideas...that's when it started going wrong for her.'

'Happy with you?'

'They're all happy with me, the girls are. I look after them, I do.'

'I'm sure you do,' Agnes said. 'Presents, no doubt.'

He smiled at her. 'Jewels. Chocolate. Flowers.'

'Flowers. Especially when they die.'

His empty gaze dropped. He stared at the ground. The dog began to nuzzle at his legs, growling softly. When he looked back at Agnes, the swagger seemed to have left him. 'That weren't my idea.'

'The roses?'

He shook his head. 'Weren't me.'

'Who was it, then?'

He sucked his teeth. 'Don't want you thinking that were me.' He slouched, all preening gone, replaced by a toe-scuffing hesitancy.

'Murchie—' Agnes put out a hand towards him, but the dog bared its teeth at her and she withdrew it. 'You could help us.'

She expected mockery, an instant rebuff. Instead he looked at her, a softness around the blue eyes, his mouth open as if to speak. She waited, searching the depth of his gaze. He caught her eye, and in an instant the rude-boy sneer reasserted itself. He drew himself up, laughed a harsh, empty laugh, looped the dog's lead around his wrist. 'How am I going to do that, then? You tell me, sister.'

'But, if you cared about Abbie—'

'Cared?' he interrupted her. 'No. You got me wrong. Don't look to me to care about no girl. Where Abbie come from, there's plenty others.' He flashed her an ice-cold smile, began to walk away from her, his hands in his pockets.

'Murchie,' she called after him, but he didn't look back; the dog, too, trotted at his ankles, its head held high. They reached the corner of the street and disappeared towards the main road.

'For the Lord looked down upon the Earth, that he might hear the groan of the prisoner, set free those that are condemned to die...'

Agnes slipped into a pew at the back of the convent chapel, and joined in the recitation of the psalm.

'He has brought down my strength before my time,

shortened the number of my days; and I said, "O my God, do not take me away in the midst of my days…" '

She had a sudden image of Pauline Stipes, sitting immobile in her dressing gown, railing against a life cut short.

'I saw you creep in late this morning.' Sister Louisa smiled at her as she handed her a mug of coffee.

'You and everyone else,' Agnes said. She sniffed the coffee. 'This is better than the usual fare here…'

'Yes.' Louisa bent her head to her mug. 'I started a bit of a campaign. Under the guise of fair trade. They seemed to accept that.' She looked up at Agnes. 'I can't bear instant, can you?'

Agnes smiled as they settled down in a corner of the kitchen. 'You've got further in half a week than I have in half a lifetime.'

'Yes. Must be to do with not caring so much.'

Agnes saw again the weight of sorrow in her face. 'Caring about what other people think?' she asked.

'Oh no.' She shook her head. 'I gave up caring about that some years ago. Decades, even. No – ' she leant towards Agnes. 'I meant, caring about being here. Vows, all that.'

Agnes considered her. 'I never took you to be a reluctant nun.'

Louisa's eyes rested on her, a stillness in their clear grey gaze. She began to speak. 'At the start, I embraced this life wholeheartedly. It felt like a homecoming. It was so much better than anything that had gone before. In that first Order, in the States, I felt I could be truly myself.' She paused for a moment, then went on, 'The problem was, I didn't know what being myself was. That's the way I see it now. As the years went on, and I really did become more truly myself, I began to part company with that younger, frightened version of me, the self that accepted all the rules, enjoyed them even, thrived within the structure...' She looked at Agnes, and her expression lightened, the hint of a smile around her lips. 'I'm sorry, I don't usually talk like this to a complete stranger.'

'Sometimes it's easier,' Agnes said.

She nodded. 'And I felt a kind of recognition...' She stopped.

'As you said last time – we both ran away into monastic life rather than running towards it.'

Louisa nodded. 'Although it seems to me that your older self is allowing you to stay.'

'And yours isn't?' Agnes lowered her voice, although they were now the only people in the kitchen.

'My spiritual director lent me a book a month or two ago. I think she had a sense that I was struggling. And there was a line in it that came to mind this morning in chapel, during the reading, which you missed, by the way.' She smiled, then went on, 'It was all about meeting Jesus in the Gospels. Walking with Him...you know the stuff. I suddenly thought, but we don't, do we? We don't meet Jesus, or God, or Our Lady, or anyone. It's all just stories. And I don't mind that. As stories go they're pretty good – but to give up your whole life for a story? It gets like believing in fairies. At best it's wishful thinking, at worst it seems to me it's self-deception.' She stopped, breathing hard.

A break in the clouds washed the window with light. After a moment, Agnes said, 'Have you told anyone that you feel this way?'

She shook her head. 'The minute I say it out loud, it will become true.'

'But you just have.'

Louisa smiled at her. 'You don't count.'

Agnes smiled back.

'Up in Yorkshire, I was working on this women's health project.' Louisa's face was serious again. 'It was a drop-in centre, for women who work on the streets. I was working with some wonderful people, and not one of them needed to believe that they were meeting Jesus. And they had such commitment, such a moral engagement with their fellow human beings...they didn't need fairy tales.'

'But surely...' Agnes gathered her thoughts, then went on, 'surely there is still a truth behind the stories. A real, living truth.'

'I envy you your faith,' Louisa said, and Agnes wondered that anyone might say such a thing to her. 'Even if there is a truth behind the fairy stories,' Louisa went on, 'what happens when they start to do damage?' She smoothed her skirt over her knees. 'The women's health centre supported women who wanted to leave the streets. But it also offered sexual-health services, including giving out condoms. What happens when the stories by which we live tell us that we're doing evil? All I could see was that we were doing good.'

'What did you do?'

Her hands were clasped tight together in her lap. 'During the days I gave out the condoms. During the nights I prayed for forgiveness from God and from our Holy Mother Church.'

'That must have been hard.'

She nodded. 'You can see why I have doubts about my future as a nun.'

'What will you do?'

Louisa frowned at her hands. 'For now, I'll carry on. I'm looking forward to this new women's health project. And when we start handing out condoms, then I'll have to make a choice. And this time, it might be a big public choice.'

'My father—' Agnes began, then stopped.

'Your father?'

'He believed in public assertions of faith.'

'Was he religious too?'

'Well, yes. Not really when I knew him, but later in life...he became a creationist, it turns out. He wrote tracts to prove that the earth is six thousand-odd years old. Including all the fossils.'

'He must have been quite an influence.'

'Oh – no – not on me. Not at all. Well, only by default. Only by being so negligent that the idea of marrying a bully seemed quite appealing. Someone who might actually look after me. I didn't know at the time it would come at such a price.'

'Hence the running away to join an Order.'

'Yes.'

'Although it seems to me, you've succeeded in growing into it.'

'It's nice of you to say so.'

'Like I say – I envy you.'

'My father wrote that his faith was a gift that had come to him late in life, but not too late. He said he would be grateful for the rest of his days.'

'And was he?'

Agnes put her empty mug down on the table. 'I didn't know him at the end. But according to those that did, then yes, I think he was.'

'Another thing you have in common, you and your father. You must take after him.'

Agnes looked up at her.

'Accepting the gifts that God puts your way. Unlike me...' She lowered her eyes again. 'These days I seem to be incapable of acceptance.'

Agnes reached out and touched her hand. 'Perhaps your doubt is also a gift.'

Louisa raised her eyes to her. Sorrow was etched across her face, although her eyes were dry. 'I pray so. God knows, that's all I pray these days.'

Agnes checked her watch. 'Louisa – I have to go back to the hostel. There's a lot of trouble there.'

Louisa managed a smile. 'Sounds like my kind of place.'

'I'm sure our work will overlap.' Agnes laughed. 'I'll see you very soon, I hope.'

'I hope so too.'

The bus inched along in the heavy traffic. The clouds had thickened overhead. Agnes looked out through the dots of rain on the window, and wondered how it was she'd become someone enviable, someone of unshakeable faith; someone who took after her father. It was not a self she recognised at all. At what point had the story changed, under her very nose, without her noticing?

The bus stopped at the traffic lights. She watched the red light melting into rain, then clearing, as the windscreen wipers swished to and fro.

CHAPTER EIGHT

She stood in the hostel hallway. There were voices coming from the kitchen and she went towards them.

The first thing she saw was Dermot, sitting at the table, his head turbaned with a large white bandage. He was laughing, holding a mug and sipping at it with some difficulty.

Gilroy was laughing too. 'Man, it's tomato, your favourite, drink it, boy.'

They were watched by Rob Coombes, who was standing by the cooker, stirring a spoon around in a mug. He looked up as Agnes appeared in the doorway. 'Ah,' he said. 'There you are.'

'Maybe a bowl?' Gilroy was saying. 'And a spoon?'

Dermot shook his head. 'Even worse, man. Can't feel my lips.'

'How about a straw?' Rob sat down at the table.

'You got one on you?' Gilroy said, and Rob shook his head.

The toaster popped up. Agnes retrieved two burnt slices of cheap white bread and handed them to Gilroy.

'Just how I like them,' he said. He began to smother them in thick layers of margarine.

Agnes turned to Rob. 'I bumped into Murchie,' she said. 'Earlier today.'

Rob looked up. 'Where?'

'Just outside here.'

'Wish I'd been there,' he said. 'We've got a few questions for that lad.' He turned to Dermot. 'Right, son. Shall we have a bit of a chat?'

Dermot struggled to his feet. Agnes put out her arm and he leant on her as they made their way to the office, Rob following behind.

'How was he?' Rob addressed Agnes.

'Murchie? He seemed very well.' She helped Dermot into a chair by the wall, then sat down next to her desk.

'I wasn't enquiring about his health.' Rob leant back in a chair and took out a notebook.

'His character, then?' Agnes picked up a pink, flower-shaped rubber from her desk. 'Pretty dodgy.'

'More than dodgy.' Rob waved a hand towards Dermot. 'Homicidal, more like.'

'I didn't see who it was.' Dermot turned towards Rob. 'I were lying on the ground, weren't I?'

'Who else would want to attack you?'

Dermot shrugged.

'We've had the matter of your rat, haven't we? We've got to conclude this is personal.'

'There was a bike. One of them little ones. I could see the wheels from where I was lying.'

'Kavin.' Rob glanced at Agnes.

'Kavin,' she agreed. 'I met him today too.'

'Another one we could do with getting off the streets.' Rob balanced his biro between his two index fingers. 'Murchie's little helper.' He turned back to Dermot. 'Any sign of the dog?'

Dermot nodded. 'Baby, you mean? Yeah. I could see him from where I was lying too.'

Rob made a note in his book, then looked back at Dermot. 'If we presented our Murchie to you in an identity parade, would it prompt your memory?'

Dermot leant back in his chair, resting his head against the wall. 'Man, I can't say. I could feel blows. There was more than one guy there. Three, maybe four. I could hear their voices. That's all I know.'

'When you say their voices – what were they saying?'

Dermot screwed up his face, from pain, from remembering, Agnes wasn't sure. 'Abbie,' he said. 'They was talking about her.'

'What were they saying?' Rob's pen was poised over his notebook.

Dermot frowned, shook his head. 'Calling her names and that. Then they said, this'll teach me a lesson for going to the feds.'

'You mean, because you talked to us?'

Dermot closed his eyes, his head still resting against the wall. 'Yeah,' he said. 'After what they did to Nige.'

Rob put his pen down. 'It all points to Murchison. It's just a question of whether he was there or not. Could you recognise his voice? Did you hear anyone call anyone by name?'

Dermot shook his head. 'Not his name, no. Only once – someone they called Zip...I heard someone call his name.'

Rob sighed. He leant forward, patted Dermot's arm. 'You've done very well, lad,' he said. 'Very well.' He stood up.

Dermot opened his eyes. 'When I'm feeling better,' he said, 'when my head's clear, I might remember more...'

'That's all right, son. We'll come and take a statement in the morning.' He glanced at Agnes. 'If that's OK?'

'Sure.' Agnes got up and showed him out to the hallway.

'Look after him.' Rob's voice was low. 'He's a brave lad.' He went to the front door, paused, his hand on the door handle. 'He's changed his story. After the attack, he was naming Murchie. Claimed to have seen him.' He gestured with his head towards the office door. 'Now he's not so sure.'

'He's scared,' Agnes said.

'I see it all the time. People ready to accuse their attackers, then withdrawing the accusation. Happens a lot in these cases. Makes my job very hard.' He opened the front door and looked out into the street. 'Nothing to lose, you see, the Murchies of this world. They don't care. They've been on the wrong side for so long, they can make up their own rules.' He turned back to her. 'Or are you going to try to tell me that Murchie is just a poor, neglected child who needs our sympathy?'

Agnes remembered the empty blue gaze. 'Not exactly, no.'

He shook her hand. 'Thought not. See you tomorrow.'

A police car was parked outside the hostel. Rob loped down the stairs, got into the passenger side, raised his hand as the car drew out and pulled away down the street.

Agnes watched him go. Making up their own rules, she thought. Causing such fear in a young woman that she takes a suicidal dose of heroin.

She glanced down at the empty milk bottle on the doorstep; a flash of memory of wilted roses.

She heard footsteps approaching, the click of high heels. A

thin young woman teetered at the foot of the steps, gazing up at the door. 'Are you that nun?' she said.

Agnes looked at her short denim skirt, black stilettos, wispy blond hair. 'Yes,' she said. 'I am that nun.'

'You knew my friend Abbie,' the girl said. 'I'm Lindy.'

She seemed frail, shrivelled with age, and yet very young. 'Would you like to come in?' Agnes said.

Lindy started up the stairs. Agnes led her through the hall and into the empty lounge.

She stood in the space of the room, flicking nervous glances around it. Then she sat down on the edge of one of the chairs, her hands locked together in her lap.

'Abbie mentioned you,' Agnes said, sitting down opposite her.

'We were that close,' the young woman said. 'We looked out for each other.' Her face clouded as she stared at her hands in her lap. 'Except at the end. None of us thought she'd do something like that.' Her voice drifted into silence.

'She didn't mean to,' Agnes said, after a moment.

Lindy faced her. 'None of us can believe it. We all feel really bad, all us girls. And the thing is...' her fingers entwined together... 'she'd been clean. She'd been clean for weeks. She'd done so well here. None of us can understand why she'd suddenly OD like that.'

'When you say us...?'

'Us. The girls. We all work out that way...by the river...' She tilted her head towards the window.

'Do you know Murchie?' Agnes said.

Lindy almost smiled, an empty lifting of her mouth. 'Course I know Murchie. Anyone don't know Murchie round our way, they soon will. He rules this manor. It's like what he said about Abbie, no one leaves him and gets away with it.'

Agnes looked at her. 'He said that?'

'When he heard she'd died, yeah. That's what Connor said, anyway.'

Agnes ran her fingers through her hair. 'I've been asking the police to ask more questions. I still think it's odd, Abbie's death. Like you, I can't understand what would make her come back here and inject like that. I've been worrying it was my fault...' She looked into Lindy's wide eyes and stopped.

'Why your fault?'

Agnes sighed. 'I encouraged her to challenge Murchie. She'd taken up with Dermot here. I thought he'd be good for her, I decided to interfere. It was really stupid of me.'

'He's sweet, Motty is. Bit of a mouth on him, but he's cool.' Lindy leant down to reach her bag. She took out a packet of cigarettes, opened it, counted the few that were left and put it back in her bag. 'Thing is, even if she did go out and see Murch, and even if he did threaten her – she still came back here on her own with the gear, didn't she? I'd love to see that fella behind bars, but we've been talking about it, us girls, and none of us can see how he snuck in here and killed her, and anyway, he wouldn't do it that way, these days he's so wired, if he gets angry he just shoots, or gets someone else to do it for him...' She stopped, breathing hard.

There were footsteps on the stairs above them, running, then laughter and a door slam.

'It's still out of character,' Agnes said.

Lindy raised her eyes to her. 'Yeah. It is. I've been wondering whether she saw anyone else. Like, either Murchie put the wind up her, or maybe someone else made her feel like life weren't worth living no more. Donna, one of the girls, she asked Murchie what he'd said to her, and he said, nothing, and she said he looked right shifty. He told Donna that all he said was that she was all right as she was and it's not as if any other guy could look after her like he did, and that Dermot wasn't going to be able to keep her safe like he does...' She seemed drained by speaking. 'Safe,' she said, then clicked her tongue. 'Like it's safe being one of Murchie's girls—' A musical beat filled the room, and she pulled her phone out of her bag. 'Wassup?' she said into it. 'What? How does he know I'm here?' She listened, her face chalk white. 'He's a bastard. I don't care. Yeah, OK. Laters.' She hung up. She put her phone into her bag, then stood up. 'Gotta split,' she said.

'Murchie?' Agnes asked.

'Kavin. Little bastard. He thinks he's so big. He should wait till Murchie turns on him like he always does. Kavin'll be out on the wrong side then, like all the others. And none of us'll care.'

Agnes followed her out to the hallway. At the door, she rested her hand on the girl's arm. 'Keep in touch,' she said.

'Will there be a funeral?' Lindy's face seemed to tremble as she met Agnes's eyes.

Agnes nodded. 'Eventually. I'll let you know when.'

'We'd like to be there. Us girls. Pay our respects.' Again, the urgency in her gaze. 'Will it be Catholic? She were Catholic, she were. Her mum's buried in Connemara. She always wanted to go back there. She said, if she had one dream in life, it was to go back to Connemara and put a bunch of violets on her mother's grave.' She shook her head, blinking. 'Well, now it's too late. Maybe I should do it for her.' She opened the front door and glanced down the street, with an edgy nervousness; just like Abbie, Agnes thought. She took her cigarettes from her bag, took one out and lit it. She breathed in the smoke, scanned the road again, then ventured down the steps and out into the street. Agnes saw her give a little wave at the corner before she disappeared.

No one leaves Murchie and gets away with it.

The words hung in the damp, drizzly air.

Agnes went back into the hostel and shut the door.

Dermot had gone to his room. The girls were nowhere to be seen. Eddie and Gilroy had taken the van to the garage to have its brakes fixed, yet again. Agnes settled at her desk in the office and ploughed through a pile of paperwork; follow-up forms for former residents, a reference for an ex-employee, applications for a hostel place for a sixteen-year-old from Dundee, police checks, banking correspondence, a parking fine for the van...

She typed letters, filled in forms, each time putting her name, Sister Agnes, and the name of the Order, then her signature. Where it was required she put her surname: Bourdillon, her husband's surname. It seemed increasingly odd to her, writing it down. She hadn't seen him for years. She assumed he was still alive, still living between a cottage in Gloucestershire and a small flat in Paris, or maybe he'd gone up in the world; maybe it was a huge country mansion somewhere, and two or three flats in various parts of France, a yacht on the south coast...

Bourdillon. How extraordinary that this should be my name. And what a relief, as a nun, to so rarely have to use it.

And if not Bourdillon, then what? My father's surname? Gardner? That would be just as strange.

She signed the last of the heap, deliberately left off her

surname, folded it up and put it in an official envelope. She picked up the parking fine and put it on Gilroy's desk. She checked the rota for the next day, finding she wasn't due in until the afternoon.

The house was strangely quiet. She called out her goodbyes and left.

'And just as it behoved our Lord to give to Adam the permission to name the animals, so does He also give to us the freedom of Paradise. For it is my contention that, far from exiling us from Eden, the Lord in His wisdom has allowed us to roam within it, offering us clues, in the rings of the trees, the lava layers of the mountains, in fossils, in the strata of the earth itself; showing us by these signs that we are still in Eden. And this is the heresy of the theory of evolution; pursuing a man-derived chronology does indeed exile us from Eden. And it is an exile that *we* choose, not God. To trust in the story of Genesis is to reconcile us to Paradise.'

Agnes lay on her bed, leafing through the close-typed pages. There was more, in a similar vein. At one point she found a list of names: Reuben, Simeon, Judah, Issachar, Ephraim, Benjamin...

She put the pages down and picked up the fossil that had been taped into his notebook, and which now lay on the shelf by her bed in her flat, next to the prayer book in French that had been her mother's.

She held the fossil between her fingers. It was impossible that a shell frozen in stone could only be as old as biblical time allowed; in other words, well within the collective memory of the human race. She thought that Brett must know that the box of fossils would either prove to be extremely old, or fake.

She wondered why he was so prepared to pursue her father's thesis, to the extent of borrowing expensive scientific equipment to do so.

She got up from her bed and lit her candle and arranged her prayer cushions.

'Our Father, who art in Heaven...'

She remembered the tears on Paul Moffat's face. 'I was her father,' he'd said. 'I was all she had.'

'...And Jesus said, "Abba" which means Father...'

She recalled Brett's hesitation when she'd asked him a direct question about her father. And yet, here he is, a link to my father, probably the only person alive who could give me anything like a clear picture of him.

She got up from her cushions and retrieved his card from her bag. She took out her mobile and dialled his number.

'Hi.' He sounded pleased to hear from her. She could hear restaurant noises in the background.

'Would you mind...' She hesitated.

'Would you like to meet up? I'd be delighted. I had this feeling you'd need to talk.'

'Oh. Good.' She hoped she didn't sound as relieved as she felt. Athena would disapprove.

'The question is when. I'm off to Oxford tomorrow evening, taking your pa's relics with me. How about before that? Tea? I've discovered Fortnum's. It's bliss. Upstairs, the fourth floor.'

'Yes. I know it.'

There was a tiny pause. 'Of course,' he said. 'Of course you would know it. Well, tea, then. Half past three?'

She agreed that three-thirty would be fine. She rang off, switched off her phone, settled back to her prayers.

* * *

The bright morning sunshine seemed garish in the suburban restraint of the Stipes's street. The neat front garden cowered in the unaccustomed brilliance; the hydrangea looked wilted, as if craving shadow.

She reached the Stipes's door. She thought she could hear raised voices, which stopped abruptly as she rang the bell.

Jeremy Stipes stood in the doorway, blinking in the brightness. 'Oh.' He put his hand up to his face and stared at her. 'It's you.'

'I should have phoned,' Agnes said.

'Yes.' He continued to look at her, as if wondering what to do with her.

'Is your wife there?' Agnes realised the words sounded wrong.

'Where else would she be?'

'Perhaps I could see her.'

He didn't take his eyes from her, and Agnes wondered whether those door-to-door salesmen actually did put their foot in the door, wondered whether to risk it.

'I'll go and see.' He left her standing there in the intrusive sunshine. After a moment he reappeared. 'She says she'd be very glad to see you,' he said. The words were sticky with resentment.

The hallway was dark and chilly. Agnes hung her coat on a peg, then followed Jeremy into the lounge. Mrs Stipes was sitting in the same chair as before, wearing the same pink dressing gown.

Agnes crossed the room and sat down next to her. Mrs Stipes reached out and squeezed her hand briefly in her thin fingers. She looked up at her husband and waited. Her husband stared back at her in the silence of the room.

He was the first to blink. 'Well,' he said.

'Perhaps our guest would like some coffee,' Pauline said.

He nodded, tight-lipped, turned to Agnes. 'Coffee?'

'Yes, please,' Agnes said.

'Milk? Sugar?' *Weedkiller?* he looked as if he wanted to add.

'Just milk, please.'

They could hear him out in the kitchen. Pauline gripped her hand again.

'What can I do?' Agnes's voice was low. 'How can I help you?'

'Hospice,' Pauline whispered. 'Old people's home. Anything.'

'What does Dr Kitson say?'

Her eyes held Agnes's gaze. 'He's so sure I'm in good hands here. He doesn't understand...'

'Should we get social services involved?'

Pauline's thin lips tightened. 'I can't accuse him of anything. No physical abuse, you see.'

Agnes leant in close to her ear. 'Promise me he hasn't harmed you physically.'

'I promise,' Pauline whispered. 'He's never laid a finger on me. It would be better if he had. Then I'd have left him. Before it was too late.'

'It's not too late,' Agnes said. 'You deserve to live in peace.'

'Live in peace, die in peace.' Pauline managed a thin smile.

'I'll think of something,' Agnes said, as Jeremy reappeared carrying a tray.

'Coffee,' he said, setting the tray down on a low stool. 'Milk?' He poured milk from a jug. The jug was terracotta, made in a thick rustic style. The mugs also had a hand-hewn look, fired clay with visible ridges from the potter's wheel. They sat oddly in the ordered neatness of the lounge.

'How is my friend Vaughan?' Jeremy turned to Agnes with a conversational tone.

Agnes frowned, then remembered. 'Dr Kitson? I saw him yesterday morning. He's fine, I think.' She wondered whether to make polite conversation about the doctor's concerns; decided that the sudden death of a drug addict was probably not a suitable topic. She sipped her coffee, which was strong and surprisingly good. She noticed he'd only brought two mugs, and was drinking from the other himself.

'Do you not drink coffee?' she turned to Pauline.

'I like it—' she began.

'We've decided it's not good for her,' her husband interrupted.

The space around them seemed to have gently chilled. 'But – if you like it—' Agnes addressed Pauline directly.

'The medication.' Pauline shrugged weakly. 'That's what he says...'

'We can't risk it, you see.' Jeremy seemed to think the conversation was at an end. 'We want to make sure she's as comfortable as possible.'

Agnes leant across to Pauline. 'Would you like a cup of coffee?'

Pauline looked at her. A nervous smile flicked across her face. 'Yes please.'

Agnes went into the kitchen, poured another mug from the expensive coffee pot and brought it through into the lounge. 'Milk?'

'Just sugar, thanks.'

Agnes handed her the mug, and Pauline sat, stirring the

spoon around in it, breathing in the scent.

With one hand, Jeremy smoothed the crease of his trousers.

In silence, Pauline sipped her coffee. In silence, Agnes drained her cup and stood up. 'Well,' she said, her voice loud in the room, 'I'd better get going.'

Jeremy breathed again. 'I'll show you out,' he said.

She took her coat down from its peg, and reached for the door handle. Before she could open it, Jeremy's hand had grabbed hold of hers. 'You shouldn't have done that,' he said.

She pulled her hand from his grasp and faced him.

'The coffee,' he said.

She looked at his eyes, narrow in his plump face. 'Perhaps it was rude of me,' she agreed.

'More than rude.' He breathed out, heavily. 'Do you have any idea what it's like nursing someone with cancer?' His voice was a rough whisper. 'When it's your life partner?' he added.

She wondered whether the terror of Julius's near death would count. 'No,' she conceded.

'We're fighting to keep her alive,' he said. 'And we shall win.'

Agnes gazed up at him. He was pink-faced, breathing fast. 'I won't be overruled,' he went on. 'I know about illness. I learnt the hard way. This time I refuse to fail.'

'How did you learn so much?'

'What I don't know about caring for the sick...' He looked down at her. 'At my mother's knee. Literally.'

'Your mother was ill?'

He nodded. 'I did everything I could. Years, it went on. I say to people, I had no childhood. I was born a little man.' He smiled, as if he'd cracked a joke.

'What did she have?'

'A wasting illness.' He fiddled in his pocket, produced a packet of cigarettes and a lighter. 'We did what we could, my father and me.' He lit the cigarette, took a long in-breath of smoke. 'And the end, when it came, was terrible. That's what I believe, you see. We must fight death to the end. We mustn't let him win. And sometimes death is so slow, we must fight him then too.' He lowered his voice. 'If I thought for one minute that Pauline was suffering beyond what a human being can bear – if at any moment it comes to that – then I would fully support her right to die. These poor people who have to go off to Switzerland, and then the husband gets arrested when he comes back on suspicion of causing his wife's death, when all he's done is take his wife to a place where she can die with dignity, in control of it all, instead of...' His words tailed off. He took another drag on his cigarette. His gaze was distant, clouded with memory. He saw Agnes standing there, and made a little movement, as if shaking off the past. 'I shouldn't keep you,' he said.

Agnes returned his gaze. 'Don't you think there's a place for acceptance,' she said. 'I mean, if there's a possibility that Pauline accepts she's dying—'

'I won't have her give up.' His voice was harsh as he interrupted. 'One of us has to have hope. And I don't mind if it's me.'

'But what if you're hoping in vain?'

He stared down at her. 'Perhaps you can choose to live like that. Praying for life but finding that you're meeting death instead. Being told to trust in God, only to find that he's not trustworthy after all...' He shook his head. 'For me, that's defeat, to live in that world. I learnt a long time ago, you have to fight.' He paused, exhausted with speaking. His hand went to the door. The sun had gone in, and he looked out across his front garden. The hydrangea seemed to be flexing its leaves once more.

'Well—' Agnes offered her hand.

He looked at her, then slowly took it. 'I don't wish to forbid you coming here,' he said. 'But—' He pursed his lips, then went on, 'I won't have anyone here who upsets her. Is that clear?'

Agnes nodded, and withdrew her hand. 'I understand,' she said.

She turned and went down the garden path and out into the street. She wondered whether it might be possible to hide a packet of decent ground arabica in the kitchen somewhere. She wondered what he'd say if he found out. She wondered whether Julius could pull strings to find a hospice place.

She stood at the bus stop on the main road. In the traffic's rumble, the words of the psalm echoed in her mind: 'And I said, "O my God, do not take me away in the midst of my days."' She thought of Jeremy Stipes drinking high-quality coffee from his craftsman-made mug, determined to fight on; determined not to see the death of his mother in the death of his wife.

CHAPTER NINE

'A wasting disease?' Julius sat opposite her in his office, his mouth open in surprise. 'Did Jeremy tell you his mother died from that?'

Agnes looked up from her cup of green tea. 'Why – what was it?'

'It was alcoholism, his mother. She died from drink, did Rosie Stipes. At the end, nothing would keep her from her gin.'

'Not even her little boy?'

Julius put down his cup. 'It was before my time here. But there was an elderly parishioner, she died some years ago, do you remember Lily Ivey? She knew them. Terribly sad. He used to hide her bottles, and she used to scream and shout at him, Lily said.

'Alcoholism?' Agnes traced a circle around the rim of her cup. 'Perhaps that explains a lot.'

'Perhaps it does.' Julius eyed a brown paper bag that she'd put down on his desk. 'That wouldn't be lunch, by any chance, would it?'

She smiled at him. 'What would you do without me to look after you?'

He shrugged. 'Oh, I'd have to put up with the various offerings that the good women of the parish bring me. Mrs O'Leary brought me sushi the other day. Nasty slimy stuff, she insisted I eat it.'

She drew out two parcels. 'There's Parma ham on olive ciabatta, or mozzarella with sun-dried tomato.'

'See what I mean? Shall we have half and half?'

She went to the corner of his office where the kettle stood, and bent to the shelves, taking out plates and knives. 'The thing is...' She brought them over to the desk, carved equal halves of mozzarella sandwich, '...it's out of the question that Pauline stays there, in that house.'

'It is?' Julius took the plate she passed him.

'She's desperately unhappy. He controls everything about her, he won't even let her drink coffee.'

'Oh dear.' Julius broke off a piece of bread. 'I suppose I should have known, when I got you involved...'

'It's too late now.' She smiled at him. 'You've only got yourself to blame.'

'Without you, they'd have carried on as they were, I suppose.'

Agnes finished a mouthful of sandwich. 'She said she meant to leave him years ago. And now it's too late.'

Julius leant back in his chair and surveyed her. 'I've known that couple for about fifteen years and I had no idea. You meet them once—'

'Twice.' she corrected him.

'Twice. And you end up knowing their life story.'

'It's just knowing which questions to ask, Julius.' She

picked some sun-dried tomato out of her sandwich and began to eat it.

'So, is the plan to spring her from her marriage, then?'

'I wondered whether you'd know anything about a hospice place, a nursing home, anywhere, really.'

Julius paused mid-chew, considering. 'There are hospices of course. But I thought her doctor's view was that she's better off at home until the end.'

'Dr Kitson? Well, he's wrong.'

'Can you raise all this with him?'

'I intend to,' she said. 'In fact, he's due at the hostel to see Dermot this afternoon, I'll grab him then.'

She ate another piece of tomato.

'You're right, of course.' Julius drained his cup of tea. 'When it comes to people, it seems I'm hopeless about the detail.'

'I wouldn't say that.' She smiled at him.

'No, really. For example, I've always thought of you as someone who doesn't like tomatoes. And there you are, picking them out of your sandwich and eating them.'

'These are sun-dried. Completely different from eating fresh tomato.'

'Ah. Right.' Julius frowned. 'So, it's not people I can't tell apart. It's just different kinds of tomato. That's something, I suppose.'

She passed him half a Parma ham sandwich. 'Silly old Julius,' she said.

The clouds had thickened, threatening rain. Agnes walked towards the hostel, rehearsing her conversation with Dr Kitson: it's not fair on Mrs Stipes to stay there, she's very unhappy, for all we know the stress might be making her worse...

A gust of wind flicked at the litter, whirled a torn crisp packet at her feet. As she arrived at the hostel she felt the first drops of rain.

She waited for him in the lounge. The door opened and he peered round it. 'You wanted to talk to me, Sister.'

'If you've got a moment—'

'Of course.' He crossed the room and flopped into one of the armchairs.

'I've seen the Stipes again,' she said. 'Jeremy and Pauline.'

'Oh.' He looked at her over the top of his glasses. 'Your "counselling" role?'

'Yes.'

'Unofficial, presumably.'

'The boundaries are all a bit blurred,' she agreed.

He leant back in his chair. 'And...?'

She sighed. 'I will be frank with you. It seems to me that her home situation is not doing Mrs Stipes any good.'

He considered this for a moment, then said, 'To be honest, Sister, there's very little that can do much good for Mrs Stipes. We're living in hope, her husband and I...'

'She's very unhappy. I'm telling you this in complete confidence, but she told me today that she wished she'd left him a long time ago.'

Dr Kitson gave a twitch of his shoulders. 'Left him?' He stared at Agnes.

She nodded.

'Well, well.' He frowned. 'I've known that couple for quite some time, and neither has given me any such indication...' Again, he shifted in his seat. 'Are you sure?' His look was searching and intense.

'That's what she told me.' She felt unsure; she found herself doubting Pauline's honesty. 'Perhaps she was exaggerating a bit...'

He leant back in the armchair. The tips of his fingers touched together.

'Julius thought he might try to find a hospice place.' The suggestion now seemed weak and inappropriate.

He smiled at her. 'It's very helpful of both of you, and I'm sure when the time comes we'll be very grateful, Jeremy and I. But you see...' He rested an arm along the back of his chair – 'In these cases timing is everything. Can you imagine what Pauline will think if we move her at this stage, when there is no sign that her illness is becoming any worse, into a place for the terminally ill? It will only upset her, and that's the last thing any of us want, isn't it?'

Agnes mumbled in agreement.

'I do appreciate your involvement, Sister,' he went on. 'Please don't think I'm undermining your expertise in any way. But, speaking as a doctor, I have some experience in dealing with people who are undergoing such difficult and painful challenges. One does what one can. There is always this feeling that there might be a better solution, a more positive outcome...' He broke off, his attention caught by something outside, the rain pattering against the window, perhaps. He turned back to her. 'It's always the same. They rely on me to make it all right again. And of course, sometimes there's nothing I can do.' He seemed to focus on the distance once more.

Agnes wondered what else to say, but then he blinked at her, looked at his watch. 'I'm sorry.'

She smiled at him. 'Don't let me keep you. I'm glad we had

this conversation. I don't wish to get in the way of your professional role...'

He returned her smile. 'Well, as much as you're intruding on one of my professional relationships, I'm doing the same where you're concerned. Sister Louisa, is it?'

'Louisa – she's in my community.'

'Yes.' He smiled. '

'When did you meet her?'

'I haven't, yet. But she's in discussion with one of my practice members about a women's health outreach project. Apparently she has a lot of experience in the field.'

'Yes. She does.'

'There's a meeting this evening of the working group. They've invited her, apparently.'

Agnes tried to imagine Dr Kitson and Louisa working together. Perhaps they'd get on very well, she thought, as she stood up.

'Sister,' He offered her his hand.

'Do call me Agnes.'

'Vaughan,' he said, as they shook hands.

Out in the hallway, Agnes turned to him. 'You really are of the view that a hospice is inappropriate for Pauline?'

'A hospice would be an admission of defeat. And while there's life in Jeremy, it would be an admission of failure, of lack of faith in him.'

He slung his raincoat over his arm. 'I'm glad you're in touch with Pauline,' he said. 'It's important she has someone to confide in.' He opened the front door. 'Other than her husband, of course.' He smiled at her. 'See you around.'

She went back into the lounge. Someone had found a vase

and put an arrangement of flowers in the window, carnations and chrysanthemums. Aysha, Agnes thought. It would be just like her to think to ask the supermarket for some flowers past their sell-by date, as well as the cakes, bread and fruit that had appeared in the kitchen overnight.

She pulled out a wilted carnation and closed the others around it. While there's life in Jeremy... It was an odd thing to say.

Or perhaps not, she thought, wandering out to the office. Perhaps as a doctor you get used to the family dynamics; perhaps it's us monastics who don't quite understand.

Gilroy looked up from his desk. 'Didn't know you were working today?'

'I'm not. Just wondered how Dermot is?' The carnation drooped between her fingers.

'Doing really fine. And it's all gone quiet where them rude-boys are concerned too. Maybe just a lull. Maybe they think they've taught Mots a lesson and they don't have to come back and teach him another.'

'That would be nice.'

'Dr Kitson is arranging for a practice nurse to pop in, so Mots don't have to risk walking the streets for a bit.'

'That's nice of him.'

'We thought so too.'

'Well...' Agnes hesitated, watching Gilroy open another file of paperwork on his desk. 'If you don't need me...'

He looked up and smiled. 'Man, we don't need you. You not on shift, we don't need you. You get me?'

'All right then.' She turned to go, went to the door.

'As far as I know, even them holy Sisters are still human.'

She turned back to smile at him, but he was concentrating on his heap of paperwork.

She was still holding the flower. She looked at it, in the dim light of the hallway, at its crimped edges. She remembered the roses left on the doorstep; the scrawled, rough letters: 'There are promises that no one can break.'

She threw the carnation into the kitchen bin. Tomorrow I'll put in a call to Rob Coombes, she thought.

The lift of Fortnums was gilded and mirrored. Alone in the lift she smoothed her hair. On impulse, she took out the lipstick that Athena had given her and applied a quick slick. She walked out into the fourth-floor restaurant, into sunlight and white linen and creamy draped curtains, and a dinner-jacketed young man playing a grand piano at the centre of the room.

She saw a hand raised to her from a corner table.

'I hope I'm not late—' she began.

'I was early.' He gestured to her to sit down. 'I nearly had a glass of champagne, but I thought it might be too early even for you.'

'How well you've come to know me in such a short time.' She arranged her bag next to her.

He was studying her. 'You look – different somehow. More—' He hesitated, then said, 'But I shouldn't say such a thing to a nun.'

'Perhaps it's just the daylight,' she said.

'Perhaps it is. Well,' he picked up the menu, 'if we're not having champagne, afternoon tea it is, then.'

They gave their order, watched the pianist, commented on Piccadilly in the rain. 'Really, it's archetypal,' Brett said. 'The architecture, the umbrellas, the buses, I'd send everyone postcards of it, if I knew anyone back home who'd be the slightest bit interested...'

Elegant tea things were placed in front of them, 'Darjeeling for monsieur, Assam for madame...'

Brett passed her the jug of milk. 'Julius would disapprove,' Agnes said.

'Oh really?' Brett raised an eyebrow.

'Milk in last. He says it scalds the milk, changes the taste of the tea. You should put it in first, apparently.'

'That's a relief.' Brett added a thin slice of lemon to his cup. 'I thought you meant morally.'

'Probably that too. Julius has perfected the art of merging his moral self with everyday life. He ought to write a book.'

'The sinfulness of scalding the milk?'

'Oh no.' Agnes shook her head. 'Not sinfulness. It would all be about living well and joyfully. It would be entirely redemptive and would make everyone who read it feel that they were in some way loved, cherished by the universe, even in the midst of terrible pain or grief.'

'Redemption in a cup of tea?' Brett laughed.

'The Zen masters have been doing it for years.'

Brett watched her as she took a cucumber sandwich. 'So,' he said.

'My father.' She glanced at him, then, 'What happened?'

'What do you mean?'

'You know what I mean. He changed. He went from being someone whose emotional needs were always unmet, someone dried up, calcified – to this impassioned optimist, author of a retelling of the creation myth.'

'I didn't know him before—' Brett began.

'Did he fall in love?' Agnes faced him.

Brett hesitated. 'Yes,' he said. 'He did.'

'Who was she?'

'A schoolteacher. English, originally, but she came to live in Charleston. She got involved in the same church as your father.'

'And the fossil stuff?'

'They explored all that together.'

There was a silence. The piano tinkled in the background. Agnes was aware of the murmur of conversation around them. 'What was she called?' she asked him.

'Monica,' he said.

'Did she always love him?'

He nodded. 'Until he died.'

There were camera flashes behind them, a party of tourists taking photos of each other.

'Where is she now?'

Brett's words were reluctant. 'In England. On the south coast. Charmouth, in Dorset.'

'So...' Agnes looked at him.

'Please don't be like that. I haven't been hiding anything from you.'

'Only that my father's last love is barely a hundred miles from here. Is that what triggered your visit over here? Are you seeing her? Does she know you're here? Does she know about me? Is the whole fossil thing a kind of front, all this carbon-dating research trip—'

'Whoa there.' His voice was loud. The camera flashes stopped. He took a deep breath. 'Firstly, there are no secrets. She doesn't know I'm here. I haven't seen her for years. She moved to Dorset soon after your father died. If I've been shifty about my reasons for coming to England, that's entirely to do with my own circumstances, and nothing about your father. Secondly—' He paused and looked at her. On the next table the photography resumed; a portly, pink-faced man took a close-up of his chocolate eclair.

'Secondly, what?'

He frowned. 'Why should Monica's existence cause you such upset?'

She stared at her plate. 'I don't know. Something about fathers, maybe.' She fiddled a breadcrumb around her plate. 'Abbie's dad said—' She rubbed her forehead. 'It's all too late now.' She reached for the teapot, refilled her cup, accepted the scone that he passed her.

'Does Julius have views on the state of your soul depending on whether you put the cream or the jam first?'

She smiled a brief smile at him. 'I expect so.' She cut her scone in half and spread jam on it. 'So,' she said.

'I know what this next question is. What is my reason for being here?'

She nodded. 'Uh huh.'

'Do I have to tell you?'

'Yes,' she said. 'You do. Given that you and I are about to prove from those fossils that the universe is only as old as the Bible tells us, it can't be anything like as earth-shattering as that.'

He smiled at her.

'Love, then?' she said.

He nodded. 'A woman.'

'Who is she?'

'Must you know everything?' he said, as Agnes's phone started to ring.

'Sweetie,' Athena began as Agnes answered it. 'I'm sure you're very busy, but it's an emergency.'

'I am very busy.'

'The thing is, I'm all alone in my flat tonight, Nic's still at his mum's, anyway, I bought this fish from the supermarket and now I'm panicking because I don't know what to do with it, and I thought if you came over you'd know what to do and you'd be able to eat most of it too because if I am going to get married, not that I am, of course, I've just got to lose some weight...sweetie, where on earth are you? It sounds like tea at the Ritz or somewhere?'

A version of 'Moon River' was coming from the piano. 'Fortnum's,' Agnes said.

'You old tart. That's one of our places. The dishy American, presumably.'

'You presume right,' Agnes said.

'I thought you said you were busy.'

'I am. He was just about to tell me who he's in love with, and now you've spoilt it.' Agnes watched Brett's expression and tried not to laugh.

'Oh, kitten, I am sorry. Trust me to interrupt at such a crucial moment. Seven o'clock do you? That gives you time to cook before dinner.'

'Seven it is,' Agnes said. 'Oh, and Athena, can you manage to track down some tarragon and lemons before then?'

'Will do.'

Agnes clicked off her phone and put it in her bag. She met his eyes. 'There's no need to look at me like that,' she said.

'Do you know, if I didn't have proof you were a nun, I'd be beginning to think that your Order was some kind of cover.

That really you and this Athena are spies, or high-class call girls or something.'

'You don't have proof I'm a nun,' she said.

'No,' he agreed.

'So—' Agnes took a miniature pear tart from the cake stand and put it on her plate. 'Who is she?'

'Oh—' He flicked his hand past his face. 'It's all rather dreary.'

'A fellow scientist?'

'A dancer.'

'Are your feelings reciprocated?'

He leant back in his chair. 'What is this? Are you writing a book or something?'

'My friend Athena is going to write a best-seller about how to catch your man. But no.'

'The short answer is that I thought it was mutual, and now it seems it isn't. And I've come over here to try to make it work.'

'How very romantic.'

He considered her. 'It's just as well your Order isn't one of the silent ones. I can't imagine you'd survive at all.'

'Oh dear. You're right. I ought to practise restraint.'

'Not at all.' He waved a hand towards her. 'This is much more becoming.' He looked at his watch. 'I ought to be going, I'm afraid. I'm catching one of those buses that go direct.'

Out in the street, he presented her with the leftovers, the raspberry pastry and the chocolate tart that they'd been unable to finish, gift-wrapped in a pink box. 'I asked the waitress,' he explained. 'I think she was shocked at an American not eating everything up there and then.'

'Thank you.' Agnes took the box from him.

They stood in the street, in the late afternoon light, jostled by passers-by.

He shifted his weight from foot to foot. 'When I said about high-class call girls...' he began. 'I didn't mean it. You must know I didn't.'

She patted his elbow. 'I know.'

'I do believe you're a nun. Really. However unlikely it seems.'

'Thank you.' She bowed her head, then turned towards the tube.

'See you soon,' he said.

She turned back. 'I hope so. Enjoy Oxford.'

He gave her a brief wave and began to make his way up Piccadilly. She watched him merging with the crowd, watched him disappear into the mix of luxury and squalor, grand porticos and closing-down sales.

'High-class call girls?' Athena slapped a large piece of salmon fillet down on her wooden chopping board. 'And do you think we should be flattered by this, sweetie, or insulted? At our age, I find it's difficult to decide.' Her dark hair shone against the matt-white walls of her kitchen; her navy blue chef's apron hung awkwardly from her neck.

Agnes arranged the two leftover pastries on a chunky, multi-coloured plate which she placed on the pale wood table. 'I think it was a compliment. It was because he didn't believe I was a nun. And if we weren't call girls we could be spies instead.'

'Ah, now, that I could go for. Foreign travel. Loads of different outfits...'

Agnes settled down on an etiolated chair in pale leaf green. The window looked out to the tree-lined street.

Athena frowned at the fish. 'They said it was organic, even though it's farmed. So that's all right, isn't it kitten?' She threw an uncertain glance at Agnes. 'Organic means it's OK, doesn't it? No exploited African fish farmers, or poor baby salmon being flown miles in cruel crates or anything?'

'I'm sure it'll be fine. Do you have any foil?'

'Somewhere. I think. I used it last time I tried to do home highlights on my hair, terrible mistake, do you remember? That's the last time I try to economise on something really important.'

'Athena, that was ages ago.' Agnes got up and began to open cupboards. 'What about tarragon?'

Athena passed her a supermarket bag. 'And the fuss they made when I asked for a carrier bag. As I said to the girl on the checkout, I'm not going to put a fish into my best Anya Hindmarsh, am I?'

Agnes turned down the oven, began to chop herbs, slice lemons, oil a baking tray. 'So, how is Nic?'

'Lovely.' Athena opened a cupboard, pulled out a bottle of gin, squinted at it. 'Can't think where all that's gone.'

'Where's his mum?'

'Devon. Honiton. She's in the old family house, it's much too big for her and she's not at all well.' She eyed Agnes's chopping board. 'Can I pinch some of your lemon slices? Nic's down there trying to help her move into something more appropriate, sheltered housing or something. He's borrowed my pride and joy again.'

'The Audi?'

'I love it, sweetie. The only thing that mars my enjoyment

is all these darned sly cameras hidden everywhere. You can't even put your lipstick on without one of those things flashing. Anyway, Nic's moving some of her stuff out to his sister's, in fact, I know – I can use those lovely crystal glasses he brought back last time, I've been wanting to get them out.' She bent to a low cupboard, brought out a cardboard box, unwrapped two crystal tumblers from yellowing newspaper. She ran them under the tap, dried them off, then splashed the remains of the gin into them. She lifted one up to the light. 'We'll just have to make do,' she said.

Agnes wrapped the fish in foil and put it in the oven. She washed her hands, dried them on her apron, took the glass that Athena handed her.

'That's not too much tonic, is it, kitten? One doesn't want to drown it.'

'I'm sure it's just right.' Agnes took a sip, put the glass down on the table, began to clear a space to prepare the salad. She picked up the old newspaper from the glasses box. '...malpractice case dropped against local doctor,' she read.

'Athena, do you want to keep all this—?' 'Dr Vaughan Kitson'. The words jumped out from the faded newsprint.

She sat down at the table, smoothed out the paper until the paragraphs appeared in full. 'A local patients' support group has dropped its legal action against Tavercombe Health Centre, following the alleged malpractice of one of the GPs. Their spokeswoman, Joyce Tamplin, said the campaign hadn't managed to raise sufficient funds to meet the rising legal costs. The Area Health Authority's spokesman, Dr Peter Latter, expressed his relief that the campaign was over. "We have always maintained that the safety of our patients is our paramount concern," he stated. "We would also like to state categorically that the initial police investigation found no fault whatsoever in the medical expertise that was offered to patients at this practice." Dr Latter went on to say that the doctor at the heart of the complaints, Dr Vaughan Kitson, was entirely exonerated of any blame. Dr Kitson has since left the practice. When it was put to her that some people felt the campaign had been a witch-hunt, Mrs Tamplin said that their comments had been taken out of context, and that "they hadn't meant to point the finger at any individual." Mr Latter ended the press conference by expressing the hope that the matter was now at an end.'

'...pumpkin seeds,' Athena was saying. 'They're supposed to be terribly good for you. Shall we add them to the salad?' She glanced at Agnes. 'Are you OK? Not enough ice, maybe? What have you found to read in those old bits of paper?'

'Oh. Nothing.' Agnes folded up the press cutting and slipped it into her bag.

'I just hope Nic gets back soon – even with both of us eating all this stuff there's going to be loads left over. Mind you, if we're really going to get married, he's got to lose weight too – even if he doesn't wear a kilt, those dress suit cummerbund things are pretty tight. Oh, what a shame the gin bottle's empty, I'll just have to open the wine, I've chilled a lovely rosé. I thought pink fish, pink wine, it's got to work, hasn't it?'

CHAPTER TEN

'I met your nice doctor yesterday evening.' Sister Louisa had tucked herself into the corner of the community kitchen near the radiator, her fingers wrapped around a mug of coffee.

'It's freezing in there.' Agnes could hear Sister Helen, out in the hall.

'Something funny happened to the timer,' someone was saying. 'The heating's only just come on.'

'Dr Kitson?' Agnes sat down next to Louisa.

'Yes. His practice is involved with this women's health initiative.'

'Did you like him?'

'Oh, yes.' Louisa's face was bright above a thick polo neck and a scarf. 'He's so can-do, isn't he? So ready to take on the powers that be and fight for what he believes in.'

The kitchen window was frosted with the cold. In the garden, the dew dripped from stiff, chilled branches.

'...even in that one meeting he was so impassioned about the street women that the Trust was virtually shamed into promising some funding...'

Agnes pulled her attention back to what Louisa was saying. 'Dr Kitson did that?'

'Oh yes. You can see why he annoys people sometimes. He said he used to work in a more provincial practice, but he felt too constrained there. He said he was aware he'd begun to get on the wrong side of people, and that's when he realised he needed a wider canvas, as he put it.'

'Oh.'

Louisa tapped the radiator with her fingertips. 'It's beginning to warm up at last. Were you in chapel? It was so cold, our words turned to ice before they reached the Lord, I reckon.'

'Yes, I was.' Agnes had sat at the back, watching the dawn creep across the east window. She had knelt in prayer, wrapping her coat around her against the cold. She'd prayed for Abbie, and for Abbie's father in his grief; she'd prayed for Dermot, with the enemy lurking at his gates.

'We were all shivering,' Louisa said.

'Yes,' Agnes agreed. She'd prayed for Pauline Stipes, imprisoned in her home, with her husband and Dr Kitson united in knowing what was best for her.

'And he's such a committed GP as well,' Louisa was saying. 'Apart from all this outreach work, he's determined to do as much of his on-call work as he can.'

'It's funny you got on with him so well.' Agnes wondered if she'd spoken out of turn, if the cold had made her blunt.

'You mean, from my sheltered background?'

'No, I didn't mean—' Agnes began, but Louisa laughed.

'It's true I've worked almost exclusively with women. All I meant was, I was impressed at his commitment.'

Agnes watched her drink her coffee. And what would I say,

she thought. That I found a dusty old press cutting accusing him of nothing at all? That he's a bit bossy where the Stipes are concerned? That there is something I can't quite put my finger on, something that makes me feel things aren't quite right about him?

And perhaps I'm just tired, and perhaps Abbie's death and the attack on Dermot, perhaps all that has made us all feel nervous and twitchy, and perhaps Bretton Laing appearing in my life and making me question my relationship with my father is setting me off balance...

'Tea,' she said to Louisa. 'That's what I need.'

The clouds were lifting as she walked through the streets, and the early sun glinted from wet roofs. The hostel kitchen was empty. She made some toast, more tea, carried her tray into the office.

Gilroy looked up from a heap of papers. 'Hi,' he said. 'Did you hear the rumours? Kavin's been arrested. We think. No one's quite sure.'

She sat down at the other desk. 'Kavin? When?'

'Last night. There was various activity outside, then police cars, the works, I went out in time to see Murchie on the run. I cornered another of his homies who said that they'd arrested someone, maybe Kavin, maybe for dealing, no one was prepared to say. I've put in a call to Rob Coombes, waiting to hear back.'

'Well, that would be progress. Of sorts.'

'Mmm.' Gilroy went back to his paperwork.

'How's Dermot?'

Gilroy put down his pen and leant back in his chair. 'Not good. Too quiet. It might be the head injury affecting his mood. It might be the medication. He just seems very low. I mentioned it to Dr Kitson and he said he'd have a look at the prescription again.' He picked up his pen and turned it over in his fingers. 'We're lucky with him, you know. All the time I've been in the hostel, never had such a good doctor here.'

There was a clatter from the staircase, laughter from the girls. Agnes stood up. 'I might just go and help with breakfast,' she said.

'No worries.' Gilroy leafed through the pages in front of him. 'Can you make sure Lizzie eats? I'm not happy about her so-called diet.'

Rob Coombes put his head round the door as Agnes was ladling baked beans on to slices of toast.

'Oi, Paz, that's my special mug!' Sari shouted across the long bench table.

'I was here first—'

'And now they've sent the cops to make sure we behave,' Lizzie said, looking up at the door.

'Morning.' Rob addressed the room, sat down at one end of the table. 'I guess you've heard the news – Kavin was arrested last night for robbery.'

'Robbery?' Agnes distributed plates, then poured him a mug of tea from the large teapot and brought it over to him.

'Unfortunate commuter got jumped on near the tube – some brave lads gave chase. Even got mobile-phone pictures of him, so we might get to court with this one. Of course, he wasn't acting alone, but he's the only identifiable one.'

'Does Murchie know?'

'I expect so. I expect he's denying all knowledge of the lad too.' There was a hush in the kitchen, a rapt eating of beans.

He looked around the table. 'No Dermot?'

'He don't eat breakfast,' Sari said.

'He don't eat nothing,' Lizzie said.

'You're one to talk, ain't you?' Paz said.

'Oi – Paz.' Sari flapped her hand across his cheek. 'Leave her alone.'

Rob leant towards Agnes. 'Any chance of a quiet word with him?'

The noise levels in the kitchen rose behind them. Rob and Agnes went upstairs and knocked on Dermot's door.

Dermot opened the door for them, then dragged himself back to his bed and flopped back on the pillows.

'I'm sorry to be a nuisance.' Rob sat down next to the bed. 'I have two more questions. In your recollection of what happened to you, would you be able to say that Kavin was there? It would just help the case we have to make against him.'

Dermot frowned at him. 'He was there, yes. When Murchie…'

'He was one of the kids taking part, then?'

Dermot gave a faint nod. 'Yes.'

Rob leant forward. 'The second question is, and you may not have an answer for this – our intelligence is saying that the supply of drugs around here had a bit of a wobble recently. There seems to have been an influx of heroin on to the streets, quite a flood of it. And from what we can gather, it's very high-quality stuff; forty, fifty per cent. It's unusually high quality for street dealers like Murchie. So, given your connections with him, would you have any information about that?'

Dermot had closed his eyes, but now he opened them. 'Listen, mate—' His gaze was direct. 'The way I feel about Murchie at the moment, if he jacked a packet of chewing gum from the local shop I'd grass him up. If I had anything to tell you about the dealing of wares round here, I'd tell you, I swear I would. But...' he shook his head. 'Can't help you, I'm afraid.'

'Well.' Rob stood up. 'That's all I need to know for now. We'll be back in a day or two to take a statement properly.' He leant his hand on Agnes's shoulder. 'I'll see myself out.'

Dermot closed his eyes. He appeared to have aged in the last two days; the lines on his face seemed somehow deeper.

Agnes broke the silence. 'Dermot – do you have family we should talk to – if only to inform them?'

He shook his head, his eyes still shut. 'Told you. All dead.'

'There's someone in your files. A woman in Clapham.'

'I don't know her really. She's something to do with my dad's aunt. You asked for next of kin, I wrote her.'

'You mentioned a cousin.'

His eyes flashed open. 'Connor? You don't need to tell him nothing.'

'You mean he'll already know?'

Dermot closed his eyes again.

'Murchie said—' Agnes recalled the steely blue eyes, the street-corner conversation punctuated with Baby's growls.

'Murchie said what?' Dermot shifted on his pillows, wincing.

'He said that you'd tried to dump him and Connor in it.'

He looked at her. His eyes were still shadowed with the bruising. 'Anyone believe anything Murchie says, they're a fool.'

'So, you and Connor—?'

'Connor's been like a brother to me. He's all the real family I got. When me and Abbie started seeing each other, he was that pleased for me. And then he started seeing Abbie's mate Lindy, so it were really like family then. And now Lindy's moved in to where Abbie used to live, before she tried to come off the streets. She's trying to get Connor to live there too, but he ain't the kind to settle down.'

'How long have you known Connor?'

Dermot leant back on his pillows. 'He came over to England a few months ago. His mum died, and he said there weren't nothing left for him no more in Mayo, so he decided to try his luck here.'

'How did he know you were in London?'

Dermot smiled. 'His mum was a lovely woman. I hardly knew her, but everyone in the family spoke well of her. And then, that woman in Clapham, she knew I was here 'cos I wrote it on the form, didn't I? But that's it you see, they're all the other side of the family, she wouldn't welcome a visit from me.'

'Dermot—'

He looked up at her.

'From what I can gather, you were the last person to see Abbie alive. After Murchie had had a go at her, you walked her back here.'

His expression drooped. He nodded. 'I went to find her. I knew she was talking to Murch, I knew it would be bad news. And you're right, she were that upset, and I started walking her back here.'

'Did she talk of harming herself?'

'She wasn't saying much at all.'

'Did she give any clue about having access to heroin?'

He shook his head. 'But you see – I didn't come in here with her, did I? I've been reproaching myself ever since. I left her on the corner there, and went off. And I keep thinking, if only I'd come back with her, sat with her, been there for her. In the end, I let her down.' He passed his hand across his forehead.

'In the end, we all let her down.' Agnes stood up.

He stirred from his pillows. 'Can you pass me my phone? I need to talk to Connor. I might meet him later.'

'Dermot – you're not strong enough to walk around.'

'It's cool.' He checked his phone, then lay back on his pillows, breathing hard.

'Dermot—'

'What?'

'It's really important you stay safe.'

'And how do you reckon I do that, then? I nicked Murchie's girl.'

'But – did he really care about Abbie?'

Dermot flashed her a glance. 'Yeah.'

'There wasn't anything else – stuff you know about him, maybe? Things he thinks you might have told the police? All this drug-dealing business that Rob was talking about?'

'Nah. Nothing like that.' He spoke with emphasis, despite his weariness.

'Oh. OK.'

His face was pale.

'I should leave you in peace.' Agnes stood up.

'Is that doctor coming again?'

'Gilroy said he was.'

'These pills...' He pointed at the table next to him with a

trembling finger. 'They don't seem right.'

'No. Well, I'm sure he can fix that.' Agnes turned back to him, her hand on the door handle. He was immobile, his eyes closed, his breathing slow.

She sat in the office, flicking through Dermot's notes, hoping to find a note of what he'd been prescribed. I should have picked up the bottle in his room and read it, she thought.

Her mobile rang.

'Are you sitting down?' Brett sounded far away and more American than she remembered him.

'Is it bad news?'

'Not bad exactly. Those relics of your father's...'

Agnes leant one elbow on the desk. 'Go on.'

'Your father might have been telling the truth. That piece of Noah's Ark—'

'Go on.'

'It's giving a reading of about five thousand six hundred years. That's with a plus or minus of about seven hundred and fifty years either side.'

'But how could it have survived so long?'

'The guys here are saying it could have fetched up in an anoxic layer, say it ended up sunk in a lake bed under an area that then became desert. We've been running some other tests, looking for seeds, pollen, spores, trying to locate it geographically.'

Agnes sat back in her chair. 'But—'

'I know. And the even weirder thing, there's a couple of fossils he claims were found in the same strata as the fragment of Noah's Ark. We're doing some tests on the fossils too, to try and correlate them with the Ark. Obviously we can't date them, but your father believed that they were living things at the same time as the wood was buried, and often an anoxic layer can be like a time capsule.'

She listened to his silence for a while. Then she said, 'If that so-called fossil is six thousand years old, then it must be fake.'

'Fake fossils. The question is, whether your father knew they were fake. Or whether he was hoodwinked. Also...'

'Yes?'

'It leaves quite a few unanswered questions. Like, why would someone in four thousand BC think it was a good idea to make a fake fossil, when they didn't even think in terms of fossils?'

'Oh.' Agnes allowed the truth of this to settle.

'If it was a hundred years old – two hundred, even, we'd have some idea of what its provenance might be. But I've never come across an ammonite of that age, fake or otherwise. And neither have the rest of the team here. It's the same with the Ark, or whatever that chip of wood really is. If it was medieval, we'd all understand why. The relic industry was a thriving business in the twelve and thirteen hundreds. There were enough bits of the real cross to crucify about six million Christs—' He checked himself. 'I'm sorry – that's in poor taste.'

'I get the main point anyway.'

'The main point being that in four thousand BC, no one would have faked an ark any more than they'd have faked a fossil.'

'Where are you?'

'In Oxford. With the geologists.'

'What will you do next? With the fossils, I mean?'

'We're trying the pollen testing. Then there are the shells

too, the guys here are talking about amino acid racemisation, although my view is it's controversial.'

'And there's my one too.'

'Yours?'

'You know that book he was writing? There's one taped into it. It's a little pebble, like a shell.'

'Well, maybe I'll borrow that back from you.'

'I'm not sure it's mine.'

'All this stuff is yours. It was your father's and now it's yours. There's other stuff too, I'm having a box shipped over from the States.'

'But I'm not allowed to own anything.'

'Is that part of your vows?'

'Us high-class call girls have to live by the rules.'

'Oh, God, look, when I said that, it really did not come out how I meant it.'

'It's all right. Athena says it's a compliment when you get to our age.'

'Thank goodness for that.' She heard his smile. 'I must go,' he said. 'I'll be in touch when I'm back in London.'

Agnes put her phone back in her bag. She took out the shell-shaped stone from her father's notebook and held it in her hand.

Julius looked up from his desk. He closed his book, pushed his glasses up his nose. 'No sandwiches this time?'

'I assumed you'd had lunch.' Agnes stood in the doorway of his office. 'I've been cooking omelettes in the hostel.' She took off her coat and hung it on the coat stand, which swayed slightly and then righted itself. The crisp chill of the morning had given way to rain, and Agnes brushed raindrops from the shoulders of her coat.

'Oh.' Julius looked at his watch. 'So I have. Tea, then? Cakes? Heavens, I'm going to have to do the four o'clock Mass in a minute.'

She sat down opposite him and patted his hand. 'I've come empty-handed. Apart from a fossil which turns out to prove that the Genesis story is entirely, factually, true.' She leant into her bag and produced the shell stone and placed it on the table in front of him.'

He looked at it, then back at her. 'And how does it do that?'

'Bretton's clever colleagues have proved that my father owned a piece of the original Noah's Ark.'

Julius picked up the shell and turned it between his fingers.

'I'm exaggerating slightly,' she said. 'But the piece of wood is giving a reading which implies it's about as old as the Ark would have been, assuming you take the biblical account of all the generations to be true.'

'You mean – counting all the sons of Adam to Abraham, then to David, all that?'

She nodded. 'And the fossils that my father claimed were buried at the same time might turn out to be the same age too. It's something to with strata and time capsules.'

He looked up at her, the shell still poised in his fingertips. 'Really?'

'They're going to do more tests.'

He considered the shell, then passed it back to her. 'Of course, it can't, can it?'

'Can't what?'

'What I mean is, none of this could ever prove that the account in Genesis is factually true.'

She put the stone back into its little box. 'No. But it's funny, isn't it?' She looked up at him. 'You and I, sitting here, determined to argue against the literal truth of the Bible.'

He took off his glasses and began to polish them. 'I see nothing odd in that at all. I know there are some people who claim to belong to our faith, and who are prepared to argue the literal truth of the Bible – indeed, who set great store by its literality. But speaking personally...' He put his glasses back on and blinked at her through them. 'Speaking personally...I find my job is made a great deal easier if I allow it all to breathe. The Torah, the Psalms, the Gospels – they are the sort of poetry to which one's soul can respond. If I began to squash all those thousands of words written over thousands of years into a neat, flat, provable account, I'd be doing everyone a huge disservice.'

'And yet, my father, who never seemed to be a man of faith, turns out to need just such an account.'

'Case in point. This chunk of the Ark that your man there has had carbon dated – let's just say that it really is a real bit of the real Ark in which Noah set sail. I have to say that for me, it makes no difference to the truth of the story. Can you imagine what would happen to the greatest stories of the human race if we demanded evidence for every telling of them? We need the stories to tell us who we are, we need beginnings, middles and ends. The great wonder of the Bible is that those stories were written for the collective, for the tribe; they define an Us. And now of course, in our post-Freudian world, we have a different kind of story, the psychoanalytic narrative that tells us who we are, who I am, the account that gives meaning to the individual self.' He smiled at her. 'Oh dear, I don't half go on, given the chance.'

She traced the edge of his leather blotter with her fingertip.

'So, my father's relic of the Ark – it's part of his story, then?'

'I'd say it tells us more about your father than it does about Noah, yes. But then, here I am living in the post-Freudian world. If I encountered such a thing a hundred and fifty years ago, I'd probably reach a different conclusion.'

She sighed. 'We all have our stories, I suppose.' She stood up. 'I'd better go. There's trouble at the hostel still, I don't like being away from it for too long.'

'Talking of your workload – I might have made progress on finding a place for Mrs Stipes.' He stood up, and followed her to the door. 'It's a hospice, in Sydenham, I know the administrator a bit, he used to be a Brother with us, a long time ago. He was Father Gustave then. He gave it all up, declared it all to be nonsense, went back to college. He decided he could care for the dying just as well without believing they were going on somewhere afterwards. Anyway, I've explained the situation, and he's going to see what he can do. Of course, such things usually require a medical referral, which might be a bit tricky...'

'I'm seeing her tomorrow. I'll see how things stand with her husband.'

They ascended the small flight of spiral stairs into the church itself. It was deserted, unlit; the rhythm of the rain in the guttering echoed around the roof. Julius followed Agnes to the front door of the church, which he unlocked, peering out into the gloomy afternoon.

Agnes turned to him. 'It's still collective.' She waved her arm towards the altar, the stained glass behind it. 'All this. It still talks about an Us and not just an I.'

'Oh, yes. Of course. That's why it's so important.' He patted her arm. 'See you soon. Let me know about the fossils – I might have to change my account of things.' He turned to go back into church. 'That'll wake them up, won't it?'

She laughed, gathered her collar around her neck, and went out into the rain.

She arrived back at the hostel to be greeted in the kitchen with a chorus of sympathy. 'Oi, Agnes, don't them nuns let you have an umbrella?'

'You can lend Lizzie's hairdryer—'

'It's not fair, everyone borrows my hairdryer—'

'If you dressed like a nun at least your hair would be dry—'

'Oi, Paz, don't be gettin' rude to our Sister here.'

Agnes hung her coat by a radiator, found a clean towel to wrap around her hair, put on the kettle for tea. The kitchen windows were misted up, criss-crossed with fingered messages, various hearts and arrows, parts scribbled out, water trickling from the names. Agnes carried her tea into the office, which was empty. Gilroy had left her two notes. The first said that Dermot had gone out: 'He went about five p.m., I'm a bit worried, he seems half asleep from his medication. He's promised to be back for supper.' The other note said that the sheltered flats might have a place for Sari, if she could be trusted to live independently and not get back into trouble. He wanted to call a case conference with her social worker to discuss it.

Agnes picked up the phone, put it down again. The hostel had fallen silent, and in the quiet she sensed the absence of Abbie, still unburied. She took the stone shell from her bag and put it on the desk in front of her. She thought about her own father, searching for the true story in a handful of bits of old wood. She thought about Abbie's father lost in grief, lost in his 'if onlys'.

A chirping from her bag broke the silence.

'Am I interrupting?'

'Only maudlin thoughts. I'm glad you have.'

'Oh, dear, I have more maudlin thoughts to add to yours. Nic's come back from seeing his mother and he's in a bit of a state. She's not at all well, in terrible pain, it's quite clear she's been pretending to manage on her own for some time when she's quite beyond it. And Nic was very upset because one of her neighbours, a nice old chap, he's been nursing his wife for years, she had some dreadful debilitating thing, one of those things where you get worse and worse, and finally she asked him to help her end it all, and it didn't work and she's still alive and now the husband is being questioned by the police for aiding and abetting an attempt at suicide or something, when the poor chap was only trying to help because he loves his wife, and this is someone that Nic's known for years, used to take him fishing out in his boat when he was about nine, he's very upset...' She stopped for breath. 'I don't know,' she went on. 'We're only young, you and me, and yet here we are surrounded by death. By endings. I really don't want to think about it, you know. The idea that I could end up like Nic's mum, she can barely see, it turns out, and she's in terrible pain with her arthritis.'

'That's no reason to die, though, is it?'

'Well, no, obviously, sweetie. But there must come a point when we know it would be better to be dead. And there's no point you going all Catholic on me, because the truth is that when our pets are having terrible suffering we put them out of their misery, and yet this poor chap next door to Nic's mum, having to put up with his wife pleading to end her pain and now finding he's being treated as a criminal...'

The rain lashed the windows of the office. Agnes could see the silhouettes of branches swaying in the gusts of wind.

'...and that wasn't even why I phoned you up,' Athena was saying. 'The main reason I called was to say that Nic's come back keener than ever on us getting married. I'm sure it's about seeing his mum so frail. He's been going on about commitment, and I can see he's absolutely right, but it still frightens me really. It's the sense that it's all sewn up, then, isn't it? Like, you can say, "So that's how it all turned out, then." It's the ending of the story.'

Agnes looked at the fossil on the desk in front of her. 'It may be the end of one story. It's the beginning of a whole new story, though, isn't it?'

'The story of my marriage.' Athena laughed. 'How very dull. Oh, look, I'd better go, I said I'd cook for Nic, I'm not risking fish again, obviously, but I found a foolproof recipe for a chicken-and-noodle stir-fry, I've got all the ingredients. Well, it says it's foolproof but they don't know me, do they? And the magazine I cut it out of also said that this autumn's maxi-skirt look is flattering to everyone. If they're that wrong about skirts they're probably hopeless when it comes to noodles too.'

Athena rang off. Agnes put her phone back in her bag. She picked up the office phone and dialled Sari's social worker.

Much later, after a rowdy supper, a certain amount of worry about Dermot, who hadn't come back, an initial meeting with Sari about finding a flat – 'I don't care so long as my mum can't track me down, but if she gets wind of where I am then

I'm out of there'– and lots of washing-up, Agnes unpacked her bag in the spare bedroom of the hostel. She sat at the table and wondered where Dermot was. She wondered whether to call Rob Coombes. She wished she had a number for Dermot's cousin Connor, who seemed to be the only relative he had left in the world, apart from some kind of aunt in Clapham.

She picked up her Bible and turned the pages.

'In the six hundredth year of Noah's life, in the second month, the seventeenth day of the month, the same day were all the fountains of the great deep broken up, and the windows of heaven were opened. And the rain was upon the earth forty days and forty nights…'

She thought of Brett's account of her father's theory, about the rings in the tree trunk. And Adam's navel, what was the word? Omphalos.

If Adam had no navel…

She closed her Bible.

If Adam had no navel, if the tree trunks had no rings… There would be no story. Just a sudden, random, coming into being.

And my father?

She went over to the bed and lay down.

What happened in his life that caused him so desperately to need a story, to hang on to a story, to write pages and pages of explanation of why there is a story; why it all makes sense?

She heard footsteps pass in the street two floors below; she waited, hoping to hear Dermot's feet on the steps, his key in the door.

The footsteps passed by and faded away.

She turned out the light and went straight to sleep.

*   *   *

A thump. A cry. Darkness. She was wide awake. A dream, perhaps. She looked at her clock. It was three a.m.

Not a dream. She knew, as she sat bolt upright, as she got out of bed, pulled a dressing gown around her, hurried downstairs; she knew that something terrible had happened.

The house was stirring. She heard doors opening, footsteps above her. She was the first into the hall, she was the first with her hand on the handle, undoing the bolts, aware, as she tugged at the door, that there was something weighty against it; and then, the body falling at her feet as she opened the door, the half-open eye and swollen face, the sound of someone screaming in the silence of the night.

CHAPTER ELEVEN

There was rain against her face, her skin tight and cold in the sharp wind. Agnes walked the familiar streets, watching the cars, the passing feet, shoes tapping out their everyday beat in black and brown, flat and heels. She marvelled at the crowd, strolling along to work as if everything was perfectly all right; as if the natural order of things hadn't been blasted to bits by death, by violence, by her own voice screaming in the silence; by a young man's body slumped bleeding against a white front door.

It was nine in the morning, and she'd been awake for six hours. Six hours since she'd found Dermot, groaning, dying. Six hours since she'd dialled 999, since she'd run shouting through the hostel; six hours of crash teams, resuscitation units, the screech of sirens; then questions, notetaking, Rob Coombes arriving, grey-faced and dishevelled; the hostel residents, motionless, murmuring like shadows in the corners of rooms.

Rob had left about half an hour ago. Agnes had found herself out on the steps, slamming the front door behind her, not looking down, walking away. She was walking still. The rain clouds had passed. She could hear the distant tolling of church bells.

She thought of those straggling Friday morning churchgoers, seeking comfort in Julius's collective narrative. How wrong they are, she thought, when it turns out that the story ends with a life cut short, with a young man's blood watered by the rain on a dark stone step.

She turned back towards the hostel, back along the main road, the car windscreens glinting in the sudden flash of sunlight. But all she could see was Dermot, clay-faced and empty-eyed as the life drained from him. She walked back towards the hostel, found herself by the police tape across the pavement. At her feet there was an empty milk bottle; in the bottle was a roughly cut rose, its leaves torn, its yellow petals fading to brown.

A scruffy card lay beside the bottle. Agnes picked it up. She knew what it would say.

Until now, she had not shed a single tear; all night, a tightness in her throat had been her only clue that grief was near. Now, wrapping the stalk in tissue, holding the single ragged bloom between her finger and thumb, she found she was crying. She ducked through the tape, let herself into the hostel and fled into the office and, finding herself alone, she curled into one of the shabby armchairs, put her head in her hands and wept.

'Agnes?' The voice was soft, northern. She lifted her head from sleep.

'Oh.' She looked up. 'Rob.'

'They left you alone.' He was standing in the office

doorway, and now he approached her.

'How long have I been asleep?'

'Couple of hours.' He perched on the arm of her chair.

She rubbed her neck, rolled her shoulders, shook some feeling back into her left arm, which was numb. Muted voices floated towards her from the kitchen. Aysha, she thought. And Gilroy. And perhaps some of the residents, although it was difficult to tell. It was as if the air around them was compressed, dampened and dimmed like the misty afternoon outside the window.

She smoothed down her hair. 'What are we going to do?'

'Keep going,' he said. 'Try not to blame ourselves.'

'We knew...' She raised her eyes to him. '...We knew he was in danger. We could have done more...'

A sharp image pierced the fog, Dermot twisted in pain, his eyes rolling in his head. She felt the tears coming. Rob put his hand on her shoulder. 'You can't begin to think that way. Once you go down that path...'

'And Abbie.' Her thoughts were active now, chasing ahead. 'Both of them in danger—' she remembered Lindy's words, about Abbie being clean, questioning her sudden return to heroin.

'We've got Kavin,' Rob was saying. 'It's all a matter of making him talk. He'll lead us to the others.'

'No.' Agnes rubbed her forehead. 'The roses,' she said. 'The card, look—'

She reached for the card that she'd picked up from the doorstep. 'Look.' She pointed to the ill-formed pencil lettering:

'There are promises that no one can break.'

'It's the same,' she said. 'With the flowers, look. Like Abbie.

It's the same words. Same handwriting,' she said. 'Look.'

Rob took the card and stared at it, then put it down again. 'I'll get the boys to take it away,' he said. He stood up. 'But it's all pretty clear, isn't it? It's just making it stand up in court, that's where the job gets hard. Abbie was Murchie's girl, Abbie tried to leave Murchie, Abbie gets so bloody terrified by Murchie and his lads that she finds her own way out, either by mistake or on purpose. And that leaves Dermot, swearing revenge for the death of his girl, ready to talk to us. So Murchie has to get him out of the way too. It's a simple, tragic tale. Shakespeare would have made a work of art of it. It's just Shakespeare didn't have to face a court tearing it all to bits. Lucky old him.' He went to the door. 'There's a cup of tea in the kitchen when you're ready. Just don't expect a bundle of laughs in there.'

Aysha put a mug down in front of her. The fluorescent lighting in the kitchen seemed to beat down on the empty space. There was only Aysha, and Rob, taking up one corner of the table scribbling notes. Lizzie was upstairs. Paz was in the lounge, plugged into his iPod, Aysha said. Sari was out in the garden in the rain, weeping by the grave of Nige the rat. Agnes felt like joining her, but remembered her promise to Pauline Stipes.

'Aye, you're no use here.' Rob managed a smile from his place at the kitchen table. 'You might as well go and do your charitable work or whatever it is you do.'

'Mostly it seems to be causing trouble,' Agnes said, pulling on her raincoat.

'I wouldn't say that.' He waved his notes at her. 'I'll be needing to talk to you soon.'

'You'll know where to find me, then.' She headed for the hallway.

'I'd use the back door,' Rob called after her. 'Forensics all over your front steps. Not helped by the weather neither.'

The hydrangea bush drooped under rivulets of rain. The gravel path squelched underfoot. Agnes rang the Stipes's bell and waited. She heard movement, the inner door opening, and then at last the front door. Pauline stood there, leaning heavily on the doorframe. She took Agnes's hand and led her inside.

Agnes could feel the tiny bones of Pauline's fingers in her own. They reached the lounge. Pauline went to her usual chair and flopped down into it. She waved towards the kitchen. 'Help yourself. Nothing for me.' She seemed breathless and her eyes were glassy.

Agnes sat down on the chair next to hers. She leant towards her. 'Are you alone?'

Pauline nodded. 'Shopping,' she said. 'Won't be long I expect.'

'Julius thinks he can find a hospice place. It's not entirely suited to your situation, but he knows the chap in charge.'

Pauline managed a smile. 'You religious types are so well-connected.'

'Are you sure it's what you want?' Agnes fixed her gaze on Pauline.

Pauline's eyes met hers. She nodded. 'More than anything. I just want peace.' Her hands were clasped tightly together in her lap. Agnes saw that her nails were painted a frosted pink. She wondered whether it was intentional, to match her dressing gown. 'I'm so tired,' Pauline went on. 'He thinks it's a fight. A battle. For all I know I've got months left. If I go into remission again, I might have more than that. Whatever life I've got left, I don't want to spend it fighting. I want to spend it living.'

'If we can get you into this hospice—'

'It would be breathing space. I can think, then, about what I want to do.' Her hand reached out to Agnes's. 'I can't think here. He tells me what I'm thinking, I lose track of my own thoughts.'

Agnes looked at the fingers resting on her own. 'Does he love you?'

Pauline withdrew her hand and began to rub the dry skin on her arm. 'He would say so, yes. The problem is...' She paused, then went on, 'The problem is that he has no idea what love is.'

'Julius told me about his mother.'

She nodded. 'Yes. When I think about it, I feel sorry for him. He didn't have a childhood. It wasn't even nursing his mother, it was more acting as a kind of prison guard, trying to keep her from harming herself, and then she'd just get angry with him.'

'Did he tell you about it?'

Pauline shook her head. 'I pieced it together. He doesn't talk about it. He has a cousin, Shelly, over in Derry, she told me most of what I know.'

'What about his father?'

'A weak man, from what I can gather. He came up from the south-west to find work, but he had a big family down there, Truro way, he never really thrived away from them all. And he didn't live long after Rosie died.'

She fell silent. There was a tapping at the French windows, as the rain spilt out of the guttering and pattered down the glass.

'I'll talk to Julius,' Agnes said. 'I'll try and get things moving as speedily as possible.'

Pauline looked up at her. 'That would be wonderful. Just to have hope...' Her voice tailed off into more silence.

'I like your nail varnish,' Agnes said.

Pauline's face softened into a smile. 'I have to remind myself, sometimes...' She fell silent again.

After a moment, Agnes said, 'And is that person gone for good?'

'That's what I'd like to know. But I'll never find out by staying here.'

Agnes stood up. 'I'll let myself out.'

Pauline seemed exhausted. She reached up and took Agnes's hand. 'Thank you,' she said.

'I haven't done anything yet,' Agnes said.

'Yes you have.' Pauline's voice was hushed against the noise of the rain. 'I thought I was going mad. All these feelings, this rage... I thought maybe it was the illness affecting my mind.' Her hand dropped back to her lap. 'All the things you've said,' she went on. 'You've allowed me to see that I'm not mad at all.'

'You're not mad,' Agnes said. 'Just trapped. It's something I recognise, that's all.' She glanced at the mantelpiece clock. 'I should go. Before—'

'Before he gets back,' Pauline agreed.

At the doorway, Agnes turned back. 'I'll be in touch. I'll try to find a time when your husband is shopping.'

'Our best weapon is surprise.' She seemed rounder, pink-cheeked and cheerful. Agnes waved from the door and then left.

*   *   *

She got off the bus and rounded the corner towards the hostel. The sky seemed to dim, the air to grow heavy around her as she approached the front steps. She was greeted in the hostel hallway by Gilroy. 'Dr Kitson's here.' Gilroy too seemed to be finding it difficult to breathe. He led the way, moving slowly, towards the lounge, opened the door for her, then melted away towards the kitchen.

Dr Kitson looked up from his armchair. He appeared gaunt and dishevelled, but then, Agnes reflected, we probably all do.

'Rob Coombes phoned me,' he said. His hand went to his hair, rubbed his head. 'Terrible news.'

Agnes sank into the sofa. 'We all feel we should have stopped it somehow.'

'Guilt.' He nodded. 'Knowing the poor boy was in danger... There I was, arranging a nurse for him, when I should have been sorting out a bodyguard.'

'We weren't to know.'

'That's what Rob Coombes said too.' He curled forward in his chair, shook his head. 'I feel so useless now. I popped by to check on everyone else, really.'

'Two deaths,' Agnes agreed. 'It's really shaken everyone up.'

He glanced at her, his eyes blank.

'Abbie,' she said.

'Ah.' He frowned, nodded. 'Yes. Of course. Different sort of thing, though.'

Agnes watched him as he leant back in his chair, ran his fingers through his short hair. She thought about Athena's press cutting. What would he say if I mentioned it, she thought. And what would I say? I gather you left your last job under curious circumstances...

He looked across at her. 'Seen any more of the Stipes?'

'No,' she said. Her voice was loud with emphasis, and she wished she were a better liar.

He gave a heavy sigh. 'Vale of tears,' he said. 'This thing called Life.' He stood up. 'And there I was, all upbeat and raring to go, before the police phoned me.'

'Upbeat about what?' She looked up at him.

'Your fellow Sister and her women's health centre. So much good we can do between us. We had a second meeting this morning. I mean, I know those women from the Area Health Authority outreach team mean well, but Louisa knocks spots off them when it comes to having a true grasp of the issues affecting street workers – and her a nun as well.' He gave a dry bark of laughter. 'She's a credit to your Order.' He glanced at his watch. 'I ought to be going. I've got evening surgery in half an hour, and I said I'd have a word with Gilroy in the kitchen before I go.'

'I've got to go too,' Agnes said. In her mind she saw candles, smelt incense. 'Evening prayers,' she said.

'Oh. Right.' At the door he raised his arm in a wave. 'Say hello to Louisa for me.' She heard him make his way down the corridor to the kitchen.

The bus was crowded with rush hour commuters. Agnes stood near the doors, watching the twilight streets pass by, the lights in the shop windows, the cyclists weaving to and fro, the undulation of umbrellas.

God's creation. Not a bustling collection of random molecules at all, but a plan, an intention, every stage worked out; a beginning, a middle and an end.

She thought of Dr Kitson's easy familiarity with Louisa. I lied, she thought. When Dr Kitson asked me about Pauline, I lied.

* * *

The convent chapel was almost full. Agnes took her place in the pews, feeling herself warmed by the glow of the altar candles. Louisa was near the front, ready to do the readings.

They obviously get on, Agnes thought. 'Say hello to Louisa,' Dr Kitson had said. And here I am, allowing a news story found quite by chance to taint my view of him.

The chords of the opening prayer were played, the nuns sang the first psalm. Agnes felt her breathing settle with the rhythm. Then Louisa stood up to read.

'"And the Lord said to Cain, 'Where is your brother Abel?' And Cain replied, 'Am I my brother's keeper?' And the Lord said, 'What have you done? The voice of your brother's blood cries to me from the ground. And now you are cursed by the earth, who has received the blood of your brother from your own hand.' This is the word of the Lord."' Louisa finished, and sat down again.

The candles had lost their warmth. In Agnes's mind there was only the splash of crimson against the hostel door.

CHAPTER TWELVE

Louisa found Agnes in the convent lounge. She was sitting alone, in darkness, the curtains still open, the street lighting outside casting long shadows across the room.

'I heard about that boy in your hostel.' Louisa sat down next to Agnes on the sofa.

Agnes dabbed at her cheeks with her fingertips. Louisa passed her a clean tissue. She stood up and drew the curtains, then came to sit down again. After a while Agnes turned to her. 'They trust us to keep them safe. Before they come to us, they're never safe, they know what danger is, they know it all too well. And then one day, they find the courage to turn to us instead. And then this happens...' her voice cracked. She held the tissue to her lips.

Louisa rested her hand on Agnes's arm.

'It was bad enough with Abbie,' Agnes said. 'I pushed her back into danger. And now Dermot – we knew he was in danger, and we didn't do enough to protect him.'

'Vaughan was very upset,' Louisa said. 'Dr Kitson,' she added.

'Ah. Yes.' Agnes leant back into the sofa.

'He said they'd arrested someone.'

'Well, sort of,' Agnes said.

'He said it was something to do with revenge.'

Agnes turned to her. 'Dr Kitson said that?'

Louisa nodded. 'Revenge over a girl.'

Agnes sighed. 'He's probably right. That's what the police think. That's what we all think.' She turned back to Louisa. 'That's what's so awful. If it was so simple, why couldn't we prevent it?'

Louisa was silent. They sat, side by side, gazing out at the darkened window. After a while Louisa patted her arm, stood up, and left.

In the darkness, Agnes's phone was ringing, muffled by the sofa cushions. She rummaged for it.

'Hi, it's me.' Brett's voice sounded bright and sunny.

'Oh.'

'You OK?'

'No,' Agnes said. 'Not really.'

'I'm back. I have news. News from biblical time. Perhaps you don't want to hear it.'

'I'd rather be in biblical time than real time at the moment.'

'Tomorrow? Lunch?'

Agnes reached across and switched on the table lamp. The room softened in the glow. 'That would be lovely.'

'Come to the hotel, we'll go on from there. One o'clock OK for you? I'll tell you all then. Your father was an extraordinary man.'

He'd gone. She had a flash of memory, a sunlit leather chair, studded with heavy nails, turning to and fro; bare feet on warm oak; the rhythm of cicadas. She felt the threat of more tears. She got to her feet, grabbed her coat and bag and left the convent.

The anglepoise lamp enclosed her in its circle, in the pool of light on the wood of her desk. Beyond was only shadow. Agnes turned another page of her father's book.

'For does not the Lord say to Job as follows: "Where wast thou when I laid the foundations of the earth? Who shut up the sea with doors, when it brake forth, as if it had issued out of the womb? Hast thou entered into the springs of the sea? Or hast thou walked in the search of the depth?" Thus we hear in the very words of the Lord himself, as Burnet's thesis verified, that the Flood was caused by the earth sinking into the subterranean waters, and not by any deluge of rain. Who can argue, against such evidence?'

The next page returned to more mathematical reckonings of the passage of time; Agnes yawned and closed the book. She stood up and went to her tiny kitchen and washed up the plate and glass left from supper.

She thought about the piece of wood that Brett had carried so faithfully to Oxford. She remembered what Julius had said, that it told more about her father than about the Great Flood.

Evidence, she thought. The white-coated experts who had been at the hostel all day with their painstaking work, gathering fragments that would together make up the whole picture, tell the whole story of Dermot's death.

And then, there were her father's shells and stones and bits of wood; evidence of a different kind of story. She wondered at her father, approaching the end of his life, making the choice that, rather than reflect on his own, individual story, he would instead retrace the steps of the whole of humankind.

An extraordinary man.

She bent to put a saucepan away, jumped at the ring of her phone.

'There you are, sweetie. Are you all right? Just had this feeling, don't you know...?'

'No,' Agnes said. She walked back into the main room and sat on her bed. 'I'm not all right.'

'Thought so. What is it this time? Gorgeous Americans being troublesome?'

'I wish that was all.' Agnes caught her breath, then said, 'Dermot died. One of our residents.'

'When you say died...'

'Murdered. Stabbed on the hostel doorstep.'

'Oh no. How awful. And after that girl last week...When did it happen?'

'Thursday night. Not long after we spoke, that evening when you were talking about euthanasia and marriage.'

'Oh. Yes.'

'He managed to annoy some very dangerous people, Dermot did.' Agnes watched a shadow on her ceiling, a moth flitting across her desk lamp. There was silence from Athena. 'Are you still there?' Agnes said.

'I was just thinking about how fragile it's all become. Life, I mean, sweetie.'

'More than usual?'

'I don't know. Car bombings. Random stabbings. Stella, our new receptionist at the gallery, she was telling us this morning about a friend of hers who has a shop in Camden Town, and one day last week this young woman walked in, and it turned out she'd just escaped from slavery. She'd been kept in a house up the road for years, since she was a child. She thought she was Nigerian but she wasn't sure. She's stateless. No birth certificate. No passport. Apparently it's happening all over London.'

Agnes listened. The moth circled closer to the bulb, then away; its shadow contracted, expanded.

A thought at the edges of her mind.

'Poor you,' Athena said. 'Have you had police everywhere?'

'It's all about evidence.' The moth landed on Agnes's hand, sat there quite still, as if pinned down. 'Tiny fragments,' she said, 'pieced together.' She was still searching for the thought. 'Stories.' Like that bit of a press cutting, she was about to say, but Athena interrupted.

'You sound like Nic. Getting married to me is about merging our two pasts or something. I said to him, how does that square with his ideas of rebirthing, and he said, all belief systems are welcome in his universe. How's the gorgeous American?'

'Oh, him. He has news on the carbon dating. For all I know my father really did prove that the universe is only six thousand years old and we're all descended from Noah.'

'I bet there's more to him than that. I bet there's all sorts of dark secrets he knows about your father. It's just a question of whether you want to know or not.'

'I'd quite like to know the age of the Earth.'

'That bit's OK. It's not as if knowing that is going to change anything important. It's just the rest. When are you seeing him?'

'We're having lunch tomorrow.'

'You see? You sound much brighter than when you answered the phone. At least there's always a gorgeous

American to cheer you up. Oh, and tell him we'd rather be spies than call girls if it's all right with him.'

Agnes smiled. The moth flew from her hand and disappeared above the curtain rail.

'We must see each other soon,' Athena said. 'Lunch or shopping or both. But if I start cooing over bridal wear, give me a good slap. I know, Sunday? That God of yours can give you an hour off for brunch, he gets the rest of the day, doesn't he?'

'Sunday brunch would be lovely.'

'See you then. We'll talk before. Night night.'

Agnes lay down on her bed. She scanned the ceiling, looking for the moth.

And what would I have said? That something odd happened when I was with Dr Kitson? That when I mentioned Abbie it was as if he'd never heard of her?

That, for a moment, I was frightened of him.

Her sleep, when it came, was fretful and full of dreams about Noah's Ark and pairs of giant moths.

Brett was already in the hotel foyer. The lilies had been replaced by a towering tropical arrangement, all flame-red and spiky purple. It went with the rain hammering on the atrium roof, Agnes thought, as she emerged through the revolving door, shaking large drops from her umbrella.

'This weather.' He pulled a face. 'London living up to its reputation.'

'We had a drought this summer,' she said.

'And you Londoners living up to your reputation for stoicism too. Where would you like to eat? I booked a table at a nice fish place by the river, but I can always cancel and find something else.'

'Your nice fish place sounds lovely.'

Back through the revolving door into the rain, umbrellas again, hers pink with large white dots, his a business-like black.

'Not very convent,' he said, indicating her umbrella.

'No,' she agreed. 'Someone left it behind, I think. If it was up to me I'd have a plain colour.'

'Chanel, probably.'

She smiled at him. 'That would be nice. Although not very convent either.'

Rain trickled down between them, and he frowned at the sky. 'If this carries on we'll need an Ark of our own, not just a scrap from your dad.'

The restaurant was a light, airy space, the windows silvery with the wet weather. The tables were neat hexagons of white linen, a bowl of white roses at the centre of each.

They clinked glasses of Pouilly Fumé.

'Go on, then,' she said.

'No,' he said. 'You first. Why are you so low? Why is Noah's time preferable to now?'

She sighed, put down her glass. 'Because my hostel is surrounded by danger.'

'Even more?'

'That boy – the one you called the ambulance for – he's dead. Stabbed.'

For a while he stared straight ahead of him. Then he took a sip of wine, put his glass down. 'Poor you,' he said. 'Poor everybody.' He looked up at her. 'And that's why you want to live in a different time to now?'

'Yes,' she said. 'Because all the consolation prizes that life offers us don't seem to outweigh the deadweight of just having to carry on in the face of destruction and terrorism and people meaning us harm—' She broke off; a flash of an image of Dr Kitson sitting in his armchair at the hostel. 'And because I'm not really thinking straight about it all,' she added.

'And,' he went on, 'and because I've turned up here with a new way of thinking about your past and maybe...' He hesitated, then said, 'Maybe it's unwelcome.'

She reached across and took an olive. 'Not unwelcome,' she said, after a while. 'But difficult, yes. Athena was saying that there'll be stuff about my dad that I don't want to know.'

'When am I going to meet this Athena?' he said.

'Oh, you're bound to meet her. She'll make sure of that.'

He laughed. A waiter came, so neatly French, his English so heavily accented, that Agnes almost replied to him in French, but couldn't remember the words for skate wings with capers.

'Isn't that awful?' she said, when he'd taken their order and gone. 'I'm so exiled, I've even lost my language.'

'No,' he said. 'You're like Ralph. He said he was the citizen of everywhere. England, France, the States, he just fitted in.'

She shook her head. 'Not me. I live on the edges.'

'Perhaps that suits you.'

She looked at him. 'Yes,' she said. 'It does.'

He met her eyes, then said, 'Why didn't you keep in contact with your father?'

She broke a breadstick. It lay on her plate in two neat halves. 'I think I was angry with him.'

'Because he left your mother?'

'No. Not because of that. The marriage was very bad for both of them.'

'Why, then?'

'Because, when I was married to a violent man and in fear of my life, he did nothing to rescue me.'

Brett was reaching for a piece of bread, but stopped, mid-reach. He stared at her. 'When?' he said at last.

'A long time ago. Before I became a nun.'

'But the Ralph I knew...' He shook his head. 'He wouldn't have let his daughter suffer like that, surely?'

She shrugged. 'You asked me why I was angry. That's the only explanation I can come up with.'

'And did you consider other explanations?'

She was about to answer, but their first course arrived, and she occupied herself with crab salad instead.

He looked up from his calamari. 'You were saying?'

She put down her fork and met his gaze. 'We Christians have a tradition of forgiveness. I have no desire to dwell on the shortcomings of my parents.'

'I don't believe you,' he said. 'Forgiveness can't be that easy.'

'You don't have to believe me.' She arranged a cherry tomato on the side of her plate. She looked up and smiled at him. 'How's your dancer?'

'Georgie? She's OK. I saw her last night.'

'Where?'

'Here. She's rehearsing a show.'

'And?'

He pushed his fork around his plate. 'She's OK,' he repeated.

Agnes took a large mouthful of crab. She stared at the tablecloth, aware of his silence. It was as if the smooth white linen was tangling itself around them, tightening its grip.

Fighting her way out, she said, 'So, go on. What have you found out about my father's relics?'

He too seemed to stretch, breathe again. 'Firstly, the seed and spore tests seem to indicate that the piece of Ark was indeed buried somewhere quite specifically in the Middle East, probably Palestine. And, even weirder – we've run similar tests on the fossils that your father claimed were buried with it, and, I know it sounds strange, but our tests seem to confirm what he believed.'

She stared at him.

'I mean, obviously, there might be other explanations...'

'But—' she began.

'I know.' He nodded at her across the table. 'It is extraordinary. 'Those sort of ammonites should be several millions of years old.'

'Why should only my father have access to this?'

'We have to conclude that it isn't just your father. That this stuff, real or fake, is kicking around. I've looked up various internet sites and it's quite a common subject for discussion, particularly amongst the evangelicals.'

'But – how can fossils be so new?'

He looked at her and shrugged. 'You're the one who believes in creation – you tell me.'

'I think I'd rather believe in your tests.'

He waited while the waiter cleared their plates, then said, 'It's a very small Venn diagram. The people who believe this stuff and the people who have access to any kind of kit – it's pretty mutually exclusive.'

'And presumably, for most of them it's enough just to believe. They don't need proof.'

He looked at her. 'I guess that's true.' There was another

silence, then he said, 'Your father was a very clever man. Brilliant, in a way.'

'In a misguided way?'

He glanced at her. 'As a scientist, I'm bound to say, yes.'

'And I would agree with you,' she said.

'As a nun?' He smiled at her.

'Yes. As a nun.' She smiled back.

Their main courses arrived, and for a while the conversation turned to the ideal way of oven-roasting cod, and whether parsley was always the best herb for a salsa verde.

Agnes covered her potatoes with butter, then caught Brett's expression. 'I like butter,' she said. 'Just because you Americans have never lost your Puritan streak—'

'It's so like your father,' he said. 'That amount of butter...' He shook his head.

'One of the few things I've inherited, I suppose.'

'No – there are lots of things...' He seemed to stop himself.

'Not our beliefs. We couldn't be more different by the sound of it.' She ground black pepper over her potatoes.

He frowned in thought, then said, 'There was always something about your father – a restlessness, a searching...it was as if he'd left something behind, somewhere, a long time ago, as if he was constantly trying to turn back to look for it. When he met Monica, it was a resolution, in a way. Her beliefs, weird as they were, allowed him to settle. They gave him a safe place – a place of certainty, I suppose you'd say.'

'Monica,' Agnes said. 'Does she still live...where did you say?'

'Oh, somewhere here. In England. The coast, somewhere, down south.'

She glanced at him, hearing his evasiveness. 'Didn't you say Dorset? Last time we spoke about it?'

'Did I? It's years since I've seen her,' he said.

It was like the wash of the tide, flattening the sand, dragging away with it all intimacy.

We could go and visit her. Agnes heard the words circle in her mind. Brett and me, together. I could close the gap between the father that I knew and the Ralph that he knew. I'd like to meet her. She was about to say it out loud – 'I'd like to—'

He cut in. 'How's your skate?'

'Lovely. Thank you.'

They sipped their wine in silence, finished their main courses, decided not to bother with coffee. He told her about Georgie's dance show – 'It's classical ballet, but abstract, very formal.' He told her about the company, 'ex-Royal Ballet, some of them,' and she listened, wondering what had happened; wondering why he had closed down the conversation when it began to edge towards a meeting with Monica.

The rain had passed. They left the restaurant. Agnes looked at the mist across the Thames, the watery pink of the sunset. He walked at a slight distance from her, waited for her to catch up.

'I'd call you a cab, but—'

She shook her head. 'I'd rather not.'

He looked down at her. She was aware of his hesitation, his uncertainty. They both knew that something had happened, some wedge driven between them; neither of them knew what to say.

'It was a lovely lunch,' Agnes said. 'Thank you.'

He stood hunched, his hands in his pockets. 'You're more than welcome.'

'Well…' She reached out a hand to him.

'Well…' His hand brushed hers. He turned to go. 'See you around.'

'Let me know about the fossils,' she said.

He glanced back towards her. 'And will it make any difference to you? In all honesty, are your father's ramblings going to change anything for you?'

He was hostile now. She reached out her hand, took a step towards him. 'But – we both know, surely—'

'You mean,' he said, 'why did I take them on?'

'Yes,' she said. 'Unless it really was just to chase your dancer to London?' Her hand dropped to her side.

He shook his head. 'No, not that.'

'A huge distraction, then? A way of delaying committing to your own life in the States?'

He shot her a glance. 'No.' He pulled a cotton handkerchief from his pocket, stared at it, pushed it back again. 'I suppose I was trying to do a favour for an old friend. Your father thought that by bringing his ideas over here, something would come of it. Some kind of redemption. But…' He shrugged. 'He was wrong.' He pulled his collar up around his neck. 'If I seem to have changed my mind, it's just that I've come to the end of being able to help him.'

She tried to close the gap between them. 'Perhaps it was enough to have tried.'

He looked down at her. He nodded. 'Yes,' he said. 'Perhaps.' He held her gaze for a moment, and she thought he was about to speak, but he turned away.

She watched him go, watched him stride along the embankment, the wet pavements deepening to crimson in the setting sun.

Her bus dropped her at the crossroads. She walked through the twilight, passing the corner that led to Julius's church. A group of young men loitered, baggy-trousered, kicking at the wall. Eyes flicked towards her, then away. One boy's gaze stayed fixed on her.

She saw his blue eyes and sculpted hair. 'Murchie,' she said. The dog at his feet growled as she approached.

A moment's flinch, hands in his pockets, then he drew himself up to face her. 'What?'

His friends watched now, sensing drama.

'I gather Kavin was arrested,' she said.

Glances cracked between the youths.

'So?' Murchie said. 'They can't do nothing to him, he's only fifteen.'

'I think they're hoping to find out what happened to Dermot,' Agnes said.

One of the other boys laughed. 'They know what happened to Dermot, don't they? Everyone knows.'

Murchie's face hardened. His fist collided with the boy's shoulder as he shushed him, loudly. The dog jumped around, barking.

'Your friend's right,' Agnes said.

He turned to face her.

'We all know what happened to Dermot,' she said.

'Yeah?' His gaze was locked to hers.

'Yeah,' his friend said. 'Like we all know what happened to Abbie.'

'Oi, Zip.' Murchie turned to him, and the others froze, waiting. 'I warned you, didn't I?'

'What – about not saying nothing about Abbie?' Zip was wearing a trilby, which he pushed towards the back of his head, revealing a long fringe of dark brown curls.

'If it was up to me she'd still be alive.' Murchie turned back towards Agnes. 'Your hostel,' he said. 'Her room – is someone else there now?'

The softness of his voice took her by surprise. Agnes stared up at him. She hesitated. 'Well,' she said. 'Not quite yet. But there will be...'

'Don't like to think of someone else taking her place.' His eyes shone in the street light.

The boys had begun to melt away. Murchie was alone, standing there on the street corner. He hopped from foot to foot, the dog's lead tight round his wrist, his eyes on hers, waiting.

'Murchie.'

'Yeah?' His gaze was locked with hers.

'The police are after you.'

'So?' With his free hand he reached into his pocket and took out his phone and offered it to her. 'Call them, then. Say I'm here. They can come and get me, innit?'

She stared at the large, shiny phone in his hand.

'Go on,' he prompted. 'It's 999.'

She breathed out. 'Murchie—'

'Cos they're going to get me in the end, the feds. My life is all about staying out as long as I can. Keeping one step ahead of them, innit, tho?'

'But – surely—'

He smiled at her, his head on one side. 'Surely what? Surely

I could mend my ways? Go straight? After the life I've lived, Sister?' He shook his head. 'I've done my time, see? I've served my apprenticeship and now I'm reaping the rewards. There ain't nowhere else for me to go but to carry on until the music stops.'

She couldn't think of anything to say.

His friends had gathered on the next street corner, talking to a boy who was circling on a bicycle.

Murchie offered the phone to Agnes. 'No? You ain't going to call the feds, then?' She shook her head, and he smiled. 'Another time, maybe?' He put his phone back in his pocket, turned towards his friends.

'Murchie – do you know anything about Dermot's rat?'

He flashed her a glance, shook his head.

'He loved that rat,' Agnes said. 'Like you love your dog here.'

He glanced down at the dog. 'No one could love anyone like I love my Baby.'

'So if someone crept up one night and poisoned her—'

'I'd kill them first.' His fists were clenched at his sides.

'It would be a horrible death, too, wouldn't it, I imagine…' Agnes held his gaze. 'An animal doesn't die quickly with an injection like that, does it? You'd have to watch it twitching.' She stared into his eyes. 'You love animals,' she said.

His hand grabbed her wrist. His gaze was intense. 'It weren't my idea, OK? It was supposed to be a warning. It was a crap idea.'

He blinked. He scuffed his shoes on the pavement.

'If someone did that to Baby…'

He crouched down to the dog and put his arms around his neck. 'They'd be dead,' he murmured.

'Why did you need to give Dermot a warning?'

Murchie straightened up. The dog nuzzled his leg. He held her gaze, smoothing his hair across his head. 'It's like I said. It's too late for me. And it was too late for him.'

'Too late for what?'

His friends were calling him, waving a phone at him. Baby jumped to his feet and barked back at them.

He turned to Agnes. 'If you've been a soldier, you can't just go back to Civvy Street again. Can you?'

He hunched his jacket over his shoulders, and began to walk away. His pace quickened towards the crossroads. 'See you around,' he called back over his shoulder.

She watched him join the others, watched as they all sauntered away, laughing.

CHAPTER THIRTEEN

'The wicked wear their pride like a necklace, they wrap their violence about them like a cloak; they set their mouths against the heavens, and their evil speech runs through the world…'

The windows of St. Simeon's were indigo in the evening light. The candles flickered in the heavy shadows.

She looked around the church, at the shrouded figures hunched over their prayer books. She thought about Murchie. A warning, she thought. A warning to Dermot in the shape of his dead rat.

'O, how suddenly do the wicked come to destruction; come to an end and perish from terror…'

It was too late for Dermot. Too late for him to turn his back on his former life.

Afterwards she lingered in the church, while Julius straightened chairs and gathered up stray prayer books.

'I heard the news from the hostel.' He blew out a candle. Soft wisps of smoke rose towards the roof. 'All rather bleak, isn't it?'

'Terrible.' She perched at the edge of the choir stalls.

Julius extinguished the last of the candles. The rows of pews lengthened into the shadows. She yawned.

'Long day?' He glanced across at her.

'A rather nice lunch with Bretton Laing,' she said.

'Ah. No peace for the wicked.'

'Thanks.' She stood up, waited for him as he locked the front door, followed him through the church to the side entrance. 'They think the fossils are the same age as the Ark. If you go by biblical time.'

'Good heavens.' He stood and faced her in the darkness. 'So Thomas Burnet was right. Him and all the others.'

'Up to a point. I'm not sure my father managed to prove that the Flood was caused by subterranean oceans.'

They stepped on to the gravel path, and he locked the door behind them. Their feet crunched the stones underfoot as they walked towards the lighted street.

Julius took her arm. 'What's your American going to do with this new theory, then?'

'I'm not sure.' Agnes was about to say more, to pour out to him her misgivings about Brett – 'He seemed to be withholding something, and now everything seems wrong, and I'm worried about Dr Kitson and I don't know why' – but just then her phone rang.

'Is that Sister Agnes?' The voice was familiar, tetchy and male.

'Yes,' she said. Of course, she thought. It's—

'This is Jeremy Stipes. I'm saying this once and once only. Keep away from my wife. Do you hear?'

'Oh, hello Mr Stipes.' Agnes spoke loudly. 'And why do you wish us to keep away from your wife?'

'I don't know what you've been saying to her, but she's talking of leaving. She's a very sick woman, Sister, and it seems to me you've been criminally irresponsible to give her such ideas.'

'I'm sorry to hear you feel this way, Mr Stipes.' Agnes raised her eyebrows at Julius. 'Perhaps I could speak to your wife, and then I might understand—'

'You certainly cannot speak to my wife. You're to keep away from her from now on. If I see you near my premises, I will have you arrested for trespass.'

'But if she needs care—'

'I will care for her. I won't have anyone get in the way. And when I can no longer care for her, when her life is no longer worth living, then I will help her die, if that's what she wants. I don't suppose we'll meet again, you and I. Goodbye.'

The line went dead. Agnes put her phone back in her bag.

'Trouble?' Julius was looking at her.

'Jeremy Stipes says he'll call the police if he sees me near his house again. His wife wants to leave and it's all my fault. "She's a very sick woman", he said.'

'Good heavens. And there I was thinking we were helping by finding her a hospice place.'

'And—' Agnes ran her fingers through her hair. 'He said that he'd help her to die if that's what she wants.'

They began to walk; Julius took Agnes's arm again. 'That sounds rather serious,' he said. 'And not in accordance with the teachings of our Church either.'

'Pauline said he was never a proper believer. She said it was always conditional with him.'

'Ah.' Julius nodded. 'Yes. I can see that.'

They reached the main street. The wet tarmac was ribboned

with silver and red in the lights from passing cars.

Julius turned to her. 'I'll say goodnight, then.'

She leant up and kissed his cheek.

He gazed down at her. 'Some times more than others, it feels as if we were only put here to suffer.'

'And is this one of those times?'

His hand went to the cross at his neck. 'Those two young people at your hostel should still be alive,' he said. 'And as for poor Mrs Stipes...' He scratched his chin. 'It's difficult, sometimes, to see redemption in any of it.'

'Dear Julius,' Agnes said.

He squeezed her elbow, turned to go.

'We should go and see her,' Agnes said. 'Pauline Stipes.'

He turned back. 'Yes,' he said. 'Even if we risk being arrested for trespass.' He glanced towards the sky. 'How would tomorrow be? I'm free after midday Mass.'

She smiled up at him. 'Tomorrow will be fine.'

'Ugh, how creepy. What a creepy thing to say. He'd kill his own wife? How awful.' Sunshine poured in through the café windows; crowds passed by outside, smiling in bright clothes. 'Mind you,' Athena was saying, 'when I think about Nic's mum, perhaps some of these euthanasia people are right. Nic said she was crying in pain when he saw her, and the doctors really can't do much. But there's a big gap between that and actually bumping someone off, isn't there?'

Agnes nodded, stirring her cappuccino.

'Anyway, kitten, at least you'll have Julius with you when you go and tackle this man. You'll be quite safe.'

Agnes looked up at her and smiled.

'How was the gorgeous American? Rhett, isn't it?'

'Brett. As you know very well.'

'Well, how was he? See, now you're pulling one of your faces. I knew he was trouble as soon as you mentioned him.'

Agnes shook her head. 'It's not that he's trouble. It's just that he's digging up all these memories, all these different stories about my father, my past...' She looked up at Athena. 'I don't want that stuff reawakened. I don't want to have to reassess my version of events.'

Athena spread butter on her croissant. 'You mean, you don't want to end up feeling sorry for your parents after all.' She cut the croissant in two and put half on Agnes's plate.

Agnes picked up the croissant and took a bite. 'It might be too late for that. How are the marriage plans?'

'Oh, don't. Nic hasn't stopped talking about it. As far as I can see, it's all about his mum and dad, how happy they were, how important it is to mark your commitment, "that's what that generation got so right and we've all got so wrong..."'

'I don't think my parents got it right.'

'No. And I'm sure Nic's glamorising how it was for his two, too.'

Agnes stirred the foam around in her cup. 'Anyway, I'm not likely to find out any more. Brett's decided he's come to the end of the road with helping my father's legacy. His goodbyes yesterday were all rather final.'

'You mean, it's over, you and him?' Athena's eyes were wide.

Agnes smiled at her. 'Whatever "it" is, then yes. Maybe.'

'Has he got moon in Pisces? I bet he has. That would explain all this ambivalence.' She sighed. 'Sometimes it does seem to make life so much more difficult.'

'What does?'

'Having men in it. It would be so restful just not to bother with them, don't you think? It's like all this business with Nic and getting married – even if Nic's mum and dad were a match made in Heaven, what's that got to do with me and Nic anyway? I said that to him last night and he went into a sulk – sometimes he can be so Virgoan – what's the matter?'

'Look—' Agnes was staring out of the window. 'That boy there, that young man – Murchie.'

'The one with the fancy jacket? The one who's just disappeared round the corner?'

'Everyone thinks he killed Dermot. He says no one can prove anything.'

'Perhaps you should call the police.'

'That's what he said last time I bumped into him. He offered me his phone.'

'Doesn't sound like the behaviour of a guilty man.' Athena drained her cup of coffee. 'Hadn't you better be going off to Julius? And I said I'd meet Nic after this, we're going to the garden centre, he wants to plant things in our window boxes, vegetables, can you believe it?'

'What things?'

'Oh, I don't know. Carrots, maybe? Beans? All I know was that he said he needed to buy stuff, compost, a trowel, that kind of thing. I mean, us, visiting a garden centre? They'll give us a marriage certificate just for that I reckon.'

The sun had gone in and the clouds threatened rain. The hydrangea bush in the Stipes's front garden had its usual hangdog weariness. Julius stood on the front path next to Agnes. He turned to her.

'Any idea what we do now?'

'I thought you were the one with the ideas.'

'Well—' He took a step forward. 'I suppose we ring the bell and see what happens.'

The bell sounded loud in the chill air. They heard footsteps, a grumbling male voice. Jeremy Stipes opened the door and saw Julius.

'Oh,' he said. 'It's you.'

Julius fixed him with a clear blue look. His hand seemed to be on Jeremy's chest, then Jeremy stepped aside, his mouth wide open as Julius walked past him into the hall, followed by Agnes.

'But—' Jeremy began to flap behind them. 'I said you weren't to – I'm not letting you in.' The flapping got louder as they approached the lounge. 'I'm calling the police. If you don't leave at once, that nun especially, I said she wasn't allowed here – I'm dialling 999...'

The lounge seemed smaller and darker. The carpet was littered with newspaper. Dirty mugs stood on the low table. There was a used ashtray. There was a plate, greasy with half-eaten toast. The curtains were partly drawn.

Pauline Stipes was in her chair. Her eyes were closed, her head lolled back against the seat.

Julius took a step towards her. 'Pauline?'

She opened her eyes. Her gaze swivelled slowly from Julius to Agnes. She raised her arm towards them, made a wordless noise in her throat. Agnes sat down in the chair next to her. Pauline's hand moved to hers, clasped it in a thin, bony grasp.

'She's a very sick woman,' Jeremy said. 'You have no right to upset her like this.'

Julius turned to him. 'What medication is she on?'

'She's in a lot of pain. The drugs help with it.'

'She ought to be somewhere where they can help her,' Julius said.

'No—' Jeremy's voice was raised.

Agnes felt her hand gripped harder. Pauline fixed her with her gaze, her eyes liquid with feeling.

'I won't have her leave me,' Jeremy said.

Julius was standing by him. He spoke quietly. 'No one wants to take her away from you,' he said.

'But they do. Hospice place, you said.'

'She's your wife,' Julius said. He ushered Jeremy to a chair, and Jeremy sat down as if his legs had given way. Julius sat next to him. 'Surely you want what's best for her?'

Jeremy turned to Julius. He slumped in the chair, his pink clammy face round like a child's. 'Then I'll be all alone,' he said.

Julius rested his hand on Jeremy's arm. 'Of course you care about her. But if she's moved elsewhere, that doesn't mean you've failed. It just means you care about her enough to do the right thing for her.'

Jeremy was tugging at the cuffs of his jersey. 'I don't want her to go,' he said, in a small voice.

Julius was silent. He clasped his hands together in his lap. Jeremy sat blinking, pulling at his sleeves.

A dustbin lorry outside broke the silence, the clattering of bins, the shouting of the dustmen. Jeremy got to his feet as if he'd been woken by the noise. 'I don't want her here,' he said, loudly, pointing at Agnes. 'I never said she could come into my house.'

Agnes glanced at Julius, then turned to Pauline. Pauline hung on to her hand, mouthing words. Agnes thought she was saying, 'Get me out.'

Agnes squeezed her hand, bent to say goodbye, whispered, 'We will.' Then they were out in the street, Jeremy still at his front door, shouting now, 'Bloody do-gooders, just don't come back or it'll be the worse for you.'

The door slammed shut.

'Well.' Julius brushed at his cassock, as if flicking crumbs. 'That went really well, I thought. Well done us.'

'Oh dear. It's all my fault. Interfering old busybody.'

'Not just you. Two interfering old busybodies...'

Agnes glanced up at the front door, thinking of Pauline trapped on the other side, numbed and wordless.

'Isn't that—?' Julius was gazing along the street and Agnes followed his line of vision. A tall, pale-coated figure was approaching. 'The doctor,' Julius said. 'Kitson. Isn't that his name?'

The figure raised its arm in greeting.

'Yes,' Agnes said. 'That is Dr Kitson.'

'Hulloa,' he said. 'Father Julius, isn't it? And Sister Agnes. What a lovely surprise. Have you just been to see...' He hushed his voice, gestured with his head towards the Stipes's house.

'Yes,' Julius said. 'We have. Not that we were welcome.'

Dr Kitson leant towards Julius. 'Between you and me, I'm a bit worried about Jeremy. I don't know how well you know him, but his own experience is rather getting in the way when it comes to dealing with his poor wife. His mother...' His words tailed off. He glanced towards the garden, then continued, 'Pauline could live for a long time yet. Jeremy's taking a rather defeatist view.'

'That was rather our impression,' Julius said.

Agnes wondered at the doctor's affability, the ease of his conversation.

'Well,' Dr Kitson said. 'Now I'm here, better do my duty. Keep in touch, eh?' He reached out and shook Julius's hand, waved towards Agnes who was standing further back. 'See you very soon, Sister, no doubt.'

He loped up the steps. The door opened and swallowed him inside.

They sat side by side on the bus back to Southwark. Brief flashes of afternoon sunlight brushed the windows. Agnes broke the silence. 'He's too plausible,' she said.

'Jeremy?'

'No, silly, Dr Kitson.'

'You don't like him.'

'No, I don't. And I don't know why.'

'He seems to be well-meaning.'

'I found this press cutting at Athena's—' She hesitated.

'Go on,' he said.

'It sounds silly now. It was just a coincidence. He was accused of some kind of malpractice, down in Devon, but nothing was proved.'

'Perhaps he's just the kind of person who gets people's backs up.'

Agnes looked at him. 'Yes,' she said. 'Perhaps that's all it is. He's very committed, he's really helpful with our residents. He spent a lot of time with Abbie...' She felt suddenly cold, pulled her coat more firmly around her.

'On the other hand, you're the one who finds out more about a person in two minutes than I do in two years.'

She nudged him gently. 'Silly old Julius,' she said. 'You know how clever you are with people, you don't need me to tell you.'

An image hung in the air before her, of Abbie's body, lying as still as clay. She leant closer to Julius, watching the sunlight fleck the passing shop fronts, the red-brick terraces.

'You were missed this morning.' Louisa found a seat next to Agnes in the convent kitchen.

'When you say missed...?'

'Let's just say, various glances were cast in the direction of your empty place.' Louisa was looking rounder, brighter, although Agnes thought perhaps it was to do with her cardigan, which was chunky, striped with pink and orange.

Agnes smiled at her. 'I went to Mass at Julius's church last night.'

'And you're here in time for compline.'

'I just bumped into Dr Kitson,' Agnes said.

Louisa flashed a glance at her. 'Vaughan? Where?'

'Outside the Stipes's house.'

'Oh. Pauline and Jeremy. Of course. He raced straight off there after our meeting this morning. It's just as well he has no family, really, they'd never see him.' She smiled, fondly.

'Meeting?'

'Our women's health project. He wants to start seeing clients by the end of the month. He's so dynamic.'

Agnes studied her. 'You're very involved with all this, aren't you?'

Louisa picked at a bit of fluff on her cardigan. 'I don't know what to do. He doesn't believe in anything, apart from the power of medicine. And there he is, being selfless and moral, more than many Christians I know.'

'When you say you don't know what to do...'

Louisa looked up at her. 'For a long time, as you know, I

have felt that my faith was growing thin. Well, it seems to have become even thinner.'

'Because of Dr Kitson?' Agnes tried to keep her voice low.

'Not directly, no. But—' She hesitated. 'As an example, perhaps.'

'An example of what?'

Louisa's fingers returned to picking at her sleeve. 'I could get a job as an outreach worker in the field of women's health. Vaughan said so himself. What I mean is —' she turned to Agnes, her voice hushed — 'I don't have to stay in the Order.'

'But—' Agnes began, then stopped.

'I feel alive,' Louisa said. 'I feel as if I'm awakening from sleep. I feel…' she paused, then said, 'I feel like me.'

Agnes looked at her. 'This has been brewing for some time, hasn't it?'

Louisa nodded. 'And I'm loving every minute. I've watched Vaughan at work. And the others on the team. Vaughan was so upset about that boy in your hostel, Dermot, wasn't it? And that girl. He'd spent a lot of time with them both, and the girl, he told me he'd been helping her with medication so that she could come off the heroin, methadone I guess it was, he's so caring…' She raised her eyes to Agnes. 'And the women on the team, they go out on the streets talking to the working girls, trying to get them to come to the clinic… I've realised, you see — you don't have to call it God. To care about other people — it's just being human.' She stopped, flushed and breathless.

Agnes swallowed, tried to speak. Methadone, she wanted to say. How come we didn't know that Abbie had been given methadone — but the chapel bell began to ring for compline and they could hear the nuns gathering in the corridor.

Agnes took her place in the chapel. In the candlelight long

shadows jumped against the walls, flickered from pillar to pillar.

'Let our cry come before you, O Lord; grant us understanding, according to your word...'

The thin female voices rose with the incense smoke. Agnes looked at the heavy, leaden outlines of the stained-glass window, dulled by the darkness outside.

'The eyes of the Lord behold the world; He weighs the righteous and the wicked, but those who delight in violence He abhors...'

In Agnes's mind she saw an ornate suburban porch; the wince of the hydrangea as the front door slammed shut.

CHAPTER FOURTEEN

'You've seen him twice?' Rob Coombes wrapped his fingers around his mug of tea and leant across the hostel kitchen table.

Agnes nodded. 'He offered me his phone, so that I could call you.'

'And why didn't you?'

Agnes glanced towards the windows, which rattled with rain. The kitchen was subdued in the grey morning light.

'Methadone,' she said.

'What about it?' He pulled his notebook out of his pocket.

'Was Abbie on methadone, according to your reports?'

He shook his head. 'Not to my knowledge. Everyone said she'd been clean until that last day. We found no evidence of anything else apart from the morphine that killed her. Dermot, on the other hand...'

'What?' Agnes felt her breathing tighten.

'Traces. In his room. Methadone. No one knows why.'

'And in—' She bit her lip. 'In the body?'

'Not that we can find. But he was on all those painkillers,

the picture's a bit muddy. Still, it's not as if the cause of death is an issue there.'

The cause of death. Agnes felt the words forming in her mind, the sentence falling into place. Dr Kitson, she was about to say. And then what? Dr Kitson looked after them both. Dr Kitson was responsible for their medication. Dr Kitson...

'So, Murchie.' Rob interrupted her train of thought.

She brought her attention back to him. 'I'm sure if we go out there together we'll bump into him. Has Kavin said anything more?'

'We've had to let him go for now.' He opened his notebook, sucked on the end of his pencil.

'Murchie poisoned Nige the rat. As a warning. Although he says it wasn't his idea, and he was quite upset about it.'

Rob watched her. 'Right,' he said. 'Anything else? Do we know what it was a warning for?'

'I asked him and he wouldn't say. He said once you've been a soldier it's hard to go back to Civvy Street.'

'Soldier.' Rob rubbed his chin. 'It's creeping in, this terminology. The glamorisation of petty criminality.' He smiled at her. 'Seems to me you've been walking my beat for me. Next time you see him, could you let me know?'

'What about the flowers?'

'Flowers?'

'The roses, and the notes, that were left here?'

'Ah, yes. We've had them fingerprinted. Pretty inconclusive, I'm afraid. One of those kids that hangs around with Murchison, someone trying to show some respect, we reckon.'

There were voices at the door, giggles, Sari's voice, '...it's well cool here, you'll love it, won't she, Aysh?'

Gilroy and Aysha appeared, with Sari and a young woman.

She was round and pink and smiling, with a mop of blond curls and a torn black T-shirt.

'This is Bex,' Gilroy said. 'She's our new resident.'

Rob stood up to make room, the kettle was put on, Agnes shook hands with Bex and exchanged a few words, enough to establish that she'd been picked up by the police in Soho the night before and that originally she was from Sunderland but had run away. 'I'm sixteen,' she said, her blue eyes fixed on Agnes's, and the flushed urgency with which she spoke was enough to convince Agnes that she was fifteen or under and desperate not to be sent home.

As Agnes slipped out of the kitchen, she could hear Sari's voice again. 'You'll have Abbie's room, she were great, Abbie were, best mates she and I were, shame she's dead...'

The office was deserted. She took Dermot's file from the cabinet, sat at a desk and flicked through it. There was no record of his prescription from Dr Kitson, although there was no reason why there should be. She found the papers he'd filled in when he'd come to live there almost two months ago. Her eye fell on the name Carole O'Keefe. There was an address in Clapham, a phone number. She wrote them down, closed the file and left the office.

On the front doorstep she encountered Rob. 'Knocking off, are we?' he said.

'Things to do,' she said.

'Me too.' He glanced at her. 'I'll check the post-mortem on Abbie, after what you said about methadone. But to be honest, you'd have to drink pints of the stuff for it to kill you.' He surveyed the street. 'See? Deserted. The minute I leave you on your own, they'll be crawling out of the paving stones.'

'Who?' She smiled at him.

'Murchison. And his pals.'

'I'll ring you if I have a sighting.' She descended the steps, Rob following. He got into his car, she headed for the main road, her head bowed against the rain.

Zip was standing on the corner by the traffic lights, his trilby hat pulled right down over his eyes. He seemed to be waiting for her.

'Hello,' she said to him. There was another boy standing next to him; he seemed very small, but it might have been his huge baggy top, or the way he scuffed his trainers on the pavement without looking up at her.

'All right?' Zip said.

'All right.'

'You looking for Murch? You won't find him.'

She met his eyes, which searched her own from under the brim of his hat. 'And why's that?'

'Murchie?' The other boy looked up at Zip. 'Gone, hasn't he?' His voice was young and reedy. 'Police after him, someone grassed, innit?'

'Someone trying to say that he had it in for Abbie.' Zip held her gaze. 'Like, he wanted her out of the way.'

'It is a possibility.' Agnes waited.

'What you have to know about Murch—' Zip glanced at a sports car as it revved loudly past them. 'The thing about Murch is, that he don't care enough about any of the girls to kill them.' He turned to his friend. 'Look at that Bim.'

Both boys followed the car with their eyes until it went out of sight. It was a metallic blue, with a customised go-faster stripe.

Agnes looked at Zip. 'It wasn't Murchie I was looking for.' She was aware of the younger boy's eyes on her.

'You that nun?' he chirruped, but then was shushed by a cuff on the ear from Zip.

'Oi, Frankie.' Zip turned to Agnes. 'Sorry about him, miss.'

'I am that nun, yes.' Agnes smiled at Frankie, who was holding the side of his head. 'And I was wondering if you knew where I might find Lindy.'

Zip pushed his hat to the back of his head, scratched his forehead. 'Lucy Locket?'

'Is that what you call her?'

Frankie began to hop from foot to foot. 'Lucy Locket lost her pocket, Katy Fisher found it...'

Agnes looked down at him. 'Funny you know that old nursery rhyme,' she said.

'Nursery rhyme?' Frankie looked up, blank-faced.

Zip rearranged his hat on his head. 'It's from that film, innit? It's what he sings when he goes to get the chainsaw.' He took his phone out of his pocket and glanced at it.

'And Lindy?'

Zip shook his head. Frankie did the same.

'Nah,' Zip said. 'We ain't seen her.'

'If you do, can you say that I want to talk to her a bit more about poor old Abbie?'

'Abbie? Like I say. Old news.' Zip patted the top of Frankie's head. 'We got to go now.'

They spun round on their heels, and began to walk away. Agnes watched them go, then crossed the street and headed for the main road. The sun broke through the clouds, sprinkling ripples of light across the puddles.

She let herself into her flat, flung herself on to her divan bed and clicked Brett's number on her phone.

'Hi.' He sounded distracted. She could hear music in the background.

'Are you busy?' She lay back on her pillows, watching the midday sun trace patterns on her ceiling.

'Yes. As busy goes, I am.'

'I wanted to ask you—' she heard someone, a woman's voice, address him by name.

'Sorry—' He came back on the line. 'What were you saying?'

She held the phone firmly in her hand. 'Why did you come over to Britain now? Why did you choose this moment to track me down when you've had my father's stuff for years?'

'I told you before, it was a question of funding.'

'If it was that important, you could have phoned me – you could have emailed me – you could have sent all those documents of his without physically being in London.'

'You don't understand.' His voice was sharp. 'The circumstances changed.'

'Your circumstances – or his?'

She heard his silence. 'I don't know what you mean,' he said.

'I mean, what did you find out about him, or about me, that meant that it became urgent to meet me? And what has happened since to close it all down again?'

His voice was muffled, drowned out. 'Nothing. I've told you. There's nothing more to say.' Again, someone was speaking to him, a woman's voice, and he turned away from his phone. 'No, honey, wait – I'll be right there. I've got to go,' he said to Agnes. 'See you around.'

The conversation clicked off.

Agnes lay on her bed in the sudden quiet.

What has he found out about my father? Or about me? What won't he tell me?

She jumped up from her bed, reached down all her father's books and placed them on her desk. She began to sift through them, flicking through pages, looking for – for what, she wondered? Clues?

'As a father loves his only child…' The words were written across the top of a page in ink. The sunlight fell on the yellowing paper. Agnes read on.

'The Old Testament reveals to us a Creator who is the Father of the tribe, of His chosen people. The Gospels give us a reshaping of this notion, so that it extends beyond the tribe. The wonderful message of the Gospels is that we have an individual relationship with our Creator; that we respond on a unique basis to the energy within the universe that brought us into being. Thus we can call to our Creator, as Jesus did to His father in Hebrew: Abba. Father.'

A sudden flash of memory: Agnes tumbling, winded, the taste of the wet mud of the paddock in her mouth. She sits up, clutching her elbow which feels numb and strange. She sees her father in the distance, his untidy, pale hair as he bends to inspect the grapes on the vine; she hears the breathing of her pony as he stands there, puzzled, wondering how it is that he is here and she is there, on the ground, when a minute before they'd been about to jump the paddock gate. He nuzzles the top of her head.

'Papa' she calls out, and then in English, 'Daddy'. The figure retreats behind the vines. She rubs her elbow and waits. He did hear, she thinks, he's just walking round that way, he'll be here in a minute. Through the ringing in her ears she fancies she can hear the crunch of his approaching steps on the old stone paths, his familiar, uneven gait; but then the ringing subsides until there is just the sound of the birds in the trees, the breeze through the branches, her pony blowing through his nostrils, tired of the game now, impatient for her to get back on and make everything all right again.

Agnes looked at the careful script of her father's handwriting. In her memory, she got back on her pony, urged him into a fast canter, headed for the fence at the bottom of the orchard which was twice the height of the gate, sailed over it and galloped off across the field beyond. In her memory, she ignored the numb feeling spreading down her hand into her fingertips. In her memory, she told herself that her father hadn't heard; not that he'd raised his head at the sound of her voice and then deliberately turned away.

And can I rely on my memory? All I can remember with any certainty is that a week later, when my arm was still swollen, my mother reluctantly called the village doctor who diagnosed a fracture; and then my father scolded me for 'trying to jump that bloody pony over the paddock gate last week...'

Agnes sipped her cold coffee and turned the page. 'I am indebted to the writings of Enos Ephraim, in whose work I first encountered the theory of prochronism in Creation, which was of course brought to a wider public some years later by Philip Gosse. Like Gosse, I too, a century or so later, consider myself to be a co-searcher with the geologists. We are all, surely, engaged in the same process; we all wish to understand the world in which we find ourselves, through an investigation of the many wonders which Creation lays before us. The strata of a rock, the rings of a tree trunk, the formation of an ancient shell; all these signs point out the way, allow us to uncover the true story of our creation.'

She continued to read, skimming detailed descriptions of the development of various forms of plant life which were supposed to prove, from what she could gather, her father's theory that the creation of the universe followed a non-linear chronology and therefore the timescale as described in the Bible could also include fossils, tree rings and the fact that Adam was born with a navel.

She put the book down and picked up the next pamphlet. She read the date written in the front, in the same neat ink writing.

July 1996: three months before his death.

There was an inscription typed underneath: 'For some years I have joined my small voice to those of greater men in promulgating the truth about the work of our Creator. But now I have learnt an even greater truth; that the greatest gift of our Creator is love itself. I have come to see that for years I have been walking in the desert, blind to those for whom I might have cared; until at last came one who opened my eyes to the Truth; who allowed me to see that in tracing the Great Work of our Creator in the signs He left behind, I have failed to see the greatest work of all; that He gave to us the gift of love. There are those whom I have failed in my blindness, and should they ever read this, I ask for their forgiveness; but to the one who opened up my eyes, to my helpmeet in the great task, in deepest gratitude I dedicate this work.'

Agnes stared at the words. Monica, it must be, although he hadn't named her. She thought back to that summer, and remembered the conversation she'd had with him on the phone, on a crackly line between her former enclosed Order and his house in Charleston, West Virginia. She had stood in

the curtained cubicle where the single phone was kept,
watching the worn woven telephone flex swing in the
draught, listening to his voice which sounded young and light
and sunny; 'It would be great to see you, my dear. I'm hoping
to visit England soon, I could always come to you if those
nuns could spare you a few moments to see me...'

And her reply, which was as cold and dusty as the stone
wall in front of her. No, she wouldn't get permission, she was
sorry, but she wouldn't like him to waste his time coming all
this way to the middle of nowhere...

In truth, she was in crisis, waking each day in the
knowledge that she was in the wrong place, feeling her spirit
shrivel a little more each day, barely eating, barely sleeping.
She had been paralysed with terror, doubting her own
judgment, in the belief that her own will was not the same as
God's will, and that her own feelings were there to be ignored.
Listening to her father's voice on the phone, she knew that any
glimpse of the outside world at all, even a part of it as distant
as he had now become, would risk bringing with it the
shattering of her fragile state of mind.

And so she had said, no. Now, reading the uneven typing,
she felt again the heavy black phone receiver in her hand; and
she heard, through the crackles and the distance, the whisper
of regret, the ghost of his apology that she had slapped away.

Three months later he was dead.

Agnes closed the book and put it down on her table. She
sat, unmoving, in the dim grey light of the rainy afternoon.
She stared at the book in front of her, picked up her mug and
sipped from it, unaware that the coffee was cold, until the
mug was empty and she looked at it in surprise.

* * *

By the time she left her flat for Julius's church, the rain had stopped. The evening sky lent dull office blocks the romance of a stage set; their twilit silhouettes sparkled with little squares of light.

Agnes slipped into church and joined the service.

'And Joseph made ready his chariot, and went up to meet Jacob his father, to Goshen, and he presented himself to him; and he fell on his neck, and wept for a long time. And Jacob said to Joseph, "Now let me die, since I have seen your face."'

Afterwards Julius found her, still kneeling in her pew. He coughed, slightly, and she opened her eyes.

'I thought... I thought we might go to the pub,' he said.

The night was clear and cold. Agnes walked next to him through the evening crowds. She thought she could hear footsteps behind them, and at one point turned, but no one was there.

The pub was warm and mostly empty. Julius turned to her 'Whisky? Lager?'

'Lager,' she said.

'French, presumably.'

'Yes please.'

They sat in a corner. She watched the condensation form on her glass.

'What's up?' He smiled at her, a moustache of Guinness foam on his lip.

She looked up at him. 'Did you love your father?'

He studied her. After a moment, he said, 'What kind of question is that?'

'What it says.'

'I don't know,' he said. 'I didn't see that much of him. But yes, I suppose, had you asked me, I'd have said, yes.'

'They sent you away to school.'

'Yes. But it was really the only way I could have got any kind of an education. There was nothing in the village.'

'What was he like, your father?'

Julius leant back in his chair. He fiddled his spectacles further on to his nose. 'Well...he was a true Kerry man. He liked a pint, and he liked the horses, and as for us children, he greeted the arrival of each one of us as if we'd been brought by a stork to make his life even more troublesome.' He smiled.

'But—'

'But he loved our mother. He always said, that midsummer's day in Dublin when it poured with rain, and he was waiting at the stop for the number nine tram, and he gave away his umbrella to the prettiest girl in the queue – he always said that was the luckiest day of his life. So—' He peered at her over the top of his glasses. 'What's brought this on?'

'I was reading my father's writings today, and I found what amounted to an apology. And now I feel really bad.'

'Oh.' He frowned at her. 'Oh dear.'

'Why oh dear?'

He scratched his head. 'Well...' He hesitated, then said, 'It seems to me...'

'What?'

He sighed. 'From what I know of your parents, it is really not for you to feel bad.'

'But – forgiveness...?'

'Oh, yes, of course, by all means, forgiveness... All I meant was, you've managed to live your life so well, you've succeeded so admirably in not allowing your past to drag you down with it, it would be a shame if a misplaced sense of regret about an attempt at an apology, which, let's face it, you'd be completely unaware of if it wasn't for this rather odd American – it would be a shame if you allowed something as passing as that to trip you up after all this time.'

Agnes stared at him. She was aware of tears constricting her throat. After a moment, she said, in a small voice, 'Admirably?'

'Yes,' he said. 'Admirably.'

'Oh.' She blinked at him.

He nodded at her. 'That's what I think, anyway.' He leant across and patted her hand. 'Now, Pauline Stipes. What is to be done?'

She looked at his hand on hers but didn't speak.

'I've had a word with ex-Father Gustave,' Julius went on, 'at that hospice in Sydenham. His worry is that it's rather a long way, unless we actually want to kidnap her and hide her from her husband altogether, and I said that although we have our reservations about him, we probably felt that was going a bit far. He said, if we need a place urgently he'd be happy to help, perhaps temporarily, but he was going to see if he could find one closer to home. Of course, he's terribly busy, what with his museum too.'

'What museum?'

'Since he ceased to be a Brother, he's become interested in ancient history and archaeology, and he's started an amateur collection...' His voice tailed off as they both became aware of someone standing over their table.

Agnes looked up, to see cold, bare legs in a short denim skirt. 'Hello Lindy,' she said.

'You been looking for me.' Lindy stared down at her. 'The boys said.'

'Yes,' Agnes said. 'I have.'

'They said it was about Abbie.'

'How did you know I was here?'

'Followed you, didn't I?'

'Will you have a drink?' Julius stood up, and Lindy surveyed him, then nodded. 'Vodka and tonic. Please,' she added.

She sat down at the table, pulled out a packet of cigarettes and fiddled with it.

'You can't smoke—' Agnes began.

'Nah, you're all right. I won't light up.' She waved a cigarette at Agnes. 'Though I've got such a record as a common criminal, I might as well add this to it.' She gave a short laugh.

Julius reappeared with a large vodka, two more beers and two bags of crisps. Lindy grabbed the vodka and downed half of it.

'It was about methadone,' Agnes said.

Lindy started on a bag of crisps, taking one, then another. 'What about it?' she said, through crumbs.

'Someone said that Abbie was using it to come off heroin. And also, there were traces found in Dermot's room.'

She faced Agnes. She shook her head. 'Nah,' she said. 'Not our Abs. Not unless it was ages ago, she might have done it then, when she was still on the streets. But then she was working for Murchie and Murch wouldn't have his girls taking meth, would he? There wouldn't be nothing in it for him.'

'And Dermot?'

Lindy downed the rest of her drink. She put the glass down on the table. 'I wouldn't know.'

Agnes sensed her hesitation. 'But—'

Lindy looked up at her. 'He was no angel, that Dermot. You ask Connor about Dermot...' She reached for the second bag of crisps and pulled it open.

'Dermot's cousin?'

She nodded. 'Everyone thinks Mots was such a cool guy, but he had a bad side, I know it's not right to say it now he's dead. But it's been right hard for Connor, having to listen to everyone feeling bad about Dermot, and there's Connor knowing the truth about him.'

'What truth?'

'Well, for a start—' She picked out another crisp.. 'He had a mouth on him, that Dermot. When I heard that Murchie and his bredren were out for him, I weren't at all surprised. Just like Mots to get the wrong side of someone like Murchie. And I've seen Mots when he's angry, and it's not something you want to be near, even women, I've seen him go for one of the girls, once, when he thought she'd nicked something off him or something. Connor said it was in his blood, his dad wasn't someone anyone wanted to get the wrong side of. Brothers with Connor's dad, but Connor said he got the right one, Desi, the little brother. His big brother, Tommy, everyone was scared of him. And then their dad, Big Louie, he wouldn't let Tommy take over the fairground business, he gave it all to Desi who everyone loved. And after that Dermot's dad was even worse, and in the end he came over to England and tried to make a life for himself. And that's when he met Mots's mum, and they had Dermot.'

'In Liverpool?'

Lindy nodded. 'But Dermot's mum died when he was quite little, and Tommy was a violent man, so after a while he ran away to London.' She reached for another crisp. 'Anyway, this methadone?'

Agnes glanced at Julius, who had found an old newspaper and was reading it with interest. She picked up her glass and took a sip. 'Would Abbie have lied if she was still taking it?'

Lindy shook her head. 'Why would she? All us girls, the stuff we've seen. Why lie about a little thing like that?'

'And is it the sort of thing that someone might trade, like Dermot, or Murchie?'

Lindy smiled. 'Nah. Not meth. Not when you could do H. Or coke. The only people who swap meth get it from the clinic, innit, when they're trying to come off the gear. It's what doctors have.'

'Doctors,' Agnes said.

Lindy fished inside the crisp packet. She turned it upside down and shook the crumbs onto her hand. 'It's all money, innit? It makes me angry. Like Connor, I really like him, you know. He's not like the guys he hangs around with. And I say to him, you and me, we could make a new start, that's what you wanted when you left Ireland and came over here, so why you hanging around with a gangster low life like Murchie? Just because he thinks he's so cool and he flashes his money around...'

'And what does he say?'

Lindy shook her head. 'He says, give it time, girl. And I say, I don't have time. He says, a year, babes, and I say, in a year I might be dead...' Her voice faltered. Her eyes welled with tears.

Agnes passed her a clean tissue.

Lindy dabbed at her eyes. 'It's like Abbie. She was about to start again. A new life. It came to nothing, didn't it?' She stood up. 'I'd better go. The boys don't know where I am. I said I'd meet Connor, but knowing him, he's vanished again – just when I think I know where he is, he disappears.'

'Lindy.'

'Mmm?' Lindy turned back to her.

'Do you know who left those roses?'

She shook her head. 'I think about that a lot, you know. I think, if someone cared enough to do that for her in death, why couldn't they have cared enough when she was alive?'

'And Dermot's one?'

Lindy shrugged. 'Maybe it was some kind of sick joke.'

'The note said something about promises.'

'Yeah, well. That was Dermot, weren't it, making promises to Abbie that he couldn't keep. She should have known better.' Her lip trembled. She clutched her bag to her chest and turned to leave.

Agnes and Julius watched her cross the floor, watched the eyes scanning her thin, bare legs. The pub door swung shut.

Julius sipped what was left of his drink. 'If you just remove people from a bad situation and put them in a good one...' He spoke with feeling.

'Lindy, you mean?'

'Well, yes, her too. I was thinking of Pauline.'

'We must rehouse her. I'll work on it tomorrow.'

Julius scribbled down a phone number and passed it to her. 'Ex-Father Gustave,' he said.

She glanced at the writing. 'You could just call him Gustave, you know.'

'Yes. I suppose I could.'

They left the pub. Julius walked Agnes as far as the main road. A three-quarter moon had risen in the clear sky.

'Well,' Julius said. 'See you tomorrow. I expect.'

She nodded. 'I expect so.'

He squeezed her arm.

'What you said, earlier – about me – I had no idea...'

He watched her. 'Maybe I'd just never said it before.'

She looked up at him. She shrugged. 'Maybe,' she said. She turned to leave.

'Tomorrow, then,' he said.

She hesitated, then leant up and kissed his cheek. 'See you.' She turned to go, then turned back, and watched him as he headed back towards his church.

She set off along the main road. Through the wail of distant sirens she could just make out the hooting of an owl.

CHAPTER FIFTEEN

The Nonesuch Gallery was fronted with huge plate-glass windows which reflected the exclusive shops on the other side of the street. Sunlight glanced off soft-leather handbags and exquisite shoes.

No wonder Athena's always buying stuff, Agnes thought as she pressed the bell. The temptation must prove too strong.

The door buzzed open, and Agnes crossed the polished wooden floor to the desk where Athena sat. Athena watched her approach with a blank expression.

'I've spent all morning trying and failing to find a hospice place for someone who needs to be removed from her husband because she's in fear of her life, and I wondered if you wanted lunch?'

Two other faces looked up from their desks. Athena smiled up at Agnes. 'How very tiresome for you, sweetie. Yes, I'd love lunch. If Simon can spare me, of course.'

Simon got up from his high-tech desk chair, his arm outstretched towards her. 'Agnes, what a lovely surprise. It's been years, absolute years, far too long.' He kissed her on both cheeks.

'You're looking well,' Agnes said. He was taller than she remembered, or perhaps it was the clean-shaven linen-shirted look, the tortoiseshell spectacle frames.

'You mean, thinner,' he replied, tapping his chest. 'Finally started going to the gym, should have done it years ago. Well, when I say gym...' he giggled. 'Sauna, spa, general all-round pampering and pick-up joint. Have you met the family? Stella, this is Agnes.'

Stella's blond hair was tied back in a way that managed to be careless and elegant at the same time; a long, well-cut skirt swirled softly against her knee-length boots. 'Hi,' she said.

'Nice boots,' Agnes said.

'Thank you,' she said.

Agnes glanced at the walls. They were hung with wide, dark frames, portraits, it appeared, heavy swirls of paint from which seemed to emerge likenesses. Agnes saw the face of an elderly man, an angular nose, a pipe, a background of bookcases, brought to life in thick curls of brown and beige and white.

'These are nice,' she said to Stella.

'Oh?' She raised an eyebrow. 'I prefer less old-fashioned stuff.'

'Such as?'

'I did my thesis on geometry and movement in American abstract painting.'

'Well, I'm sure Simon's got some of that lined up for the next show.' Agnes glanced across to Simon, who winked at her.

Athena stood up. 'Did someone say lunch?' She gathered up her coat and bag and went to the door. 'I may be some time,' she said.

Out in the street, Athena peered up at the sky. 'Look,' she said. 'I believe that stuff up there is called sunlight. This means only one thing.'

'What's that?'

'We're going to sit outside.'

'But it's practically winter,' Agnes said.

'Us Englishwomen have got to make the best of whatever the climate throws at us. Anyway, the place I have in mind has outdoor heaters.'

They settled at a pavement table, their green metal chairs wobbling on the cobbled stones. 'Mmm.' Athena pointed across the road. 'I like that look, don't you, in that window there? That sort of military coat and those tailored trousers. That would look good on you, you know. I must have a word with your Mother Superior about updating your uniform. Now, they do a great crab salad here, and I would suggest Sancerre too, only we've got a big stocktaking bee this afternoon and it wouldn't be fair on Simon if I just fell asleep, so I think I'll slum it with mineral water. What about you?'

'I'll have exactly the same, please,' Agnes said, as the waitress approached, dragging herself to their table as if she'd much rather be somewhere else, struggling to write their order down with a stub of pencil.

Athena pulled her jacket around her shoulders. She helped herself to a breadstick. 'So, what did you think of Stella?'

'Well…' Agnes hesitated.

'Go on.'

'She seems very nice.'

'And…'

'I said, nice boots. And she said, thank you.'

'Exactly.' Athena waved her breadstick at her. 'What real woman behaves like that? Every woman I've ever counted as a friend would say, "Do you know, they were a bargain, half price in the sale…" '

'Mmm.' Agnes sipped her water. 'Perhaps they really were terribly expensive. She looks like someone who could afford the full price.'

'That's not the point. She could at least make the effort and lie. Apart from that she's OK, and her coffee-making is fantastic. Although that might just be because Simon bought a Gaggia machine last month, at last. Anyway, kitten, this poor woman whose husband is trying to kill her…'

'Oh, no, not the husband.'

'Oh.' Athena looked puzzled. It's usually the husband, isn't it?'

'Is it?'

'Your husband nearly killed you.'

Agnes broke a breadstick in half. 'Pauline's case is completely different.'

The waitress thumped two angular white plates down on the table; the lettuce leaves flinched.

'The point is,' Agnes said, 'I have to get her away.'

'But – if she's dying anyway…'

I just have this hunch, Agnes was about to say. I just feel she'll have a better chance of living out whatever life she has left. Dr Kitson was in Devon, you see—

'Devon.' Athena interrupted her train of thought. Agnes blinked. 'What about it?'

'I was just saying, Nic's had to go to Devon again. His mum is so frail now, and she really can't stay in her own house. It's awful to see someone so diminished. Do you know, during the war she drove a tank in Albania or somewhere…or was it an ambulance? Anyway, it's so sad when you think of what she was, and what she's become. And, it means he's forgotten about getting married. For now, anyway.' She bent over her salad.

'You seem disappointed,' Agnes said.

Athena looked up. 'What, me? Goodness, no, did I ever want to get married?'

'Well, no, but I thought perhaps now the idea had sunk in a bit…'

'You mean, having a special day where I'm the most gorgeous person of all, and having a fab new dress, and getting all my favourite people together so that the man I adore most in the whole world can swear undying love to me in front of them all…?' She shook her head. 'Can't see the attraction, really, can you?' She began to attack a crab claw.

'I'm sure if you feel like that,' Agnes said, 'I mean, I'm sure once Nic realises you're keen, he'll be there with a marriage licence and a booking for a chateau somewhere…'

Athena pulled a face. 'Maybe.'

'What else is wrong?'

'Oh, nothing.'

'Go on.'

'No, really, it's fine. I mean, why should I mind if his ex-wife is helping out with his mum, and being such a great support, so wonderful that she lives down in the South-West, what a coincidence, they always did get on…'

'Really? His ex-wife?'

'Ben's mum. *So* lovely she can see more of baby Daisy too…'

'Oh.'

'So, you can see, it's rather taken his mind off a wedding. Just as well I don't mind.' Athena took a large mouthful of mineral water. 'Anyway, talking of men who don't know what they want—' She looked up at Agnes. 'How's the lovely American?'

'Oh, him.'

'Misbehaving too, eh? I don't know, these men, it must be something astrological. Saturn being retrograde or something. What's he up to, then?'

'Hiding from me. Talking to me on the phone whilst addressing someone else as "honey" in the background.'

'Oh. That is serious.'

Agnes laughed. 'It would be if I was interested in him.'

'And after all the effort you made. Wearing lipstick and everything, see you're blushing, no use pretending, kitten.' Athena dabbed her lips. 'I'm really thinking moon in Pisces. Either that or lots of Gemini somewhere.'

Agnes speared a piece of cucumber. 'What gets me is that he parachutes into my life, completely rewrites my sense of who my father was, and then buggers off and leaves me to try to piece it all together. Julius says I shouldn't dwell on it, he says I've moved on and it would be best not to start digging up regrets...'

Athena sipped her mineral water. 'I'm with Julius on this one. As usual.'

'But there's all this stuff in my father's writings, this sense of wasted opportunity, as if right at the end of his life he realised what he'd missed. It leaves me feeling that he and I could have had a relationship, if only...'

'If only what? If only he'd been sufficiently mature at the time to be like a proper father to you, to give you the template of what a functional relationship might be like, instead of leaving you so cast adrift that you had no defences when Hugo caught you up in his lying and deceitful net?' She shook her head. 'No, Julius is absolutely right. This is one of those cases where there's nothing to be gained in looking backwards.'

They ate in silence for a while. Athena put her fork down on her plate. 'Do you ever wonder what happened to Hugo?'

'Rarely. Do you?'

'Hardly at all.' She took a compact mirror out of her handbag. 'It might be amusing to find out. We could add him to our friends on Facebook.'

Agnes laughed. 'Do you think you can get Facebook if you're living on a seedy yacht somewhere off St Tropez?'

'Oh, that's where you have him, is it? I was thinking more debtors prison.'

'Anyway, I'm not adding him to my friends on anything.'

'No, you're right. Good riddance.' She reached across and took a tomato from Agnes's plate. 'It might be fun to know, though.'

'I think that Facebook would spell the end for my community. We're much too chatty as it is.' Agnes drained her glass of water. 'So, no gazing backwards into the past. Not my father, not Hugo. Not anyone.'

'If I had a glass of anything that counted, I'd raise it to that.'

'Although...' Agnes fiddled the sugar spoon round and round in its bowl. 'I wouldn't be what I am now, without either of them. My father, or Hugo.'

'As far as Hugo's concerned, he just gave you something to run away from.'

'Yes, but in my case, eventually anyway, that became a good

thing. I suppose. Sister Louisa, in my community…she became a nun from running away, and now she's regretting it. After years and years. And now she's very taken with Dr Kitson and I think he's dangerous, but I can't think what it is about him that's so wrong, he's really helpful, and he's fantastic with the residents, they really like him…'

'Ooh, dear…'

'I know, you're going to tell me I'm getting distracted because of all this business with my father, and I should just get on with my work and try to find a hospice place for Pauline without getting all paranoid about it.'

'You took the words out of my mouth.' Athena gathered her bag on to her lap. 'After all, which of us can honestly say we haven't been blinded to the faults of a man? And doctors are the worst of all, I imagine, if you're into that kind of thing. All you can do with this Sister Louisa is to remind her that playing hard to get never did anyone any harm.'

Agnes laughed. 'I'm not sure that's exactly the advice she needs at the moment.' She checked her watch. 'I'd better get going. I'm visiting Pauline this afternoon. I've got one possible hospice place but there's a complication about signing a form. And Julius and I have plotted to have her husband out of the way so that I can talk to her properly.'

They paid and left. Agnes glanced up at the stripes of sunlight that fell across the green umbrellas. 'You were right about coming here.'

'It's my manor, isn't it? And we didn't linger. Just as well, I really don't want to encourage Simon in his belief that you're a bad influence.'

*   *   *

The bus made its stop-start journey towards Streatham. The sun began to fade behind thick clouds, and by the time she walked up Atherton Road a fine rain was falling.

The curtains in the Stipes's windows seemed to be more limp; the paintwork on the door more faded. It was a long time before Agnes's ring was answered, and Pauline's face appeared in the crack of the door.

Agnes was shocked by her appearance. Her hair stood up in tufts; the brightness of her eyes was gone, replaced by a clouded, hollow despair. Her arm was as thin as porcelain. Pauline leant on her heavily, as they made their way slowly back into the lounge, and Pauline took up her place on her customary chair.

She sat with her eyes shut, and her laboured breathing filled the room. After some minutes she opened her eyes and looked at Agnes. 'Get me out,' she said. Her voice was hoarse.

'We've found you a hospice place,' Agnes said. 'It's a bit of a long way away, but the problem is you need to be referred. And the form needs a signature from your next of kin.'

'Not going there to die,' Pauline said. 'He doesn't need to sign anything.' She leant back in her chair and closed her eyes again.

'But – Pauline...' Agnes wondered what to say.

'Listen—' The eyes flashed open again. 'I know I'm not well. Not at all well. But me leaving here – it's to get away from him. That's all. If I die there too, that's as maybe. But what I write on your damn form, where it says reason for admission, I write "escape". Escape from my prison. In big bloody letters.' The effort of speech seemed to revive her. Her eyes flashed briefly with life.

'Well,' Agnes said. 'Do we ask Jeremy to sign this, then?'

She shook her head. 'He won't sign. Don't ask him. Just make him even nastier.'

Agnes studied the form again. There was a space where it said, 'Name of GP', followed by a dotted line for a signature. 'Well...' She took a breath. 'We could ask Dr Kitson. His name might be enough.'

Pauline sat motionless, her fingers gripping the armrests of her chair. She looked at Agnes. 'What do you think of him? Of Dr Kitson?'

Agnes wondered what to say. She searched for a form of words that would be diplomatic yet honest. Pauline spoke again. 'I think he's dangerous.'

'In what way?' Agnes leant towards her.

Pauline reached for her glass of water, held it between both hands. She took a sip, then put it down again, spilling a drop as she did so. 'I don't quite know,' she said. 'I mentioned this hospice plan to him, last week, just in passing. He was adamant against it. He said I wasn't to talk of dying. I said, I'm not talking of dying, I would just rather not be here. I didn't go into detail about Jeremy, I flannelled on about not wanting to be a strain, that kind of thing. Then Dr Kitson said, "He needs you." He said, "Your husband needs you." He was quite cross, kind of angry. And after that he didn't say anything else.' She lifted her head towards Agnes. 'Don't you think that's an odd thing to say? I was quite frightened of him.'

Agnes straightened up in her chair. 'Yes,' she said. 'I do think that's an odd thing to say.'

Pauline's breathing was shallow as she struggled to regain it.

'He might be our best hope, even so,' Agnes said. 'I could just ask him to sign the form, I could insist it's what you want.

I can catch him at the hostel later, he's due in.'

'Doesn't he frighten you?' Pauline's gaze was searching.

Agnes met her eyes. 'Yes,' she said. 'Yes, he does frighten me.'

Pauline clasped her hands together in her lap. 'I'm glad it's not just me. These days I worry that I'm going mad.'

Agnes went over to her and rested her hand on her shoulder. 'I should go,' she said. 'There's a limit to how long Julius can delay your husband in a discussion of helpful books for his crisis of faith.'

Pauline shook her head. 'I can't imagine my husband will listen anyway. He is a man without faith. I think perhaps he always was.'

'We'll get you out of here. I'll tell Julius to confirm with ex-Father Gustave that we want the room, and I'll make sure that Dr Kitson sees how urgent it is.'

Pauline reached up and grasped Agnes's hand. 'Thank you, Sister. You...' She took a breath, then went on, 'You've saved my life.'

Agnes squeezed her hand. 'I'll show myself out. Don't get up. Have you got everything you need?'

Pauline nodded. 'He'll be back soon. You go.'

Agnes closed the front door. Behind her the house settled into silence. She hurried away, back towards the bus stop, fearing to meet Jeremy Stipes coming the other way, then remembering that he would have gone to meet Julius by car.

The sound of laughter came from the hostel lounge. Agnes found Lizzie and Bex sharing an iPod, trying to dance while joined together by headphones. It was even funnier being watched, and they collapsed in hysterics on the sofa.

'Is Dr Kitson here?' Agnes asked.

'He was in the office with Gil,' Lizzie said.

'And you can tell Gil that if it's cauliflower again for dinner then I'm going back to Stoke Newington.' Bex stamped her chunky black boot on the carpet.

Agnes left them both helpless with laughter and went to the office.

Dr Kitson was sitting on his own at Gilroy's desk. He looked up, then smiled. 'Ah. Sister Agnes. Did you want Gilroy? He's gone to deal with supper, I think.'

'Let's hope it's not cauliflower,' Agnes said. 'Else we'll be way off our targets for retention of clients.' She sat down next to Dr Kitson. 'Actually, it was you I wanted to speak to.'

'Oh. Good.' He glanced at her through his pale lashes. 'I was rather hoping to have a word with you too.'

She looked at him, surprised. 'Why?'

'Well, it's rather a delicate matter, to discuss one nun with another. But your Sister Louisa...' He blushed, fell silent.

'She's working on that project with you,' Agnes prompted, wondering what was coming next.

He sighed. 'Yes. That's just the problem.' He gave an exaggerated sigh. 'I worry that I'm challenging her – shall we say, her beliefs.' Again, he was silent.

'She seems very happy.'

He leant forward, resting his elbows on his knees. 'That's just the point, Sister. There are one or two things she's been saying over the last couple of days, to the effect that she wishes she could do more of our kind of work and less of your community's kind of work.' He bit his lip, struggling with the words, then said, 'I don't wish to make her unhappy.'

He seemed awkward with concern, sitting there so crookedly, his limbs all awry. Agnes found herself wondering why she'd allowed him to frighten her. Perhaps it was all about my father after all, she thought.

'It's not your fault,' she said to him.

'Do you think not?' He looked up at her.

'I think Louisa has been doubting her vocation for some time. If your project has given her an opportunity to express her doubts, then for her that's helpful, not destructive.'

He seemed to untangle with relief. 'Ah,' he said. One arm came to rest along the back of his chair. 'Yes. I suppose you're right. These things are part of a long process, I suppose.' His eyes were bright as he held her gaze. 'She's a very valuable part of the team, you know. Bags of common sense.'

Agnes smiled at him. 'We could all do with that. Especially us nuns.'

He smiled back. 'Only the most narrow-minded kind of atheist would accuse you nuns of having no common sense.' He leant back on the chair, 'What did you want to see me about?'

'Well, like your question to me, this one to you is also rather delicate. It's about Mrs Stipes.'

He nodded. 'A difficult situation,' he said. 'Do go on.'

'There isn't a nice way of putting this. She needs to leave that house. She needs to be away from her husband.' Agnes bent to her bag to find the form from ex-Father Gustave. 'We think we've got her a place in a hospice, it's somewhat unorthodox, but if you could sign as her GP—' She pulled out the papers and glanced towards him.

He had become angular; his face was sharp, his knees twitched together as he met her eyes.

'Why?' His voice was harsh. 'Why should she leave?'

She didn't know what to say, how to reply. 'Dr Kitson,' she began, 'Mrs Stipes has made it very clear—'

'Made what very clear?' He was louder now, and colour blazed on his cheeks.

'Please listen to me.' Agnes tried to keep her voice calm.

One of his feet drummed on the lino floor. 'No. I will not. I will not have it suggested to me that I participate in some half-baked plan to remove one of my patients from the only person who truly cares about her, who truly has her best interests at heart, when that patient needs constant care and attention. The idea that she might leave...' His voice cracked with rage. He stood up. 'The idea that I, as a medical man, might connive in her leaving...' He headed for the door, his steps uneven. He flung the office door open. 'I wish you a good evening. Sister,' he added.

The door stayed swinging on its hinges. She heard the front door slam behind him as he left.

Agnes leant back on her chair and took a deep breath, then another. She held her hand up and watched the trembling of her fingers.

Yes, she thought. Yes, I am frightened of Dr Kitson.

CHAPTER SIXTEEN

'The dead do not praise the Lord; nor all those who go down into silence...'

They chanted the evening psalms. Agnes tried to join her voice with her Sisters in the community chapel, but her breath was shallow in her throat.

'The sorrows of death entangled me, the pains of the grave took hold of me...'

In her mind she could still see the figure of Dr Kitson as he loomed to his feet, still hear the rage of his voice. She glanced across the pews and caught sight of Louisa, who was mouthing the psalm, her eyes tight shut.

'...Hide me, O Lord, under the shadow of your wings, for my deadly enemies surround me...'

What am I going to do? she thought.

After the service, she sat alone in the convent kitchen, leafing through a newspaper.

'Hippo bones older than Roman times,' she read.

She looked up as someone approached, and was relieved

to see Louisa, hesitating by the table.

'Agnes—'

She looked troubled, and Agnes gestured for her to sit down next to her.

'I haven't dared say this out loud to anyone, not anyone at all.' Louisa smoothed her skirt over her knees. 'But I'm going to say it to you and then it'll become true.'

Agnes waited.

Louisa's hands continued to stroke the dark blue fabric. Then she said, 'I'm thinking of going back to the States. There, I've said it.' She faced Agnes, pink-faced with effort.

'You mean…' Agnes hesitated, then said, 'You mean, not as a nun.'

Louisa nodded. 'That's right. As a civilian. I've been wondering about giving up my vocation, as you know, and it's been great working with Vaughan and thinking about other ways of living well without being in community, but whenever I thought about it, all I could see was that I'd be unhappy. I'd be neither one thing nor the other. But now this old friend has emailed me, out of the blue, she's setting up a safe house for women who want to leave street work, in Philadelphia, and that's where my sister lives too, she has a disabled grandson who lives nearby, it would be a great opportunity, he's a lovely boy and I don't see enough of him… And the more I thought about it, the more it all fell into place.'

Agnes listened. Louisa's face seemed to lighten as she imagined her new life.

'I feel I've been carrying a deadweight,' she finished. 'And I feel that now's the time to be brave enough to just put it down.'

'You haven't told anyone else?'

Louisa shook her head.

'So, now you have – how does it feel?'

Louisa considered for a moment, then said, 'It feels even more like the right thing to do. I thought of mentioning it to Vaughan today, but I'm so enjoying working with him, I didn't want to burn my boats. And as he said the other day, he's tired of people letting him down. So I've really got to be sure before I say anything to him.'

Agnes's hands were gripped together in her lap. She ungripped them. 'Dr Kitson—' she began.

Louisa turned to her. 'What about him?'

A gap opened up in front of Agnes, which she was about to fill with words: I don't trust him; I don't like him; he frightens me.

Louisa broke the silence. 'He's been really helpful in my thinking. Not directly, but he said the other day that he thought that sometimes people search out a God to replace the father that they never had, and I've been thinking about this ever since, because it's true, my father was not a great presence in my life, and I think I fell too easily into a simplistic relationship with God, a childlike one, you might say.' She smiled. 'I don't think he meant to be insulting, it was just a passing comment but it touched a chord with me.'

'Are you going to tell our provincial, then?'

'Oh, dear.' Louisa puckered her lips. 'Then it really will be true, won't it? I think I'll carry on saying nothing to anyone for a while longer yet.' She stood up. 'Thank you for listening. It was important to see what it sounded like out loud.'

'Well, I won't tell a soul.'

'You'd better not.' Louisa wagged a finger at her, and then was gone.

* * *

The convent kitchen was quiet, with only the electric hum of the fridge, the whine of the fluorescent light; but Agnes was aware of a darker pulse, a beating tremor of anxiety.

What am I going to do? The question circled in her mind.

The ringing of her phone made her jump; seeing Brett's number displayed made her even more tense.

'Hello – Agnes?'

'Hello Brett.'

She heard him pause, then he said, 'How are you?'

'I've been better,' she said.

'Not more ambulances, I hope.'

'No,' she said, 'not since last time.'

He was silent, and she could hear music in the background. 'Where are you?' she said.

'The thing is—' He paused again, and Agnes thought she could hear a woman's voice. 'The thing is...we wondered...I wondered, whether you could meet up with me. I mean, us.'

'You and Georgie?' Agnes heard herself ask.

'Yes. Me and Georgie.'

'Why?'

She heard him breathe, then he said, 'I guess I've kind of come to the end of the road with your father's quest. And the truth is, I feel really bad about that.'

'Oh.'

He said nothing.

'But what about the fossils?' Her question sounded empty to her. 'What about all those exciting results from the labs?'

'Well, yes,' he said. 'That's the other thing, the guys in the lab were on to me this morning – in the end, there were no surprises. They've done all the tests. As far as the fossils are concerned, it's all pretty inconclusive. It's true that the seeds and things seem to indicate that they all originated from somewhere in the Middle East, but without knowing exactly how they were all recovered, and where, we can't prove a thing. All we had, in the end, was a very old piece of wood and a couple of fossilised shells of indeterminate age. And in the end, they're probably exactly what they look like. Just ordinary Jurassic stuff.' He gave a heavy sigh. 'And what else did we expect? I'm a scientist. The beliefs that your father held with such conviction, I can't share in that. I've honoured his memory as best as I can, which isn't much. And now we're sitting here with all the rest of his stuff, and Georgie thinks that at least if you have it, I'll have done what I can—' he broke off, and Agnes could hear muttering in the background. 'She says that's not exactly what she meant. Anyway, if you came and met us, you could take it all away.'

Agnes felt a heaviness in her limbs. 'Where are you?' she said.

'At the hotel.'

No, she wanted to say. No, I don't want any more fossils and notebooks and jottings and memories...

'What will happen if I don't take it all away?' she said.

There was another pause, another murmured consultation. Then he said, 'Please. At least meet us. You can decide then.'

Agnes looked up at the darkened windows. She could hear a distant bell chime the hour.

'I can call you a cab.' he was saying.

'It's all right.' Agnes stood up, gathered up her coat. 'I'll find you in the bar. Half an hour?'

'Half an hour,' he agreed. 'Thank you,' he added. 'I appreciate it.'

*　*　*

The hotel's revolving door transported her from the damp autumnal night to a spring-like explosion of red and yellow tulips. Agnes looked towards the bar. Brett waved to her from the same place as before. As she approached his table, she was aware of his companion; auburn-haired, snub-nosed and green-eyed, draped softly in a floral shirt, she was sitting on the long leather bench. In front of her stood a cocktail glass containing clear liquid and a green olive.

The young woman put out a hand. 'I'm Georgie,' she said. 'I've heard so much about you.'

'Oh.' Agnes took the hand she offered her. 'I'm used to anonymity,' she said, and Georgie smiled.

Brett got to his feet. 'Single malt? Or something else?'

'Actually—' Agnes met his eyes. He looked tired, older somehow, and she realised she was very glad to see him again. 'I'm starving,' she said.

Georgie laughed. 'I told him we should invite you to dinner,' she said. 'But he wouldn't have it. I think he's scared of you.'

'Crisps,' Agnes said. 'Nuts or something.' She glanced down at Georgie, who had stretched out her legs on the leather bench. She was wearing high-heeled strappy sandals in patent navy leather with diamante buckles.

'And a glass of dry white wine, please.' She settled down next to Georgie as Brett went to the bar. 'I can't believe he's scared of me,' she said to her.

'Oh, he is. He said you saw into his soul.'

'Oh, nonsense.'

'No, really.' Georgie clasped her hands around her blue-denimed knees. 'He said that you could see that he was lost, and that chasing me halfway across the world, and using your dad as an excuse, was just a way of delaying finding himself.'

'Well, I suppose I did say something of the sort. I'm not sure about the finding himself bit...'

'There you are then.' Georgie stretched out her legs again and wiggled her pink-painted toes.

'Nice shoes,' Agnes said. 'My friend Athena would love those.'

Georgie leant towards her. 'They're Jimmy Choo but I got them from a warehouse sale – such a bargain, you wouldn't believe it.' She looked up as Brett returned with a tray.

He distributed drinks, handed Agnes a dish of olives, passed a bowl of nuts to Georgie.

Georgie ignored the nuts but speared her cocktail olive and popped it in her mouth.

'So—' Agnes turned to him. 'How much more stuff is there?'

He leant down to his chair and produced a large carrier bag and a cardboard box roughly tied with string.

'This – the bag – is the rest of his writings. And this box is the rest of the fossils. There's some bones – mostly animal. Apart from this.' He passed her a cardboard box. She lifted the lid and peeped into it.

'A skull?'

'Probably brought back from his travels by some colonial treasure hunter.'

'I can't have a skull in my room.' Agnes tried to keep her voice low. 'It ought to be buried.' Agnes had closed the box and now sat with it, her arm across the lid.

'Yes, but by whom? Where? All the connections to anything are lost.'

'And what on earth do you want me to do with it? Give it a full Catholic service?'

Brett turned to Georgie. 'You see – that's exactly what I said she'd say.'

Georgie sighed. She turned to Agnes. 'I'm sorry. It was my idea. Brett was getting more and more neurotic with all this, I didn't know what else to do. You're right. We'll take it all away again.'

Georgie looked like a child in her disappointment. Brett was gazing absently away, towards the hotel foyer. Agnes felt suddenly cross with him, protective towards Georgie, whom she now addressed directly. 'I'll take it all. He was my father. It's still my legacy. Signing up for religious orders didn't mean absolving myself of responsibility for my past.'

'Worse luck,' Georgie said, and they both laughed.

He looked from one to the other, frowning, then stood up. 'Will you ladies excuse me – I have to make a call.' He wandered off towards the foyer.

'Well,' Agnes said. She took a handful of nuts.

'He drives me mad.' Georgie's gaze followed him. 'He's never honest. That call could be anyone. His spymaster. MI6. The CIA. He's so secretive. And then he wonders why I don't want to commit to him.'

Agnes picked up her glass. 'Another woman?'

Georgie shook her head. 'No. Oddly, that's the one thing I don't think he's lying about. But that's why I keep trying to keep a distance from him. Sometimes I think he really is the man I want to spend the rest of my life with, but then he'll do something evasive, something secretive again, and I have to keep my distance just to rescue myself. If he can't be honest with himself, how can he be honest with me? As you said.'

'He's lying to me too,' Agnes said. 'He's withholding something.'

'What I don't understand is why he didn't mind when you said it, but he hates it when I do.'

'Because you're gorgeous and a dancer and someone he wants, whereas I'm just a nun.'

Georgie looked at her. 'Don't say "just".' She held her gaze, then said, 'Come to my show. Next week. Here.' She scrabbled in her handbag and produced a flyer. 'It opens on Thursday. Phone the company manager, he'll arrange it, lovely Adrian will.'

Brett was striding back into the bar. He smiled at them both. 'Had to talk to my seminar group leader. He wanted a different time tomorrow.'

Agnes stood up. 'I'd better go.'

'This time you must let me find you a cab. With all—' he waved his hand towards the cardboard box.

'OK. This time.' She turned to Georgie. 'See you next week.'

'Looking forward to it.'

The wind was getting up. Clouds scudded across the night sky. There was no sign of a taxi.

They waited by the pillars, in the pool of warm light.

'She's nice, Georgie.'

'Yes.' He glanced back towards the hotel door.

'Brett – what is it you're not telling me?'

'Nothing.' She watched his familiar veiled expression.

'It's about my father, isn't it?'

'I've told you all I know.'

'Would Monica know more?'

He looked down at her, as a lone taxi approached, braking loudly. 'I've no idea,' he said. He opened the car door for her, handed her the box. 'If all this is too much for you, just get rid of it,' he said. 'At least I know I've done what I can.'

The door slammed, the taxi pulled out. He was hidden from view behind a pillar, and Agnes couldn't tell whether he was waving or not.

She settled at her desk with a cheese sandwich and a cup of hot chocolate. She glanced through the carrier bag. More notebooks; more of the same, she thought, from a rough glance.

She untied the string on the box and peeped at the skull. It looked polished, like ivory. It had markings on it, lines, fragments of writing in black ink, single words; a list of names. Reuben, Simeon, Levi, Judah...

She closed the box. She wondered whether she'd feel differently if someone told her it really was ivory, rather than human.

She wondered who had owned it when it was alive. She imagined a corpse, buried, headless. Somewhere there is the true story, she thought: an attack, vengeful and bloody. Or a quiet death, followed by a silent theft. And then, there is the story that my father made of it. Whoever owned these bones couldn't possibly have known that they would end up as part of another story, my father's thesis of creation.

She placed the box on her desk. *Memento mori*, she thought. Remember you must die.

Memento mori. She felt once again Pauline's fingers in her own, heard her whispered words, 'You've saved my life.'

The box cast a shadow on her desk. She felt her fear return. She grabbed her phone, dialled Julius's number.

'It's me,' she said. 'We must get her away. Pauline.

Tomorrow. Can you tell Gustave to expect her?'

'Oh. Well, the thing is, it's all the red tape...'

'Julius, she'll die from rage if she stays there.'

'Yes. I can see that. The problem is, either her husband or her GP has got to sign that form thing. I've checked with Gustave.'

'He refuses. Dr Kitson. I asked him. He went into a rage, went on about Jeremy being the best person to look after her. Julius...' Her voice cracked as she tried not to cry.

'Agnes, what is it?'

'Julius – I'm scared.'

'Of what?' She heard the concern in his voice, blinked back her tears.

'Dr Kitson. There's something wrong. All his patients die. There's methadone, or something, it's all wrong, and today he shouted at me, he got kind of angry in a really odd way...'

She heard Julius listening. Then he said, 'I tried your phone earlier. You didn't answer.'

She glanced at the phone. 'I can't have heard it,' she said.

'Where were you?'

'I was with Brett. He's given me all my father's things. It's as if he's signed them all away to me. Something's changed. He's finished with it all.'

'And you've got all that stuff now?'

'Yes.' She looked at the bag on her floor, the pile of notebooks. 'Yes,' she repeated.

'Agnes, it's bad for you. What have you got, fossils? Bones?'

'A skull,' she said.

'Human? No wonder you're worrying about mortality. He had no right to dump all that on you. I've a good mind to punch him on the nose. After all you've done, escaping from your upbringing, and this busybodying American comes blundering into your life and leaves you weighed down with all the rubbish...'

The tears receded. 'Julius—'

'Well, really. If he knew you as I do, he'd see that there was a risk of doing you terrible harm. Put all that nonsense of your father's into a bin bag and I'll take care of it.'

'Oh.'

'You can't have a skull sitting on your desk.'

'No. You're right. It has various Hebrew names written on it. The sons of Jacob...'

'I don't care.'

She listened to his silence, looked at the cardboard box on her table. 'But—'

'But what?'

'What about Pauline?'

'Oh. Pauline. Shall we kidnap her?'

She smiled at the phone.

'I'm serious,' Julius went on. 'Gustave has a place for her, we know that. First thing tomorrow, you borrow your Order's car, go and fetch her, meet me back here and we'll go on to Gustave from here.'

'Are you sure?'

'What else can we do? I'm not having you feeling tearful and defeated. If I'm not allowed to punch presumptuous Americans on the nose, at least I can do something useful. See you tomorrow.'

'OK.' She clicked off her phone. The tears returned, but the fear had disappeared.

* * *

She was woken by the sound of rain, beating against the window. The sky was pale with the dawn. The community was busy and silent, preparing itself for early chapel. She found Sister Helen in the kitchen, and after a whispered conversation, Helen brought her the keys to the community car. They jangled in her pocket as she filed into chapel for lauds.

'Let the rivers clap their hands, and let the hills ring out with joy before the Lord, when he comes to judge the earth...'

It will be all right, she thought. Today, everything will be all right.

She got into the Community's VW Polo. It still had the dent at the back where Sister Thomasina had collided with a bollard in the supermarket car park. Her recent letter from the Order's house in Nurnberg had expressed bewilderment that she wasn't allowed to drive, something about permits, the sisters here are most insistent...

Agnes drove east, then south. The noise of the city was muffled by the rhythm of the windscreen wipers. She put on the radio:

'Police in Shropshire have arrested a man in connection with the disappearance of a Ludlow woman twenty-five years ago...'

She switched it off again.

At last she was on Streatham High Road; at last she was taking the road towards the Stipes's, turning left into their street, wondering how close to get, wondering in fact what on earth she was going to do, how to just walk in and take Pauline away, particularly as the street seemed full of cars and there didn't seem to be space anywhere, let alone near the Stipes's which was most clogged of all; not just cars but police cars and an ambulance too...

Agnes was aware of her heartbeat loud in her ears, of someone flagging her car down, indicating that she could go no further.

She stumbled out of the car, leaving the door open, a rising sickness, a sense of panic as she went towards the activity in front of her, someone trying to restrain her, calling after her; a man in uniform, shouting, 'Madam, you can't go that way—'

'Pauline Stipes,' she was saying, out loud, as if somehow that would fight a path through the noise and chaos. 'I'm a nun,' she tried, finding her way barred by people and cars. 'Mrs Stipes!' she shouted, as someone put his hand heavily on her shoulder. Her walking stopped mid-pace.

'You know her?' the voice was saying, a young, uniformed police officer, dark-skinned and boyish.

'She's expecting me,' Agnes lied.

'Could you come this way, Madam?' the young man said and led her towards a dark blue car. An older man was standing beside it, and the younger man spoke to him. 'She says she's a nun,' Agnes heard, 'she says she was expecting her...'

The house was taped off. Neighbours gawped from windows. Across the road, a woman in a nightdress was sitting on her front wall, talking on a mobile phone. The hydrangea bush was barely visible behind all the busyness, all the people, some in uniform.

It was as if she was at the centre of the noise, which came and went in waves. She tried to think, tried to block out the din. She looked up at the house. She could see a figure standing at an upper window, outlined like a shadow. He was smoking a cigarette, staring down blank-faced at the street below.

CHAPTER SEVENTEEN

'Streatham?' Rob Coombes's voice was loud on the phone. 'Yes, I'd heard. Not my patch, though.'

'But... Couldn't you find out?' Agnes tried not to shout into her mobile.

'I'm sure the lads there are dealing with it. I'm sure they'll be happy to answer your questions when it all settles down a bit.'

Across the hostel office, rain streamed in rivulets down the windowpane. 'It's just –' she began, then stopped.

'We're checking Murchison's alibi – if only our friend Kavin hadn't been swearing blind he was with him. But we're on to it, should be able to haul him in soon.'

Murchison. 'But it's another—' Agnes said.

'Did you say something?'

'It's another. Pauline Stipes. Abbie. Dermot...'

'Can't hear you,' he said. 'It's right busy here. Call me later, will you? Be good to catch up.'

'They've taken her husband in for questioning,' she said.

'Routine, in these cases. Sudden death of spouse. He'll be

out soon. She was ill, wasn't she? Unless there's a will worth a fortune. Give me a ring later on.'

She wandered into the kitchen. Aysha was there. 'Have you seen Dr Kitson?' she asked.

'No. We called his practice about Bex's prescription, but he never got back to us.' Aysha continued to stack ready meals into the freezer.

She went into the office, dialled the community house, asked to speak to Sister Louisa.

'Hi, Agnes—'

'Louisa – have you seen Dr Kitson?'

'Not since yesterday. But he's with his brother, he's not due back with the project till tomorrow. Is there a problem?'

Agnes settled her voice. 'No. Not at all. See you soon.'

She hung up, sat by the phone. For a while she watched the rain beating against the windows. Then she picked up her bag and left. She stood on the hostel steps, trying to open her umbrella, fiddling with the catch. Someone was calling her name, and she looked down to see Lindy, waving at her through the rain, followed by a taller, shaggy-haired figure.

Agnes descended the steps. 'Hi,' she said.

'I've brought him,' Lindy said. 'Connor.' She turned round, beckoned him forward. He shuffled towards her, mumbling. He had bad skin and the young fluff of a beard.

'Hello,' Agnes said.

'We need to talk to you.' Lindy glanced around them. 'But not here.'

Agnes pushed open the door of the Mercury Café on Borough High Street, aware of a sudden hunger for bacon. She sat them at a table tucked away in a corner and ordered three full cooked breakfasts and three mugs of tea. Connor spooned several spoonfuls of sugar into his mug. Agnes looked at the odd blade of straw sticking out of his hair and wondered where he'd been hiding out.

'So—' Agnes began. 'You're Dermot's cousin?'

Connor nodded, his mouth full of toast.

'Did you know each other in Ireland?'

Connor shook his head. 'Never met him till I came to London.'

Lindy leant forward. 'Dermot never lived in Ireland, did he?'

Connor glanced at her, then back at Agnes. A silence fell. Their food arrived, brought by a wispy, waif-like girl who looked at each plate as she put it down with an expression of disbelief, before fleeing back to the kitchen. Agnes watched Connor as he layered thick margarine on to his toast.

'So—' Agnes looked from one to the other. 'What did you want to talk to me about?'

Lindy looked at Connor. Connor speared a piece of bacon, chewed it slowly. 'Go on,' she said.

He finished his mouthful.

'It's about Murchie,' Lindy said. He looked at Lindy, and she nodded at him. 'Go on, tell her,' she said.

He leant towards Agnes. 'I told the feds that I were with Murchie when Dermot was...you know... But I weren't. I were that scared of Murch, I did what he said. But I weren't with him, I wasn't even in these ends, was I?' He looked up at Lindy, then back to Agnes. 'She said I should tell you, so here I am, and I'm telling you.' His voice was very low.

'So—' Agnes met his eyes. 'You're Murchie's only alibi?'

He nodded, staring at the table.

'Have you told the police?'

Connor managed a smile. 'What would I do that for?'

'No one's going to grass to the feds about Murchie, are they?' Lindy pushed her bacon to the side of her plate.

Agnes picked up her mug of tea. 'So, if I tell the police…?'

They flashed a look at each other. 'Just don't say it were us,' Lindy said.

Agnes sliced a mushroom in two. She thought about Dermot's last days, last hours; the bruised, sleepy face, the complaints about his medication. She recalled Murchie, handing her his phone: 'It's 999,' he'd said.

I could have had him arrested then, she thought. She turned to Connor. 'Did you get on with Dermot?'

Again, a sideways look at Lindy. Then he said, 'I tried to look after him. He was only a kid. When I came over from Mayo, made contact with him…' His voice tailed off, his gaze fixed on the distance. He blinked, looked down at the table, took a sip of tea. 'I liked him, though. Family, he was.'

'He was difficult to like,' Lindy said.

'Not when you got to know him.'

'So—' Agnes began. 'You think Murchie was with him the night that he died?'

'Man, I know he was.' Connor leant towards her across the table. 'Mots had a deal with Murchie. He was trying to get out of it. That's what the beating was, a warning. No one messes with Murchie. So, he was locked into the deal. And the night he died, he'd come to see me, and we talked it over. About him getting out. I warned him, I tried to make him see, but he weren't having it. So then he went to see Murchie about getting out of the deal.'

'What kind of deal was it?'

Connor glanced at Lindy. Lindy nodded at him. He turned back to Agnes. 'Heroin.'

'And he was trying to get out of it.'

Connor nodded. 'That's all I know. He left me that evening, and then I came over to yours, didn't I?' he turned briefly to Lindy. 'And it was after that that…' He stopped. He picked up his mug, gulped some tea, put it down again. 'Later that night, I've got Murchie on the phone saying he was with me that night. It's happened before. I know what it means. So, I said, OK.'

'And now you've changed your mind?' Agnes saw the tears well at the corner of his eyes. He nodded.

'Why?' she said.

He stared at his plate.

'Family, innit?' Lindy smiled at him, but he ignored her. 'Cousins, see,' she went on. 'Dermot comes from a family of hard men, but Connor's side is just as hard. Didn't you say, Con, where your mum comes from, they'll kill you and then leave flowers on your grave?' She laughed.

He looked at her. 'It's not like that,' he said.

'Yes it is. You kept going on about it. Dermot being cousins with you.'

'That's not the point,' he said. His voice was harsh.

Lindy shrugged. 'Blood thicker than water—'

Connor nudged her, hard. 'That's enough.' He took a last mouthful of baked beans.

Lindy pushed a piece of toast around her plate. 'He's going to go on about his mum now.'

'I said, that's enough,' Connor hissed at her.

'His mum was perfect, you know?' Lindy went on. 'Raised him on her own, over in Ireland, never wanted for anything, did you? And on her deathbed, she sent him over here to make his fortune. And all he's done is hang around with a load of drug-dealing gangsters. What would she say, eh? Ow!' Lindy's words were cut short as Connor slapped her face.

'I told you, girl, that's enough.' He stood up.

His plate was wiped clean. 'Thanks for the breakfast,' he said to Agnes. He threw a look towards Lindy, and she stood up too. Agnes was on her feet, her fingers gripping Lindy's arm. She turned to Connor.

'What?' He faced her.

In the silence, Lindy shook herself free.

Connor turned on his heel and walked towards the café door. Lindy gave a thin smile, then followed Connor out of the café.

Agnes sat back at the table. She sipped her cold tea. She knew she had to phone Rob Coombes, and she knew what she would say.

'So your nice policeman was relieved, was he?' Julius fumbled in the cupboard in the corner of his office. 'I know they're here somewhere,' he said. 'Mrs O'Leary gave them to me. Ah, here we are...' He came over to the desk. 'Oatcakes. She says they'll lower my cholesterol.'

'I'm not hungry.' Agnes pushed away the plate he put in front of her.

'Not hungry?' Julius sat down in his chair. He took an oatcake from the packet, and studied it. 'Something up?' He looked across at her.

'I don't know.' A brief burst of afternoon sunlight filtered through the window above. She frowned at the heap of papers on his desk. Inquisition Revisited, she read. The New Catholic Voice.

'Surely if this chap's a bad 'un, and the police now know that his alibi was false, then everything's a lot more straightforward, isn't it? We know that poor boy in your hostel was stabbed, and now they can prove it was this Murchie character who did it.'

Agnes looked up. Julius's face was tinged with concern. 'Yes,' she said. 'That's roughly what my nice policeman said.'

'Well then.' He held the packet out to her. 'Oatcake? After all?'

She looked at him and laughed. 'And I've just eaten one and a half full English breakfasts at the Mercury.'

'Ah. Well, then. Perhaps not.'

'Rob said that Jeremy had been questioned and released.'

'How does he know?'

'I asked him. He'd phoned the boys in Streatham, as he put it.'

'Yes.' Julius nibbled on his oatcake.

'You knew?'

He met her eyes. 'I – I've been helping him to hide.'

'Jeremy?'

'He came here. Earlier on. He said he couldn't go back to his house, it's surrounded by press, apparently. So – he's at my place.'

'Your place?'

Agnes stared at him. Julius had lived alone as long as she'd known him, and even though the house that he was provided with by the church was large, he'd never even had a housekeeper. He always maintained that he liked cleaning. The garden was looked after by various parishioners, mostly elderly women. Agnes felt that they pottered in Julius's garden, doing 'a bit of weeding', just to have an excuse to spy on him.

'There are enough empty rooms,' Julius said. 'And he's in rather a bad way. I said I'd look in on him before midday Mass. You coming with me?'

He stood up and gathered up his keys. She followed him out of the church, down the side alley that led to the vicarage.

It was a double-fronted, red-brick house, which surveyed the street in front of it with a puzzled hauteur, as if accustomed to looking out on to green fields and surprised to find these tower blocks spoiling its view.

The red paint on the front door was peeling. Agnes wished that the busybody parishioners had more skills than a bit of weeding. 'Perhaps you could find some nice young Polish people,' she said, but Julius had already opened the door, and was standing in the shadows of the hall. The angle of the thick walls seemed to prevent daylight from intruding. There was a smell of damp.

'Jeremy?' he called.

From upstairs came the sound of a door opening.

'It's me. Father Julius.'

There were footsteps above them. 'Oh.' Agnes heard Jeremy's voice. 'It's you.' The footsteps began to descend the stairs, then stopped. 'And you,' Jeremy added, seeing Agnes. He turned to Julius. 'Why did you bring her? She's the cause of it all—' His face grew red, and his arms flapped at his sides.

'Never mind that.' Julius took a step towards him and began to lead him down the stairs, his grip firm on his arm. 'The point is, we both want to help and at the moment we're the only help you've got.'

'But – but—' Jeremy still stared at Agnes. Julius steered him past her and led him into the sitting room.

Here there was sunlight, falling fitfully across the bare wood floor. The walls were painted a bright salmon pink, as if the church authorities had managed to find a job lot of paint and thought that it would do. Jeremy flopped into an armchair and put his hand across his eyes. Julius and Agnes sat down too. Through the silence, Agnes could hear faint fragments of music, someone singing, a female voice, phrases here and there, repeating.

After a while, Jeremy raised his head. 'I can't believe she's gone.' He stared from one to the other. 'I simply can't believe it.' He looked as if he was waiting for them to tell him that it wasn't true, it was all a mistake, Pauline was alive and waiting for him back home…

Julius was the first to speak. 'She had been very ill.' His voice was quiet in the room. Agnes could hear the soprano trilling above the low traffic rumble.

Jeremy spoke with great effort. 'Yes,' he said. 'She was very ill. She was getting worse.'

'So, finding that she'd died…' Julius prompted.

'Not yet.' Jeremy's hands moved in his lap, his fingers entwined. 'That was what I told myself. She wouldn't go yet.'

'But—' Julius looked at him. 'It's not as if you could control it.'

'But I could.' His hands twisted together, round and round. 'I always said, it was my promise to her, when things got so bad, I would help her go.'

Agnes glanced at Julius. Julius went on, 'So, things hadn't got that bad, then?'

'Oh, no.' Jeremy leant back in his chair. 'Not at all. She was getting better. I told her, you're getting better, love, you're on the mend. Even Dr Kitson says so.'

Agnes thought of Pauline hearing this news from her husband. She reached for Julius's hand, glad that he was here, glad not to be facing Jeremy alone. Jeremy addressed Julius again. 'I know all about death.' His voice was louder now, harsh against the bare walls. 'I watched mum go through it. So I knew, when I married Pauline, I knew I was safe. Even the first time, with her illness, I knew it would be all right. So, when they told me that it had come back...' His voice faltered. He glanced at Agnes, then back to Julius. 'I knew it was up to me to make it all right. Dr Kitson understood, you see. He knows what it's like, and he knew it was the most important thing, to make it all right again. That's why I knew she wouldn't die, I knew she couldn't, not until the end...' His words stopped, choked. His eyes reddened. He put his hand to his forehead.

To make it all right again. Agnes heard the echo of Dr Kitson's words: They rely on me to make it all right again. She wrapped her arms around her against the chill of the room.

Jeremy leant towards them. 'It makes no sense. Can't you see? I knew when she'd die, I had the medicine ready, she trusted me to make it all right, she needed us both to make it all right for her. Not this...'

'Jeremy.' Julius held his gaze. 'Are you really saying you had contemplated killing her?'

Jeremy blinked at him. 'Of course.'

'And you'd discussed this with her?' Julius went on.

'Oh yes. I promised her she wouldn't suffer.'

Agnes's fingers tightened as she recalled the urgency of Pauline's grip at her last visit, her terror at having to stay in her husband's home. I told her I'd rescue her, Agnes thought. And I failed.

'Did you love her?' Agnes hadn't meant to speak out loud.

Jeremy's gaze flashed in her direction. 'What?'

'I said, did you love her?'

The singing outside faded to silence. Jeremy's hands twitched in his lap. 'She was my wife,' he said at last. 'Of course I loved her.'

'Enough to kill her?' Agnes was aware of Julius's warning glance.

'If necessary, yes.' Jeremy's gaze was steady now.

'And is that really love?'

'Yes. I would assert that it is.' His voice was clipped. 'Far better that someone chooses the moment of their going, than that they linger, in pain, causing suffering to others as well as to themselves...'

'To others?' Agnes said.

'You don't know what it's like...'

'Your mother, you mean?'

He glanced at her, then down at his hands. 'My mother suffered, yes.' His tone was muted now. 'I resolved then, that no one else should suffer as she did.'

'As you did, you mean.'

He shot her a glance. 'What are you implying?'

'All she means—' Julius cut in. 'What concerns us both,' he went on, 'is that all this talk of helping her to die won't serve your cause one bit if the police get to hear of it.'

Jeremy seemed to wilt in his chair. 'Police?'

'Assisted death is illegal in this country,' Julius said. Agnes thought he added a murmured 'thank God', but she couldn't be sure.

'I'm aware of that.' Jeremy frowned at him. 'But I didn't do anything. That's what I've been trying to tell you. My wife's death, it doesn't make sense. I found her, dead, the syringe was in her hand, the one I'd told her about so that she wouldn't be frightened when the end came… I didn't mean that she should do it herself, if I'd thought she was thinking that way I'd have hidden it from her…' He shook his head, his eyes moist.

'So—' Julius spoke again. 'You're saying that she did it herself?'

He looked up at them both, with a blank expression. 'Of course.' His gaze flicked from Agnes back to Julius. 'Of course,' he repeated. 'What else would anyone think?'

Julius breathed, then said, 'The police will want to question you.'

'But they already have. They were very kind. I don't know how they got there, I called an ambulance and then they all turned up too. I suppose it's routine in these cases, can't be too careful, can you…?' He looked at Agnes again, then back to Julius. 'But they can't possibly think…'

Julius appeared to be studying the rather dusty floor.

'I told them everything I knew,' Jeremy went on. 'I told them about the syringe, they wanted to know where it had come from. They'll know I've got nothing to hide.'

'You told them about the syringe?' Julius stared at him.

Jeremy nodded. 'I had to. My wife was holding it when I found her. They were very understanding.'

'Oh.' Julius stared at the floor again. 'Oh dear.'

A quiet descended on the room. Faintly, the trilling began again, a series of arpeggios up and down a scale. Agnes allowed her thoughts to follow the pattern, four notes up, three down, then again a note higher. 'C' major; 'D' major.

She tried to imagine Pauline's last hours; a lethal injection, it appeared; a syringe clasped between her fingers.

'E' major. The soprano voice rose higher.

Pauline did not want to die.

Agnes turned to Jeremy. 'Are you sure that your wife would have known what was in this syringe?'

'Oh yes, we'd talked it through often enough.'

'Might she not have mistaken it for something else – for pain relief, perhaps, rather than something lethal?'

'I don't see why she would think that. When Dr Kitson prescribed it for us, he made it perfectly clear.'

Agnes felt her breath catch in her throat. 'Dr Kitson?'

'Yes. He was very understanding.' Jeremy leant forward conversationally. 'He's a very good doctor, you know.'

'When?' Agnes tried to keep her voice level. 'When did you talk about all this?'

'Oh, it must have been...' Jeremy paused to consider. 'About three months ago, I suppose. Pauline had had a bad day, and I was at my wits end, and he happened to pop by. And I confided in him, and he said, "You don't have to worry." Those were his words. He said, carers like me have enough to worry about, and he saw it as part of his job to take on the fear, about what would happen at the end if it all got too much. He said he understood, he'd been through something similar himself.' Jeremy allowed himself a brief smile at the memory. 'He was quite tearful, in fact. Anyway, after that I felt I could trust him with anything. We became quite close.'

Three months ago. But when I met Pauline, barely ten days ago, she was well, and optimistic, and talking about a future. A future without her husband.

Julius broke the silence. 'Did you – did you share these thoughts with your wife?'

'Oh yes. We discussed it. I wanted her to know that she didn't have to worry if it all got too much.

'So, she knew where the syringe was?'

'Yes. It was just in the cabinet, with her other pills.' He looked at Julius, his face tight with anxiety. 'I told you – I told you both – I've got nothing to hide.'

The final arpeggio hit top 'G' and then scrambled down again. There was silence. Jeremy stared at the floor, his hands now motionless. Agnes stood up. 'I think I should go,' she said.

Julius followed her out into the hall. In the damp darkness she whispered, 'He can't stay here.'

'He can't go home,' Julius whispered back.

'They're bound to arrest him.'

Julius's eyes were a flash of blue in the dim light. 'Do you think he killed her?'

'All I know is...' Agnes lowered her voice still further, '...the Pauline I knew wouldn't have killed herself.'

'Even if—' Julius's words were barely audible. 'Even if the alternative was staying with him?'

Agnes breathed in the stale air. 'She thought we were going to rescue her.'

Julius was silent at the truth of this.

Agnes patted his arm. 'I'll ring you tomorrow. And when this nightmare is over, I'll help you apply to the diocese for funding to do this place up.'

'You'll get nowhere. It's part of the job description; poverty, chastity, and enforced lack of taste.' Julius went to the door to open it for her. A wash of afternoon sunlight flooded in, turning the dust to glitter.

'At least it has potential.' Agnes leant up and kissed his cheek. 'Good luck with your house guest.'

'I might be busy in my office this evening,' Julius whispered in reply.

Agnes made her way slowly towards the main road. The singer had returned to her practice, and Mozart's highest notes sliced through the soft pink sunset, then faded out altogether as Agnes reached the main road and headed for the Embankment. Across the river, the City skyline made fairy-tale shapes against the rainbow sky. She paused, aware of the beauty of the evening, the gentle lapping of the Thames; but all she could feel was a vice-like terror, like the grip of pale fingers on a syringe.

CHAPTER EIGHTEEN

'Well, frankly, I'm very glad I phoned you. The thought of you spending the rest of the evening alone, with all these terrible thoughts...' Athena raised a glass of rosé wine.

Agnes clinked her glass with Athena's. 'I'm glad you phoned me too. Otherwise I'd be sitting in my flat, with only my father's old bones for company.'

'Bones?' Athena's eyes widened. They were sitting at a low table in a bar. The evening was clear and cool; through the window, straggling city workers headed for the tube, or to the bars on the Embankment.

'Only some old relic that he'd collected, and that Brett has now passed on to me.'

'Well, that's not very nice, is it?' Athena huffed in indignation. She was wearing a fuchsia pink jacket with large buttons, and lipstick to match.

'He seems to have run out of steam. I met his nice dancer last night.'

'And?'

Agnes looked at Athena's expression of eager curiosity and smiled.

'That's better.' Athena smiled back. 'I hate to see you so bogged down when it's all other people's problems. So, this dancer?'

'She's very pretty. And very nice.'

'And?'

'You mean, him?'

'Uh-huh.'

'I think she's trying to give him a chance. And I think he's failing to take it.'

Athena sipped her wine. 'It never does to be that subtle where men are concerned. It's like Nic at the moment – here I am, on my own for yet another evening, while he has yet another meeting to sort out his business, and if he's not doing that he's down with his mother, or on the phone to various people trying to sort out her care, and when anyone asks her all she says is that if they move her from her home it'll be the end of her, which is hardly helpful, is it?' She broke off to take another sip of wine. 'All of which means that even if I wanted to talk about weddings, I wouldn't get a word in edgeways.'

'Even if you wanted to?'

Athena put her glass of wine down on the elegant glass surface. 'Well, of course, sweetie, it's not as if I'm that bothered. Luckily.'

'What's happened?'

'Did I tell you he calls his ex-wife Mack? What kind of name is that for a woman? Some old nickname apparently.'

'And?'

'Oh, it's fine. I mean, even if she is trying to scupper any possibility of me and Nic getting married, it really doesn't matter seeing as I don't even want to...'

'She is?'

'The other night Nic said how impressed he was with the way she lives her life. She has some kind of long-term partner, apparently, but as she said, according to him, "it's so much better without anything contractual between us" or something. Silly cow, it's obvious what she's up to. And then Nic comes home and goes on about how well she's aged.'

'Bloody cheek.'

'I know. He just can't see through her. He never has been able to. Still, at least I don't want to get married. So that's OK.'

'Mmm.'

Athena topped up their glasses. 'Do you know, I found this fab venue in Hampshire, it just turned up when I was just messing about on the internet, it's an old castle, absolutely beautiful, and it turns out it's licensed to do weddings. Isn't that extraordinary? Part of the building is Elizabethan, absolutely gorgeous...' Athena looked up at her. 'Still, as I say, just as well I have no wish to get married. Perhaps I'll hire it for a big birthday party one day. What do you think?'

'As long as you invite me.'

'Goes without saying. I'll tell Nic. That's the answer. I'll say, let's organise a party for a big birthday. You just have to be clear with them, don't you? It's like your chap's poor dancer – there's no point "giving him a chance" if you don't spell it out to him loud and clear, saying, for example, you're bloody lucky to have me and unless you start treating me as the absolute catch that I so clearly am, I'm going to run off and find someone who will.' She looked up at Agnes. 'I've learnt from experience. It's the only language they understand.'

Agnes laughed, and for a moment everything returned to normal, as if life could be just this, sitting in a bar on a cool autumn evening, drinking rather good wine, laughing with Athena. But then the clouds drew in again, and the space around her seemed to shrink once more.

'Sweetie.' Athena looked concerned. 'What is it?'

Agnes shook her head. 'As you said – other people's problems.'

'Yes, but knowing you, they've become yours. I mean, as you say, this woman was dying anyway, but as you'd intended to rescue her – you're bound to feel that you've let her down. And as for her ghastly husband hiding out in Julius's house – salmon pink, did you say? How awful. And for Julius, of all people, when he's such a lovely man, he needs tasteful colours, matt surfaces, pale wood, the odd touch of black, chrome too, maybe. Honestly, these religious authorities have a lot to answer for, it's like some of the clothes you'd end up wearing if I didn't rescue you from time to time. And there's poor Julius having to sit in his salmon pink lounge with a possibly murderous husband. He deserves better, he really does.' She topped up their glasses with the rest of the wine. 'So, do you think she was helped on her way, this poor woman?'

Agnes picked up her glass. 'I don't know,' she said.

'It would be awful if she was. If it was her husband. It really is an argument against getting married.'

'They're not all like that.' Agnes took a sip of wine.

Athena looked at her. 'And you're no one to talk either.'

Agnes sighed. 'It's true. What do I know? I'm no judge of character, it turns out.'

'What?' Athena was wide-eyed. 'Of course you are.'

'My husband—'

'Oh, your husband, that's different.' Athena waved pink-varnished nails at her. 'You were a child then.'

'And Jeremy.'

'Jeremy? You mean, this possible wife-murderer?'

Agnes nodded. 'I don't know what to think.'

'Hmmm.' Athena finished her wine.

'It's like Louisa, one of the Sisters. She thinks Dr Kitson is wonderful, and for all I know she might be right, and all my doubts about him are wrong. And there she is saying that her whole vocation as a nun was just running away, and she's thinking of leaving the Order and going back to America. And then I think about Hugo and my lack of judgement, and I think, did I do the same? Did I just run away?'

'Do you really think that, kitten?'

Agnes fiddled with the cuff of her jumper. She noticed it was worn, the black fabric so thin it was beginning to fray.

'I mean, it might have been that way once...'

Athena went on. 'But it seems to me, you've made something good of it all. Not running away after all.'

Agnes looked up at her in surprise. 'Really?'

'Yes. Really. I mean, obviously not my cup of tea at all, but then, here I am sitting here contemplating marriage. If you told me last year that I'd be looking up venues for marriages on the Internet, I'd never have believed you. We can all make excuses. I expect even this murderous husband thinks he can justify his behaviour.'

'His mother was an alcoholic.'

'See? But in the end, we all have to make the best of things, don't we? I could talk about nearly being sold into marriage in my village in Greece and having to run away. You could talk about your violent husband, or the fact that your father was "never there for you", but it seems to me we have better ways of dealing with all this.'

'Like becoming a nun?'

'Or getting married.'

Outside the sky had clouded over. Athena stared into her empty glass. 'Or in my case, not getting married.' She looked up at Agnes. 'We ought to go.'

Outside they scanned the street for a cab. 'So, what are you going to do?'

'About my doubts?'

'I meant about murderous husbands.' Athena raised her hand and a taxi drew up. 'And poor old Julius's ghastly decor.' She turned to Agnes, clapped her hand to her head. 'Of course, darling, why didn't I think of it before? TV makeover shows. It's the obvious answer. He's so cute, they'd be bound to take him on. It would be a ratings winner. Of course, you have to put up with ghastly telly people invading your house, but Julius would be lovely to all of them, and at least it would be free. And at the end of it he'll have a properly decorated house. Even all those mean bishops couldn't object, could they?'

She sat by the window, in the dark, turning her father's relics over in her hand. She picked up the fossil shell. Its pinkish sheen seemed to glow in the dim light. She wondered what her father saw when he looked at it. According to his writings, he saw proof of his own version of creation; he saw what he wanted to see. And I, too, am seeing what I want to see; I see my father choosing to tell a new story, as a way of making up to me for years of absence, years of neglect.

Moonlight glanced off the stone in her hands. She felt afraid. It was a clue, this cold dead chunk of history, and she felt its weight; as if it might reveal its meaning, if she only knew how to look for it.

She imagined her father, too, weighing the fossil in his hands, determined to find the truth in nailing its age. And did it scare him too?

She had a sudden picture in her mind of Louisa, yesterday evening, chatting happily about her future, her sister in Philadelphia: 'I've been carrying a deadweight,' she'd said...

Agnes put the fossil down on her desk. It landed with a heavy clatter. She turned to her prayer book, lit her candle with hands that shook.

'For I have eaten ashes for bread, and mingled my drink with weeping; you have lifted me up and thrown me away. My days pass away like a shadow, and I wither like the grass...'

She felt the brush of Pauline's fingers on her own.

The ringing of her phone brought her blinking into pale daylight. She reached out and answered it.

'Agnes, hi, it's Rob Coombes. Just thought you'd like to know, we've arrested Mr Murchison.'

'Oh. Good.'

'You don't sound so thrilled.'

'No, it's fine.'

'We're having a very useful chat with him about Mr O'Hagan's death.'

Agnes sat up in bed. 'You didn't mention Connor, did you?'

'Didn't have to. It's high time that lad was hauled in. Thanks for your help, eh?'

'Oh, you're welcome.'

'Take it easy. We'll be in touch.'

Agnes clicked her phone off. She lay back on her pillows.

Outside her window the city awakened, yawning, stretching, the rumble of traffic, the rattle of metal shutters.

Perhaps Murchie did kill Dermot, she thought. She remembered how he'd handed her his phone, challenged her to turn him in.

Perhaps he was just waiting. Perhaps he knew it was a matter of time.

A lorry thundered past, shaking her windows.

The image of Pauline, never far away, surfaced again.

'Luckily he's back now.' Louisa crossed the kitchen to Agnes, carrying two mugs of tea. 'He was with his brother in Sussex, and I thought, how are we going to introduce this new person without him, but he called last night to say he'd be there.' She smiled. 'So that's a relief.'

Agnes made room on the bench next to her. 'Dr Kitson?' She took the mug of tea.

'Yes. He had a couple of days leave. He's meeting us there, I'm going over there after this.'

'Over where?' Agnes tried not to let the tension sound in her voice.

'To the project. We've got a meeting with the new co-worker. It'll be a good time to tell him that I'm leaving.'

'Yes.' Leaving, Agnes thought. She imagined Louisa on a plane, soaring into the sky, away from London, away from Dr Kitson. For a moment she breathed normally again, almost turning to her, to say, leave now. Leave while you can...

'Are you all right?' Louisa was watching her. 'You seem tired.'

'Me?' Agnes held her mug tightly in front of her. 'I'm fine. Really. A bit tired, yes.'

'I'm not surprised, of course. These awful misfortunes at your hostel. It must take it out of you. I know Vaughan feels it terribly.'

Vaughan. The ease with which Louisa used his name. Agnes felt the knot tighten. 'Can I come with you?' She heard herself blurt out the question.

'What – to the project?' Louisa was smiling at her. 'Whatever for? I would have thought your workload was heavy enough.'

'Just...just out of interest...' Agnes mumbled.

'Of course. We'd better get going, if we're going.'

The sun had broken through the early clouds. Louisa led the way, striding through the city streets in her brightly coloured mackintosh, her scarf trailing nonchalantly in the breeze.

Perhaps I should tell her, Agnes thought. Perhaps I should tell her to beware. Perhaps...

Agnes caught up with her, took her arm. 'Louisa,' she said.

'What?' Louisa turned, her pace unslowed.

'Be careful.'

Louisa smiled at her. 'Oh, no, it's fine. My mind's made up. If I'm choosing damnation, it's too late.'

'No, no, not your soul.'

Louisa saw the expression on Agnes's face and slowed to a halt. 'What then?'

'Dr Kitson. I don't trust him.' There. The words were out, out in the fresh morning light.

'Vaughan? Why ever not?' Louisa patted Agnes's hand where it lay on her arm, and set off again.

'Because...'

Because nothing. I have no proof.

Agnes fell silent as they rounded the corner.

The women's health project had its headquarters in a rented ground-floor room in a crumbling Victorian terraced house. Louisa had a key to the peeling front door, and let them both in to the damp hallway.

The office was high-ceilinged and bright with sunlight, papered with information posters in bold lettering: helplines, emergency phone numbers, slogans of self-help and empowerment.

Dr Kitson was sitting at one of the two desks. He looked up as they came into the room. He was spectral, his eyes dark-ringed, his lips a thin, nervous line as he tried to speak. 'Oh,' he said, after a long moment. 'Oh. It's you.' He stared from one to the other.

'Vaughan,' Louisa greeted him, smiling. 'Did you have a good break?'

'What? Oh. Yes.'

'Your brother?' She seemed amused.

'Yes, yes, of course. My brother. Yes, thank you.' Something switched back on. Agnes watched the life return to his face. He jumped up, found her a chair, smiling as he gestured to her to sit down. 'Just had rather bad news, that's all. Got back from Sussex to hear that one of my patients—' He glanced at Agnes. 'You'll know this, of course. Mrs Stipes. I've only just found out. The police came to see me at home first thing.'

Louisa looked at Agnes.

'One of Dr Kitson's patients,' Agnes said. 'Someone I knew. She died...'

'Yesterday morning. Poor Jeremy's been trying to get hold of me. Cancer,' he said, turning to Louisa. 'A matter of time, of course, but it's still upsetting.'

'Oh.' Louisa cast him a sympathetic look. 'Oh dear.'

'Particularly as there's a bit of a question mark over how it actually happened. She may have...' he hesitated, glanced at Agnes again. 'Well, it's not for us to speculate. The authorities will, I'm sure, do whatever they have to do...'

Agnes found she was gripping the arms of her chair. She loosened her hold, her eyes still on Dr Kitson.

Perhaps I'm wrong.

I thought I was looking at a monster. And now, in front of me, all I see is a rational being; an ordinary man, a doctor, expressing his natural concern for one of his patients.

'So—' he interrupted her thoughts, leaning forward conversationally. 'You've come to see us at the hub of our new project, have you?'

'Of course,' Louisa laughed, 'she's got nothing better to do.'

'They obviously don't keep you busy enough at your Order.' He smiled at Agnes. 'Well, I'm afraid there's no vacancy here.' He glanced at Louisa. 'What with Cath coming to join us today, we're very well staffed, aren't we?'

'Ah. Well.' Louisa hesitated.

'What?' He smiled across at her.

'That's what I need to talk to you about.'

His smile died. 'What do you mean?'

She went on, 'Various things in my life have come to a head, and it looks as if I'll be going back to the States. I mean, of course, we can talk about a timescale, I'm not going to just up sticks and leave just like that, I'll help you find someone to replace me...'

His face had clouded. His eyes narrowed as he stared at her. His mouth worked, but he said nothing.

'It's funny isn't it, how things kind of come together.' Louisa chatted on. 'It's like it was the right time to make this decision...'

Agnes watched the beads of spittle form on his lips. Her fingers curled around the arms of her chair.

Dr Kitson opened his mouth. 'No!' It was more of a shout than a word, fracturing the air around him.

Louisa stopped, mid-chat.

He was absolutely still, apart from his chest which moved up and down, his breath coming in uneasy gasps.

'But—' Louisa stared at him, puzzled. 'Vaughan,' she said.

Agnes reached out a hand towards her. They watched him as if frozen, transfixed by the pent pallor of his face.

There was a ring at the front door bell.

Louisa looked at Dr Kitson. He was staring straight ahead, his face twitching. She looked towards the door, then back to him again. She stood up, and went to answer the door.

Agnes heard greetings, a female voice, laughter. Louisa came back into the room, followed by a tall, afro-haired young woman in scarlet high-heeled boots and a red tartan coat which swung at her knees. She reached out a hand to Dr Kitson.

'Vaughan, how are you?'

He stared at her, glassy-eyed.

'Man, I am just so excited about joining this project.' Cath smiled from one to the other. 'And Louisa, I've heard so much about you from Vaughan. We'll be such a great team, eh?'

An odd croaking sound came from Vaughan. Cath was standing directly in front of him. His hand reached out and grabbed her coat pocket, and began to tug at it. 'No...no...' he seemed to be saying.

Louisa glanced at Agnes.

'Dr Kitson?' Cath looked down at him, smiled in confusion. He stared up at her, his expression empty.

'Dr Kitson?' Cath said again. Her voice was loud, and he blinked.

It occurred to Agnes later that it had been like watching a computer-generated image; the way that the black and white angles of the doctor's features filled suddenly with colour and rounded out; the way his smile returned, his breathing settled, his voice lightened as he stood up and said, 'Cath, great to see you,' resting his hand on her shoulder. He turned to Louisa and smiled at her. 'Let's have this meeting, shall we?'

Louisa's eyes darted nervously towards Agnes.

'Maybe I should—' Agnes began.

'Listen, don't you worry about a thing.' Vaughan crossed the room towards her and took her arm. 'I know this Pauline business is upsetting. Listen, why don't we meet up later, maybe with Father Julius too, and share our feelings?' He began to steer her towards the door. Behind him, she saw Louisa relax, exchange a few words with Cath, begin to smile again. She found she was out in the hallway.

Dr Kitson leant towards her. 'I didn't want to say this in front of Louisa,' he said. 'The police had quite a few questions for me this morning. They wanted to know what kind of drugs Mrs Stipes had access to. I told them what I could. They kept going on about the syringe. I know I'd prescribed it, but to be honest, there wasn't enough morphine in it to kill anyone. My view is, the syringe was for show. Some kind of crazy theatricality. I told them to check for pills, stuff taken orally. If she stockpiled her medication without anyone noticing, then maybe...' He frowned down at her, and once more his face had softened. 'I worry about Jeremy. He was so attentive – if he thinks she managed to do that in spite of all his care…' He squeezed her arm. 'I'm sorry, I imagine it's upsetting to us all. I'll call you later on.' He smiled at her, opened the door for her.

Out in the street, she glanced back. He waved, briefly, then the door closed shut.

CHAPTER NINETEEN

The sky had clouded over. Agnes walked, north towards the river, west towards Tower Bridge. The Embankment was chilly in the damp air. She found she had stopped still, staring across the river, with its low, edgy waves. She glanced down at a stone bench, and dropped on to it, unable to take another step.

It had come on to rain, but she didn't see the drops of water falling around her; she didn't see the blue-grey blur of the City skyline. In her mind, there he was again, smiling, concerned, anxious for the bereaved husband – 'I worry about Jeremy...'

The river slapped against the stone.

In her mind she saw the door slam shut; with Louisa on the other side. In her mind hung the words: I don't know what to do.

It was still raining when she hammered on the front door of Julius's vicarage. He opened it, blinked at her appearance, led her through the dark hallway into the lounge.

'I tried the church,' she was saying, 'I thought you might be there, and then I thought, with Jeremy here, you'd be bound to be here with him, and thank God you are, I'm soaked through, I've been walking in the rain for what seems like hours…'

'He's not here.' Julius's voice was quiet.

'What?'

'Jeremy. They came for him. He's been arrested on suspicion of killing his wife.'

Agnes looked across at him. He seemed small and frail; even the pink walls were muted in the dull light.

'Can we see him?'

'I was waiting for you.'

Jeremy looked up at the clink of keys. His eyes were blank, as if nothing surprised him any more, not the cell door opening, the duty sergeant greeting him, 'just started my shift – Mr Stipes, isn't it?'; not the appearance of Julius and Agnes, squeezing into the tiny room, sitting one on the end of the bed, one on the sole chair.

They were left alone. Jeremy looked from Julius, next to him on his bed, to Agnes, opposite him. He seemed to be waiting.

'Well, Jeremy…' Julius patted his hand. 'How are they looking after you?'

Jeremy stared at him. He nodded, but said nothing.

'I'm sorry you were arrested,' Agnes said.

His gaze turned towards her. He looked puzzled, as if trying to put a name to the face.

'Particularly given that you didn't do anything wrong,' she went on.

He breathed in, his eyes still on her face. Then he said, 'I didn't. I know I didn't.'

Agnes imagined the rumours being breathed around the house, the hydrangea bush turning to and fro to catch the whispering.

'They say it wasn't suicide.' Jeremy's voice had shrunk to a whisper. 'They know she didn't want to kill herself. I could have told them that, I said to them, she was getting better, there's a nice policewoman upstairs, she's got funny hair all in twists, she listened. And she agreed with me. But then she said, Mr Stipes, if your wife didn't kill herself, then who did kill her?'

The silence was thick in the tiny cell.

Jeremy rubbed the top of his head. 'You see,' he said looking across at Agnes again. 'If it wasn't me, then who was it? Who can have taken out that syringe? Someone would have had to come into the house, someone we trusted, she'd have had to open the door to him, and I keep thinking, but it can't be him. How can anyone think such a thing of such a good man?' His eyes were round and anguished as he stared at her.

'You mean Dr Kitson?'

Her words cut through the air in the cell. A rhythmic tapping came from the pipes which snaked along the gloss-painted ceiling.

He still held her gaze. His mouth opened, as if to speak, but no words came. After a moment, he said, 'It was the same.'

'What was the same?'

'The bottle. The morphine. Oramorph. Dr Kitson brought us some more, that evening. He said he was about to go away for a day or two and he knew we needed a top-up, as he put it.'

'That evening?' Agnes stared at him.

Jeremy nodded. 'He often called in after his evening surgery. I didn't think anything of it. But the thing is...' His cheeks were flushed, his breathing was fast. 'Afterwards...when I found her...The thing is, I looked at the bottle of Oramorph. And it said 100 mls. And her normal one was 10 mls. But then I thought, he'd know best. And maybe she did need something stronger. And anyway, it was me who gave it to her, that night. No one else.'

Agnes reached across and touched his hand. 'Jeremy,' she said. 'I know you didn't kill your wife.'

They followed the duty sergeant back up the stairs, out to the street, blinking in the daylight. Julius turned to Agnes. 'Are you sure?' he said.

'About Dr Kitson?' She looked up at him. Behind him she could see the terracotta brick porch of the police station. A woman with a pushchair struggled up the steps and disappeared inside. 'No,' Agnes said. 'I'm not sure about anything at all.'

'What will you do?' Julius took her arm and they began to walk to the bus stop.

'I know what I've got to do.'

They sat side by side on the bus. The afternoon sunlight broke through the clouds; the misted-up window sparkled with light.

Agnes sat alone in the hostel office. A mug of tea sat in front of her, half-filled, cold. The room was dark; rain pattered against the window. There was a knock at the door. Gilroy showed Rob Coombes in, and then left the room.

'It's really nice of you to pop by,' she said.

'Part of the job.' He pulled up a chair.

'Pauline Stipes died.' Agnes met his eyes, willing him to understand.

'Yeah. I heard. They've hauled in the husband.'

'It wasn't him.' She watched the flicker in his eyes, watched him lean forward, waiting for her to speak.

She picked up her mug and took a large mouthful of cold tea. 'What I'm going to say will sound mad, but please listen. I think I'm right. No,' she added, 'I know I'm right.'

He studied her. 'Go on.'

'Doctor Kitson.' She was aware that just saying the name out loud had eased her breathing.

'What about him?'

'The thing is – Abbie's death, Dermot's death, and now Pauline's death...'

Rob was staring at her, blank-faced.

'They're all his patients. And they were all on medication that he prescribed. And he signed all three death certificates. And no one really had a motive for any of them to die.' It was like stepping off a mountain, finding that you're running down the slope, free and unrestrained and much too fast. 'Abbie had everything to live for,' she stumbled on. 'Pauline was determined to get away from her husband and live her last few weeks or months on her own terms. Neither of them would have killed themselves, and although they were both tied up with rather odd men, I don't believe they were in danger from them. And Dermot—'

'Hang on a moment.' Rob was leaning back in his chair, his fingers teasing at a spot on his chin. 'Dermot had got on the wrong side of a very dangerous group of young men in the neighbourhood. They'd given him enough warnings, what with the rat and the beating and all—'

'Dermot was on very toxic medication. He should never have gone out the night he died.'

'He died of stab wounds.'

'And Murchie's denying having anything to do with it.'

Rob leant back in his chair. 'You think he'll own up to it?'

'And Abbie—'

'That girl made the mistake of going around with the same crowd. You said she was trying to get away from them. And then, that day, she lost all hope, thanks to that bullying pimp of hers. Both of them, Dermot and Abbie, tried to stand up to him and failed. And what I can't stand is that he thinks he's got away with it.'

The room had grown even darker. There was a distant rumble, perhaps thunder, perhaps a passing lorry. Agnes felt the ground beneath her tremble. She tried again.

'The heroin that Abbie used – it was much purer than anything she'd normally get hold of.'

'We think that Murchison has got a very high-quality supply. We're still running tests. Your friend Mr O'Hagan was pretty shifty too about helping her out with stuff from time to time. There was a bit of a scene with people swapping methadone, too.'

'I'm not saying he was an angel.'

'So, what are you saying?'

The tea seemed to have congealed in its mug. She looked back up at him. 'I'm asking you to consider the possibility that Dr Kitson is not what he seems. He left his last job in a hurry, there was some worry about malpractice although it came to nothing…'

Rob crossed one leg over the other.

'He had access to the hostel when Abbie died. He'd been in and out of here that day. And he visited the Stipes the evening that Pauline died. He brought her a very strong morphine mixture.'

In the dim light, Agnes saw him glance at his watch.

'I know it sounds mad,' she said, and heard in the words her own defeat.

He looked up at her. He rubbed the side of his face. 'No,' he said. 'Not mad. It's what we're taught, not to just go with the obvious.'

'So you might look at these cases again?'

A car revved up outside, then pulled away, filling the room with silvery threads of light.

'It's true, I suppose,' Rob said, 'that someone like a doctor, someone who seems respectable...' He looked at her. 'This Mrs Stipes. Are you saying that Dr Kitson supplied her with the wherewithal to end her own life?'

'I'm saying that Dr Kitson had provided some very strong pain relief. And he knew what was in that syringe that she was found with—'

The office phone rang, shrill in the darkness. Agnes reached across and answered it. She listened, nodded, replaced the receiver.

She leant back in her chair. 'That was my friend Father Julius.' She bent to the anglepoise lamp on the desk and switched it on. 'He's spoken to Jeremy's solicitor. Apparently Jeremy wants to plead guilty.'

The passing traffic outside was muffled by the silence.

She looked up at Rob. 'It doesn't change anything,' she said. 'Everything I've just said, it doesn't change it...'

There were raised voices outside the door, which then

opened. 'He wouldn't let me in.' Lindy flew through the door in a rush of floral skirt. 'That Gilroy, he said you were busy, and I tried to tell him this is important—' She flung herself into a chair. She looked pale and tear-stained. 'It's even worse. You know how Connor said he lied about his alibi for Murchie when the feds were asking him about Mots? Well, now he's told me something else, something worse, poor Connor, he's been that scared of Murchie. But what he said was, that day that Abbie died, he'd seen her. And she was that upset, running through the street, back towards here. And he stopped her and said, what's up, and she was crying and that, and she said, she wanted to die. She said that she'd tried to tell Murchie she wasn't having nothing more to do with him, and Dermot was there, and I thought Dermot was so great, but it turns out, Dermot wouldn't back her up. He was just standing there, next to Murch, and there she was pleading with him to take her away from Murchie, and he didn't say nothing. And then she ran away, crying, and that's when Connor saw her, and she told him the whole story and said she wanted to die…' She shook her head. 'It's like she had nothing left to live for. And she said she'd got some gear and she was going to use it, and Connor tried to stop her, and he said he didn't think she meant to kill herself but that maybe it just went wrong because she was so upset…'

She lifted her feet to the desk in their strappy sandals, swinging her chair round, blinking as she noticed Rob sitting in the other chair.

Her face tightened. Then she leant forward and held out her hand and threw him a thin, sweet smile. 'Sergeant Coombes, isn't it. How lovely to see you again.'

* * *

Agnes circled a beer mat around the table in front of her. 'And then after that, she wouldn't say anything else.' She looked up at Julius. 'Which was hardly surprising, as none of that lot will talk to the police. For obvious reasons.'

Julius sipped his pint. Through the window behind him, Agnes could see the blurred edge of the full moon.

'And Rob would have listened to me,' she went on. 'I was just about to convince him that Pauline's death, and Abbie's death, and Dermot's death, all involved drugs supplied by Dr Kitson, when Jeremy goes and pleads guilty, and then Lindy comes in with this story of Abbie being suicidal.'

Julius looked up at her. 'But – presumably – Lindy was telling the truth?'

'That's what Rob said.'

'I mean, doctors have to supply drugs. That's part of their job.'

'Yes.' Agnes inched the beer mat towards the edge of the table. 'That's what Rob said too.'

She sighed, picked up her glass of lager and took a large mouthful.

'Poor Jeremy,' Julius said. 'He got himself into a terrible tangle, it turns out. An awful sense of failure, all about his mother, of course. And then, trying to pre-empt it by taking control of Pauline's death.'

'So he says. He's given up, that's why. He's grief-stricken.'

'I see no contradiction,' Julius said.

'If he'd killed her—'

He met her eyes. 'He could still be grief-stricken.'

'He didn't kill her.'

Julius held his glass of beer up to the light.

'What?' Agnes waited.

He put his glass down, looked at her, then looked away again. 'It's a wonderful moon out there,' he said.

'I know what you're about to say.' Agnes edged the beer mat further, watched it waver for a second before it fell to the floor.

'Agnes—'

'Go on, then.' She faced him.

His hand moved towards his crucifix. 'It's been a strange time for you,' he said. 'All this business with this American waking up old feelings about your father, and then it turns out your father, too, turned to God seeking a paternal relationship. At the risk of sounding a bit too Freudian about all this, I can't help wondering whether your worries about this doctor aren't all caught up in some kind of crisis brought on by this Bretton character...'

'Julius, it's nothing to do with him. He's not even involved any more. He seems to have abandoned the whole idea of my father's theories.'

'Which is why you feel even more burdened by it all, perhaps.'

'If you're suggesting that my worries about Dr Kitson are connected to my sense of betrayal about my father—'

'Agnes—' He raised his hand to silence her. 'Please remember that if I speak like this it's only because I care about you. I have no wish to make you doubt your perception of the truth. But the fact is, this unreliable American has invaded your life, bringing with him a trail of fossils and a load of confused theories about the origins of humanity, and it wouldn't be at all surprising if, on top of all these terrible goings-on at the hostel, and given your fine intellect, you have perhaps intertwined too many things together.' He met her eyes, and almost smiled. 'And now I'll be quiet.'

She found she'd reached for another beer mat and was pushing it around the table in circles. 'Julius—'

He leant across the table and his fingers brushed her sleeve. 'You don't need to answer me.'

She looked up at him. She couldn't think of anything to say.

The skull sat on her desk, cowering in the unaccustomed light from her desk lamp. Agnes traced her finger along the ink lines. Outside the city churches chimed the lateness of the hour.

If Julius is wrong...

Julius is never wrong, she thought.

The skull watched her, empty-eyed.

Memento mori.

She studied the neat black calligraphy: Reuben, Simeon, Levi, Judah...

'Everything is wrong. Murchie is about to be arrested. Jeremy is going to plead guilty...' Her voice broke the silence, and she realised she'd spoken out loud, confiding in the blank dead bone in front of her.

She stood up. She took out her phone and dialled the convent house and asked for Louisa. She waited, hearing neat footsteps on polished wood floors, receding, approaching.

'Hi, Agnes.'

'Louisa.'

'Everything all right?'

'Please—' Agnes's voice sounded small. 'Please,' she said again, much louder. 'Keep away from him.'

'Are you OK?'

'Dr Kitson.'

'What about him? Is he OK?'

'Louisa – I'm very worried... I'm worried that you're not safe.' Out loud, her words seemed drained of reason.

'I'm fine, really. I know it's a big decision, but I've told Sister Christiane now, so that's the scary bit over now.'

'But Vaughan—'

'Oh, you mean that scene at the project? It's OK, I was worried too, but he's calmed down now. I think that patient of his dying really threw him. But it's all clear now, I've got a timescale for leaving, and I've got to support him all I can in the meantime.' She continued to chat, about the meeting with Christiane. 'Do you know, that horrible cat of hers was with her, that huge black and white thing, he must be about fifty, she had him on her lap the whole meeting, and he just sat there looking daggers at me, I'm sure she does it on purpose...'

They said their goodnights. Agnes clicked off her phone.

The skull was silent, waiting. She stared back, aware of a sudden wave of rage. 'There's no point you sitting there looking as if you know the answer. You should have stayed with Brett,' she said. 'I feel like taking you to that hotel of his and throwing you through his window.'

She flung herself into her desk chair, began to go through her father's papers, leafing through mathematical formulae, lists of the descendants of Adam, until she found the pages where she'd slipped the press cutting.

'A local patients' support group has dropped its legal action against Tavercombe Health Centre, following the alleged malpractice of one of the GPs. Their spokeswoman, Joyce Tamplin, said the campaign hadn't managed to raise sufficient funds to meet the rising legal costs...'

She went to her bookshelf and retrieved a battered road map. She turned the pages, traced lines of routes south from London, picked up her phone again, dialled Athena.

'Athena, I'm sorry—'

'Poppet, it's fine, I'm still up.'

'It's a car question, I'm afraid.'

'You want to borrow my pride and joy? Oh, really, have it. I'm not going anywhere.'

'It may be a day or two.'

'A week's fine. A month. I'm just stuck here planning a wedding which is clearly never going to happen. Nic's off with the lovely, helpful Mack again, his mum seems to be failing fast, and of course I'm terribly fond of his mum but the truth is I hardly know her, and there's Mack who was very close to her for years...and I wouldn't mind if it wasn't that he'd suggested this blasted wedding in the first place. There he is spending days with his ex-wife and here's me finding myself going through brochures for specialist caterers and flower arrangers. I'm going to be like that woman in that old film, the one in the wedding dress with the cobwebs and the cake rotting on the table...'

'I'll be round quite early, if that's OK.'

'I'll be here.'

Agnes rang off. The moon was high in the sky; a fleck of silvery light glanced off the eyeless sockets of the skull.

CHAPTER TWENTY

The receptionist had tight curls of grey hair. Her gaze was flinty behind the glass screen.

'Yes?'

Agnes looked around her at the bored stillness of the health centre waiting room. People turned the pages of their papers, stared into space. No one returned her glance.

'I said, can I help you?' The voice was sharper, rattling the glass.

Agnes cleared her throat. 'It's about Dr Kitson. Vaughan Kitson.'

There was a flicker in the steely eyes, a hardening of the line of her lips. 'What about him?'

'I was wondering...' Agnes searched for words. 'I wanted to know about—'

'I'm sorry, madam.' The receptionist's fingers went to the handle of the blind above her. 'We don't answer queries of that nature.' The blind slammed down between them.

*　*　*

The car park was a windswept plain of concrete. Agnes stood by Athena's Audi and surveyed the view. Dull terraces of housing huddled together; stick-like trees twitched in the gusts of wind.

She thought about Julius, back in London. He'd be visiting Jeremy this morning, trying to encourage him to change his plea, to give himself a chance, as he would put it, even if…

Even if Jeremy had killed his wife.

She glanced at her watch. It was ten past one. In a few hours I could be back in London, she thought. I could get back up the motorway, I could meet Athena, we could go to that tea room and eat pink cake and remind ourselves that life sometimes contains order, and joy, and rightness, and that there are times when it doesn't do to dwell on the wrongness, the disorderly, the possibility of evil—

'Excuse me.' It was a woman's voice. Agnes turned towards it. 'I'm so glad you're still here, I hurried out of there as fast as I could but I had to sort out my prescription first and that receptionist can be so slow sometimes…' She was short, and limping, with a shock of jet-black hair and, Agnes noticed, a nicely cut tweed suit. 'Only I heard you asking about Dr Kitson, and I thought to myself, they won't tell her, of course they won't, not now it's all over.' She stopped, wheezing. Agnes saw the line of grey hair at her roots where the dye was growing out. 'You see, at the time, everyone thought he'd actually caused the poor woman's death, and then other people, patients of his, they came forward and for a while it looked like we had a serial killer in our midst, the local papers had a field day. But then nothing could be proved, apart from poor Mr Blacklock, and then it came out that his wife had been very ill, and then lots of people spoke up for Dr Kitson, he was a popular man, a good doctor, people said, I didn't know him that well, I've always had Dr Sergeant after he was so good with Mother, but anyway, what I came out to say is that the person you need to talk to is Joyce, of course – she's the person you need.' The wheezing was stronger now; she leant against the car to catch her breath.

She had bright brown eyes. Agnes held out her hand to her. 'Agnes.' she said.

The woman took her hand. 'Sylvia,' she said. 'Joyce will know who you mean, just say Sylvia from the committee. Here.' She handed Agnes a scrap of paper. Agnes read the wobbly biro: Joyce Tamplin, and a phone number. 'Thank you,' she said.

Sylvia bent towards her. 'We don't think it's over, you see. The supporters' group ran out of money, but we're still encouraging people to put their side of the story. That's why I followed you out here, I hope you don't mind.' She peered at Agnes. 'Mind you, if you were one of those news people, it would be a different story, awful nuisance they were, but you don't look like that sort of person.'

'No,' Agnes said. 'I'm not. I'm a—' nun, she was going to add, but Sylvia interrupted.

'Goodbye, then.' She patted her arm and turned away. 'I hope you won't think me rude but the bus doesn't wait, if he doesn't see you he just drives away and it's two hours till the next one these days. Oh—' She turned back. 'Could you tell Joyce that the dahlias won't be needed this week after all? Save me a phone call. Thanks very much, dear.'

Agnes watched her uneven step as she made her way down the hill towards the small parade of shops.

She drove south towards the coast, finding herself suddenly

on the seafront. She stared out of the car window at the churning ocean, the thick expanse of water flecked with white, the seagulls squawking, the unlit fairy lights trailing in bleak festoons. She felt her spirits lift, a feeling that lasted the rest of the drive, up the hill away from the parade until she reached a street of faded guest houses. She got out of the car.

'Sea View', she read. 'Gull's Rest'. 'Nora's Delight'. One was painted bright turquoise and had a slightly crooked sign which said 'Chez Nous'. Next to it a plastic tag said 'Vacancies'. Agnes rang the bell.

Her room was surprisingly large – 'we've only got the deluxe left, I'm afraid, chuck,' the woman who'd answered the door had explained. She had introduced herself as Doreen, had led Agnes up the dark staircase, teetering on black patent heels. She'd unlocked the room for her, explained the rules of the house – 'I lock up at eleven sharp. That's your shower in there, all en suite now of course...' She'd tossed her bleached-blond curls, pouted her very pink lips which matched the nail varnish on her very tanned hands. 'Though, the hot water's not very reliable, mornings are better than evenings. No music to be played in rooms after nine p.m.' She ticked the list off on her long fingers. 'No smoking, obviously, else we'll all find ourselves up before the beak, for myself I don't mind, gave up years ago, but it drives my old man barmy, don't get him started on the subject, chuck, not that you'll see much of him, the time he spends down the Whistle these days.' She flashed her a smile. 'I hope you enjoy your stay with us.'

Agnes heard her heels retreating down the stairs again.

She went to the window and opened it. The sea was a wide stripe beyond the line of rooftops. The air was salty. Agnes wondered why her mood should lift at the sight of this grey ribbon of ocean under heavy clouds. She watched the gulls circle overhead. Further out to sea there was a tiny white triangle of sail, and Agnes watched its dainty progress until it disappeared out of sight.

She went over to the bed, sat down and pulled her phone out of her bag. She dialled the number on the scrap of paper. A man's voice answered and she asked to speak to Joyce. There was a pause, and murmurings in the background, then the phone was picked up again.

'Joyce Tamplin speaking.' The voice was soft and well-spoken.

'I was given your number by Sylvia from the committee,' Agnes said.

'Ah, yes, dear Sylvia.'

'She was in the health centre at Tavercombe when I was asking about Dr Kitson, and she said I should talk to you.'

There was a pause, a taking stock. Then Joyce said, 'Might I ask why you were asking about Dr Kitson?'

'Of course. I'm a nun, you see, from London.' Agnes kept a conversational tone. 'Dr Kitson has been looking after someone who has died in, shall we say, odd circumstances, and I needed to find out more.'

'London? I say. I had no idea word had travelled that far. That silly old judge would have a fit if he knew.'

'Which judge?'

'The one who warned us at the hearing that any further aspersions cast on Dr Kitson's expertise would be treated as libel and we would be pursued through the courts accordingly. Those were his words, or something very similar.'

'Tell me, Mrs Tamplin—' Agnes hesitated, then said, 'Do you think Dr Kitson is dangerous?'

There was a silence. Then Joyce said, 'That's why you should talk to Mr Blacklock. I'll give you his number, have you got a pen? It's Mr Eben Blacklock...'

Agnes wrote down the number. 'Thank you,' she said.

'They said it was a witch hunt.' Joyce's soft tones hardened slightly. 'We didn't mean any harm. We were just being a voice for the voiceless. Or so we thought.' She was silent for a moment, then said, 'Lots of people came forward in his support. Even now, people will tell you what a good doctor he was.' She sighed. 'I'm glad it's over, to be honest. It got to the point where I didn't know what to think any more.'

'Yes,' Agnes agreed.

'Well, goodbye.'

'Oh –' Agnes remembered. 'Sylvia said to tell you that the dahlias won't be needed this week after all.'

'Well, it's all very well for her to say that, but they're already in water, red and gold just as we agreed, they won't be much use next week, I do wish she'd told me earlier, I'm going to have to have a word with Barbara now about the christening...'

Agnes managed to interrupt to say goodbye. She rang off.

She looked at her phone, looked at the scrap of paper with Eben Blacklock's number on it. Outside the clouds had lifted; the sky was daubed with pink, echoed by the sea. She took the heavy key that Doreen had left in the door, and went out.

The buildings along the seafront had a weary look, as if they too were bored, like the teetering girls in strappy tops making their way along the pavement, or the three swaying, loud young men sitting on the wall. The smell of fish and chips made her realise she was hungry.

The café had neon signs outside and greenish strip lighting inside. The television on the wall was showing motor racing, and the drill-like buzz of car engines drowned out the background music. Agnes sat by the window. The sea was flecked with purple light. She tasted a chip. She leant back in her chair and marvelled at this easy contentment; a sea view, a sunset, and a plate of surprisingly good haddock and chips. Tomorrow, she thought, I will go home. She breathed in the scent of fried fish and sea air, and wondered what had happened to the knot of anxiety that she'd carried for so long.

'...husband in mercy killing.' Agnes glanced up at the television screen, astonished to see Jeremy's face. 'Mr Stipes spoke only to confirm his name,' the reporter was saying. 'Outside the court there was a small protest in support of euthanasia.' Agnes could see placards, slogans: 'Mercy not murder.' There was a brief interview with one of the demonstrators, a fidgety, balding man; 'In a more civilised country he'd be treated as a caring husband, not a criminal,' the man said.

Then the report was over, and the television was talking about a hurricane somewhere, Jamaica, Agnes thought she heard, but the young woman behind the counter had turned up the music, and a sickly voice singing of betrayal drowned out the television.

It was dark when Agnes left the café. She walked along the seafront. The tide was in, splashing dark waves along the beach.

If Jeremy killed Pauline...

She thought about Joyce's words. I didn't know what to think any more.

A flight of stone steps led to the beach. Agnes picked her

way down them. The wet shingle made silvery circles in the moonlight, like coins strewn across the beach.

The wind tugged at her coat. She remembered a summer long ago. Her father had vetoed the usual trip to the French coast and insisted they come to England. Why, she wondered. And where? She had a memory of tall cliffs, and moors: somewhere further north, perhaps. It had rained, she remembered that. She remembered being cold. One day her mother had taken her to a department store in the town and bought her winter clothes, a coat, a jersey, extra socks. Agnes had liked her new clothes and yet even at that age – nine? ten? – had sensed that she now stood on her mother's side in a silent, invisible battle, and that by wearing her lovely new jumper she had somehow joined her voice to her mother's list of complaints about the weather, the food, the people...

The stones underfoot bruised her feet through the thin soles of her shoes.

So often I betrayed him, she thought. And yet I never meant to.

She looked out towards the black horizon. 'And the Spirit of God moved upon the face of the waters...'

She thought about her father, retelling the story of creation as an absolute truth, with no room for doubt. What was it that he needed to rewrite? Was he trying to make amends? And for what?

The wind ruffled the dark waves with foam. She pulled her sleeves down over her hands. She remembered the feeling of creamy Aran wool tugged over her fists. She wished she'd been brave enough to take his side.

*　*　*

Doreen was sitting at the tiny front desk. She looked at her watch. 'You took your key,' she said.

'Oh.' Agnes felt the heavy fob in her pocket.

'We prefer our guests to leave them.' Doreen opened a drawer in the desk, closed it again.

'I'm sorry.' Agnes started up the stairs.

'Just in case. You never know when someone might need to get hold of someone. You know, in an emergency, like.'

Agnes reached her room with relief.

She switched on the lights, went to her bag and unpacked her father's notebook, with its cardboard cover, its watercolour border of insects. 'For it is Written in the Book of Names,' she read, then the name, Ralph Gardner.

She flicked through the thin paper.

'...in spite of our exile from Eden, we are still living out our days within the creation of our Father.'

She sat at the table by the window and turned the page. 'We have all lived for so long in exile, and yet we know in our hearts we are God's people. So, why do the children of God choose exile? For in so doing we are being obedient to the serpent, who wanted to see us in exile, but disobedient to God, who still loves us as his own.' Then there was a quotation: '"Blessed is the nation whose God is the Lord; and the people whom He hath chosen for His own inheritance."'

Agnes gazed out of the window into the night. She could hear the soft background rumble of the sea.

What had changed, she wondered. Who was this new version of her father? If the handwriting wasn't so familiar, if she didn't, in spite of her doubts, trust Brett to be telling the truth, she would be beginning to think that these writings were those of an imposter, of someone pretending to be Ralph Gardner.

And yet…

In her mind, she saw, once again, the sunlit corridor of the house in Provence; her father, emerging from his study. She had lined up her dolls on the wide window ledge, it was a school, she remembered, and she was the teacher. At the sound of the heavy iron latch of her father's door her chatter ceased. He had approached, along the corridor; she recalled the thump, thump of his uneven tread, as if one leg was longer than the other. He'd paused beside her, studied the dolls for a moment; he'd patted one on the head, Delilah, she'd been called. Agnes recalled untidy tufts of blond hair and wide-open, long-lashed eyes. Then he'd gone on his way. But even then he'd had bundles of notebooks tucked under his arm.

She flicked through the pages in front of her. Perhaps it had been this very book; perhaps, even then, he'd been engaged in an exploration of the age of the universe. He was silent about so many things; it wouldn't be surprising if he'd been silent about this too.

She closed the book and put it down on the table. Her eye fell on the scrap of paper with the phone number that Joyce had given her. She looked at her watch. There was still time.

The morning sunlight was bright and persistent. Agnes had eaten Doreen's eggs and bacon, alone in a dining room awash with light, as if the rays of the sun were magnified by the strip of sea view. She had stared around the threadbare, empty space and wondered about the de luxe room being the only one available. But Doreen was cheerful, and Agnes, too, felt happy enough to overlook the soggy, cheap toast and instant coffee. She had paid Doreen, promised that indeed, she would come back soon, and now she walked up Culverton Drive looking for number seventy-three.

It was a large, red-brick house, with an imposing gate and a rather incongruous turret emerging from the roof. The door was answered by a tall, weathered-looking man in well-cut trousers and a navy shirt. He peered down at her. 'Ah,' he said. 'The nun, is it?'

'Sister Agnes.'

'Blacklock.' He shook the hand she offered him, and led her inside. 'They knocked the church down, you see,' he said. He waved vaguely around him at the large hall, with its thick picture rail and oak panelling. 'Next door. Used to be a church. This was the vicarage.'

Agnes followed him down a passageway into the kitchen. She thought of Julius's salmon pink walls; even this oak panelling and glimpses of faded cream paintwork would be preferable.

She watched him fill the kettle and put it on the hob. His hands trembled slightly, and she realised that he must be older than his still-dark hair suggested.

He gestured to her to sit down at the blue formica table. 'They do keep sending people to me still,' he said.

'I hope you don't mind.'

'Oh, no, I don't. I don't mind at all. Not that I have anything conclusive to add, but it was my wife's death that became the centre of the brouhaha.'

'What happened?'

He sat down opposite her. 'She'd been ill for a long time. One of these auto-immune things, no one really got to the bottom of it, they called it ME in the end.' His hand went to the back of his neck. 'She was in a lot of pain. Her back, her knees. Life was hard.'

'And Dr Kitson?'

'Well, this is the thing, you see...' He leant back. 'He was marvellous. A great support. He was new to the practice, he ordered tests, took it all more seriously than our previous doctor had done. And, Evelyn began to get better. We thought it was Dr Kitson, we thought he'd helped. Perhaps he did. He was very careful with her medication, very concerned.' He turned to check the kettle.

'So, then what happened?'

He turned back. 'She had a new lease of life. This was, what, two years ago now – no, more, it was the summer...' His eyes seemed hooded, cast in shadow. 'In her new optimism, she signed up for a degree, life seemed easier. But, it was a remission. After a few weeks she got worse again, until...until she died.'

'So—' The kettle began to whistle, and he got up. Agnes watched him find teapot, tea bags. 'So, what caused all this movement against Dr Kitson?'

He shook his head. 'I didn't mean it to. I didn't want all that at all. Joyce means well, but – the thing is, around the time of my wife's death, Joyce had been talking to a woman at the health centre who said that Dr Kitson had been very rude to her, and then the next thing was that one of the nurses there accused him of improper behaviour, but immediately withdrew her claim, and it turned out she'd done similar things before, the practice managed to get rid of her after a while. And then the last straw was an elderly lady, a patient of his, who died very suddenly and he signed off the death certificate rather hastily, and, because of the worries about

Evelyn's death, all these ideas took hold, and the local papers got wind of it all, and of course, it sells papers, doesn't it?' He brought the teapot and two mugs to the table.

'And what do you think?'

'About my wife?' He sat down heavily into his chair. 'In the end, I had to conclude that nothing untoward had taken place. There was a post-mortem. She had an inflamed heart, and a pituitary malfunction. It explained some of her symptoms. But Dr Kitson couldn't live with the murmurings, he had to go. The funny thing is, I felt quite sorry for him. He came to say goodbye to me. Decent sort of chap, isn't he?'

Agnes took the mug of tea that he passed her. 'Yes,' she said. 'I suppose he is.'

'I passed Joyce in the street the other day.' He clicked two pills of sweetener into his mug. 'Hadn't seen her for a while. We exchanged a few words, but—' He glanced up at Agnes, then away. 'I think we wonder what got into us all.' He turned back to Agnes, and she felt he was weighing her up in some way. Then he said, 'The truth is, and I feel I can say this to you because I'm never going to see you again – the truth is, that I was angry with Evelyn. And I buried it. Instead of allowing myself to be angry with her, out loud, I let all that strength of feeling spill on to other things. Instead of challenging my wife about her infidelity, I pretended it wasn't happening. Instead of being angry with Evelyn, and her pathetic twerp of a lover, I decided to get angry with her illness, with her doctor...with fate, in a way.' His face was still, but his fingers twitched where they rested on the table's edge. 'Perhaps if I'd had more of a family, children...perhaps if I'd had religious faith, I'd have coped better.' He looked at the ceiling. 'Ironic, isn't it? I'm Jewish by birth, but I'm not religious at all. And now here

I am, living in a vicarage.' He threw her a small smile.

She smiled back. 'If it's any consolation, I'm not sure that faith makes much difference where death is concerned.'

'A great leveller, isn't it?' His mood seemed to have lightened. 'Unless you think that Heaven is guaranteed.'

She shook her head. 'I'm not one to make deals with God.'

'No,' he said. 'Neither am I.' For a second their eyes met, and she was reminded of her father, although she wasn't sure why; something about the creases around his eyes, or perhaps it was the untidy hair at his temples.

'Are you all right?' His voice had softened.

She blinked, nodded at him. 'Yes. Yes, I am. It's just, I really do have to get back to London.'

The sun cast short shadows, flattening out the grey ribbon of road, the strips of farmland. She drove away from the coast, towards the A30.

What a nice man, she thought. What a shame his wife found someone else. And there he was, repressing his rage, putting all that feeling into some other story...

And what if I'm doing the same? What if all this is about what Brett has brought into my life? And I've decided to make up stories about my father instead of just getting on with my life.

She remembered how she'd promised to arrange a meeting with Sari and her mother, through social services in Birmingham. I bet they've replied to my email and I haven't done anything about it. And I said I'd get a quote to replace the carpet on the top landing where it got burnt by a bin fire. Eddie never owned up to that, either. And there's the funding bid to employ a new co-worker...

She thought about Eben Blacklock; the sadness around his eyes. The A30 seemed to have come to an end, and there was still no sign of the motorway. The road signs said A35. There were towns listed; Dorchester, Axminster. She wondered what had happened to Honiton. She thought about Nic, trying to do the right thing for his mother, neglecting his wedding plans. She imagined herself driving into Honiton, tracking him down... I could meet his ex-wife with the peculiar name, get a sense of things, report back to Athena. I wonder what she's like, Mick, no, Mack, isn't it...?

The route had diverged. She seemed not to be on a main road at all. She wondered how it was she'd got so lost. She drove, on, waiting for an opportunity to turn back. Then she found she was heading down the hill, and there it was, a line of sea, sunlit and blue.

I ought to turn round, she thought. I need to get back to London. They'll be worrying, she thought, although she knew this wasn't true.

She parked the car at the top of town. Her bag was on the passenger seat beside her. She unzipped it and took out her father's books, flicked through until she found the letter to Monica, tucked into its envelope, the biro scrawl of her father's handwriting.

She folded the letter into her pocket and walked down the hill.

The beach looked like a postcard, the artificial brightness of the sea, children playing and paddling in spite of a sharp wind.

Agnes walked along the beach, enjoying the breeze against her face. She walked down to the sea's edge, watched the foamy waves lap around her toes. She found herself worrying about salt stains on the leather of her ankle boots. Her eye was drawn towards the stones, and she realised that many of them seemed to carry the marks of their own fossil stories; in shades of beige and pink and brown they tumbled over each other, glistening in the clear light, each one imprinted with the sign of the creature who had once lived; each one, in death, carrying a calligraphy of life.

She stood absolutely still, transfixed by the scene before her. Even the wind seemed to pass her by as she stared at the fossils, each one a fragment of a story, painstakingly written in stone.

And is that what my father saw, she wondered, as he stood on this same beach? And did he find it unbearable, to see it stretching away into the distance, with no beginning, no middle, no end?

She bent down and picked one up.

A violent interruption, she thought. A violent interruption to the cycle of creation. A way of creating a structure to the story, a way of holding up one's hand and saying: Here. Now. This is where the story starts. From here on we can find its meaning. We can look back to a past we can trace. We can say, 'This is what happened'.

She took out the envelope and stared at her father's handwriting.

All this time, I have denied him. All these years, I have said, my father and I were very different. All those times I've said it: Oh, I wasn't at all like my father...

And yet, here we both are, my father and I, standing on a beach, trying to find meaning in the chaos, to uncover the true story. For him it was about the Earth, an explanation of the beginnings of our universe itself. For me...

An image occurred to her. Rose petals, crumpled on a doorstep. Pink and cream and marbled, like the stones spread at her feet.

To uncover the true story.

A sudden gust of wind caused her to stumble. She looked at the envelope still clutched in her hand.

By the time she reached the house the sun had gone in. She pulled out the envelope again and checked the number. This was the house. This is the house.

She imagined her father walking up the gravel drive. She wondered if the door was the same pretty shade of apple green in those days. Perhaps Monica had had it repainted since.

There was a wisp of movement behind the windows, a flick of a curtain.

And what would I say, she thought.

Hello. I'm Agnes. You knew my father.

Maybe she'd be delighted. I'd be welcomed in and offered tea, and she'd ask me all about my father, and I'd say…

I'd say what?

Or perhaps she'd be appalled, to be confronted with the part of my father's life she never knew.

The front door was surrounded by an ornate porch, delicate curls of dark wood, with a large ceramic doorbell on one side. She took a step towards it.

From the street came the sound of approaching footsteps. A young man was walking towards the house. He had a shock of blond hair, a straight-backed, tailored look to his coat, and an uneven gait, as if one leg was longer than the other.

Agnes hurried away along the street. When she glanced back, the young man had disappeared.

CHAPTER TWENTY-ONE

By the time she reached the motorway the rain had set in. Against the steady beat of the windscreen wipers, she saw once again the glistening stones, the rose petals scattered on stone steps.

She'd walked away from Monica's house, back into town, back up the hill to her car. She said to herself it was because of the heavy clouds crowding the sky, the damp wind which threatened rain. But that didn't explain the tightening in the air, the sense of space shrinking around her.

She tried to warm up the car, but the dry roar of heat made it difficult to breathe.

Rose petals. Bruised and frayed, the rose stem still standing in the milk bottle on the hostel's doorstep. She'd said to Murchie, did you leave the roses on the doorstep?; he'd denied it, stuttering and red-faced.

Returning to the scene of the crime, that's what Rob Coombes had said.

And what had Zip said? Murchie didn't care enough about any woman to kill them.

Dermot, too, had set himself up against Murchie. But didn't the boys make it perfectly clear that Murchie had no liking for knives? If his other, more shadowy enemies had been dispensed with a single bullet, why make an exception for Dermot?

Roses. Roses left on a step, filthy and mocking. It's not the style of south London drug barons. It's more poetic, more dramatic, like an opera, something Italian…

Perhaps the roses mean nothing at all. Perhaps one of Murchie's boys saw it in a computer game.

She remembered Lindy's tears for Abbie. Why? she'd asked. She had no motive to kill herself. And no one had any motive to kill her. Even if Abbie had started a relationship with Dermot; even if she was talking of leaving…

How we cling to life, cling to our plans, plan for a future…

She remembered what Pauline Stipes had said, about a future. Even if it's only months. And Evelyn Blacklock, her health briefly restored, making plans for a future. A future without her husband.

Agnes was aware of a swerve of the car, loud hooting behind her, flashings of headlights. She steadied the steering wheel, braked, moved into the left-hand lane, tucked herself behind a lorry, tried to settle her breathing…

They all left. Abbie was leaving, Pauline was leaving, Eben's wife was leaving, Louisa is—

There was a service station ahead. She sped into the car park, braked hard, took out her phone and dialled the convent.

'Is Louisa there?' She was shouting, she realised.

'I'm very sorry, who is this?' The voice was clipped and well spoken – Sister Michaela, she thought.

'It's Agnes. I need to speak to her.'

'Oh, of course it's Agnes. Well, no, you can't speak to her.'

'What? What's happened?' Agnes was hoarse now.

'But you must know. She's very ill.'

'Ill?'

'Hasn't anyone told you? Oh, dear.'

'What's she got?'

'We think it's pneumonia. That's what that nice doctor thinks, anyway, he's been ever so helpful, he's allowed us to keep her at home rather than move her into hospital. It came on so fast, though...'

Agnes had started the engine and was driving out of the car park, one hand on the wheel. 'Keep him away from her,' she shouted down the phone.

'I'm sorry, Agnes, I don't know...'

'Send her to hospital. Please.'

'But Dr Kitson said—'

Agnes clicked off her phone and threw it on to the seat. She joined the motorway, grateful that Athena had upgraded to the Audi. She moved into the right-hand lane, wondering how to arrange it so that the Order would pay her speeding fines with all these darned sly cameras hidden everywhere.

Louisa was lifeless. She lay absolutely still, her eyes closed, her face skeletal. The only movement was a tremor in her throat with each shallow, hesitant breath. Agnes watched her. The convent seemed slowed and still, as if the flow of time itself had silted up.

Louisa's eyelids flickered, and Agnes whispered her name. Her eyes opened, gazed emptily on Agnes for a brief moment, then closed again.

Agnes stared at the papery, hollowed face before her. She

was gripped with fear. In her mind, the words circled; this is my fault.

She ran from the room, into the community office. She snatched up the phone, even though Sister Michaela was sitting right next to it. She dialled 999. She spoke to the operator, gave the information, hung up. Other Sisters had appeared in the room, people were asking her questions, but she found it difficult to hear, impossible to speak, standing in the hallway, waiting for the ambulance to arrive, only breathing again at the sound of the siren outside. It was Agnes who led the ambulance men to the room, and when Sister Lucia said, 'Pneumonia, we think,' Agnes grasped the paramedic by the arm and said, 'Please check for poisoning. Morphine. We think she's been poisoned,' she said, loudly.

The ambulance drove away. The convent was hushed once more; then, gradually, came back to life. Sisters gathered in the hall, asking what had happened, was Louisa worse, what was all this about poisoning?

'…We were all managing perfectly well until she appeared,' Agnes heard. 'Some people do have a heightened sense of drama…'

Agnes slipped away. She went back to Athena's car where it was parked on the corner right by the convent. She saw the plastic envelope stuck to the windscreen, and wondered how to persuade the Order to add the parking tickets to the speeding fines.

She left the car outside the hostel. At the top of the steps she turned, scanned the street. There was no one there.

The hostel was quiet. She remembered that Gilroy was taking Eddie to see his new accommodation. Aysha and the others would be at the weekly staff meeting in the lounge. The odd thump from upstairs reassured her that Sari and Lizzie were at home, Paz too, she hoped. She went into the office, checked Abbie's old file, wrote down the address of the squat where she'd lived.

Then she dialled Rob Coombes's number, heard the recorded message, asked him to come to the hostel as soon as possible; she had urgent information, she said.

She hung up, stared at the receiver. If only I did, she thought. If only I knew anything at all.

The air felt charged. The silence seemed to carry an electric hum within it. In her mind she saw Louisa's empty eyes, the strands of pale hair stuck to her forehead. Agnes leant back in her chair.

She heard the click of the door. In the glass window, the shadow of a face. A push of the handle, and the door eased open.

Dr Kitson took a step towards the desk. He appeared unaware of her presence, until she said, 'Hello.'

He jumped, startled, stared at her. 'Oh.' His smile seemed to take some effort. 'Hi. I didn't see you there. Catching forty winks?'

She smiled back. 'Sort of.'

'Staff meeting.' He jerked his head towards the corridor.

'You go to those, do you?'

'It really helps with my work, you know?' He sat down at the other desk; the chair swung to and fro with a rhythmic squeak.

'Louisa's in hospital, you know.' There. The words, spoken out loud. She waited.

The twitch of his lips. He stared at her. 'H-Hospital?'

'Well...' Agnes leant back in her chair. 'With that amount of toxin in her system, we couldn't take any chances.' She was surprised to find her voice was level.

The swaying ceased. He was stock-still. His lips worked, silently.

'I was in Devon yesterday,' Agnes said. 'Tavercombe. I gather you know it. I met Mr Blacklock...' Here we both are, she thought, Dr Kitson and me, having a chat. Except, that if this was a chat, he would be joining in. Mr Blacklock, he'd say. How is he? What a shame about his wife...

'He spoke very highly of you,' she said. Dr Kitson was still silent, although his breathing was coming in short gasps, and his knuckles were white on the sides of his chair.

'I mean, I know there was all that controversy over his poor wife, but it's not as if they found anything, did they? It's just like Mrs Stipes, it's not as if doctors can be expected to work miracles, can they...?' Agnes wondered how much longer she would have to fill the air with words.

He began to sway again, to and fro, staring straight ahead. The squeak of the chair was the only sound in the room.

Agnes tried more words. 'And there's poor Jeremy arrested for Pauline's murder—'

The squeaking stopped. His eyes fixed upon her, as if seeing her for the first time. He murmured something. Agnes caught the word 'unfaithful'.

'I'm sorry?' She leant towards him.

'She was unfaithful.' He spoke as if the language was foreign to him, each word spelt out.

'Who?'

'Evelyn.'

'Ah.' Agnes nodded.

'She said she was leaving.' He nodded. 'Yes. Leaving.'

'Leaving?' Agnes prompted.

He frowned at her, as if wondering who she was. 'The hospital,' he said. 'Louisa—' Now he appeared distressed. His grip tightened on the sides of the chair. 'She mustn't go, you see.' He met her eyes. 'I don't want her to go.'

'I'm sure Louisa is quite all right.' Agnes's voice was soothing.

'No—' His head jerked upright, his voice was loud. 'No, she's not all right.' He stared at Agnes. 'I had to make it all right. Make it all right again.'

'Yes. Of course.' Her fixed smile was beginning to ache.

'It's not my fault,' he said.

'No,' she agreed.

'They try to blame me, but I didn't do anything, I haven't done anything wrong.' He let go of the chair; his hands clenched into tight fists, banging on the sides of his knees. 'I tried to make her stay,' he said. 'You can't blame me if she went.' He continued to bash at his legs, harder and harder.

Agnes reached across and took hold of one of his hands. 'When did it start?'

He looked at her hand on his. He shook his head.

'With Evelyn? Or before?'

He glanced up at her. He shook his head again.

She kept her grip on his hand. 'Before?'

His lips were moving, but he said nothing.

The light in the room seemed to have grown dim. Agnes took a deep breath. 'Abbie,' she said. 'And Pauline. And Evelyn. And it would have been Louisa too, wouldn't it? And how many before?'

He seemed not to have heard. He was sitting absolutely still now.

'You can tell me,' Agnes heard herself say. 'You can just say, yes. Yes, I killed them. Abbie was easy, I imagine. No one would think to ask whether someone else had administered a dose of morphine to a girl known to be a junkie. Pauline was more complicated. So you gave her something slow-acting before you went away, and told her that the syringe you'd left with her was an antidote should anything go wrong, and you knew she'd trust you, even then, despite her misgivings...' Agnes heard the words spill from her lips. Still he didn't look up. He seemed hardly to breathe. The only sign of life was a strange, fast blinking of his eyes.

'I suppose the question is why,' Agnes said. 'A privileged man like you, growing up with your father, loved and supported, given a good education, everything that money could buy...'

Any reaction would be better than this, she thought; tears, rage, anything. 'And your mother.' She glanced at him. In her mind, a flash of memory, Cath coming into the room, the swing of her coat, Dr Kitson's fingers grabbing at the red tartan pocket.

He turned to her, frowning, as if seeing her for the first time. His lips worked, then he said, 'We were happy, my father and I. He did everything he could for me. He was proud of all my success.' His voice was a low monotone. 'I don't know what you're insinuating by all this.' He snatched his hand from her grasp. 'I've a good mind to report you.' The colour had returned to his face, and he stumbled to his feet.

'A tartan coat,' Agnes said. 'When your mother left, she was wearing a tartan coat.'

He turned back to her, reached an arm out into thin air, swaying.

'The pocket,' Agnes said.

He stared down at her.

'And she never came back.' Agnes gazed up at him.

He fell back into his chair. He gazed straight ahead. Out in the street a child bounced a ball; the sound came towards them, then faded away again.

'Pockets,' Dr Kitson turned to Agnes and smiled. 'You could keep your hand warm in them when you were walking along next to her.' He patted the side of his jacket with his hand.

'When did she leave?'

'She was in the doorway.' Dr Kitson stared at his feet. 'She was standing in the doorway. She had a suitcase. I knew she meant it this time. If she was coming back, she wouldn't be wearing her winter coat. Red. Red tartan. It was summer,' he said, as if to explain. His hand dropped to his side. 'It was the last time I saw her.'

'Why did she leave?'

He shrugged.

'Is it because he was cruel?'

'He wasn't cruel.'

'Why didn't she take you with her?'

He breathed as if gasping for air. His face was open, like a child's; his eyes were moist.

'Did she say why?'

He shook his head.

'She must have been very unhappy, to leave you behind.' She reached out her hand towards him again.

'I can't remember...' He lowered his head. His voice was

low. 'My father used to say she left because I wasn't good enough. But I'm not sure he was right, because there's one bit I do remember, I'm sure I do...' He stopped. Agnes waited.

'I ran up to her. I had a bear, a little knitted one. Someone had made him for me...a great-aunt, I think. I put my hand in the pocket of her coat, like I used to do. And I tucked the bear in with it. And she patted the pocket, with the bear in it, and she looked at me, and she was crying. And then she picked up her suitcase and walked away...' He covered his face. When he took his hands away, his eyes were dry. He turned to Agnes with an empty smile. 'And you see, when I remember it, I hear her say that she'll come back for me. And I remember them arguing, on the doorstep, and my father shouting, You can't afford to keep him, what about that school, it's very expensive – something like that...' He met her eyes, then looked away again.

'Did you really never see her again?'

He stared at the floor. 'She was American. Something happened with her visa. My father wouldn't sign something. They weren't married, it turned out. He wouldn't marry her.'

'She was deported?'

He nodded.

'And then you went to medical school.'

The warmth in his face was fading. His expression seemed to shut down.

'But – surely...'

He flashed her a glance. 'Surely she kept in touch, you mean?'

'Or her family?'

'She had no family. She had a cousin. I think it was a cousin. Someone sent me the death notice, anyway.'

'Death notice?'

He was drained of colour. His eyes were blank. 'Sudden death. Might have been suicide.' His voice was expressionless. 'They didn't say so in the papers in those days.' He gave an odd, coquettish smile.

She looked at him. His gaze was fixed straight ahead, as if at a picture on the wall. He began to rock, backwards and forwards.

I could say nothing, she thought. We could sit here for a while, and then after a bit he'll snap out of it and stand up and – and what? Pretend nothing's happened? Chat about his evening surgery?

Agnes broke the silence. 'So your father said you weren't good enough.'

'He said if I'd been a good boy I'd still have a mother.' His voice was reedy and child-like. 'But it wasn't my fault.' He turned towards her. 'It wasn't my fault, was it?'

'No,' Agnes said. 'It wasn't your fault.'

He began to hit his leg with one hand.

'How old were you?' Agnes tried.

'Nine,' he said.

In Agnes's mind, a picture began to form; but he interrupted. 'He told me I had to be a man now, not a boy. When he hit me, he told me not to cry. "You're not a baby now, son," he'd say.' Again, the odd smile.

'He hit you?'

Dr Kitson looked at her. 'Well…no. Not really. Not much, anyway. Only when I deserved it.'

The room seemed suddenly cold. How I remember that, she thought. All those years spent living with violence, dependent on the perpetrator of the violence, until you believe them too, yes I deserved it really, yes, it was my fault, yes, if only I hadn't done that or neglected to do this, he would have had no reason to hit me...

'No one deserves it,' she said.

His breathing had become laboured. He sat, motionless, his blank gaze fixed on her.

'Your father was wrong,' she said.

A passing siren cut through the silence; it was as if a spell was broken. Dr Kitson jumped to his feet. He was huge, red-faced, towering over her, his voice a roar of rage. 'You think you're so bloody clever, don't you? Coming in here with your do-gooding, your faux psychology, throwing around your accusations...What do you know about it? You don't understand the first thing about it.' His legs were almost touching hers, the stream of words so close that she shrank back in her chair. 'I could take action against you, you know, I could have you arrested. Slander!' he shouted. 'Sending her to hospital. You shouldn't have done that. I knew when it was right, no one else knows, no one...' He stepped away from her, turned towards the door. 'I expected better from you. I'm always disappointed. Always...' He strode to the door, still shouting. 'I'm going now, and there's nothing you can do—' He threw open the office door, stepped out into the corridor.

Agnes flung herself from her chair. She tried to run after him, but her legs felt strange and weak. He was already at the front door as she stumbled to catch up with him, his hand on the latch. He opened the door.

Rob Coombes was standing there. 'You've saved me from ringing the bell,' he said.

CHAPTER TWENTY-TWO

'Yes, I know they're all at vespers...' Agnes tried to steady her voice. 'But can you leave a message – it's about Louisa? Yes, in hospital, I know...' She listened while Sister Mary explained that they'd phoned up about visiting her tomorrow and the nurse had been a bit cagey, no one knew why, it was all rather worrying...'That's what I'm trying to tell you,' Agnes interrupted. 'She's survived a murder attempt. The police will be questioning her tomorrow, now she's regained consciousness. Yes, I did say murder. Yes, that's the point, they've arrested someone...'

Her mind replayed the scene on the hostel steps, as Dr Kitson had tried to push past Rob Coombes; Rob, seeing the state he was in, had grabbed his arm and said, 'Whoah, what's all this—?' And Agnes, standing behind him, had begun to gabble – he killed Abbie, and Pauline, he tried to kill Louisa—

Rob, struggling to understand, had looked up at the doctor; and Dr Kitson, raving still, had aimed a punch at him with his free hand. At which point, Rob, listening to Agnes's stream of explanations, produced handcuffs, radioed for help, and within minutes Dr Kitson had been manhandled into a police car and driven away.

'He's being questioned now,' Agnes said in answer to Sister Mary's new flurry of worrying. 'They're waiting for test results from the hospital. Yes,' she agreed. 'Louisa's going to be all right. Thank God.'

She clicked off her phone. Outside it was dark. The windows of her flat were streaked with rain.

She dialled Brett's number, which went straight to voicemail. 'Please call me,' she said. 'It's Agnes. I went to Charmouth. I need to talk to you.'

The third call was to Athena's home number. There was an answering machine. 'Oh. It's me.' Agnes hoped she was screening calls and would pick up, but nothing happened. 'Well, I'll try tomorrow. I hope you don't need your lovely car quite yet. There's one more thing I've got to do.'

She checked the piece of paper she'd copied from Dermot's file. She dialled another number. 'Hello,' she said. 'It's Sister Agnes. As I promised…Yes,' she said, in answer. 'Although I'm sorry to disturb you on a Saturday evening…Well, if you're sure, that would be very kind of you.'

She drove west along the Embankment, glad of the efficient heating in Athena's car. She headed south, inching her way around Elephant and Castle, finding herself driving through Kennington, Clapham Road, Stockwell. It goes on and on, South London, she thought. She was surprised Athena's car hadn't simply refused to go any further.

And then the junction with Clapham High Street, another turn right, and she found herself in a pretty Victorian terrace. She parked the car.

The street was dark with unpollarded trees. She searched for number seven – 'It's the one with the overgrown garden, you can't miss it.'

There was a neat electric bell. Agnes pressed the button.

The woman who opened the door had untidy blond hair streaked with grey, and large sheepskin slippers. 'Ah,' she said. 'There you are, then.'

She showed Agnes into a bright kitchen of terracotta tiles and wooden worktops. 'Do sit down.' She waved towards a broad pine table. 'Sorry about the mess. Find a space somewhere.' Agnes lifted a heap of magazines from one of the chairs and sat down.

'Actually,' she said, switching on the kettle, 'I don't know why I apologise for the mess. This is how I live since our Cheryl left home. I'm not really sorry at all.' She smiled across at her. 'And I don't know why I'm putting the kettle on, either, because I'm halfway through a really nice Merlot, and you might as well help me finish it.'

She fetched a second glass, and sat down opposite Agnes, pushing a newspaper and a bowl of fruit out of the way. 'There,' she said. 'Now I can get a proper look at you. Mind you, you don't look like a nun.' She pointed in Agnes's direction. 'I'm used to the nuns back home. You know where you are with them, and it's usually in the wrong.'

Agnes laughed.

She poured some red wine into a glass and handed it to Agnes, then topped up her own. She peered at the glass. 'All these units we're supposed to count these days. But the O'Keefes have always been drinkers, and it's done us no harm so far. So,' she said. 'Dermot O'Hagan. Poor kid. The police told me what had happened. They even came here, asked me about him, but there was so little I could say. I barely saw him, you know? And then you called, and I was about to say the same to you, until you said it was Connor you wanted to know about, and I thought, well, at least he was our side of the family. Sweet boy too, what I saw of him, which wasn't much when I was back home. And I know they said he was in London, but I never saw him here neither. So—' She leant on one elbow. 'What did you want to know?'

The wine glass in Agnes's hand was curved and elegant. She turned it round between her fingers. 'The thing is, Carole – I'm not sure what the question is.'

Carole smiled at her. 'Do you know the answer, then?'

Agnes met her eyes. 'The answer seems to lie in a faded rose left on someone's grave. In Ireland, perhaps.'

Carole blinked. Her expression grew serious. 'Cosima's husband, then? That's who you mean. My cousin Desi. She loved him all her life, in spite of the terrible tragedy. Cosima and Desi, they were made for each other, she'd say so herself: "A match made in heaven," she'd say, in her lovely Italian accent. And every Sunday she'd go to his grave and take a single rose. And when there were no roses to be found, she'd take a wild flower, a branch of tree blossom, anything. Even right at the end of her life, when she could hardly walk, she'd set off from the village to walk the two or three miles to the church graveyard.'

'So, Desi was Connor's father?'

Carole frowned at her. 'I think we'd better start at the beginning.'

Athena's car seemed faster on the journey back, racing towards Tower Bridge with an eager instinct for home. Still south of the river, though, Agnes thought, as she parked under a lamp about three streets away from the hostel. She wished the Audi didn't look quite so new and shiny, surrounded as it was by boarded-up windows, faceless low-rise housing, graffitied walls topped with fearsome metal spikes. The rain had eased, but the night air was damp. She checked the address and approached the house. It was part of an older terrace which stopped abruptly – bombed, perhaps. Agnes saw uneven brickwork, dark, curtainless windows. There was no bell, so she knocked, loudly.

The door opened into a dark hallway, and Lindy stood there. 'Hi,' she said. 'I got your message on my phone. We ain't going nowhere anyway.'

Agnes followed her through the dim passageway, into the room that passed for a lounge. Lindy sprawled on to a mattress on the floor. 'You can have the chair. Can't she, Connor?'

Connor grunted from the corner. He stood up and moved to sit next to Lindy.

Agnes sat down in the armchair, its chintz arms greasy with age. The room was lit by a single light bulb, which cast shifting shadows as it swung very slightly to and fro. The window frame was rotten, the glass cracked. A makeshift curtain drooped across part of it in off-white folds.

'So—' Lindy curled her knees under her. 'That doctor killed Abbie. The bastard. If I saw him now, I'd – I'd – wouldn't I, eh, Connor?'

Connor was hunched over, hugging his knees. He grunted again.

'She had everything to live for. Didn't she? Didn't I tell you?' She turned her face to Agnes. 'Everything to live for. The bastard. I suppose he thought he'd get away with it.'

Connor reached into his pocket and took out a packet of cigarettes.

'She and Dermot would've been so happy, you know.' Lindy watched Connor take out a cigarette and light it. She turned back to Agnes. 'Did he kill Dermot too?' Her eyes were wide and shining, perhaps with tears, Agnes thought.

'No,' Agnes said. 'He didn't kill Dermot.'

'It were that Murchie. For once them feds have got the right bloke. All along, that's what it were, a fight between Mots and Murchie, and Murchie couldn't bear him winning. It's like I said all along, didn't I Connor? Here, give me one of them—' She reached across and grabbed the packet of cigarettes. Connor barely looked up. 'A feud,' Lindy said, 'that's what it were.'

'Yes,' Agnes said. 'A feud.'

Lindy lit her cigarette, threw the packet back to Connor. It landed in front of him. 'And then there was the wares—' Lindy exhaled a curl of smoke. 'I knew Mots had been up to something, and it was just like him to try to go straight when it were too late. Someone should have tried to warn him that Murchie weren't having nothing like that.' She turned to Connor. 'You tried, didn't you, Con? I remember you saying...' She took another drag. 'But he wouldn't listen. He was like that, Mots was.' She fell silent, watching the smoke rise from her cigarette.

'Murchie couldn't have done it without the Irish connection.' Agnes settled further back on her chair.

'Nah.' Lindy nodded. 'He needed Mots.'

'That's why it was quite convenient when you arrived in London too, wasn't it Connor?'

He looked up at her, blank-eyed. He flicked some ash into an empty mug.

'Particularly as Dermot could be trouble at times.'

Lindy smiled fondly. 'Oh, yeah. Bad shit. Sometimes his own worst enemy, Mots was.'

'You calmed him down a bit, you looked out for him,' Agnes went on.

Connor turned his cigarette between his fingers.

'You were like that, weren't you? You and Mots. Cousins, see. Blood being thicker and all that.' Lindy patted his knee. He stared at the cigarette packet in front of him.

'That's why Dermot didn't tell the truth at first,' Agnes said, 'when Abbie was killed. Because he thought she might have killed herself. And he couldn't tell the police the whole story because of his own involvement in the cocaine-shipping business from Ireland. Although, by then, he was beginning to extricate himself from it, as Murchie had a better Irish connection to work with.' Agnes glanced at Connor. A gust of wind rattled the window frame. 'Of course,' Agnes went on, 'that wasn't the main reason you came to London, was it? There was another reason.'

Connor stubbed out his cigarette in the empty mug.

'Your mother—' Agnes began. Connor raised his eyes to hers. 'Your mother Cosima asked you to come here, didn't she?'

Connor's gaze was unmoving. Lindy glanced up at Connor, frowning. She shifted on the mattress, curled her legs the other way.

'It was the roses,' Agnes said. 'I couldn't work out who would have left those roses for Dermot. And then I remembered you making that joke about your mother's family, that they'd kill someone one day and put flowers on their grave the next.'

Lindy's eyes were fixed on Connor.

Connor picked up the cigarette packet. He turned back to Agnes. 'It were a joke.' His voice was rough. 'Weren't it?'

'No,' Agnes said. 'I don't think it's a joke at all. There's a grave, in Ireland, isn't there, where your mother used to leave flowers? Every week. Right up until she died, almost, until those last few days when she could no longer walk the two or three miles to the graveyard.'

Connor was breathing heavily, his mouth open. Lindy was now staring at Agnes.

'And it was in those last few days that your mother sent for you, and told you she was dying, and made you promise something. And it was after that that you came to London, looking for Dermot.'

'I never said I'd do it.' His voice was a hoarse whisper. 'I told her not to ask me to do that. She wouldn't listen. She said her ghost wouldn't rest in peace until she'd been avenged.'

'So you promised?'

He looked down at the cigarette packet in his hands. He nodded.

'What? Con, what did you promise?' Lindy's voice was shrill. She reached for his arm and shook it. 'Tell me.'

He didn't move.

'It was just the drugs, weren't it, Con? Say that's all it was. Just the gear from Kinsale, the boats coming over like that night I heard you talking to Murch about it and when I asked you you said, nothing, babe, nothing to worry about. So I didn't. I trusted you...' Her voice cracked with tears.

Agnes broke the silence. 'It's what you said, Lindy. A feud. A feud between Dermot's father and Connor's father. Both brothers. Both from a fairground family. And that's how they

met your mum, didn't they Connor? Cosima, known as
Seema. Also from the fairs, but originally from Sardinia. Her
father had fled his home and taken up a new life in Ireland.
There was some story of a murder in Sardinia, his father being
in fear of his life. And your mother lived with the shadow of
this fear, didn't she?'

Connor's face was bone-white. He made no movement, no
sound, staring down at his hands.

'So, when she met Desi O'Hagan, your dad, through the
fairs, and they both fell in love, she was happy. She could start
a life away from the shadow of whatever it was that had
happened in Nuoro all those years ago. And Desi and his
brother Tommy, they ran their rides, and travelled their patch,
along with their father. But what no one knew was that
Dermot's dad Tommy was in love with Cosima. He watched
his little brother and his new wife, and he seethed with rage.
And he might have kept all that to himself, in spite of his
reputation for violence. But there was worse to come. When
their father Big Louie died, Tommy found out he'd left the
whole business to Desi, the younger son. And no one knew
why. Tommy was disinherited. Ousted from the family firm.
His cousins turned their backs on him. He was met with
silence. Some people thought that it must have been because
he wasn't his father's son. There'd been murmurings for years,
but no one could prove anything and their mother was long
since dead. And one night, in a terrible drunken rage, he killed
Desi, and he raped Cosima, the woman he'd always loved,
and for whom his love had now turned to hate. And then he
left Ireland.

'And as we know, he went to Liverpool, worked in
construction, married, had Dermot. Made rather a poor fist of

the whole thing. His wife left, Dermot ran away. All of this we know.

'But going back to Seema. Seema, now widowed, and as yet childless, finds she's pregnant. She raises you on her own. She's taken in by Desi's aunt Vera, a kind woman, who left the fairgrounds some years before. Her own daughter, Carole, has married and moved to London, so it's nice for her to have company and a baby around the place too. The fairground people close ranks, no one wants to see Dermot's father brought back from England, she's told to keep quiet. She raises her baby, baby Connor. And she never forgets Desi, the man she'd always loved, the man whose grave she tended every week. But she knows the truth, deep down. She knows what happened, the night she was raped. And the secret grows within her, like a cancer. And finally, when she's dying, as if the rage itself has finally eaten her away, she makes you promise to avenge her—'

Lindy shouted out – 'Tell me it ain't true, Con.'

Connor looked at her, his eyes blank. He turned to Agnes, attempted to speak, fell silent.

'You and Dermot,' Agnes said. 'You weren't cousins. You were half-brothers. And you killed him.'

Connor raised himself up on the mattress, his legs at an odd angle. He was agitated, his fingers twisting together in his lap. 'I weren't going to kill him. I knew, even when my mum told me, I knew I couldn't kill him. When I came over here and found him, we were like brothers, we got on, we did, peas in a pod...but it went wrong. When he wanted to stop dealing, Murch got angry. It was his cousin in Bristol who was the middleman, like, and Murch knew that if we stopped it would leave him exposed, and he'd get bad shit. And I tried to protect Dermot but I was angry too. And then Abbie died, and Mots was talking to the feds, and Murchie was really angry then, right full of rage, I thought he'd kill him. He battered him then, like you know. And after that I thought, Dermot's in real danger, and I said I wanted to talk to him, I wanted to sort it out, and he came to meet me. And he was right weird, like out of it, I said, what you on, boy, and he wouldn't say. So I sit him down, and I say, you've got to stop grassing to the feds. And he's telling me to get out of the business, and I say, you tell me what else I'm going to do, and he says that his dad said we were always the bad lot, always the bad side of the family. And I look at him, mouthing off, dissing my mum, dissing the man he thought was my dad. And I'm trying to say, Dermot, we're brothers, and he's going on about Desi, the one I never knew, the one my mum always loved – and I lose it. I see red. And I slice him. And he runs off. And I run after him. Only I know, I can see how he's staggering, he's shouting for help, he gets up to the hostel, and I can see he's bleeding, and I stand in the street and I'm thinking two things. One is, if I hang around I'm in deep shit. And the other is, I kept my promise. I never meant to, but now I have. And I stand in the street, and the rain's pouring on my face and I look up to Heaven and I say, Mum. I kept my promise. And then I run…'

He buried his head in his hands.

Lindy was trying to speak. 'The roses—' she said. 'Why did you…?'

He looked up at her. He breathed. 'After Abbie died, I saw them roses in a bin, and I kind of knew I had to do it. Maybe it was because I felt bad, because I was the last one to see her, there in the street, and I thought I could have said something, could have helped her. And then with Dermot, it happened again. Just one rose, sticking out of a bin. Like a sign. It spooked me. It was like I was taken over by something. I felt I had to...' He shook his head.

'It was your promise, babes.' Lindy reached out to him, but he shrugged her hand away. Tears welled in her eyes. She clasped her hands together, shifted away from him. She began to cry.

Connor slumped forwards, his face buried in his arms. The only sound in the room was Lindy's quiet sobbing. It had begun to rain again. Drops of water squeezed through the cracked glass and splashed on to the bare floor.

'...How many tears must we shed, O Lord; are the oceans of the Earth to be filled with our weeping...?'

Agnes heard Julius recite the words. The altar window was muted in the dull morning light, as if the red and blue and gold were dissolving in the rain which beat against the glass.

She thought about Lindy, waking up alone in that damp, desolate room; the empty mugs, the cigarette ash, the stained scrap of curtain keeping the rain at bay.

'You're very quiet.' Julius put a mug down in front of her. After the Mass she had followed him silently down the stairs to his office, slumped into the chair by his desk. 'It must be very bad,' Julius went on, 'for you to put sugar in your tea.'

She stirred the spoon around in the mug.

'Go on, then.'

She raised her eyes to his. 'Last night a man was arrested for killing his half-brother. And I had to see the young woman who thought he was worthy of her love have all her hopes and dreams smashed to bits.'

'This isn't—'

Agnes nodded. 'Dermot. Yes. He was killed by Connor, who we thought was his cousin but it turned out they had the same father.'

'So, they arrested Connor?'

'Poor Rob Coombes. I had to call him out on a Saturday night. I half thought Connor would run away, make a bid for freedom. But he just sat there. He kind of gave up, I think. He just stood there and allowed himself to be arrested. And poor Lindy, sobbing as though her heart would break. I've arranged for her to move into the hostel, she's going over there later today.'

'Jeremy Stipes has been released.' Julius sat down at his desk with a heavy out-breath.

'That was quick.'

'No further case against him. I popped in to see him yesterday. He's rattling around in that miserable house. The worse thing is, he's become a spokesperson for euthanasia. Two phone calls while I was there, he had to explain that he wasn't responsible for his wife's death, sent them away very disappointed. They were obviously hoping to speak to a real live murderer.'

'What will he do?'

'I don't know. He seemed to have shrunk. He was skin and bone. Kept going on about Dr Kitson. "I can't believe it of him. To think I trusted him…" That sort of thing.'

'Poor man.'

'He has a relative in Yorkshire, apparently. On the coast somewhere. Whitby, I think. I was suggesting he start again, make a new life. Anything's better than being stuck in that house with those curtain-twitching neighbours.' He glanced behind him at the window. 'Miserable weather. How was Dorset?'

'Sunny.'

'Lucky you.'

She wrapped her fingers around her mug. 'While I was there, I felt light and unburdened and – happy. I walked on the beach, I looked at fossils, I thought about my father and his writings... I thought about beginnings, middles and endings.' She took a sip of tea. 'And I saw this young man. He was walking down a street...' The mug wobbled in her hand, and she put it down.

'A young man? How old?' Julius studied her.

'Mid-twenties, I reckon.'

'And is he part of the story, this young man?'

'I don't know yet.'

'Ah, that's better.' Julius leant back in his chair.

'What's better?'

'You're smiling. I thought perhaps the burden of all these arrests was going to weigh you down for good.'

'Was I smiling?'

'You can't deny it. It must be the young man, about whom you know nothing.'

'I think, if he means anything at all, he's the reason that Brett ran away from me.'

'What are you going to do?'

'I'm going to have to track Brett down and annoy him.'

'That's all right. I was worried it might be something difficult.'

'If you're not careful I might throw something at you.'

Julius leant back in his chair. Behind him the window teemed with rain. 'Now you really are your old self. In a minute you'll be asking me if I've got a single-malt whisky tucked away somewhere.'

'What do you mean, tucked away? There's a very nice half-bottle in full view over there, right next to the tea bags.'

'So there is. Lucky my parishioners don't come down here.'

'Anyway, it's much too early, even for me, as you well know.'

'I just thought perhaps we should celebrate.'

'Celebrate?' Agnes stared at him.

'These last few weeks you've been a long way away.'

Agnes looked at her mug, clasped between her hands. Her voice when she spoke was quiet. 'I didn't mean to run away,' she said.

Julius was still gazing at her, and she raised her eyes to his. 'Perhaps you had to run away,' he said. 'But I'm glad you came back.'

CHAPTER TWENTY-THREE

'Well, honestly, if it means another serial killer has been taken off the streets, it's the least I can do. What's a few points on my licence between friends, eh?'

Agnes stood by her mirror, combing her hair. 'It might be more than a few. And there's a parking ticket too.'

'We can go and appeal.' Athena put her feet up on Agnes's desk chair. 'We can stand up in court and insist that it was a matter of life and death. Well, it was, wasn't it? How is that poor nun he almost poisoned?'

'Louisa?' Agnes turned away from the mirror. 'She's fine. She's out of hospital, back in the community house. I'm due to visit her later on today.'

'Definitely a court appearance. We can get new outfits. Something black and tailored. Hats, maybe?'

'But Athena—'

'What?'

'Aren't we saving up for the wedding?'

'Oh, that.' She flopped back on to Agnes's cushions. 'Far too many shopping days between now and whenever Nic thinks we might get married. Months. Years, probably. I'll need a new outfit before then.'

'What's happened?'

'More of the same. Iris is in hospital. They're talking of discharging her, I think they're mad, she seemed really ill to me, Nic and I were both there yesterday. And so now Nic's running around trying to find the right kind of care for her.'

'You were in Devon?'

Athena nodded. 'But no sign of the ex-wife, thank goodness. I think she was hiding from me.'

'Can you blame her?'

'Sign of a guilty conscience if you ask me. So – where are we going for lunch?'

Agnes unhooked her coat from its peg. 'Wherever you like. And then after that, I'm calling in at a rehearsal studio in Old Street.'

'Don't tell me – the dancer girlfriend of the not-so-gorgeous American?'

'Absolutely right. I've been leaving him messages ever since I got back from Dorset, and he's ignoring me.'

'Oh, they're hopeless, really. But—' Athena stood up and tied her raincoat belt around her waist – 'Do you think the girlfriend is the right approach to take?'

'I just have this hunch she might be.'

'Well, kitten...' Athena sauntered to the door, waited for Agnes. 'Your hunches are usually right. Especially where gorgeous men are concerned.'

Notes of Bach floated down towards her, as Agnes climbed the dark staircase to the studio. She pushed the door open. She saw limbs, in pink and blue and yellow, bodies in leotards and leg warmers and T-shirts. The windows were reflected in a mirror the length of the room; muted daylight bounced off the polished floorboards.

The music came from an upright piano in the corner of the space. Agnes stood by the door, watching the long forms and curves of limbs echoing the structured progressions of the notes of music. At the front there was a tall figure outlined in tight black clothes; counting, stepping, turning, every so often calling a halt, starting again.

She wasn't sure how long she'd stood there, watching the bodies make shapes that formed and changed, reflected in the mirror. Then the music faded to silence, the dancers loosened into chatter and the shaking out of limbs, and Georgie was crossing the room towards her.

'I hope you didn't feel ignored.' She kissed her on both cheeks.

'Not ignored. Large. Clumsy.'

'You're neither.' Georgie laughed. She took her arm and led her to a bench at the edge of the studio, and they sat down side by side. Across the studio, the other dancers talked, stretched, sipped from bottles.

'So—' Georgie looked at her. 'Brett.'

'He's not returning my calls,' Agnes said. 'And it's really quite important.'

'I'm having nothing to do with him at the moment.' Georgie bent over, wrapped her hands around her leg-warmered ankles.

'I don't blame you.'

Georgie straightened up, breathed out. 'I don't get what it is with him. He made this song and dance about coming over and seeing me, he couldn't live without me, the Chambers money meant he could spend some time here properly, he mentioned some unfinished business on behalf of a friend too, that must have been your father...and then what does he do?' She reached up and leant one arm over her head. 'He proceeds to tell us a load of half-truths, dumps a load of old writings on you, not to mention a dead person's head, and runs away.' She tilted her head to one side, then the other. 'Mind you I don't know why I'm surprised, he's always been that way.'

'Athena says it's moon in Pisces.'

'I wouldn't be at all surprised.'

The pianist had taken up her place at the piano again, and notes of music filled the space. The choreographer stood beside her, counting out the beats, occasionally taking a step, making a turn. 'And one, and two—' Agnes heard. 'The thing is, Rach, if we can slow it right down on the adagio, we can pick up speed in the second movement.'

Georgie was watching him. 'I feel so lucky, you know,' she said to Agnes. 'This is such a break, to work with Niklaus like this. He's got plans to tour the States and everything.'

'Is the whole show this piece?'

Georgie shook her head. Her eyes were still on Niklaus, as he walked over to one of the dancers, a dark-skinned man in layers of white, and talked through some steps. 'We're doing a Balanchine too. But this is Niklaus's piece. I love it. He asks so much of us, you find yourself opening up to ways you've never danced before. He has this idea about silence and stillness. The silence between the notes. The stillness between the steps. That's why the music works so well, the way Bach brings each phrase out of the one before, the way he endlessly postpones any resolution. We're trying to do the same with the dance. It's a kind of narrative, when each step leads to another, and all the time you don't know what's going to happen next, until at the end it all kind of resolves, and yet even the resolution is open-ended, it leaves open the possibility of the next phrase, the next part of the story.'

'Goodness me. And I thought dance was all silly stories and pretty costumes.'

Georgie smiled. 'Maybe it's a while since you went to the ballet.'

Agnes turned to her. 'What do I know? I'm just a nun.'

Georgie met her eyes. 'Don't say "just".'

At the piano, Rachel started to play, and the dancer in white came to stand in the middle of the floor. He began to move; slow, sustained steps, a pirouette turn, an arabesque, his body one long, balanced, changing line.

'I should go,' Agnes whispered. 'You're obviously about to start again.' She gathered up her bag.

'I don't know what to suggest about Brett. If I hear from him, I'll get him to ring you.'

'Thanks.'

Georgie stood up. 'You are coming to the show on Friday?'

'I certainly am,' Agnes said. 'After the preview I've just seen, I wouldn't miss it for anything.'

'One ticket, or two?'

One, Agnes was about to say, but then she remembered. 'Two, please.'

'They'll be on the door.'

She wandered south in the thin, watery sunlight, taking the road from Old Street, eventually finding a bus stop. The bus towards Hackney skirted the edge of the City, and through the tower blocks Agnes glimpsed the glass facades of the City as they blinked emptily in the Sunday sunset. She thought about the silence between notes; the stillness between steps.

Louisa looked somehow older, as if her hair had grown more grey, her face more pinched. She was sitting alone in the community lounge, propped up in one of the green armchairs. As Agnes approached she reached out and grabbed her arm and pulled her towards her. She held her like that, gripped in her embrace, for a long moment.

Her face was expressionless. Agnes sat down in the chair close to hers. The central heating was making its irregular ticking sound.

After a while, Louisa turned to her. 'I owe you my life.' The words settled in the grey twilight of the room.

'Well—' Agnes began, but Louisa held up her hand.

'Without you I wouldn't be here. I'm grateful to you beyond words.'

'I—'

'And don't start talking about God's will.' Louisa interrupted again. 'Don't let supernatural beings take the credit. You worked it out.' She tapped her head. 'Intellect. Reason. Evidence. Don't go talking to me about faith.'

'But, in fact—' Agnes tried.

'It's rationality that saved my life. I tell you, I'm done with blind faith.' She leant her head on the back of the chair, settling her breath.

The door opened and Sister Michaela tiptoed in with a tray of tea things, placed it down carefully on the table in front of them and tiptoed out again.

'Good heavens,' Agnes said.

'I know. Waited on hand and foot.'

'Best china. I haven't seen these things in use since that French deacon, or whatever he was, came to visit, the one who turned out to be embezzling from the Order's house in Brittany. Or was that before your time?'

Louisa laughed, and for a moment it was the old Louisa, bright-eyed and amused. Then her features clouded again. 'You know he's pleading not guilty? Dr Kitson, I mean.'

'I had heard, yes. Rob Coombes told me this morning.'

She breathed out with a sigh. 'It means I'll have to give evidence. As the only living witness to his homicidal urges...' her voice faltered. She busied herself pouring tea for them both.

'He's on remand in prison. He's charged with Abbie's murder, and Pauline, and Evelyn in Devon, and the attempt on your life too. And the hospital in Devon are having another look at three other cases of sudden death, all women. It'll take some time, he might change his plea. And Rob said they'd looked again at the syringe that Pauline was holding – it was full of morphine, but it was labelled Naloxone. Rob says that Naloxone is an antidote to morphine, you use it to wake people up again. So, it looks as if it wasn't the syringe that Jeremy had stockpiled at all, but something that Dr Kitson had given to Pauline, deliberately wrongly labelled. So that even if the high oral dose that he provided that evening didn't work, he knew that Pauline would try to counteract it herself later on, when he'd long since left and was hiding at his brother's.' Agnes took a deep breath. 'All of which means, when all this evidence is presented to him, that he might simply accept the truth.'

Louisa shook her head. 'Can you see him doing anything other than total denial?'

'No.' Agnes picked up the bone china cup and held it between her finger and thumb. 'No, I can't.'

Louisa sipped her tea.

'What will you do?' Agnes asked her.

'Oh, I've told them here already. I'm leaving. I'm going back to the States, going to live near my sister, help with the project for women on the streets.'

'As a—' Agnes hesitated. 'As a lay person?'

Louisa nodded. 'As an ordinary, secular member of the public. It's like I said – blind faith is not for me.'

Outside in the hall a solitary bell was chiming. Louisa put down her cup. 'I assume you're joining us for vespers?' She reached across to Agnes, and Agnes helped her to stand up. They walked towards the chapel arm in arm.

'You still come to chapel?' Agnes whispered to her. 'Despite being a secular, ordinary person?'

'What do you think? I was born a Catholic. When it comes to trying to leave, it's almost like being Jewish.'

Arm in arm, they walked through the chapel doors and found their places.

'And it came to pass that the children of Israel took their journeys out of the wilderness of Sinai. And the standard of the camp of Reuben set forward according to their armies...'

Reuben, Simeon, Levi, Judah... Agnes thought of the black ink words on the skull. The sons of Israel...

'And when the Ark rested, Moses said, "Return O Lord unto the many thousands of Israel." '

She thought of Eben Blacklock, who'd reminded her of her father.

And Brett. 'I don't like being lied to...'

Was that the lie, then? Was that what Brett had discovered, that made him turn away from the whole enterprise, that made him hand over to her all the clues, the objects, the artefacts, that added up to a picture of Ralph Gardner being Jewish?

She glanced up at Louisa, who was standing with her eyes shut.

'The Lord will visit the iniquity of the fathers upon the children, unto the third and fourth generation.'

My father's silence, Agnes thought. The silence between the words.

CHAPTER TWENTY-FOUR

Agnes was woken on Monday morning by bright sunshine and the revving of a car engine. She pulled back the curtains to see a Mercedes SL in the courtyard, with a man at the wheel who appeared to be waving to her.

It looks like Brett, she thought, rubbing sleep from her eyes. He was still waving, so she waved back, half expecting a glamorous young woman to appear below and get into the passenger side, the door of which Brett was now holding open and pointing to.

'Since when did you and I become actors in a Godard movie?' Agnes leant through the driver's window. It had taken her five minutes to find some clothes, wash her face and run downstairs, blinking in the sunshine.

'You could be Jane Fonda.'

'At my age?'

'She's older than you.'

'That's really not the point.' She straightened up and surveyed him.

'I'm – um – I'm sorry I haven't returned your calls.' Agnes said nothing, so he went on, 'Georgie told me you were looking for me. It all got rather complicated. As I think you guessed. Your father hadn't told me the whole story, it turned out, and I felt responsible for bringing news into your life that I thought might not be welcome...' He stopped, waiting for her answer.

'Do you know—' She took a step back, surveying the car. 'I always thought if I got one of these I'd get it in black. But, now you come to look at it – the silver really isn't bad at all.'

He looked at her, then indicated the passenger seat. 'Don't you want to know where we're going?'

She sat down next to him. 'I know where we're going.'

Agnes felt the engine purr as they reached London's outer reaches. The motorway curved into the distance, the swathe of silver-grey cutting across the blue of the sky.

'Georgie left me.' Brett broke the silence.

'I know.'

'She says I lie.'

'I know.'

'You know everything.'

'Nearly everything,' she replied.

He glanced at the dashboard. 'We'll be there by lunchtime.'

Agnes watched the industrial landscape slide by, the self-storage warehouses and superstores. She wondered if Brett would let her drive on the way back. She looked at the convertible roof, imagining folding it back, wondering if they'd freeze to death. She tried the CD player, the radio. She switched on the air conditioning.

Brett sighed. 'I only insured it for me.'

She flicked the temperature setting, felt her feet begin to warm up.

'I should have realised you'd be a hopeless passenger,' he said.

Agnes found her seat adjuster. She leant her seat right back, then straightened it up again.

'It's like driving a five-year-old around,' he said. 'I should have put you in a car seat in the back.'

'I'd only start asking you "Are we there yet?" every five minutes.'

'It would be preferable to you thumping your foot down every time you want me to go faster.'

'It's just a waste of a good car,' Agnes said. 'Look, there's no one in the fast lane at all.'

He threw her a sideways look. 'Do you just ignore speed cameras, then? Or is it that you monastic types are above the law?'

'Well, now you come to mention it—'

'Does your God make sure a flash of white light blocks out your number plate?'

She turned to him. 'Oh, I do hope so. I did about a hundred and ten up here in an Audi A3 on Saturday.'

He checked the mirror. His voice was quiet above the soft murmur of the engine. 'You mean you've already been to see her?'

'No.' Agnes looked at him, but he was staring straight ahead. 'I got as far as the house. I hung around outside for a bit, and then I went back to London.'

'Ah. Right.'

'Brett?' She watched him steel himself, waiting for her question.

'Go on,' he said.

'My father was Jewish.'

He seemed to let out a long breath. He nodded.

'When did you find out?' She looked at him, waiting.

'About ten days ago. One of the Oxford team put me in touch with someone who he said knew your father. I had a chat with this chap last week, amateur geologist kind of thing, lives down in Surrey, is that what it's called? He was very unhelpful about the fossils, and it turned out he'd never actually met Ralph, but he said in passing something about your father being Jewish.'

'Oh.'

'He'd read a paper your father had written some years ago, about how geology is essential to tell the story of the people of Israel. Ralph got a lot of flack for it at the time, apparently.'

The satnav piped up to warn them of their approaching junction.

'Brett?'

'Yes?'

'Why is it such a big deal?'

He glanced at her. 'Well, firstly, you're a nun. I didn't want to throw you into crisis.'

'I think I can be the judge of that.'

'I'm sure you can. Secondly, I felt I'd been lied to. Your father turned out not to be what I thought he was. I felt I'd gone to all this trouble to honour his memory, as his only surviving friend, and then it turned out he'd shown the same lack of respect to me as he'd shown to other people.'

She nodded, still listening.

He went on, 'I felt, here I was, carrying his story across the Atlantic, and now I didn't know what that story was.' Again, a sideways glance. 'I'm sorry. Georgie says that someone of more emotional intelligence wouldn't have made such a mess of it. And she's right.'

He signalled, turned off the motorway on to the A35. 'In the end, I just felt burdened with all his secrets.'

'Yes,' Agnes said. 'I know the feeling.'

The sky grew heavier, blue fading to grey. The road narrowed towards Charmouth, and at last they drew up outside the house. Again, the gravel drive, the green door, the ornate porch; and Brett's hand on the ceramic bell, which resonated loudly through the hall.

The door opened.

'Hello.' Her voice was bright. Agnes saw a kind, lined face, framed with grey, well-cut hair. She wore tailored trousers, a mauve cashmere jumper. She leant up and kissed Bretton on each cheek. Then she turned to Agnes, extended a hand. 'I'm Monica,' she said. Her gaze was searching; for several moments her eyes were fixed on Agnes. 'At last,' she said.

They followed her into a wide living room which gave the impression of space and light and warmth, perhaps from the coal fire which burnt in the grate, or the lamps dotted around. There were two wide, cream sofas, and Agnes and Brett sat down while Monica went into the kitchen area and emerged with tea things. She cast Agnes a look, shook her head, smiled.

'What is it?' Brett leant forward to help her with the tray.

She smiled again. 'She looks so like him.' She distributed cups and saucers, biscuits. 'Just shop ones, I'm afraid.' She sat on the other sofa. 'Well,' she said. She clasped her hands together on her lap. 'There'll be so much you want to know.'

'The Judaism,' Brett said. 'it's kind of news to us both.'

Her smile faded. She gave a sigh. 'It was such a shock to him. They'd lied, you see. Everyone. From when he was so small. All that loss...' She shook her head. 'It never does to lie. Even for good reasons. But I suppose, for Hannah, when she and her little boy looked so German, so Aryan, it seemed to be the best thing to do, to slip away from Hamburg, come across to England, and then after the war quietly assimilate into English life.'

'Hannah?' Agnes felt the words form on her lips. 'My grandmother?'

'Yes. She was German. They all were. Only she and your father escaped. The others were all killed. She hardened herself to a new life, sent your father to boarding school, became English. That's what I gathered from Ralph, anyway. His name, even. Ralf Garten, with an "f", became Ralph Gardner, with a "ph".'

The fire sputtered in the grate. Brett jumped up and put some more coals on.

Monica smiled up at him. 'It's a lot to take in.'

'It sure is.' Brett looked at Agnes. Agnes gazed into the fire, the smoke rising from the fresh coal.

'I always felt it explained his religious quest,' Monica said. 'The need for certainties. He only found out by chance, long after his mother's death. Some of the family property was forwarded on to him from Germany, God knows how anyone had hung on to it. Nothing valuable, of course, but bits of letters, correspondence, a horrible old skull with writing on it... That's when he became even more taken up with his fossils, with his story about the age of the Earth. I suppose, when so much of your past turns out to have been rewritten, it's understandable that you'd try to find a story that no one could argue with.'

Agnes watched the flames lick around the coals.

Monica looked at her, then stood up. 'Just a minute,' she said. She left the room, then came back with a photograph. It was black and white, framed, and showed a woman's face, the hint of a lace shirt at her neck. She handed it to Agnes.

'My grandmother?' Agnes looked up at her.

Monica nodded. 'Hannah. Taken in England. Before she died.'

Agnes stared at it. 'I always thought I looked like my mother. I thought my looks were French.'

'And here's your father.' Monica handed her another photograph. It was in colour, in a dark wood frame. A background of trees, sunlight, her father smiling out at the camera; an elderly man, but still the upright posture, the blond hair.

'I took that,' Monica said. 'It was here, in Dorset. It's a lovely garden you can visit, inland, towards Dorchester. About a year and a half before he died...' Her voice faltered.

Agnes looked at the image in front of her. She thought about the young man in the street; the same blond hair, the same upright posture. She handed the photo back to Monica.

'Let's go and walk on the beach,' Monica said.

The pebbles were salty under their feet. The sea was dark grey and wind whipped. Agnes walked next to Monica, Brett a little way behind, stopping now and then to pick up a stone.

Agnes looked at the beach stretching ahead of her. 'It was here—'

Monica nodded. 'It all made sense to him here.'

'But he died in the States?'

'Yes.' Monica pulled her collar up against the wind. 'We were based over there.'

'And the house here?'

'It belonged to my mother. I only came to live in it after Ralph died.' She glanced up at her. 'I knew you were – what I mean is, sometimes I thought I should—'

'But I didn't know about you. It wasn't your responsibility, to repair whatever breach existed between my father and me.'

Monica met her gaze. 'No,' she said. 'That's what I concluded too.'

'You—' Agnes felt the words form against the wind. 'You loved him.'

Monica looked at her. She nodded. 'I loved him very much.'

'How did you meet?'

They began to walk again, leaving Brett further behind them, still picking over stones.

'We met in the States. I'd lived there for some years.'

'But you're English?'

She nodded. 'My family was rather eccentric. Both my parents were artists. When I was in my teens, my father went off to California to "find himself". I stayed here with my mother. I got married, trained as a teacher. But my marriage didn't work out. We'd married so young, you see... I went through some difficult years, and then my father needed care, he was living in West Virginia by then, and it kind of made sense that I should go over there and look after him. And then, after a while he died, and I stayed on. I had a lovely job as a schoolteacher. I lived a quiet life; a kind of reaction to my noisy childhood, I think. And there was a church in Charleston, a very charismatic minister, Reverend Colin, a lovely man, but looking back, rather odd, perhaps. And I was drawn to having a belief system, after all those years of having none at all. And there was your father, also drawn to it. And of course, we were rather thrown together, both of us being the Brits. There was a lot of teasing…' She laughed. 'And he was all those years older than me. He was divorced with a grown-up daughter, as he told me…' She coloured slightly. 'And I was in my late thirties. But after a while, we realised we'd fallen in love. It was me who first said it out loud. He was so closed-in, so English. I think he felt he was too old for—'

'Happiness?'

She nodded. 'I think he felt he didn't deserve it. I don't know what your mother was like, but it was as if he didn't feel he could make anyone happy.'

Agnes felt the wind brush against her cheeks. 'Yes,' she murmured.

'So we began to live together.' She smiled. 'They were very happy years. It was like watching him thaw out.' She glanced up at Agnes. 'I only wish you'd had the chance to know him then. But of course, you were—'

'I'd shut myself away behind a grille by then.'

Monica threw her an uncertain smile.

'And the Judaism,' Agnes went on. 'How did that happen?'

'Oh, dear. He was tracked down by a lawyer in Germany. It was actually all about a painting, which turned out not to have belonged to his family at all. But of course, the rest of the story came out. And those few bits and pieces were shipped over…' She pushed a lock of hair away from her eyes. 'It did precipitate rather a crisis. I encouraged him to write. It was something he'd always done, as you must know. I like to think it helped. It's not as if I could have sent him to counselling or anything, he was much too English.'

'No,' Agnes agreed.

She fell silent.

And your child, Agnes thought. Tell me about your child.

'It's impossible—' Brett bounded up to them, holding out a stone. 'It's impossible to consider that it all might have had a neat starting point. Look at this. It's so obviously ancient. How can people ever think the whole story started with man?'

Monica smiled at him. 'You mean, how could Ralph?'

'Well, not him personally, but—'

'But he didn't.' Agnes reached out and took the fossil from him. 'He believed it was continuous. He just felt there'd been a violent interruption to allow it to start somewhere. To allow Adam to have a navel.'

'And if you were him—' Monica bent and picked up another stone. 'If you'd learnt about your past the way he did – then the idea of a violent interruption to a story would make perfect sense. All he did was turn it into something redemptive. Someone less good-hearted, on learning that their family had been destroyed in that way, might have become bitter, or vengeful. All he did was seek another way of finding evidence of God's love.' She smiled at Brett. 'It might not make sense, but you can't deny that the intention was good.'

They walked on. The wind seemed to ease, and the sea appeared bluer as it lapped against the shore. In the distance someone was approaching, coming nearer, a hand held up in greeting. Agnes saw a shock of blond hair, a swirl of raincoat against the wind; a clumsy stride. He was a man in his mid-twenties, she thought, and as he came up to them he smiled, laughed, ran to Brett and hugged him, then kissed Monica on the cheek.

'I didn't think you'd be out in this weather. I went home

first, I thought you'd be there.' He punched Brett on the arm. 'Great to see you. Mum's been looking forward to your visit for weeks, hasn't stopped going on about it, have you, Mum?' He smiled at Monica.

She took hold of his arm. 'Marcus – this is Agnes. Ralph's daughter. Agnes, this is my son.'

CHAPTER TWENTY-FIVE

'No, sweetie, really, I won't have it. I've obviously fallen into a parallel universe where you look just like Agnes but you've had a completely different life, involving having brothers and being Jewish. Next you're going to tell me you've never been a nun and you're just some kind of—'

'High-class call girl?' Agnes broke her croissant in two and put half on Athena's plate.

'Now, that would be OK. That wouldn't be too much of a stretch.'

'And I'm only half Jewish. And he's only a half-brother.'

'Hmmm.' Athena surveyed her half croissant. 'Perhaps I am in the right universe after all. Are you more than half a nun?'

Agnes sighed. 'I hope so. But God knows it's a struggle.'

Athena sipped her coffee. 'A brother, eh? Lucky you. What's he like? Does he look like you?'

'He's blond like my dad. And he's lovely. He's kind of quiet, but with this very dry humour.'

'Scorpio, maybe. Or Capricorn.'

'I don't know.'

'Don't know? Your own brother and you haven't asked him the most important things. What are his clothes like?'

'Expensive jeans. Trainers.'

'I'll have to see for myself. What does he do?'

'He's a historian. He's writing a thesis on sixteenth century theories of gravity.'

Athena looked at Agnes. 'Hmmm. Well, I suppose you couldn't expect anyone from your family to be practical. Or rich.' She smiled. 'Still. Jewish, eh? How fab. It's very fashionable, I gather. That pop singer, isn't it? She's adopted it. I'm sure it's all the rage.' She frowned. 'But – seriously, doesn't it prevent you being a nun? I mean, surely you can't be Christian too?'

Agnes smiled. 'Firstly, I don't count. Judaism goes through the mother, so I'm the wrong half. And secondly, there's a very long answer about the Jewish roots of Christianity. Brett was teasing me about how I'm a fulfilment of the promises of the Old Testament, although as I pointed out to him on the way back yesterday, there is a major stumbling block in the nature of the Messiah and the historical person of Jesus Christ—'

'And what's the short answer?' Athena was looking at her watch.

'Are you in a hurry?'

'Not really, only I'm meeting Nic after this, he's having a break from his mum's bedside.'

'How is she?'

'Still in hospital. She's not well enough to come out. We were down there yesterday, she was barely conscious, poor woman. She's wired up to one of those beeping things, and her heart rate was all over the place, to think they were considering sending her out in that state… Nic's very upset, as you can imagine. Luckily he's got Mack to look after him.'

'Luckily?' Agnes looked at her.

Athena returned her look. 'Oh, didn't I tell you? She's charming, it turns out, her and her partner. Bella, her partner's called. Both of them, absolutely lovely. And Mack had heard all about us getting married, and she said she used to be dead against it, but now she and Bella are considering a civil partnership, and she thinks, why not? She said, us feminists should keep our powder dry for more important parts of the 'Struggle', and I think she's absolutely right, don't you?'

Agnes smiled at her. 'So, you and Nic?'

'We'll see.' Athena raised an eyebrow. 'And, as for you? Racing round the countryside with the not-so-gorgeous American? Is he gorgeous again?'

'He was never gorgeous. But yes, we drove back last night.'

'So did we.'

'And he let me drive. He said it was preferable to having me behaving like a child in the passenger seat. I wouldn't have bothered, but I really wanted to try out the SL500. I even put the roof down for a bit, just to watch all that clicky stuff it does, until Bretton fussed about freezing to death—'

'A Merc? I was racing a Merc most of the way there. It must have been you. At least your lovely American can pick up the tabs for the speeding fines this time.' She gathered up her bag. 'When am I going to meet him?'

'How would Friday evening be?'

'Friday would be fab. I might even bring Nic if he can escape.'

'There's one problem—'

'Go on.'

'It might involve watching ballet.'

Athena's hand went to her eyes. She shook her head. 'The sacrifices I make just to keep an eye on your spiritual well-being.'

Agnes let herself into the hostel and almost tripped over a large suitcase which stood in the hallway. There was a smell of chips, but the kitchen was empty, and lunch was all washed up. The office was empty too.

A burst of loud music came from upstairs. A door slammed, there was shouting, laughter; the music stopped. Footsteps crossed the landing, then Lindy appeared on the staircase. 'Oh.' She looked at Agnes. 'It's you.'

'Didn't they tell you I was calling in this afternoon?'

'They might have done.' She smiled. 'I probably forgot.' She pointed at the suitcase. 'A lot on my mind.'

'They told me you were leaving today.'

She nodded. 'In about half an hour.'

'Ireland?'

'To start with, yeah.' She took Agnes's hand and led her into the lounge. 'Just a holiday, really.' She flung herself on to the sofa.

'And then what?'

Lindy sat hunched, her hands clasped together in her lap. 'His brief reckons five years with good behaviour.'

'Whose brief?'

She looked up. 'Connor, of course. He'll plead manslaughter.'

'Five years.' Agnes switched on the lamp, chasing from the room the dull greyness of the afternoon.

'It's not that long to wait.'

Agnes sat down in an armchair. 'Connor's sentence doesn't have to be yours.'

Lindy leant back on the sofa cushions. 'Someone has to believe in him, don't they?'

'So, what will you do for five years?'

Lindy locked her fingers together, then unfurled them. She looked up at Agnes. 'After Abbie died, I made myself a promise. I thought, we can all go on as we are, living our lives, blaming everyone else. Or we can make a decision, find a way out. And I thought Connor was my way out. And then, these last few days...' She shifted on the cushions. 'After all that, it was like I was in prison again. I thought, there is no way out. I might as well give up. And then I thought, no. I can still make a decision. And then I was talking to Cath at the women's health centre, and it turns out they need an outreach worker, after all this crisis with that doctor being arrested and everyone leaving... And she said I'd be good at it. And I laughed, and she said, no really. It's your choice, she said. And I thought, she's right. It's my choice. They'll pay me and everything. So, I start the week after next.'

'So, Ireland?'

Lindy met her eyes, then stared down at her lap. 'Another promise. Abbie's mum. I'm going to Connemara to put violets on her grave.' She looked at her watch. 'I've got to get to the bus station in a minute.'

Agnes stood up. She went over and kissed Lindy on the cheek. Lindy looked up at her. 'You see,' she said, 'the thing is, everything's going to be all right.'

It was already getting dark when Agnes left the hostel. She walked to the corner, towards the main road. A lone figure was leaning against a wall. He shifted, moved towards her, and she recognised Murchie, with his dog trotting at his feet.

'Hello,' she said.

Murchie slapped his hand against hers. 'All right?' he said.

They stood under the yellow lamplight. 'How are you?' She looked up at him.

He smiled. 'Free,' he said. 'They nearly had me. But I'm out, all thanks to you.'

'Well, hardly—' she began.

'No, Sister, you listen to me. You believed me. When no one else did. No one trusted my word.'

'And are they right, not to trust you?'

He scuffed his feet against the pavement, then he looked up at her. 'No one should trust me. Like I said, it's a matter of time.' He smiled a broad smile, crushed her fingers in his own once more, and set off down the street, his dog at his heels, without looking back.

It felt as if a long time had passed since she last climbed the stairs to her flat. She let herself in, thinking it was only two days ago that I opened these curtains to find Brett outside my window, only two days since I met Monica, and Marcus.

She switched on lights, opened the fridge, wondered whether the chicken liver pâté was still good.

Her phone rang.

'Sweetie, I'm sorry to bother you...' Athena sounded tense, her voice flat.

'What is it?'

'Iris died. Earlier today. Nic's there now. I'm just about to get in the car and join him.'

'Oh. Well, send him my love.'

'He sounded dreadful. Poor love. I can't wait just to put my arms around him.'

'Poor him. Losing a mother...'

'It was all so long ago for me...back in Greece...I'd already run away. Still, even if I can't actually know what he's feeling, I can be there for him. Poor love.' Athena sniffed. 'You can pray for him if you like.'

'If you're sure.'

'Oh, I think it'll be fine. As he says, all belief systems are welcome in his universe.'

'Well...OK. Athena – take care.'

'I don't risk speeding. Unlike some people I could mention.'

Agnes put her phone down on the table. A memory; walking down a dark corridor, her habit swishing at her feet, Sister John-Mary handing her the handset of the old black bakelite phone – 'bad news, I'm afraid, Sister'. Then listening to the American voice informing her that Ralph Gardner had passed away that morning, his attorneys will be writing to you...

In the end, there'd been nothing other than a letter from his solicitor. No personal effects, nothing left to her in his will, on the understanding, the lawyers said, that she'd have been unable to own anything given her religious vows. To that extent, they were right. She wondered whether her father's withholding of any mention of her in his will was a symptom of his own distance from her or of respect for her vocation. She found herself wondering why she'd never asked herself that before, but then, her father's death had become mixed up, at the time, in the confusion and anguish of leaving the old Order and entering the new one, and in her mind her father had passed away leaving very little trace.

And now: now, there was so much. Boxes of writings, of

artefacts; diaries, notebooks, fossils, skulls. And in the end, his lover; his son. My brother.

And all the time he was writing his theories of creation, his histories of mankind, the story he was struggling to tell was his own.

CHAPTER TWENTY-SIX

'You were right, of course.' Agnes picked up a tin from Julius's desk and looked at it.

'What was I right about?' Julius reached the teapot down from its shelf.

'That thing you said, the other day. That we're all post-Freudians now. That if someone believes that God created the world in six days, that tells you a lot about that person, but not much about the history of the Earth.'

'Did I say that? How very clever of me.' Julius poured boiling water into the teapot and rinsed it round.

Agnes put the tin back on his desk. Afternoon sunlight filtered through the window. 'I mean, with my father. It was all about his need for a story. Given that the one he thought he had had been taken away from him.'

Julius spooned tea leaves into the pot.

Agnes flicked through one of her father's notebooks. 'Do you think ex-Father Gustave really wants this stuff?'

Julius carried the teapot over to the desk. 'He says so, yes. He was particularly interested in the skull.'

'He's welcome to it. I asked Monica about it. She said he'd been in touch with an antique shop in Hamburg, and they said they'd seen a couple of them over the years, and mentioned a dealer in London. And then he talked to this man, he was a collector of medical artefacts, phrenology, early surgical instruments, that kind of thing, and according to Monica this chap said something about grave robbing. After that neither of us wanted to think about the skull too much.' Agnes picked up a cardboard box that was on the desk.

'Well—' Julius poured milk into two cups, then tea. 'Father Gustave says it'll be great for the museum. If it ever gets to open.' He passed her a cup. 'Oh, by the way—' He sat down at his desk and reached towards a pile of envelopes. He took out a postcard. It showed a seaside view. 'I thought you'd like to see this.'

Agnes turned it over 'Whitby?'

'It's from Jeremy Stipes.'

'So it is.' She read the few brief words. 'The air here is much healthier than London. If only Pauline could have been here, I do believe she'd still be with us. Yours, Jeremy.'

Agnes handed the card back to him.

Julius tucked it back in with the other post. 'There we are, then, eh?'

She nodded.

Julius looked at her. 'Well,' he said. 'Ballet, eh?'

'I didn't get you a ticket. I knew you wouldn't want to come.'

'You knew right.'

'I got two tickets for me, and one for Athena, even though she's complaining bitterly, but she wouldn't miss the chance to meet Brett. She says she'll just have to sit there with her eyes closed, and maybe her fingers in her ears too, depending on the music.'

Julius sipped his tea. 'And who's the other ticket for, then? Brett?'

'No, he's got his own.'

There was a knock at the door. It opened slightly, revealing a face. 'Is Agnes…? Ah,' he said, seeing her. 'She said I'd find her here. She said you wouldn't mind…'

Julius looked at the young man as he stood in the doorway, his floppy blond hair, his hesitant step as he walked towards the desk, smiling, holding out his hand to Julius. Julius shook his hand, then turned to Agnes. 'So. Here he is. As you said – the young man on the beach was part of the story after all.'

'Julius – this is Marcus.'

'Your brother,' Julius said, looking up at Marcus. 'Goodness me. Who'd have thought? Agnes's brother.' He stared at him some more, then said, 'Oh, dear, I'm forgetting my manners. She's told me so much about you. Will you have some tea, perhaps?' He stumbled to his feet, pulled up another chair.

'If we have time.' Marcus glanced at Agnes.

'We have to go in a minute.'

Marcus sat down next to Agnes. 'She's told me a lot about you as well,' he said.

'Well,' Julius settled back in his chair. 'Who'd have thought, eh? A ready-made relative.'

'Perhaps it's the best kind.' Marcus smiled.

Julius considered him. 'And do you too hold to the biblical timescale for the age of the universe, like your father?'

Agnes put her cup down. 'Oh, poor Marcus. He's only just met you and you've started already.'

Marcus laughed. 'She speaks very highly of you,' he said.

'Yes, and now you've gone and spoilt it.' Agnes patted Julius's arm. 'We have to go. There'll be plenty of time for you to frighten the poor boy with deep theology on other occasions.' She stood up.

'I hope so.' Julius held out his hand.

Marcus shook his hand. 'I hope so too. I've been trying to find out about the Judaic numerology of the New Testament accounts, the five loaves and two fishes, the number of fish caught by the apostles at Tiberias.'

'Well, it's funny you should say that,' Julius said. 'I've just been reading an article about prime numbers and their significance to Judaism at the time of the destruction of the temple – you see, if you make an equilateral pyramid, the base of which is seventeen—'

Agnes stepped between them. 'I might have known.' She took hold of Marcus's arm and began to lead him towards the door. 'Why don't you swap email addresses and then I can leave you both to it?'

Julius followed, holding the door open for them. 'Well—' He offered his hand to Marcus. 'Any brother of Agnes's is a brother of mine.'

'Silly old Julius.' Agnes kissed him on the cheek. 'You've got about nine brothers of your own who you never see, there's no point stealing mine.'

The theatre bar was a wide, curved space, bright with spotlights. Agnes walked in, followed by Marcus. The first thing she saw was Athena, her legs crossed, one red-jewelled, peep-toed wedge shoe hanging from one foot, the other planted on the floor. She was sitting at a low table, leaning towards a figure in a tailored raincoat.

'Oh, I think you were right to go for the A3...' the cultured American tones were unmistakable. 'A lot of engine for your money, and they haven't entirely solved the cornering problems on the A4.'

'Do you know, I felt exactly the same. And then, when they told me about the heated seats – oh, darling.' Athena looked up and smiled. 'We've already introduced ourselves, I hope you don't mind.'

Brett stood up and kissed her on the cheek. 'Your friend seemed to know exactly who I was.' He met her eyes. 'I can't think how.'

Behind him, Agnes could see Athena winking.

'And Marcus. How are you enjoying London?' Brett leant towards Marcus, took his hand, introduced him to Athena.

'A drink? Another of those?' Brett indicated Athena's glass, and she smiled, charmingly.

Brett went to the bar.

'Agnes's brother.' Athena gazed up at him.

'I'm getting rather used to this.' Marcus smiled down at her.

'Well, it's not every day that Agnes produces a relative from nowhere.'

Marcus looked at Athena. 'And are you keen on ballet? I really love it, it's one of my favourite art forms.'

'Ah, well...' Athena fluffed up her hair. 'I wouldn't quite say favourite... I mean, obviously, I try to keep up with current developments in the arts...'

Brett reappeared, distributed drinks. He leant his hand on Agnes's shoulder. 'I meant to tell you. I had a phone call yesterday, from the labs in Oxford. They've done some more specific tests on the piece of Noah's Ark.' He sat down next to her. 'They've pinned it down to something pretty near to five thousand, seven hundred years old. And, even weirder, they've found tree pollen that could only have come from quite a limited area of East Turkey.'

'Mount Ararat?'

Brett looked at her. 'How much more specific do you need me to be? I thought you said you didn't need evidence for your faith.'

She laughed. Behind her she could hear Athena talking to Marcus. 'Ah, you see, I knew it would be one or the other. Although, now I've met you, I'm thinking fiery ascendant, maybe Sagittarius, I wouldn't be at all surprised...'

Agnes turned back to Brett. 'I don't really need evidence. It's just...'

'You mean, it would have been nice for Ralph to have his true story after all.'

She nodded.

He squeezed her hand. 'He had two fine children. And at the end, he knew he was loved. No one can ask more than that.'

She looked up at him. Tears welled in her eyes.

Then, the bell was ringing, there were calls to take their seats.

Agnes turned to Brett. 'And Georgie?'

He shrugged. 'I've been a fool, to be honest. Once she might have married me. Now she's saying that she can't commit to someone so unreliable. And it's only now that I realise, that she's the one I want.'

'Oh, you men.' Athena was standing next to them. 'Listen.' She leant close to Brett's ear. 'I'll tell you a secret. Don't tell anyone else. But if a woman starts to say that she really doesn't care whether she gets married or not, that's the time to start planning a wedding.'

The bells were more persistent. Brett looked at her. 'Are you sure?'

Athena smiled at him. 'It's worked for me.' She took Agnes's arm as they went through to the auditorium.

'The sequel to the best-seller, then?' Agnes said to her, and they both laughed.

Agnes sat in the red plush seats gazing around her. The theatre was filling up, people filing into their seats, a hubbub of noise and expectation. Fragments of music drifted up from the orchestra pit. In her mind she saw the muscular bodies she'd seen in the rehearsal room, their bright leggings and scruffy T-shirts. She wondered what they'd look like now, all in costumes, illumined by the stage lights.

The theatre was almost full. She looked along the seats, and saw Brett, a row or two in front of them. He gave a brief wave, and Athena, sitting on one side of her, waved back.

The house lights began to fade. The orchestra played 'A'.

Agnes was aware of Marcus, sitting next to her.

My father had two children. And, at the end, he knew he was loved.

She thought about the ballet. A kind of narrative, Georgie had said. When each step leads to another; and even the resolution is open-ended, allowing the possibility of the next phrase, the next part of the story.

The conductor took his place in the pit. The first few notes of Bach filled the air. On the stage, a single spotlight pierced the darkness.